D0532383

About the author

Christine Marion Fraser is one of Scotland's top selling authors with world-wide readership. Second youngest of a large family, she soon learned independence during child-hood years spent in the post-war Govan district of Glasgow. At the age of ten she contracted a rare illness which landed her in a wheelchair and virtually ended her formal education. From her early years Christine has been an avid storyteller; her first novel *Rhanna* was published in 1978.

Christine Marion Fraser lives with her husband in an old Scottish manse on the shores of the Kyles of Bute, Argyllshire.

Praise for Christine Marion Fraser:

'Her tempestuous, all-human-life-is-there historical nov-els are testament to her ability to understand what makes a rollicking good read . . . Fraser is Scottish publishing's best-kept secret' Jackie McGlone, *The Scotsman*

'[*Kinvara*] is a story set in a small, remote Scottish com-munity where the landscape is harsh, the coast is rugged and the inhabitants are colourful and memorable . . . [A] must to take on your holidays' *Telegraph & Argus*

'Christine Marion Fraser writes characters so real they almost leap out of the pages . . . you would swear she must have grown up with them' *Sun*

'Christine Marion Fraser weaves an intriguing story in which the characters are alive against a spellbinding background' *Yorkshire Herald*

Also by Christine Marion Fraser

Fiction

RHANNA

RHANNA AT WAR

CHILDREN OF RHANNA

RETURN TO RHANNA

SONG OF RHANNA

STRANGER ON RHANNA

A RHANNA MYSTERY

KING'S CROFT

KING'S ACRE

KING'S EXILE

KING'S CLOSE

KING'S FAREWELL

NOBLE BEGINNINGS

NOBLE DEEDS

NOBLE SEED

Non-fiction

BLUE ABOVE THE CHIMNEYS

ROSES ROUND THE DOOR

GREEN ARE MY MOUNTAINS

Kinvara

Christine Marion Fraser

CORONET BOOKS
Hodder and Stoughton

Copyright © 1998 by Christine Marion Fraser

First published in 1998 by Hodder and Stoughton
A division of Hodder Headline PLC
First published in paperback in 1999
by Hodder and Stoughton
A Coronet paperback

The right of Christine Marion Fraser to be identified as the
Author of the Work has been asserted by her in accordance
with the Copyright, Designs and Patents Act 1988.

10 9 8 7 6 5 4 3 2 1

All rights reserved. No part of this publication may be
reproduced, stored in a retrieval system, or transmitted,
in any form or by any means without the prior written
permission of the publisher, nor be otherwise circulated
in any form of binding or cover other than that in which
it is published and without a similar condition being
imposed on the subsequent purchaser.

All characters in this publication are fictitious
and any resemblance to real persons, living or dead,
is purely coincidental.

A CIP catalogue record for this title is available
from the British Library

ISBN 0 340 70714 3

Typeset by Palimpsest Book Production Limited,
Polmont, Stirlingshire
Printed and bound in Great Britain by
Clays Ltd, St Ives PLC, Bungay, Suffolk

Hodder and Stoughton
A division of Hodder Headline PLC
338 Euston Road
London NW1 3BH

For Bobbie and Jack Wilson. Friends as well as neighbours.

Kinvara Light

Eilean Orsa

Kinvara Point

Eilean Crocan

Signal Tower

Stac Gorm

St. Niven's Chapel
and House

Old Harbour

Niven's Bay

Camus nan Rua

Vaul

Boat Yard

K

Inn

Balivoe Village

Mill o Bruach

Cragdu Castle

Monk's Light   Camus nan Gao

Hermit's Hut

Caves

Mary's Bay

Keepers Cottages

Oir na Cuan

Quarrymen's Cottages

Vale o Dreip Farm

Calvost Village

Mill o Cladach

Crathmore

Garden Cottage

k and Manse

Purlieburn
Cottage

Butter — Meadow

Butterburn Croft

Croft Angus

Butterbank House

ACKNOWLEDGEMENTS

With thanks to Frank for music and song when I needed both to help me along. Also to Ken who keeps everything going when I'm shut in my study and the words are just flowing.

In appreciation,
The Lady Rhanna

THE KINVARA
PENINSULA

Christmas and
New Year 1922–23

Chapter One

It was cold out there on the sea, a deep, bitter cold that penetrated the thick layers of clothing worn by the three men standing at the rails of the relief boat, their faces whipped to raw brightness in the stinging bite of the December wind that was whistling fretfully over the churning foam of the Atlantic ocean.

They were the keepers of the Kinvara Light, a lonely tower that rose sheer out of a slate-coloured sea to pierce the low-slung clouds of a grey horizon, twelve miles south-west of Calvost.

'We're going home, lads!' shouted Robert Sutherland, deputy head keeper of the light. 'Home for Christmas!'

Home for Christmas! It was a wonderful thought, one that brought smiles to the weatherbeaten faces of Rob's companions. After more than three months of confinement in the Kinvara Lighthouse, with only the gulls and the seals for company, the men were more than ready to sample the seasonal festivities that lay ahead.

They had waited long enough for this moment. Because of bad weather, the relief boat had been three days late in coming. The bleak islet on which the light was built consisted of jagged rocks which extended a considerable distance underwater, and a complex system of tides created continual turbulence, even in calm weather, making it difficult to land.

So the men had waited, getting on each other's nerves, while huge seas from the west had battered the reefs and the swell from the south had broken on the vertical sides, tossing up spray over seventy feet high.

But at last the boat had come, bringing with it supplies for the relief crew who faced spending Christmas and New Year away from their families. 'Drink one for me at the bells!' had been Donnie 'Hic' Gillespie's parting shot, his cheery pink face taking on a mournful expression as he spoke. 'There's nothing here but cocoa and tea and you can't expect a man to get happy on any o' these.'

'I wouldny be too sure o' that. It would all depend on what you put in them.' Mungo MacGill, head lighthouse keeper, had said sourly, his ferrety eyes raking suspiciously into those of Donnie Hic, as he was affectionately known. Mungo was always suspicious of Donnie Hic; as a result the two men didn't get on and had once stopped speaking to one another during an entire three-month stint on the Kinvara Light. But Donnie Hic's buoyant nature, coupled with his youthful high spirits, never allowed him to keep up grievances for long and at Mungo's words he just shrugged his shoulders, winked at the other men, and climbed up the mural stairs to the kitchen to put the kettle on.

The boat rounded Kinvara Point and skirted Mary's Bay. Robert Sutherland detached himself from the rails and strained his eyes through the gathering darkness, gazing into the bay as if he expected to see someone or something that he would recognise, a signal to tell him that everything would be as he had left it – all these long weeks ago. He always did this when he came back – back to the Kinvara peninsula and the shores of his boyhood, Mary's Bay and all it meant to him, the little cottage standing white and neat on the machair beneath Blanket Hill, the hens and the ducks poking about in the rocks, the dogs running riot on the shore, diving into the sea . . .

And Morna Jean, his beloved Morna Jean, waiting to welcome him back . . . His heart leapt. Surely that was a wisp of smoke he saw rising up from the shore below that tiny white blob of a house . . . and a bell . . . its notes ringing and winging over the water . . .

Morna had seen the boat, she knew that he was coming home and she was letting him know it. His eyes roved no further, he didn't want to look at No. 6, Keeper's Row, the end house, nothing would have changed there, it would still be the same – worse maybe . . .

He didn't allow his thoughts to wander beyond that. The Old Harbour of Calvost was coming closer, looming out of the half-light of late afternoon. Soon the boat was tying up and the men clambering ashore, delighted to set their feet on familiar ground. The wind was strengthening again, keening in over the sea beyond the harbour, whipping the tops of the waves into a creamy foam that crashed against the jagged reefs lying off Kinvara Point. 'Would you look at that now.' Jock Morgan, known as Big Morgan or Morgan the Magnificent because of his awesome height and masterful physique, inclined his head seawards. 'She's starting to blow stink again. 'Tis glad I am no' to be out on the rock tonight.'

In the distance, the Kinvara Light was winking, a beacon in the grey-blackness, a lonely indication of life out there in the midst of the dark ocean.

Moggy John MacPhee, whose brood of six awaited him in No. 3, Keeper's Row, shook his shaggy red head and grinned. 'Poor old Donnie Hic, having to spend Christmas wi' that moaning old goat, Mungo, but knowing Donnie he'll have a dram hidden away somewhere.'

'Ay, and Jimmy will keep them all going with his songs,' nodded Big Morgan.

'And maybe driving them all daft at the same time,' Rob put in drily. 'He sings the same ones over and over and he's worse when he's got a drink in him.'

'Ach, at least he's a cheerful wee man.' Moggy John rubbed his hands briskly together. 'Come on, let's get home. Cathie will be waiting to tell me all the gossip. She bottles it up for months then lets rip as soon as I'm over the doorstep and the bairns will deeve my lugs with all their talk about Christmas.

After the solitude of Kinvara, a family o' six is a bit much for any man to take.'

'You made your bed, man.' Jock Morgan grinned in the darkness. 'Ay, and a right cosy bed it must be too, your brood bears witness to that.'

Moggy John shrugged his shoulders. 'A man has to pass the long winter nights somehow, and these spells away from Cathie makes her all the nicer to cuddle when I come home. I've had to squeeze it all into a short space and somehow the bairnies just kept on coming.'

Jock nodded knowingly, 'Like a string o' sausages, one after the other, not all of them out the same factory, but you can't tell that just by looking at the skins. Your mother should have called you Tom, but then, she wasn't to know what a regular wee alley cat you'd turn out to be.'

Moggy John bunched his fists, scowling at the big man and wishing for the umpteenth time that he could take a swing at the huge craggy face towering above his own. But although he was wiry and quick on his feet he knew he could never be a match for Morgan the Magnificent. That, however, didn't stop him from snarling an oath under his breath and venting his anger on the rear end of a stray cat whose misfortune it was to cross his path when it did.

Jock Morgan roared with laughter and threw one hefty arm across Moggy John's shoulder. 'Come on, lighten up, Moggy! I'm just envious because you've fathered more bairns in a few years than I ever will in a lifetime. Janet and me have just the one and wish for a dozen more but we will never be so lucky. And if you don't mind me saying so, you shouldn't have kicked that poor old cat up the arse, he just might be a relative o' yours!'

Moggy John could never stay angry with the big man for long. His annoyance abated and all three men were in the best of spirits as they trudged over the machair to the lights winking in Keeper's Row. Caught up in their talk and their banter they were poorly prepared when a shadowy figure suddenly rose up in front of them, making them jump with fright.

'Johnny Lonely! Bugger you!' cursed Big Morgan. 'How

can you no' be noisy and normal like the rest o' us, instead o' creeping about like a ghost in the night!'

The newcomer said nothing in retaliation, instead he just stood and stared at the men for a long, silent minute, before disappearing as suddenly and soundlessly as he had come.

'God! That man!' exploded Moggy John. 'He fair gives me the creeps the way he just stands and stares at you. What's in his mind, I'd like to know.'

'More than any o' us can ever guess,' Rob said slowly. 'He sees everything that goes on, he knows more about the folk here than the rest o' us put together.'

'Ay, he could tell a tale or two.' Moggy John felt his spine tingling at the thought. If Cathie ever found out about some of the things he got up to there would be no living with her. His 'nights on the tiles', as she herself laughingly called his outings with the lads, would be no more and he gulped in dismay at the idea of having to abandon the little pleasures that lent spice to his life.

'Just as long as he keeps what he knows to himself he won't be harming anybody,' Big Morgan said thoughtfully, glancing slyly at the other man as he spoke.

Moggy John didn't notice as he voiced a heartfelt agreement to this, but Rob Sutherland said nothing as quietly he wondered just how much Johnny Lonely *did* know. Johnny was a hermit who had been around for a good many years. He was part of the local scenery, a kenspeckle figure who lived rough in a ramshackle hut among the dunes beyond Mary's Bay, though if the mood took him he would move his sparse belongings to the ruins of the Old Chapel Light above the cliffs of Kinvara Point, there to light fires on the headland as the monks of old had done long ago to warn off shipping.

To all intents and purposes, Johnny kept himself to himself; in his own way he was a likeable creature and was a great attraction for the local youngsters who were fascinated by his way of life and the stories he told about the marine history of the Kinvara coastline, particularly his tales concerning the many ships that had foundered on the treacherous rocks off the point and those around Camus nan Gao, the Bay of the Winds.

'One day there will be another shipwreck hereabouts,' he prophesied in his slow deep voice. 'The Light does its job well but it canny stop vessels being blown off course and landing up on yonder reefs.'

The children, convinced by Johnny's predictions of doom, were always on the look-out for evidence to support his claims, though Camus nan Gao, battered by storms, pocked with slimy caves, cut off at high tide by vertical cliffs, was not a hospitable place to be, especially in the long harsh months of winter when huge seas lashed the shore and strong winds transported the white shell sands far and wide.

The grown-ups dismissed Johnny's verbal meanderings as pure fancy and said he was soft in the head through living too long on his own, but that didn't stop the menfolk at least from keeping half an ear open whenever their offspring were recounting the things told to them by the hermit.

Robert Sutherland himself saw no reason why Johnny shouldn't air his opinions, since they did no one any harm. Far more disturbing was his ubiquitousness, always popping up when he wasn't wanted, never saying anything, taking his fill of what was going on before turning away and disappearing into thin air, like a puff of smoke dispersed by a breeze. But that was Johnny Lonely all over, never seeking human contact, unable to prevent an encounter with it now and then. Everybody was used to him by now though many could never forgive him for discovering their small indiscretions, unwittingly or otherwise, depriving them of their right to privacy and in the process laying them bare to such feelings of apprehension and guilt that they experienced pangs of unease whenever they came upon the hermit in his wanderings.

Moggy John and Big Morgan dispersed to their respective houses but so deep in thought was Rob that he hardly noticed them going. His earlier mood of lightheartedness was wearing off the nearer he got to No. 6, Keeper's Row. He walked on alone, hands deep in his pockets, his steps slowing as he went up the path to his house, the end one in the row, the window in its sturdy gable looking out over Mary's Bay and beyond that to the Kinvara Light winking in the distance.

Hannah, his wife, had wanted him to block up the window, saying that it caused draughts, but he had refused to do so. He liked the view; he enjoyed looking out towards the wild Atlantic ocean and the isles of the Hebrides dotted on the horizon; most of all he liked poking his head out so that he could gaze along the beach towards Morna's house, sitting there on the edge of the machair, a tiny haven of a place, snug, secure, welcoming . . .

For a long moment he stood on the step outside his house, then he took a deep breath, put his hand on the knob and slowly began to turn it.

Chapter Two

'I'm home, Hannah!' Rob shouted as he threw open the door and went inside. The kitchen was warm and cosy after the bitter cold of the night; the table was covered over with a starched white cloth and neatly set; a lively fire burned in the grate of the black-leaded range; copper pans gleamed in the glow cast by the oil lamp suspended from the ceiling; the flickering light of candles danced on the white walls, all of it combining to give the room an ambience of contentment.

But it was only an illusion. Hannah Mabel Sutherland was by the fire, stirring something in a pot, shoulders hunched slightly forward, her brow resting on the hand that gripped the mantel, her eyes gazing moodily down into the embers.

She didn't turn at her husband's entry. 'I know,' was all she said in a flat dull voice. 'Your tea will be ready in a minute.'

And that was all. No word of welcome, no sign of any kind to let him know that she was even slightly glad to see him again. Going forward he stood behind her, willing her to turn round and look at him. He could see the pulse beating in her neck, tiny strands of her hair gleaming in the fire's light, the movement of her wrist as rhythmically she guided the wooden spoon round and round in the pot.

In this light she looked young and soft and vulnerable and suddenly he was reminded of how it had been with them when first they had met. He had gone to a cattle sale in Ayr because he wanted to buy a new milking cow. Afterwards he had gone to a tiny, quaint, dimly lit tearoom and that was where he had met Hannah, sitting alone and pensive at a table near his own. After a while they had got talking and had enjoyed one another's company. She had been shy and hesitant to begin with, giving him the impression that she wasn't used to conversing with the opposite sex. She had been like a little girl, lost in a world she didn't quite understand, and had aroused the protective instinct in him. At the time, his own heart had been bruised and sore and he had been easily seduced by Hannah's obvious need to be loved and cared for.

Everything had seemed surmountable then: the expectations of her well-to-do self-made father for his only child; the displeasure of her mother for everything that didn't meet with her approval. She had not approved of Robert Sutherland, a lighthouse keeper living in a remote part of the west coast, with only a small piece of croftland to supplement his income.

She wasn't impressed by the fact that he had recently been promoted to deputy head keeper of the Light and had a house to go with his job, and neither she nor her husband had given their daughter the slightest encouragement to continue seeing him. However, by then Hannah was besotted with him and despite her parents' opposition they were quickly married and starting their life together in Kinvara.

He had soon realised it had all been a mistake, one that he regretted every day of his life. Hannah hated the isolation of her new home and made no effort to settle in; she abhorred her husband's long spells away at the Kinvara Light, yet she made no attempt to alleviate her loneliness by getting to know her neighbours. Instead she kept them at arms' length and it wasn't long before she earned herself a reputation for being a snob. And after just four months of marriage, when she discovered that she was pregnant, she immediately packed her bags and went home to her parents in Ayrshire.

They had, however, not been as sympathetic towards her as she would have liked and, after a few weeks of their reproachful nagging, she returned once more to Kinvara where she had given birth to a son, an event that had proved to be traumatic for everyone, not least Hannah.

Everything had happened in a very short space of time and Rob felt himself softening as he stood there at the fire beside his wife.

'Hannah.' Gently he nuzzled the curve of her neck with his lips. She shivered and stiffened and, turning to him, she said tightly, 'Stop that, Rob, I told you, your tea's nearly ready. Wash your hands and sit down at the table.'

She moved into the halo of light cast by the lamp and he could see her face clearly now, the early lines of discontent at her mouth, her prematurely greying hair, the dullness in her brown eyes, eyes that had once sparkled with joy whenever she had looked at him. She was only twenty-six but already she had the look of a woman for whom life had scant meaning.

At her words he felt as if he had been slapped. He had been through it all before but each time he came home there was fresh hope in him that something might have changed for the better, some small sign to show him that she still cared.

His mind was numb with hurt as he moved away from her. But he didn't go over to the sink to wash his hands, instead he went to the cot in the corner of the room where his infant son lay, a delicate little rickle of bones with no control over his limbs, his big dark eyes staring at the ceiling, mouth running wet with the saliva that continually dribbled down his chin.

Andrew William Sutherland had been born with cerebral palsy and the doctor had told Rob that it would take a lot of time and patience before Hannah got over the shock of having borne such a drastically handicapped child. She wasn't a robust lass, she was physically and mentally frail, she'd had a terrible job giving birth . . .

Dr Alistair MacAlistair had rhymed it all off, thoughtfully stroking his whiskery chin as he did so and sadly shaking his head. 'Patience, my lad,' he had said heavily. 'Just try to have patience. The weeks will pass, things will get better.'

That had been nine months ago but it might have been yesterday for all the difference it had made to Hannah. She kept the house like a new pin, she cooked and washed, darned socks and mended clothes, but beyond that there was nothing: she spoke no loving word; scorned all Rob's attempts to comfort her, implying, but never saying outright, that the baby's imperfections were all his fault.

'I want no more children, Rob,' she had told him in a trembling voice. 'It was enough to bring this one into the world – I can never take the risk of it happening again.'

In this view she was ably backed up by her parents, particularly her mother, who had stayed with her daughter for six weeks after the baby's birth, giving Rob little chance to heal the rift that had sprung up between him and his wife.

Harriet Houston was an extremely capable woman with very decided opinions about everything. She was bossy, intrusive and domineering and whenever she was around, Hannah just seemed to melt into the background, allowing her mother to have all her own way.

Not so Rob. He upheld his place in the home with a doggedness that was a match for his mother-in-law any day of the week. As a result there was a continual clash of personalities between them and he had never been so glad to see the back of anybody as on the day Harriet packed her bags and returned to the hotel in Ayrshire that she and her husband had built into a thriving business.

But by then, any spirit that had been in Hannah was locked away inside her and Rob despaired of growing close to her again. Now, as he gazed down at his son and took one of the restless small hands in his, he felt a pain like a knife twisting in his heart. The little boy's eyes were on him, unblinking, unwavering, and Rob drew in his breath. There was intelligence in that look, an awareness, a questioning wonder that might have been in the eyes of any normal infant of nine months.

'Do you speak to him, Hannah?' Rob's voice came out harsh and ragged. 'Do you play with him and take him on your knee and love him as you would any babe o' his age?'

'I feed him and change him.' Hannah didn't look up as she

ladled soup into plates. 'He's comfortable and that's enough for any bairn.'

'It *isn't* enough! He's a human being, Hannah, he needs love, he needs protection! Just because he's handicapped doesn't mean to say that his brain doesn't function. He knows what's going on, I can see it in his eyes, and if you stopped feeling so damned well sorry for yourself you would see it too! This is our son, Hannah, he deserves all the chances he can get, he deserves parents who want and love him and, by God! if you haven't got it in you to give him any o' these things I'll see he gets them a millionfold . . . !' His voice broke, his eyes glistened with a mixture of rage and pathos.

Hannah looked at him standing there, a tall strapping figure of a man with crisp dark hair and snapping blue eyes, a jawline that was obstinate and strong and a mouth that was firm and determined.

Women had always fallen for Robert James Sutherland. His rugged good looks, his passionate nature, his slow deep voice and his ability to inject an enigmatic quality into everything he said and did had captivated many a feminine heart. He had never needed to lure any of them to his bed, they had come to him, willingly and wantonly, drawn like moths to a flame by his charismatic nature and the knack he had of making each one of them feel special and wanted.

The parishes of Calvost and Balivoe, and places further afield, were sprinkled with Rob Sutherland's old flames, many of whom still sighed over him and asked themselves what had possessed him to marry so unsuitably, and him still just twenty-five with all his life in front of him; a life which each of them had hoped to share before he had ruined it by tying himself down to '*that woman*', a stranger who didn't belong in Kinvara; one, furthermore, who thought herself to be a cut above everyone else.

Ay, Rob had made a big mistake wedding himself to '*High and Mighty Miss Houston from Ayr*', as the local ladies sometimes referred to Rob's wife if they were in the mood to strip her of her marital title.

'And that mother o' hers, a real Tartar if ever there was one,' was the opinion of Mattie MacPhee, wife of Dokie Joe who worked as gardener and handyman to the laird. 'She's no better than any o' us and a lot worse than some.'

'Ay, and she has a coarse tongue in her head when she likes,' supplemented Cora Simpson, housekeeper to the Manse, her nostrils dilating with disapproval, 'even though she bows and scrapes in kirk and makes herself out to be as meek as a lamb when she's talking to the minister – and her just an occasional visitor too.'

'Well, neither mother nor daughter can afford to be so uppity now,' sniffed Catrina, Cora's sister, impatiently pushing a curl of red hair from her eyes. 'The coming o' the bairn soon took them down a peg or two.'

'Poor wee mite,' agreed Connie, who, at twenty-five, was the eldest of the Simpson sisters. 'But they'll still stick their noses in the air and pretend that they're better than folks who have lived here all their lives.'

All three sisters nodded their righteous approval of one another's comments. Give or take a pound or two they were as alike as peas in a pod, plump, pretty, rosy-cheeked, 'footloose and fancy free', as Connie was wont to say in a flippant attempt to hide the anxiety she was beginning to feel about still being single.

Each of them had harboured secret hopes of becoming hitched to Rob Sutherland at some time or other. In those days they would have torn one another's eyes out if he had dared to favour one above the others, but all that was in the past, he had been 'caught' by an outsider and now they had joined forces and thoroughly revelled in acting out their little personal vendettas against Hannah and her mother.

Rob didn't give a fig for any of these opinions, especially those of the Simpson sisters who were always trying to 'hook anything with breeks on'. Hannah didn't care what the Simpson sisters thought either; she knew how popular her husband had been with them and with womenfolk in general, but they were only locals and weren't to be taken seriously. He had other matters to think about now and plenty of responsibilities to keep his mind occupied.

'Your soup's getting cold, Rob,' was all she said in response to his outburst, her voice devoid of emotion.

But Rob wasn't finished with her. 'Why isn't Andy at the table with us?' he demanded as soon as he had seated himself. 'He shouldn't be left lying in that cot all day.'

Hannah gaped at him. 'With us? You know fine he can't sit up. He'll never sit up like a normal bairn.'

'Whatever gave you that idea? He *will* sit up, I'll bloody well make sure o' that. Where did you put the high chair I made for him before he was born?'

'In the cupboard in the lobby,' she faltered, an expression of fear coming into her eyes. She had never seen her husband as angry as he was now and she jumped a little as he tossed his chair back from the table and strode into the lobby, coming back a short while later with the high chair. Into it he installed his little son, strapping him in, packing pillows and cushions around him.

'Now put a bib on him and give him some food.' Rob was breathing hard, his nostrils aflare with temper, and Hannah rushed to his bidding. 'Feed him,' Rob ordered. 'I'm home for a few weeks now, Hannah, and before I go back on lighthouse duty again I want to see the spoon in his own hand and himself making an effort to guide it to his mouth. He'll make a helluva mess, and your kitchen might not be as spick and span as it is now, but at least we'll have the satisfaction of seeing our baby trying to do something for himself. He'll have to start learning sometime.'

In a very short time there was food everywhere, on the floor, the table, the high chair; the baby's face and hair were plastered with it as his uncontrolled muscles sent his limbs into spasms and contorted his face and mouth.

Hannah, almost weeping, tried half-heartedly to get him to hold a spoon till Rob could stand it no more. Grabbing the utensil he clamped it into the little boy's hand and holding it there with his own he began making it work, plate to mouth, plate to mouth, over and over, rhythmically, doggedly. The child spat and blew, girned and protested, food and saliva dripped over his chin and back into the plate but his father kept on till the dish was empty, half of it lost, some of it eaten. The baby's eyes were rolling in his head but he was grinning in his lop-sided fashion and banging the spoon on the tray of his high chair.

'There!' Rob was triumphant. 'He's done it! All he needs is to be helped and guided. And that's the way it's going to be from now on, Hannah. We're a family, and he's part of it. Never again let him lie alone in that cot unless it's necessary. Put him on the rug, let him roll about and discover the world he lives in. He'll never be a normal lad but it's up to us, you and me between us, to see that he gets as much out o' his life as possible.'

Hannah was feeling nauseated and kept her face averted from the sight of her own baby covered from head to chest in a slobbery mess. She had been disgusted enough feeding him milk from a bottle and had left off weaning him for as long as possible. But at least she had been able to exert a certain amount of control over the procedure, never wasting time over it, mopping up as soon as it was finished with and breathing a sigh of relief that it was over and out of the way before her stomach could start heaving. Rob had risen to fetch a soapy cloth and was now gently cleaning up his son. 'There, my wee man.' He touched the delicate small face with his lips and gathering up child, cushions and all, he deposited the whole bundle on the rug in front of the fire.

'We'll get him a dog.' Rob made the statement firmly. 'He'll need a companion if he's to be an only child. I'll see about it tomorrow. A pup would be best, then they can grow up together.'

'A dog.' Hannah went pale to the lips. 'I can hardly cope with him, never mind a pup piddling all over the place. It's all right for you, you're away half the time and I'm left with *him*, nobody to talk to, nothing in my life but a child who slavers and girns and throws himself about like a creature demented.'

'It's your own fault,' her husband stated baldly. 'You won't make friends, you won't let anybody near you, you seem hell bent on making your life a misery but I won't let you do it to him. I'm getting him a dog and that's all there is to it.'

As he was speaking Hannah was pouring the reheated soup into fresh plates. They sat down and in silence they broke bread, supped soup, ate potatoes and meat, but before the meal was halfway through Hannah said through tight lips, 'By the way, I forgot to tell you earlier, Mother is coming for Christmas. Father has to stay and supervise things at the hotel but she's managing to get away for a few days.'

'You forgot!' Rob blazed, little sparks of rage dancing in the hot blue of his eyes.

'Ay, you were so busy ranting on about *him* I had no chance to tell you anything.'

'*She's* coming here for Christmas! Your mother! Interfering, looking at Andy as if he was some sort o' monster, looking at *me* as if I was the big monster who allowed it all to happen. I had thought it would be just you and me and the bairn, our first Christmas together as a family – I imagined that we could maybe draw closer to one another – try to rekindle something of what we had in the beginning.'

'It's too late for that, Rob.' She kept her head down as she spoke, her tone gruff and cold. 'It can never be like that again, not now, now that we've got – him.'

For Rob, it was the last straw. Without another word he rose and going to the stand in the lobby he retrieved his jacket from its hook and threw himself out of the house, into the raw cold of the dark night, the muscles in his jaw working, his throat tight and sore with the pain of his despair and his loneliness.

With his departure the house was suddenly quiet. Sparks exploded in the chimney; Andy jumped, whimpered for a moment, then fell silent, his big dark eyes gaping in fascination at the shadows dancing on the ceiling. At the table Hannah stared into space for a long time, then she put her head into her hands and wept for everything that had turned sour in her life. Her heart was hard and cold in her breast. She wanted to reach out to her husband but her emotions seemed caught in shackles of steel.

The remembrance of how she had once loved him made it all the harder to bear. He was a good and loving man but he should never have burdened her with so much so soon . . . it was too much, far too much for someone like her to take. She looked at her son, lying there by the fire, his features twisted, his thin little limbs weak and useless looking. How could she ever draw close to a child like that? A changeling! That's what he was! The fairies had taken her own baby away and had left this creature in its place . . .

Oh, God, she thought, take pity on me, this child has come between Rob and me, I can't bring myself to love him. He isn't a healthy bairn, he'll never make anything of his life.

She knew it was wicked to think such terrible things but she couldn't help it and the tears that she wept were not for her husband or her child but for herself and everything that she was suffering.

Chapter Three

Passing the window of No. 5 of the row, Rob saw Big Morgan inside, his great shaggy face alight as he held his two-year-old son aloft, Janet, his wife beside him, as little as he was big, a tiny doll of a girl with long fair hair and a face as soft and as sweet as a rose. Both of them were laughing up at the child, the only one they could ever have, and the adoration in their faces was profound.

The picture they presented in the window-frame was like some old masterpiece, beautiful in its simplicity, and a lump rose in Rob's throat. That was how a family *should* look, united and loving, instead of divided and bitter. He walked on, hands buried deep in his pockets, uncertain of where he was going, yet his steps taking him away from the houses to the flat grasslands beyond.

The boom and roar of the Atlantic filled the night. It was big and it was magnificent. He inhaled deeply of the salt-fresh air till every fibre of him was filled with a surging new feeling of hope. The greatness of his surroundings was above and around him — and out there — over the infinite reaches of the ocean, the Kinvara Light was flashing.

He thought of the men on the rock, dour and solid Mungo MacGill, brash and bold Hic Gillespie with his quick tongue and fists to match, Jimmy 'Song' MacDuff, hiding a more serious side to his make-up with his stories and songs, all of them separated from their families at this special time of the year, thrown together in a tight sphere where the might of the waves reigned supreme and the voices of men were mere whispers in the pattern of creation.

And here he was, a speck of life amidst the vastness, a life that seethed and ached and wanted more than it had. Pausing for a moment he searched the twilight landscape. The hills rose up in front of him, dark and forbidding, Kinvara Point and the jagged ruins of the old chapel monastery were starkly etched against the sky, and up there on the shoulder of Ben Du, the Castle of Kinvara stood, the ancient seat of the Clan MacKernan, glowering down over the surrounding countryside, separated by the undulations of the hills from the laird's house.

Back in the mists of time, a feud had sprung up between the two houses concerning the rights to land ownership, and to this day, remnants of it still existed, though now it mainly concerned status in the community, inciting the two factions to vie with one another, albeit good naturedly, for first place in the popularity stakes.

At this moment, however, Rob wasn't giving much thought to the gentry and their little altercations, his eyes were drawn again and again to the curving white sands of Mary's Bay and the tiny pinprick of light flickering over yonder on the promontory. He tried not to look at it, to pretend to himself that he was only interested in the scenery. But it was no use. Something that might have been a name came out of him on a sigh and he began walking again, over the sodden turf to the sheep track leading down to the sand banks where deep channels carried the hill burns into the sea.

But he didn't get his feet wet, he knew where he was going, was familiar with the windings of the terrain that eventually took him to a grassy point of land and a sandy path leading to a lone cottage known as Oir na Cuan, which meant Edge of the Ocean, surrounded by sea and sand and sky and little else, except for a rough stone wall that kept the elements at bay and allowed for the survival of growing things within its confines.

There was something soft about this house, soft and warm and inviting. Rob took his fill of that impression as he stood out there on the machair, gazing at the white walls, the windows glowing with quiet luminosity. And then he heard the laughter, a muted melody of sound, muffled by brick and mortar yet so evocative he couldn't wait a moment longer to penetrate the sturdy portals.

'Morna.' The name was on his lips even as he raised his hand to rattle the door knocker. There was an immediate stirring from within, barkings and growlings, scrapings and shufflings, a voice ordering restraint and then the door opening, allowing a shaft of light to spill outwards, outlined against it the figure of a young woman, comely, shapely. Rob's heart beat fast. 'Morna,' he whispered, drinking in this first sight of her after so long.

The two Labrador dogs, Tink and Mink, one black, the other golden, were frisking and snuffling round the visitor, poking their wet noses into his pocket, obviously pleased to see him again.

'Robbie.' The girl gazed back at him. 'I hoped you'd come, I saw the boat, I rang my bell and lit the fire down on the beach, only a little one in case it would be too obvious . . .'

'I know, I heard, I saw . . .'

She pulled him inside, into the homeliness, shutting out the cold and the eyes that might lurk out there in the shadows of gloaming.

Johnny Lonely watched as the shaft of light on the path was suddenly extinquished. He blew into his hands and imagined the sweetness and warmth inside Morna's house. Johnny liked Morna, she had always been good to him, taking him in, feeding him when his belly was empty, talking to him in that nice easy way she had. He could converse with her as he could with no other: she listened, she sympathised, she was interested when he spoke about the stars, the tides, and the other things that he knew about. But Morna had Rob, always he came back to her, in the end he always came back. Johnny's eyes glistened; he rubbed his cold hands together, and then he made his way over the shore to his lonely little bothy huddled under the fortress-like cliffs of craggy Ben Du.

The rooms of Oir na Cuan glowed with more than just lamplight. There was fire and light and spirit in them, as if they had absorbed the character of Morna Jean Sommero who, with her laughing green eyes and jet-black hair, her smooth rosy face and warm smile, was the essence of everything that embodied happiness and contentment in human nature.

Rob had always thought that her name was like the morning, bright and new, yet aloof and mysterious too, filled with subtle colours and quiet shadows and little rainbows that suddenly appeared above the dreaming valleys of dawn. And like the morning there were many facets to Morna's personality. Rob knew them well, for she had come to Kinvara from Shetland four years ago at the age of sixteen to work for the laird. She had soon made a niche for herself in the community, everybody liked her, her cottage was never short of visitors popping in and out, but Rob's brother, Finlay, younger than him by two years, had liked her more than most, even though he had never been very good with women and was inclined to be awkward and shy in their company. Morna Jean Sommero was different, she put people at their ease; she did the same with Finlay and it wasn't long before he had fallen under her spell and would have done anything for her.

Then Rob came home from the Merchant Navy after serving in the war, and he and she had met one another for the first time. Romance had quickly blossomed between them. They had been so much in love it had hurt them to be parted for any length of time – it hurt now even to think about it, and Rob knew he was as much in love with her now as he had been then, more perhaps than during those stormy days of painful emotions and desperate longings, and he was captivated by the radiance that shone from her face as she stood there in front of him, laughing up at him, as pleased to see him as he was to see her.

'Morna.' Reaching out, he pushed a strand of glossy hair from her brow. She caught and held his hand, and the awareness that leapt between them was like a living thing, powerful and sweet, poignant and passionate . . .

And then came a soft little gurgle of laughter, the laughter of a little girl, and there, on the rug by the fire, was Vaila Marie, eighteen months old, her hair a cap of dark curls round her head, pearly teeth showing as she gazed up at the visitor.

'Wobbie.' The name came out, lisped but recognisable.

'I've been teaching her to speak,' Morna explained. 'She can say quite a lot now of course but she has her favourite words and your name is one of them.'

His heart turned over. Bending down, he plucked the child from the rug and held her at arms' length above his head, Morna there beside him, her expression of delight matching his in these proud moments. It was like the cameo Rob had recently seen through Big Morgan's window – but he wasn't thinking of that then, all he could see was this small bundle of rosy childhood, *his* daughter, his and Morna's, born after Morna had fled from him in rage and frustration because of an argument they'd had about Finlay who still persisted in seeing her.

When Rob had cast doubts over her feelings for him a great row had sprung up between them and she had left Kinvara to go back to Shetland to live again with her sister, Mirren, who had virtually raised her when their parents had died in a boating accident. There in Shetland, unknown to Rob, Morna had given birth to their daughter, and it was during this time that he, torn apart by heartache and loneliness, had met and married Hannah, never knowing about the existence of his baby girl until it was too late.

Five months ago Morna had returned to Kinvara and he had known instantly that Vaila was his, conceived out of the untamed love that he and Morna had shared. The realisation that he could never lay any claim to his own daughter had been a bitter blow to him, but he couldn't tell anybody, it would hurt too many people: his wife, his son, his own family, and yet he couldn't let Morna bear the brunt of the situation alone.

'It will have to be our secret, Robbie,' she had told him in that decisive way he knew so well, looking like a child herself with her hair tied back in a ribbon and her eyes big and dark in her young face. 'People will talk about me but they'll soon get over it. I'll look after Vaila here at Oir na Cuan and you'll come and visit us whenever you can manage. The laird might be an old rascal at times but he's been good to me and is letting me stay on at the cottage. In return I'll do some needlework for him which means I can be here at home with our baby. Oh, if it could have been you and me and her, all of us here together under one roof, I think I would never have asked for more out o' life.'

'It's all my fault,' he had said huskily. 'I should never have argued with you over my brother.'

'And I should never have left you in such a hurry, so we are both to blame, Robert Sutherland, and it's no use crying over spilt milk. We'll have to make the best of it and enjoy every precious minute we have together.'

After that they had snatched treasured moments out of his two months' remaining leave from lighthouse duty, and then he had gone away, so long ago now it seemed to him as he stood there with his child in his arms, gazing deep into Morna's eyes. She had come through all her earlier traumas well, with a contentment about her that he had never seen before, but she also looked weary, there were blue smudges under her eyes, a pallor about her face despite the flush on her cheeks.

But when he voiced his thoughts she brushed them aside with a laugh and told him he too would be tired with a growing infant to see to and all the creatures of God's creation coming to her door to be fed and healed. He laughed at that. It was true what she said; among all her other attributes she had a way with animals: cats, dogs, wild birds of shore and sea, even a young seal and an otter, had all found their way into her keeping at some time or another, drawn to her magnetism, unwilling to leave it when the day came for them to return to their natural habitat.

Some never did. The seal popped up regularly to visit her;

ducks and geese inhabited her woodshed; a young deer whose broken leg she had mended came to her for titbits; a rabbit she had rescued from a trap climbed the wall into her garden and ate the lettuce and carrots she had so painstakingly grown for her own table.

When she first came to live in the area the men of Calvost said she was 'daft as a fox's brush', and had a bit of the witch about her. The womenfolk, however, sympathised with her and told her she was 'a good kind lassie', though to one another they agreed that she was 'a bittie unusual' to say the least.

'Well, but of course, she *is* a newcomer,' Effie Maxwell, the district nurse, had said in Morna's defence and in such a way as to suggest that anybody other than a born and bred local had to be indulged.

'Ay, that would explain thon funny wee quirks she has about her.' Mattie MacPhee nodded sagely, her eyes gleaming at the remembrance of Morna freeing a cockerel that Mungo MacGill had so carefully confined in an upturned peet creel in respect of the Sabbath.

Morna knew that she was regarded as something of a novelty but that didn't stop her doing what she felt had to be done for God's creatures, and, as well as all that, she let nature have its way with them, and Rob smiled as he glanced at Mink with her slack belly and a row of pups swinging from her teats in an effort to suckle as she moved across the room.

'She was like me' – Morna's tone was teasing – 'too young to know what she was doing when she got caught by that big collie brute from Croft Angus. And just look at the pups, a queer mixture with their big lumpy heads and ungainly bodies.'

'Och, c'mon, Morna,' he said reproachfully, 'we weren't too young to know what we were doing. We knew all right. My only regret is how it all turned out in the end. But Mink and that big collie brute have done me a favour. I want Andy to have a dog for his Christmas, especially a puppy, I told Hannah so before I came out. She wasn't pleased but she'll just have to thole it.'

'How was she – when you came home?'

'The same as ever, distant, resentful, hating Andy, hating me more.'

'Oh, Robbie,' she whispered, her head downbent so that the firelight burnished her hair. 'I'm so sorry. We played it wrong you and me – we could have had such a lovely life together . . . Oh, what's the use . . .'

Getting up suddenly she went through to the scullery to fetch the tin tub which she filled from the bubbling pans and kettles on the fire. When the water was at the right temperature she and Rob bathed the baby between them, up to their elbows in rose-scented soapsuds, while Vaila crooned and blew and thoroughly enjoyed all the attention she was receiving.

When they were finished with her she was pink and perfumed, a picture of healthy babyhood with her damp curls clinging round her head and her face shiny and glowing.

They sat with her for a while, playing with her, talking to her, then Morna bore her to bed in her own little attic room upstairs, accompanied by the dogs who enjoyed the routine of the household and loved to be in the middle of everything that was going on, especially when it involved Vaila Marie, on whom they doted and whom they followed everywhere.

When Morna came back to the kitchen it was to find that Rob had made tea and had set the big fat brown earthenware teapot on the hob to keep warm. It was a homely scene, the pups and the cats on the rug, sleepy and contented, the firelight flickering over the room, falling on that handsome figure of a man sitting there waiting for her, his eyes on her as soon as she appeared, eyes that were dark and intense in the shadowy planes of his face.

The sight of him turned her legs to jelly and caused her pulse to race. He had always done this to her, her Robbie, her strong, brave darling of a man. She would never love anyone else the way she loved him and her heart was sore in the breast of her as she stood there, wondering how she was going to tell him the things he had to know before the night was over.

Chapter Four

Hannah was growing uneasy. Rob was later than he had ever been and she felt as if she had been alone for hours. Despite her cool welcome to him earlier, she had looked forward to having him about the place again. He was the only person that kept her sane in this barren world she found herself in.

Tonight she had chased him away with all that talk about her mother. Perhaps he was right, it would have been nice if it had just been him and her, here together for Christmas.

Hannah's mouth twisted. Her mother wouldn't be put off now: once Harriet Houston had made up her mind to do something there was no stopping her. The only way to make her visit bearable would be to get her out and about as much as possible. She came from farming stock; her own parents still ran a sizeable acreage of arable land in Ayrshire and farming was in Harriet's blood. She liked nothing better than to get on her boots and muck about with the animals . . .

Just as long as she didn't get under Rob's feet, for he enjoyed being out there too, working his croftland, seeing to the beasts, mending walls and fences, doing all the little jobs that had piled up in his absence, even though his father and brother kept an eye on everything, making sure that the cows, the hens, the geese, and the sheep were fed and cared for.

Hannah had never taken to any of that, although she had certainly enjoyed childhood visits to her grandparents' farm. In those days it had seemed all sunlight and sweetness, with her hand in the big horny one of her granpa as he took her to see chirpy little day-old chicks and tiny fluffy kittens, all helpless and wide-eyed.

The reality wasn't like that at all, the glaur and the dung, the maggots on the sheep, the dipping and the clipping, cows with mastitis, bellowing out in pain, especially when they were calving . . .

Hannah shuddered, she didn't want to think of that . . . She turned her mind back to her husband; although he was late it wasn't unusual for him to go out, he had a lot of friends he could go to, people he had known all his life, who knew him and his ways just as he knew them and how they reacted and behaved. It was as if they were all one big family, sharing things together, laughing at the talk and the banter, confiding their little troubles, arguing too but always safe in the knowledge that they would make it up to one another, somehow, sometime . . .

Hannah knew that she would never be accepted into such a close-knit community, they were suspicious of strangers, expected them to adopt habits and customs that were foreign to them and to go along with all the little oddities that seemed to be inherent in many of the inhabitants. You had to be born into a place like Kinvara really to belong. Incomers didn't stand a chance; they weren't wanted or needed, it seemed – that fact had been quite plain to Hannah right from the beginning.

Yet there *were* exceptions. Morna Sommero, for instance. It was common knowledge that she had borne a child out of wedlock and had come back with it to Kinvara, as bold as brass, looking as if she had nothing to be ashamed of, holding her head high . . . 'Like a hussy' Big Bette MacGill had pronounced – but she hadn't meant it, the people of Kinvara might never let Morna forget her indiscretions but they had soon forgiven her. She invoked curiosity, gossip, speculation in the locality as a whole but Hannah had never yet met anyone who didn't like her.

Not that Hannah had mixed with very many of the locals in the time she had lived here . . .

'It's your own fault.' Rob's words rang in her head. 'You

won't let anyone near you, you've shut everyone out and if you're not careful you'll soon become a hermit like Johnny Lonely.'

Hannah stared into the fire and bit her lip. She didn't care! They weren't the sort of people she wanted to befriend anyway. Some of them were downright coarse with their unsophisticated manners and idle chatter; the rest were no better, hiding their hypocritical ways under prim Sunday hats whilst going about casting sly innuendoes at whoever didn't meet with their approval.

She glanced at the clock. Ten of the hour and still no sign of Rob. A terrible thought went through her mind. What if he never came home again? She would be left alone with – with . . . Her eyes raked through the shadows to the cot in the corner. She couldn't be left with *him*, that pitiful wraith of a child whose appearance filled her with such repugnance she wanted only to shut him out of her sight, forget all about him as if he had never existed, had never drawn breath . . . With a stifled cry she got up and put another lump of coal on the fire when a hurried rap at the door made her glance up quickly. Who could that be at this hour? She didn't want to see anybody, was in no mood to listen to a lot of small talk that meant nothing to her . . .

'It's only me, Hannah.'

Janet's light girlish voice came from the lobby and Hannah went hastily to intercept her young next-door neighbour.

Janet was only nineteen, young for her age, a slender dainty child-woman who laughed a lot and never seemed to stop talking. Hannah looked at her standing there on the doorstep, her pretty face alight, long fair hair hanging down her back, her eyes a brilliant grey-blue in the warm flush of her face. When Hannah had first come to Kinvara almost two years ago Janet had just given birth to Joseph, an event that had brought the utmost joy into the lives of Big Morgan and his tiny adored wife. Janet had wanted to share her happiness with everyone, even though the doctor had warned her that she could never have another child, that Joss was to be the one and only.

She had tried to include Hannah in her life, eager to share with everyone the wonderful things she was experiencing, but she had found it hard going. Hannah had made it plain that she wanted to be left alone, though Janet never gave up trying to be friendly.

Then had come little Andrew, an event that had made the Morgans' new neighbour more withdrawn, more unapproachable than ever. In order to see her at all there had to be an excuse and tonight Janet had come on the pretence of borrowing sugar, an empty earthenware bowl in her hands as she waited to see what kind of reception she was going to get.

'I'm sorry, I've run out,' she imparted hastily, 'Bette was waiting for a fresh supply to come in and Jock canny seem to do without it in his cocoa. It's that nice to have our menfolk home again,' she went on happily, gazing curiously past Hannah to the open door of the kitchen. 'I fair miss Jock when he's away and like to spoil him a wee bit when I've got him all to myself again – and I'm sure you feel the same about Rob.'

The older woman did not invite the girl in, instead she took the bowl and disappeared without a word into the kitchen.

In a short while she was back, thrusting the sparsely filled container into Janet's hands, saying shortly, 'It's all I can spare and it's brown. I couldn't get any at the village store either, but it didn't overly worry me since I consider too much o' it to be bad for anybody.'

Janet reddened. 'To be truthful,' she said softly, 'I didn't really need it, I just came because I wanted to ask you and Rob to a little party we're having for Joss. He'll be two soon and we thought it would be nice to have a few friends in to celebrate.'

'I'm sorry.' The refusal sprang quickly to Hannah's lips. 'I can't leave Andy, he demands my attention day and night – and I was never a one for parties anyway.'

'Oh, but you can surely bring wee Andy along, it would be fine for him to – to get out for a whily – even if it is just next door.'

Hannah recoiled as if she had been struck. The very idea

32

of taking her son to visit the Morgans filled her with horror. All they were good for was baby talk, fussing and doting over their child, expecting everyone else to do the same, as if he was the only one ever to be created . . . that perfect, beautiful little boy . . . 'No!' she cried sharply. 'Andy's not fit to go anywhere, too much noise upsets him and it is me who suffers afterwards when he lies girning and whining and won't go to sleep.'

'Och well.' Janet retreated a step, 'If you change your mind . . .' With a dignified movement she placed the sugar bowl on the window-ledge. 'I won't be needing that after all and I'm sorry to have bothered you.' Turning away she muttered, 'I will bid you goodnight then,' and like a little ghost she was soon swallowed up in the darkness.

There came the sound of her door opening and closing and then there was silence. Hannah let go of her breath in a long sigh. Shivering she pulled her shawl closer about her shoulders and went back to the kitchen to resume her place by the fire, unable to concentrate on anything, her thoughts bleak and empty as she stared into the hot cinders and wished Rob would come home.

Chapter Five

Rob had lost all sense of time as he sat there in Oir na Cuan, watching Morna as she came further into the room to say quietly, 'Robbie, you're such a good man, thoughtful, considerate, a loving father to your children . . . How strange to think of it like that, your children, as if we were one family, instead of divided and separated, living under different roofs.'

'Don't torment yourself like that, Morna,' he whispered, a mist of tears in his eyes. 'You're all I think about when I'm away, the only person in the world I want to be with when I come home.'

They sat by the fire drinking their tea, she on a little raffia stool at his feet, both of them silent for a long time till he leaned forward and took her hands in his, his voice husky with the emotions that were tearing him apart. 'Morna, do you still love me? I have to know, it makes my life bearable somehow – just to know that you care.'

'Oh, God!' With a sob she pulled her hands out of his. 'Please, don't ask me that! It's more than I can stand. I'm sorry, so sorry, my dearest love, but there's something I have to tell you, something I've been dreading all the weeks you were away. You see, I must think of Vaila, she – she needs to have a father, one who is here all the time – and that is why I'm getting married – just as soon as the wedding can be arranged.'

'To give Vaila a father!' he blazed, his expression one of incredulity. 'She's got a father, she's got me!'

'No, Robbie, she can never call you that, that right has been denied her by circumstances she had no part in. You will always be special to her, I hope she will always look up to you and respect the part you must play in her life, someone she can turn to when she needs affection and comfort.'

'Who is it?' he asked tightly. 'Who has waited like a fox in a hole to move in like this as soon as my back is turned?'

She took a deep shuddering breath. 'Your brother, Finlay, and please don't think o' it like that, Robbie, he's been very kind to me, he's been here for me when I needed a man's hands about the place.'

'My brother!' he exploded, staring at her in disbelief. 'But he was the cause of your leaving me, the reason I ended up wedding myself to Hannah instead o' you . . .'

'I know these things, Robbie, but they're all in the past. I have to think o' the future, Vaila's and mine. Finlay has never asked very much about how she came to be, he just seems to accept that it was somebody I met when I was away.'

'My father will never condone your marrying Finlay,' Rob quickly pointed out. Ramsay Sutherland was a devout member of the Free Kirk and travelled miles to get to it, sometimes standing in for the preacher when his services were required elsewhere. When Morna had first come to Kinvara, Ramsay had expressed his doubts about her, regarding her unusual lifestyle and lack of attendance in a church of any sort as a threat to the more God-fearing members of society. He had tried to discourage his sons from seeing her, and now that she had borne a child 'on the wrong side o' the blankets', to quote Mattie MacPhee, his disapproval of her was greater than ever.

At Rob's words, Morna nodded and said quietly, 'He doesn't know yet, but he will very soon and there's nothing he can do about it. Finlay has already spoken to your mother; she came here to see me – and though she wasn't very pleased at first she came round in the end and said she would give us her blessing.'

'Her blessing! And you think that makes it all right! Mother would say anything to keep Finlay happy – and so it seems would you. He's never known his own mind, he's never been able to decide what he wants to do with his life. You're marrying him for all the wrong reasons, he doesn't really mean anything to you – unless . . .' His voice dropped. 'Was it him you wanted all along? I know he hated the idea o' me butting into what was his in the beginning. Perhaps Vaila—'

'No, Robbie!' Morna protested vehemently. 'She's yours. I never loved anyone else but you, no man ever touched me the way you did! Don't you see. I'm doing it to be nearer to you? The baby – *our* baby will have your name. She will be a Sutherland after all, and if it has to be done through your brother, then so be it.'

The tears were pouring down her face as she spoke and taking her in his arms he smoothed the hair from her brow and kissed the trembling soft lips that had always driven him crazy with desire. 'It *is* for all the wrong reasons,' he whispered hopelessly, but the anger was out of him now, another kind of fire burned within him as he held Morna close and murmured his words of love into her ears.

Hannah strained her eyes through the darkness for a sign of her husband. It was the third time she had gone out to the door that evening. She hadn't been able to settle since he'd left and now there was a strange feeling of dread at the pit of her stomach. She had never felt more alone, more cut off from the people and the places she had known before her marriage. Not that she had ever been a one for gadding about, in fact she had been inclined to keep herself to herself, even at school when all the talk and chatter around her was about boys and partying. It had seemed silly and meaningless to her; she had preferred to stay at home with her books. She had loved reading, losing herself in other folks' lives, the dramas and dreams, the romances, the heartaches. She had grown more withdrawn when her mother had joined forces with her father and had launched herself energetically into running their thriving hotel business. Even so there were always people around, especially in the summer when coachloads of visitors invaded the quiet of the seaside resort.

In her own way she had enjoyed the activity going on in the hotel, helping out with the paperwork, seeking company when she wanted it. There had been one or two male acquaintances, but nothing serious; she had never experienced any deep urges to become entangled in the physical side of a relationship, her books were enough for her; in them she could immerse herself in the lives of the characters and shut the pages on them whenever she felt like it.

Rob had been her first real contact with a man and she had been surprised at how quickly she had succumbed to the attraction she felt for him. It was as if she had waited for someone like him all along, so tall and handsome, so like one of the heroes of her favourite books. She had clung to him like a drowning person clutches at a straw, seeing her life as a mere existence without him, longing only for him to carry her off to that wonderful world of sea and sky that he spoke about in such soft, loving tones.

How different was the harsh reality. Here there was nobody worth getting to know, it was a lonely God-forsaken spot, and out there, on the black horizon, the flashing of the Kinvara Light reminding her of the times her husband was away on duty and how often she had stood outside in the darkness, afraid and alone, thinking of the miles of cold sea that separated her from him.

Her thoughts made her shiver and she scrunched the folds of her shawl closer round her neck as she listened to the waves heaving themselves against the rocks in the bay and saw the faint glimmer of lights coming from distant houses, signs of life that only served to accentuate the bleakness of the bitter night . . .

Her ears crackled suddenly, as if tiny electric shocks were running through them. Someone was coming along, walking slowly but steadily towards the house. She released her breath sharply and scuttled back to the kitchen to seat herself at the fireside and pick up the book she was currently reading.

When Rob came in and saw her sitting there she appeared

to be totally absorbed in the pages and hardly looked up at his entry. 'Where have you been?' she asked in a tone that suggested scant interest while she kept her eyes glued to the words in front of her.

'Just for a walk. I saw Morna Sommero, her bitch has had pups – I'm getting one for Andy's Christmas.'

To his surprise Hannah made no comment to this, instead she said musingly, 'Morna Sommero, I met her once or twice down in the bay, she's – different from the others here. I suppose because she's an incomer like myself. I liked her because she doesn't gossip or pry but just gets on with her life. There's – something about her that makes you feel you want to confide in her.'

'Ay, a lot o' people get on well with Morna,' he hazarded cautiously, amazed that his wife had actually admitted to liking someone in the place.

'I know that, Rob, and you seem to be one o' them. She gets quite a lot o' visitors down yonder, yet nobody knows very much about her – who the father o' her child is, for instance.'

Rob, feeling as if he were treading on eggs, replied slowly, 'Everybody has their private lives to lead. You said yourself she isn't a busybody and I suppose she expects other folks to behave in the same way.'

'I suppose so, yet it isn't natural, is it? A young woman like that, bringing up a bairn all on her own. It must be hard on her, she must get lonely – and I know only too well how that feels.'

'It won't be for long,' he said quickly, harshly. 'She's marrying my brother, Finlay. Father won't be too pleased, he doesn't know about it yet so don't say anything to anybody else.'

'Finlay?' A note that could have been relief was there in the surprised tone of her voice. 'I knew that he was quite close to her before she went away and had her bairn, but then – so too were you, Rob.'

'That's all in the past, it's now that counts, and hopefully Finlay will make her a good husband.'

'Ay, and a father for her bairn.' Hannah put her book aside

and, getting up, she set the kettle to boil on the fire, never seeing the look of despair in the eyes of her husband as he thought about Morna and how circumstances would change for them both in the months and years to come.

Morna remained seated by the fire long after Rob had gone, cuddling one of Vaila's teddy bears to her breast. She was exhausted, her heart was heavy and tired within her, all she wanted was to go to bed and sleep but she knew she wouldn't be able to rest, not just yet, when every detail of Rob's visit was fresh and vivid in her mind.

She knew that she had hurt him deeply that night, but her pain was even more for she could never tell him the real reason that had made her decide to marry Finlay. It was enough that she was forsaking the true love of her life to give her daughter a secure future. In her heart she would always love Robert Sutherland, a man who could never be hers in the eyes of the world but one she would never stop pining for as long as she lived. Her Robbie, she would never cease to think of him as such, even though he belonged to another woman . . .

Morna felt as if she were the only person in the world as she sat there with her thoughts, the firelight flickering and dancing all around her, the animals tranquilly snoring, the sea sighing and whispering outside the walls of the little house.

After a while she rose and went upstairs to go into the room where Vaila peacefully slept. Morna gazed down at the small face framed by its cap of black curls and gently she touched one of the petal-soft cheeks. 'Little girl,' she whispered. 'You will be a Sutherland after all, if it's the last thing I do you will have someone you can call Father – even if it is in name only.'

Chapter Six

Ramsay Sutherland found out about his younger son's marriage plans sooner than anybody had intended; the very next morning in fact when his own wife let everything slip over the breakfast table.

Rita Sutherland had never been a body to worry her head about the latest styles in the fashion world. Her life at Vale o' Dreip, the big rambling farmstead on the slopes of Blanket Hill, demanded sensible clothes and good sturdy footwear. The only times she changed into something more dressy was for funerals, weddings, and the Sabbath, and she was always quite happy to get back into garments in which she felt more comfortable. But on rising that morning a glance through the dilapidated contents of her wardrobe had caused her some alarm. There was nothing at all in the mothball-smelling collection worthy enough for Finlay's proposed marriage to Morna. Rita, never one to shirk anything, far less the wrath of her husband who was always ranting and raving about something, had none the less avoided broaching this particular subject, knowing how much he would rebel against it and make life awkward for everyone involved.

She had hoped that Finlay himself would have told his father by now, but the days were wearing in, nothing had been said, and clicking her wardrobe door shut, she decided that it was high time someone said something, and the sooner the better as far as she was concerned.

'Wait a while, Ma,' Finlay said when she told him of her decision. 'At least till Christmas is over, you know how unpleasant Father can be when something doesn't please him.'

Rita looked at her strapping son with his big hands and his broad shoulders. He was a tall giant of a boy, sturdy and strong, with sandy red hair and light blue eyes, and an endearingly child-like way of expressing himself – at least his mother thought it was endearing, others said he wasn't the full shilling, while his father maintained that it was time he grew up and started behaving like a man.

Finlay was very like his father to look at but entirely different in every other way. He was the timid one of the two sons and had never been able to make up his mind about anything; he didn't like facing up to the more unpleasant aspects of life and had always relied on other people, usually his mother, to sort things out for him.

Unlike his brother, he hadn't joined up at the start of the war. For one thing, he had been too young; for another, he maintained it went against his pacifist principles. Later on, when it became apparent that every man worth his salt had little option but to fight for his country, he had fallen prey to a mysterious disabling illness that had baffled every doctor who had examined him. During all of this he had been supported by his mother who told him he wasn't the sort that was cut out for wars and that his health came first above all else.

It had been a very trying period for everyone concerned. Many husbands and sons, brothers and sweethearts, had not survived to return to Kinvara, so Finlay was the odd one out in a place of mourning. Folks talked about him behind his back and called him a yellow belly; some said it straight to his face, while others kept silent but conveyed their feelings well enough by what they implied.

Rob hadn't flinched from his duties and had emerged from his naval services unscarred and more manly than ever, his experiences on the waves and his knowledge of the sea giving him the grounding he needed to realise his boyhood ambition of becoming a lighthouse keeper.

Ramsay too had returned unscathed from his stint in the Black Watch, except for nervous depression and anxiety which still troubled him and made his already fiery nature more eruptive than ever. Unable to hide his scorn at a son who had shirked his duty to his country, he continually nagged at the boy and found fault with whatever he did, especially when his malaise unaccountably vanished not long after the guns of war fell silent. But Finlay had one saving grace that did find favour in Ramsay's critical eyes. He was a born farmer, up at the crack of dawn every morning, seeing to the beasts, helping with the milking, out at first light in the fields doing whatever had to be done. These were the times he got on best with his father, when they were working together, each of them attuned to the other, knowing instinctively what had to be done without the need for idle chatter.

Rita didn't need her younger son to prove himself in any special way, she doted on him the way he was. Now she found herself softening as she gazed at his young face and noticed the tiny golden hairs glinting in his sideburns. He was such a nice lad, a bit weak where drink was concerned, possessed of quite a temper, but otherwise a good and loving son. It would do no harm to wait till after Christmas, she thought. What Ramsay didn't know wouldn't harm him; she often left off telling him things just for the sake of peace. She pursed her lips and sniffed. He was forever going on about something or other, greed, laziness, lust. Pity he didn't practise what he preached, last night, for instance. Tearing at her body, forcing himself on her like a heathen; his religion didn't stop him from wanting *that* – and quite often she had noticed a gleam in his eye at the sight of a pretty young girl passing his vision.

Finlay was waiting for her answer and she was about to give him the reassurance he wanted when she remembered the state of her wardrobe and how long it would take her to get something decent to wear. Trips into Inverness were few and far between, there were no clothes shops worth mentioning in the whole of the Kinvara peninsula, and with that in mind she laid her hand on her son's arm and said softly, 'Wheesht, Finlay, he'll have to know sometime, he'll make a fuss but that's to be expected . . .' Breaking off she was silent for a moment before asking, 'Are you really sure about this lass? It won't be easy, taking on another man's bairn, and I only want what's best for you.'

'Ay, Ma, I'm sure. I love Morna, I've loved her all along and now that she needs me I want her even more.' Despite his nervousness there was a steady conviction in his voice, a note of strength that surprised his mother. It wasn't often that he was so positive about anything and Rita knew that nothing would hold him back now, not even the wrath of the man who frowned on anything that did not come within the framework of his rigid expectations.

Mother and son went downstairs together, he to sit uneasily at the table, she to prepare the sort of hearty breakfast that her husband expected to be set before him every morning – except Sundays. Then he ate frugally and expected his family to do the same, since 'thought for food' was the order of that sacred day together with a menu of bible study and prayer.

As predicted, Ramsay Sutherland did rave and rant when the news was broken to him. His eyes bulged, he paused in the action of digging his knife into his bacon and eggs and for one long moment he simply stared at his wife as if she had gone mad. Ramsay was a tall giant of a man with good broad shoulders, ice-blue eyes, auburn hair, and a neatly clipped beard attractively flecked with red. He was a respected figure in the community, people looked up to him and came to him for advice and he was always willing to help anybody in trouble – as long as it was the sort that fell within the laws set down by the Free Church, an establishment which he attended rigorously and believed in implicitly. Rita too was a member of this church but only to pacify her husband; Rob had stopped going when he was sixteen; Finlay still went but sporadically, much to the displeasure of his father who maintained that if a family should unite in anything it should be in the church and all it had to offer. He had said often enough that his sons had gone to the dogs since their faith in the church had wavered and this latest scheme of Finlay's seemed to be proving his point.

'Married!' he repeated harshly, his eyes swivelling rapidly from wife to son. 'When did this all come about I'd like to know! And to a lass who leads the life o' a heathen! What are you thinking of, lad? She isn't in the least bit suited to you and certainly not the sort I'd visualised having for a daughter-in-law. It's bad enough having Hannah in the family but at least she led a decent enough life before her marriage to Rob. And what makes you think you can cope with the child? You don't know what sort o' father she had, there might be bad blood in her for all you know.'

Finlay hesitated before giving his answer, for his father was voicing some of the doubts he himself harboured. Although he hadn't said anything to Morna he *had* wondered about her child's background, what kind of stuff she was made of, how she might turn out in later years. Then he straightened, he wasn't going to let anything stand in the way of his marriage to Morna, it was just too bad that they would be starting off with a ready-made family but if any problems arose on that score he would soon sort them out – and they would have children of their own to bind them together, he would make sure of that.

'Well? I'm waiting.' Ramsay's voice was like a whiplash. Rita opened her mouth to say something in her son's defence but he got there first, his voice reasonably steady when he said, 'Vaila's only a baby, she'll be fine if she's given the chance to grow up happily. All she needs is a father figure to look up to and I'll make sure both she and her mother have everything they need to make them comfortable.'

'And how, pray, do you propose to do that?' Ramsay's voice was heavy with sarcasm. 'You don't have any means that I know of.'

'I've been saving a bit, so we'll manage fine. Morna doesn't want to leave Oir na Cuan, she has had a word with the laird and I'll be moving in there after the wedding. Also . . .' He looked straight at his father. 'I was hoping I could go on working here. Farming is what I'm best suited for, I can't see me ever doing anything else — and I thought, seeing that I'll have a family to keep and I won't be living here any more, you could maybe see your way to paying me a bit more than I get now.'

Ramsay gave in to this proposal with bad grace, mainly because Finlay was such an invaluable help about the place and had never been paid his full worth, despite the fact that his father was a man of considerable means, having bought Vale o' Dreip from the laird when that gentleman had fallen on lean times after the war.

Ramsay had never regretted letting go of his tenancy of the farm in favour of ownership. Good husbandry of the land, an eye for profitable dairy and beef stock, and hard work had all combined to make the place a viable acquisition, the result being that Vale o' Dreip was one of the most flourishing farms in the area.

Even so, its owner, renowned for his canny nature, was tight with the pennies and never parted with them unless it was strictly necessary. In Finlay's case, he felt that the boy owed the allegiance that any good son of the soil should owe to the land that fed and nurtured him, the monetary side of it hardly coming into prominence since most of it was swallowed up in bed and board and all the little extras that it took to keep a young man of Finlay's age happy.

He saw of course that he couldn't argue that point now that the fledgling was leaving the nest, but thank God he wasn't leaving it completely as the idea of hiring someone to take his place didn't bear thinking about. Even so, he made his son sweat a bit before giving his answer, it would never do to let the boy get too much of a sense of his own importance and he let a full minute elapse before speaking.

'Ay, you can continue here,' he growled, more annoyed than ever by Finlay's unusual boldness that morning. One would have thought he might have shown a bit of deference. Instead, here he was, outlining his wishes, asking for extra money that he might live with a fallen woman and her bastard child. Ramsay's brows drew together in a thunderous frown. He positively glared at his son when he added, 'I hope you're no' planning to marry here in Kinvara. It would be the talk o' the place. You have no right to a kirk wedding, it wouldn't be seemly in the eyes o' the Lord.'

Finlay felt himself going cold at this. 'Morna and me have every right,' he said tightly. 'As a matter o' fact, we *are* having a kirk wedding – in Shetland. Morna's sister has spoken to the minister and he's agreed to do it.'

Ramsay's fingers drummed the table, his brows blackened even further. 'You can count me out o' that one!' he retaliated furiously. 'I will not be witness to my own son making a fool o' himself in a house o' God.'

Finlay felt only relief at this. The last thing he wanted was his father there when his nuptials were finalised. 'As you wish, Father. I'm sorry you feel this way, it isn't my intention to start off my married life under a cloud but I know how you feel about certain matters and I have to respect you for it.'

'Ay, ay, so you say. In my view it would have been more respectful if you had gone for a normal sort o' lass and could have wed decently in the Free Kirk – I take it this minister you speak of is a Kirk o' Scotland minister.'

Finlay nodded and Ramsay, his face a bright shade of crimson, stood up. 'My breakfast is ruined! I won't stay here and listen to another word – but I promise you this, my lad, I don't want to see Morna Sommero or her child here in this house, she will bring nothing but shame and misery to the good family name and I, for one, don't want any part of her.' He looked pointedly at his wife. 'You do see my thinking in all this, Rita, don't you?'

'Ay, Ramsay, I see your thinking.' Rita's eyes snapped in her lively face. 'But that's no' to say that I myself will go out o' my way to avoid the lass. Since she and Finlay will be living in the same house together I don't see how I can ignore her when I go down there to visit him.'

'You don't have to visit. You will see him here, he'll surely be around every day as he has been for the last twenty-three years, therefore you will have no reason to go anywhere near Mary's Bay or to *that* house.'

'We'll see,' Rita said softly and with a note of determination in her voice that her husband knew well. He was about to argue with her further when the door opened and Captain Rory MacPherson, the laird of Crathmor, popped his head round.

'Not interrupting anything, am I?' he asked in his big bumbly voice as he came further into the room. His appearance stifled any further family disputes. Finlay rose to go and fetch another chair, which he positioned strategically at the table; Rita put out another cup and cheerily filled it from the earthenware pot that had been keeping warm at the side of the stove, glad of the diversion that the laird's arrival had brought into a situation that had been growing very uncomfortable indeed.

Chapter Seven

The newcomer needed no asking to sit down at the table: he enjoyed nothing more than a brew of piping hot tea in a homely atmosphere, and without hesitation his big hand was out to grab a buttery scone as soon as Rita set a plateful at his side.

Captain Rory MacPherson was a large handsome man of forty with a military moustache and an upright bearing. Having lost an ear whilst serving his country in the war, he wore his hair swept dramatically to the one side in an effort to disguise the blemish, thus creating a feature which only served to enhance his already distinctive appearance. Invariably dressed in clan kilt and lovat tweed jacket, he was a fine sight to see, striding about the countryside with his crook and his spaniel dogs at his side, a skinny Siamese cat bringing up the rear because she couldn't bear to remain at home when her master was on one of his rambles. He was a man who had always mixed well and was as comfortable with farmers and villagers as he was with those of his own ilk.

He loved joining in community activities and was often to be seen in the thick of any event, be it the annual Vaul Highland games or simply a jumble sale in a local hall. He thought nothing of stripping to the waist to help with the dipping and the clipping and it wasn't unusual for him to be seen drinking at the village inn and to be taken home afterwards in any kind of transport that was available, be it a pony and trap or a donkey cart piled with hay or turnips and – once – a load of dung!

Some criticised him for being mean, yet he never failed to give something to the poorer families at Christmas and was also renowned for handing out tobacco and spirits in the pub at New Year. His festive dinners for his employees and their families were much relished by everyone and spoken about long afterwards for their informality and generosity of spirit.

His pretty young wife, fourteen years his junior, had borne him three children, all still under the age of six. When he had married himself to Emily Stables Abercrombie, folks had called him a baby-snatcher; when the children arrived in quick succession, Dolly Law of Balivoe had declared him to be 'a dirty auld bodach', only to be told by Mattie MacPhee that she had a cheek to talk since the Laws were notorious for having reached seven in number after only nine years of wedded unrest.

No matter what people called Captain Rory MacPherson, most of them were devoted to him and his family and loyally stood up for them should any stranger or incomer dare to make a derogatory comment against them. Ramsay Sutherland was no exception. He and the laird were close associates, both business-wise and socially, and those who knew Ramsay best were always surprised at how lenient he could be towards the other man, even in matters that were normally tender subjects in his book.

The laird could be as liberal as he liked with his opinions about morality and the Church and Ramsay seldom took offence at his more outrageous views; rather he gave every appearance of enjoying a good-natured argument and laughed more than was his wont with anybody else. He indulged the master of Crathmor, there was no doubt about it, and it had nothing to do with the other man's higher social status. The truth was that he genuinely liked and respected Captain Rory MacPherson and was never sparing in his efforts to ensure that he was comfortable and well cared for whenever he had reason to visit Vale o' Dreip.

On this occasion, his mind seething with all that had transpired at the breakfast table, Ramsay did not feel like entertaining anyone, but for the sake of good manners, and knowing how much the laird enjoyed a dram at any time of the day, he went to fetch the whisky from the cupboard in the parlour. Ramsay always kept a good supply of drink in the house, ostensibly for his more distinguished callers though he had partaken of the devil's brew on occasions when he thought it only hospitable to do so. This little drinks cache in the 'best room' of the house was kept locked at all times, the key for the same reposing on a ring attached to his belt, along with others for various private drawers and cabinets in his study.

Going back to the kitchen he uncorked the bottle and poured a good measure into the visitor's teacup, he then poured one for himself, chinking the glass against the laird's cup before downing the contents in one swift gulp.

Captain MacPherson looked at him. 'I think you needed that, lad,' he said with a wink.

Ramsay drew the back of his hand across his mouth. 'Ay, ay, you could say that,' he agreed succintly. 'There are times . . .' His words trailed off. There was a good deal of activity in the room by now. The laird had left his dogs outside but Sheba, his Siamese cat, had come into the house with him and was presently engaged in a howling match with Ben and Bess, the Vale o' Dreip sheepdogs. The two canines, silent and purposeful by nature, obedient to the letter, were not well acquainted with the more exotic of the feline species and literally despised the cantankerous Sheba with every sinew and muscle in their bodies.

Whenever Sheba crossed the paths of these two she took a positive delight in testing their nervous endurance to the limit and today she had decided to try and unnerve them completely by growling and spitting at them and generally making a nuisance of herself. The dogs had put up with this show of ferocity for a long time, now they could take no more and lay noses to the floor, lips drawn back, snarling and whining in retaliation.

'Come ahint!' Ramsay roared at them and they slunk to his side to take refuge under his chair, leaving Sheba to glare at them from a distance and flex her claws as if preparing herself for physical confrontation, until the laird grabbed her and stuffed her without ceremony down the front of his jacket where she soon quietened and fell asleep.

Ramsay looked at the clock; the laird intercepted the message and stood up. 'I'll be going now, Ramsay,' he said apologetically, 'I only came along to ask if you would deliver a sack of potatoes and some eggs to the house. We're having guests for Christmas and without exception they have appetites like horses. A side of lamb wouldn't go amiss either and perhaps a dozen or so chickens to keep the wolves from the door.'

He chuckled at his own wit and Rita giggled as she began clearing the table. Ramsay had to smile too: the master of Crathmor could always be relied upon to lighten the day. A few more pleasantries were exchanged before the farmhands arrived for a belated breakfast, looking a bit sheepish as they blamed their lateness on Johnny Lonely whom they said they had caught stealing turnips from the sheep in one of the fields.

'The cratur' looked dead wi' cold and hunger,' emphasised one, Ryan O'Donnel, whom everyone knew as Ryan Du because of his curling mass of jet black hair with beard to match. He was a massive great figure of a man whose skill at throwing the hammer in games events all over the country was legendary. His looks and physique ensured his popularity with the womenfolk of the area while Ramsay valued him for the great strength he displayed whilst tackling the heavier jobs around the farm.

The other man, Linky Jack Black, half the size of Ryan, thin and undernourished looking, was nevertheless as strong as his partner, able to carry loads twice his own weight, toss bales of hay about as if they were feathers, and clip so many sheep in an afternoon as to incur wrath in some of the seasonal itinerants who said he was 'just a buggering show off and serve him right if he dropped dead with heart failure for his efforts'. But he had a kind heart, had Linky Jack, and when he conveyed to Rita that they had brought the starving Johnny Lonely back to the farm with them she immediately directed that he be invited inside so that she could give him something to eat as well since it 'all came out of the same pan'.

With a gracious sweep of his hat, the laird departed and Johnny Lonely was ushered in, a sullen-looking creature with unkempt black hair, a tangled beard, and dark suspicious eyes that darted restlessly about whenever he found himself in an enclosed space of any sort. Even so, his was an interesting face, nut-brown and full of character, the creases in his skin telling of a man who had lived a lot of his life in the open air. Underneath his moustache, his large mouth often wore a wry little smile as he observed the endless quirks of human nature. People were wont to wonder what he was thinking because he seldom passed judgement or remarked in any depth on the things that went on around him. But he saw, Johnny Lonely saw everything, a fact that made his fellow humans wary of him and yet respectful of him at the same time.

Johnny Lonely also had habits, odd little idiosyncrasies that had developed in him over the years. One of these was a nervous tic in his eyelid, causing it to drop rapidly down whenever he found himself in an awkward situation of any sort. Now was one of those moments; he hated being in a roomful of people, he hated being in a *room*, he disliked intensely the feeling of being trapped and if he hadn't been so hungry that morning he would have bolted right back through the door and run away to the familiar security of his bothy. As it was he kept eyeing the door longingly, his eyelid twitching rapidly, making it seem as if he was winking at everyone he looked at.

Ramsay had never got used to this habit nor ceased to be offended by it. The hermit had always made him feel uneasy, his way of life was beyond the understanding of a normal-thinking man and certainly did not meet with Ramsay's approval. He considered it to be both godless and useless and he wasn't too sure if he wanted such an odd representative of the human race in his home that morning. He sympathised to a certain extent with the man's need for solitude, but to carry it as far as Johnny did was bordering on madness.

On the other hand, Ramsay liked to think of himself as

charitable; as someone who would never deprive any living creature of sustenance and had always prided himself on lending his support to needy causes. But this man had never lifted a finger to earn his daily bread, instead he lived like an animal, trawling the wilderness for food, scraping an existence from sea and land, trading on the good auspices of anyone who was soft enough to take pity on him.

He was also poorly equipped in even the most basic of social graces and was obviously ill at ease as he stood there in the kitchen, shuffling his feet, giving every impression of wanting only to be back outside in the element he knew best. Far wiser to give him some food and let him squat behind a rock to eat it and no doubt enjoy it better.

Ramsay cleared his throat and was about to utter words to this effect but he was too late, Rita was bundling the hermit into the scullery, directing him to take a seat at the table along with the other men. A startled Johnny, remembering suddenly that he had forgotton to remove his hat when first entering the house, scraped the scuffed deerstalker from his head, stuffed it into the pocket of his duffel jacket, and thereafter sat staring at a willow-patterned plate hanging on its hook above the dresser.

In no time at all, Rita was laying dishes full of sizzling bacon, sausage, and eggs in front of the men. Ryan Du and Linky Jack seized their forks and dug in but Johnny remained motionless, still staring at the ornament on the wall as if it was about to bring him his salvation at any moment.

'C'mon, man,' Ryan Du poked him in the ribs. 'Eat up before it gets cold.' Johnny Lonely at last pulled his eyes away from the willow plate and fixed them on Ryan Du. 'I will no' eat until I've thanked God for the food that is set before me,' he intoned in a voice so deep it might have come from the 'very depths o' his empty belly' as Ryan Du said later.

'Prayers?' Linky Jack stared. 'I didny know you were a religious man, Johnny.'

'I believe in thanking God for the things He gives me,' Johnny returned politely. 'That doesny mean to say I believe

54

in religion. That is man's doing, God is too busy to be bothered wi' it.'

'Well, are you no' a man o' surprises,' Linky Jack chuckled.

'Ay, and a philosopher into the bargain,' nodded Ryan Du, adding: 'Go on then, say your piece if it makes you happy, we'll go along wi' it, whatever it is.'

Johnny closed his eyes. 'Thank you, God, for the hens who laid the eggs, the pig and the bullock who gave us bacon and meat, and for Mrs Sutherland who gave up her time to fill our bellies. Amen.'

Linky Jack blinked. 'I'll say this for Johnny, you've a different way o' doing things from anybody else I know.'

'I am different,' Johnny stated with dignity and, picking up his fork, he proceeded to demolish his meal with the greatest of gusto.

Rob had awoken that morning with his mind seething. All he could think about was Morna's proposed marriage to Finlay, an act that would change so many things for ever. In his heart he knew that she deserved to have security in her life, the sort of security that only a good and loving man could give her. But, Rob argued to himself, was Finlay the right person for the job? He was besotted by Morna, there was no doubt of that, but would he be able to handle a girl as individual as Morna and at the same time take on the task of bringing up a child who was already showing every sign of becoming as strong a character as her mother?

Sweat broke on Rob's brow at the idea of having to give up his daughter to another man, even if it was his brother. He half thought of telling his family the truth about Vaila but quickly abandoned the notion. He was a married man with a son who was going to need all the support he could get in the years to come. Hannah might just up and leave altogether if such a thing came out. She wasn't all that good a mother to Andy but at least she was here to see to his creature comforts.

Rob knew he couldn't very well ask his own mother to

take on a baby with such severe physical handicaps, and as for Ramsay Sutherland, he might blow his top altogether if even a hint of such scandal leaked out. Morna's life would become impossible with the reopening of old wounds, the wagging of tongues. Vaila too would suffer in a way that didn't bear thinking about.

If Finlay was to be her stepfather she would at least have his name and become a Sutherland after all. It was an ironic twist of fate, she would never know who her real father was, his name on her lips would be that of an acquaintance, for the rest of his life he would have to suffer that and always try to put a face on it.

In the next instant he realised that, as matters stood, he couldn't claim her as his daughter anyway and he could only hope, if Finlay had children of his own, he wouldn't neglect Vaila in favour of them.

Rob stared up at the ceiling as his mind went round in circles. Outside the window, dark clouds were scudding across the sky, signalling another morning of wind and rain. But he knew in his bones it would clear up for Christmas, just a few days away now, and he thought of little Andy and what he could get him in the way of a present. Then he remembered the pup. It would bring a bit of life into the house anyway, he would go down to Morna's on Christmas morning and get it, a good excuse to see her – very soon there would always have to be excuses to visit her, yet he knew he could never stay away from her, his Morna, his lass, he would never cease to think of her like that, even if she belonged to another man . . .

Beside him, Hannah stirred and turned towards him, her hair was spread over the pillow, one hand was outflung over the sheets. She was dressed to the neck in white flannel and looked young and strangely virginal in the half-light of dawn. If only things could have been different between them he might be more contented with his lot; as it was he felt as if he was forever grasping at straws, reaching out for things that could never be his . . .

There came the sound of Andy crying from the kitchen

below. This was where he slept during the night and lived out his little life in the daytime hours. Hannah had never shown any inclination to prepare a nursery room for him, maintaining that it was easier to look after him in the one place rather than having to trek up and downstairs all the time.

The cries became louder. Hannah opened her eyes and clicked her tongue in annoyance. Rolling on her back she muttered something unintelligible and lay for a few minutes longer before tossing the covers aside and putting her legs out of bed.

Going to the ewer on the dresser she poured cold water into the china basin, splashed her face with it then got quickly dressed, drawing her arms out of her nightdress to make a tent under which she could dress without exposing her body.

Rob too was pulling on his clothes and was down in the kitchen before her, carefully stirring the dross on the fire, sliding open the damper, putting on the kettle, going over to the cot to lift Andy up and give him a morning hug. The child's limbs jerked violently, his head lolled on his thin neck, his flannel gown was sodden, but he stopped crying as soon as his father picked him up and a crooked half-smile lifted up one corner of his mouth. 'Come on, wee man, time to change and bathe you then we'll see about breakfast.'

Hannah was rattling the fire with the heavy brass poker, causing sparks to fly up the lum. Rob glowered. She had never yet mastered the knack of getting the cinders to glow without disturbing them too much. Her violent administrations with the poker only resulted in loosening the bed of red hot cinders underneath the dross, making them rain wastefully down into the ashpan.

When first she had come to No. 6, Keeper's Row her knowledge of housekeeping had been sparse. Obviously her mother hadn't attached much importance to teaching her daughter anything except the bare rudiments of homemaking, and once the hotel business had got going they had both become accustomed to having everything done for them. But by nature Hannah was a clean and tidy young woman and she had quickly learned how to keep a home looking good. The one thing she fell down on was thrift which didn't please Rob in the least since he had been brought up in a home where the maxim was definitely to waste not and want not.

'Leave the fire,' he told her quickly, 'I'll do it if you see to Andy.'

'No,' she returned with equal asperity, anxious to do anything that would free her from tending to her son. 'I'll see to it, the kettle's nearly ready so you can wash him while I make the porridge. I prepared it last night so it's all ready to go on.'

Without ado she hooked the heavy black pot over the glowing coals and half an hour later they were sitting round the table eating breakfast. Andy, clean and shiny looking, a voluminous napkin tied round his neck, was at the table with his parents, strapped into his high chair, having been placed there by Hannah herself, though she was reluctant to let him try and feed himself.

'He'll make a terrible mess,' she protested. 'It was bad enough last night, it took me ages to get everything clean again, and I have enough to do in the morning without mopping up after him.'

A muscle moved in Rob's jaw. Grabbing a spoon he held it in the little boy's hand. 'He'll do it,' Rob said doggedly. 'In the end he'll do it, with just a bit of help from us. It will be better for him if he's able to cope with himself and better for you too in the long run. A certain degree of independence will stand him in good stead when he's older.'

There followed a scene that was a repeat of the night before. Andy's tiny body went into contortions as his father attempted to make him feed himself, a monotonous wailing sound issued from his mouth, his flaying fists sent the spoon flying several times and soon there was porridge everywhere.

'Can't you see he doesn't want to do it?' Hannah said, keeping her eyes firmly fixed on her plate in order to avoid looking at her son. 'Surely even you have to admit that, or are you just too stubborn to give in? He's useless and always will be, he'll never be able to hold a spoon, far less guide it to his own mouth. In the normal way o' things, it makes me sick just to look at him, and now you're making matters worse with these fancy ideas o' yours. It isn't him you're worried about, it's yourself and how you'll look if none o' this works in the end.'

Rob didn't answer, he was too occupied with the task in hand, his brow furrowed in concentration as he persevered in helping his son to get his food down. The breakthrough was as sudden as it was unexpected. Andy stopped fighting, he allowed his father to guide his hand to his mouth, a surprised look flitted over his face, as if he was realising what a good game this was and how it could be better if he let himself join in.

'That's a lad!' Rob let out a triumphant laugh and an answering chuckle came from Andy's lips. He sat there in his high chair, his hair plastered with porridge, the spoon in his hand, giggling infectiously as he gazed at his parents. 'He's enjoying it! By God! The bairn's enjoying it! He's never laughed like that since he was born. For the first time he seems happy — as if he senses he belongs in this house and is at last part o' the family.'

Rob's eyes were dark with delight as he looked at his wife. She too was looking bemused by the turn of events but all she did was shake her head and say doubtfully, 'He's too young to feel any o' these things you speak about. A normal bairn o' his age couldn't know them, never mind one who's mentally retarded and will be for the rest o' his life.'

'Retarded, ay, but only physically — and you're right, Hannah, he isn't normal.' Rob's eyes were burning into hers as he spoke, compelling her to look at him. 'I'd say that his intelligence goes beyond the concepts of ordinary normality and one o' these days he'll prove it to you — to all of us.'

'Neither o' us will live that long,' she returned in a voice that was heavy with sarcasm.

He stood up. 'I'm going before I lose my temper with you, Hannah, I cannot stand it when you're like this and hope you'll be in a better frame o' mind by the time I get back.'

'And just where do you think you're going? You were out last night, and no doubt you'll be gone for hours today again?'

He paused at the door. 'I'll be over at Vale o' Dreip seeing my mother. Why don't you come with me? If you wrap Andy up we could go for a walk along the beach later, it would do him good to get some fresh air.'

'No.' The refusal sprang readily to her lips. She got on well enough with Rob's mother but his father was a different kettle of fish altogether. She could never get over the feeling that he regarded her as not being good enough to be a member of his family, a feeling that had grown since she had presented him with a grandchild as disappointing as Andy. To be accepted into the Sutherland clan you had to be seen to be as strong as they were, to be upright and bold like Ramsay, as good a wife and mother as Rita, strong and determined like Rob. Only Finlay had faltered on these counts but he had his mother behind him and as long as she was there to support him he would get by.

'As you like.' Rob was pulling on his jacket and pushing his feet into his boots. At the door he turned. 'By the way, I hope you're remembering about the pup I'm getting for Andy's Christmas.'

'And I hope you're remembering that my mother will be here by then. She won't like having a piddly smelly dog about the place.'

'If she doesn't like it she can bloody well turn right round and go home again!' was his parting shot as he opened the door and closed it behind him with a bang.

Chapter Eight

Rob paused outside the door, breathing hard, every fibre in him tense and on edge after the row with Hannah. After a while he calmed down. It was a wind-fresh day, beyond the harbour the sea was grey-green, topped with white horses that were leaping to the shore from the south-east. To the right of Kinvara Point he could see the isles of the Inner Hebrides, a grey haze on the horizon, almost hidden under a blanket of purple clouds, and away to the left, beyond Niven's Bay, the rocky islets of Eilean Crocan and Eilean Orsa were dark specks in the misty spray of the ocean. Rob liked days like this, the air clean and bracing, not too cold because the wind had swung to the south and was bringing milder air currents.

A movement over in Mary's Bay caught his eye, a small figure was wandering along by the tideline. He knew it was Morna; no matter how far or near she was, he always knew it was her from the way she walked and held herself. He half thought of going down there to be with her for a while when the door of Big Morgan's house opened and out he came to stand on the step with Janet and Father MacNeil.

The curate, a brawny loose-limbed young man of twenty-four, with fair hair and laughing blue eyes, had come to the parish of Vaul a year ago to take up his post in St Niven's chapel. He had quickly established a niche for himself in the community as a whole and had become a well-kent sight in the area as he rode his rusty black bike through the villages to visit the more far-flung of his flock.

The Morgans were Catholics, but the nature of Jock's work meant that he had to live further from the chapel than was convenient for regular attendance, even though he possessed a good pony and trap and often went further afield than the Clachan of Vaul when the need arose. Father MacNeil saw to it, however, that the family were not starved of spiritual sustenance and it was not unusual to see his bike propped outside the Morgans' door at any time of the day, especially now that young Joss was getting older and able to take in more of what went on around him.

Rob liked Father MacNeil and was quite happy to spend a few minutes chatting to him till the young man decided that he'd better get going as he had another call to make and had also promised his housekeeper that he would pick up some groceries from the Calvost Village Store on the way home.

'Ach, he's a nice soul,' Janet said warmly as she watched him cycling away, his long legs on the pedals causing him to wobble a bit on the rough grassy path.

'You'll be going to see your mother, then?' Big Morgan addressed himself to Rob and the three of them stood for a while, exchanging pleasantries, seemingly oblivious to a shower of rain that came sweeping in over the sea, blotting out the islands in dark curtains of vapour.

In the course of their conversation, the Morgans mentioned the little celebration they were having for Joss's birthday, Janet saying it was a pity Rob wouldn't be coming as they had looked forward to all their neighbours from Keeper's Row being there.

'Who said we weren't coming?' Rob asked with a frown.

Janet reddened. 'Oh, I'm sorry, I thought Hannah would have mentioned it. I popped in last night to ask her but she didn't seem at all keen on the idea.'

Rob's brow darkened. 'She didn't say anything to me – but don't worry, I'll be there anyway, and it's kind o' you to ask.'

'And you'll bring wee Andy?' Big Morgan smiled down

from his great height. 'It will do him good to get out and mix with other bairns.'

'Ay, I'll bring Andy.' Rob's mind was seething with renewed anger against his wife. She was trying her best to make him a recluse like herself but in that she would never succeed. He would also make damned sure that his son too saw the light of day instead of languishing in a house with a woman who seemed determined to become old before her time.

Delighted with themselves, the Morgans went back indoors. Rob looked towards Mary's Bay but of Morna there was no sign and he went on his way, taking the path that ran round the foothills of Blanket Hill and eventually led on to the track that wound its way up to Vale o' Dreip farm.

'It is yourself, Rob!' Catrina Simpson's voice hailed him and he groaned when he saw both her and Mattie MacPhee making their determined way towards him.

'We'll just get you up to the house,' Mattie told him briskly as she hoisted the handles of her empty shopping bag up over her wrist. 'We're having a wee party for the bairns in the village hall tonight and Rita said if we called in this morning she would have some of her baking ready for us.'

'It's that nice to see you home again, Rob.' Catrina, who, at twenty, was the youngest of the Simpson sisters, showed her dimples as she spoke and eyed him flirtatiously. 'Three months seems a long time to be away and no doubt Hannah thinks so too.'

He merely grunted at that but brightened when Mattie observed solicitously, 'Ach, but it's the bairn who needs you most just now. We don't see very much o' him except when Hannah has to go into the village and brings him along in his pram. He'll be growing into a big boy now.'

'Ay, he is that,' Rob nodded. 'And clever too, he's getting the hang of feeding himself. Andy knows what's going on, all right, he's brighter than any o' us can imagine and will never be the vegetable some folks might think.'

'I quite agree wi' you there,' Mattie said, too quickly. 'I was saying to Dolly Law only yesterday that bairns like Andy have a wee special sense all of their own and only need bringing out o' themselves.'

'Hannah will encourage that, surely,' Catrina said gently, her eyes darting to Rob's face to see his reaction.

'Surely she will,' he said shortly and in tones that brooked no further talk about his wife.

The two women glanced at one another meaningfully but said no more on the subject. They were nearing the farm, a rambling, picturesque place set against the russet slopes of Blanket Hill, full of little nooks and crannies and surrounded by red-tiled outbuildings, its many chimneys prodding up into the sky, the breaking sun glinting on its attics and turning its sandstone gables into a warm shade of terracotta. Behind them the sky was lightening and brightening; the mist was clearing off the hills; and rays of golden sunlight were spilling over the fields, cascading into the sea. One or two puffers were chugging towards the harbour along with some fishing boats as the countryside came to life: down below on the road the children were making their way to school; smoke was pouring from the chimneys of the village, tossing hither and thither according to the wiles of the wind; the tiny dot that was Effie Maxwell, the district nurse, was pottering about in the garden of Purlieburn Cottage, no doubt feeding and tending her geese and her hens and seeing to her beloved sow named Queen Victoria because, as Effie claimed, no pig in all the land could be more regal and royal than hers, even when it was rooting around in its trough for scraps.

Ramsay and Finlay were just emerging from Vale o' Dreip as the trio came into the yard. Catrina made straight for the menfolk, bidding them good morning, going on to utter a few breathless observations about the weather and other such trivial matters, eyeing Finlay as she spoke. Then her roving glance shifted to Ramsay, silently inviting him to share the intimacies that were always there in her gaze whenever she was in the company of males, whatever their age.

Ramsay purported not to notice but when she looked away for a moment there was a strange expression on his face as he took in her comely figure, her red hair gleaming in the sun, the flash of her green eyes when she brought them back to him and treated him to a wide, secretive, knowing smile.

'Shouldn't you be working?' To hide his momentary confusion, Ramsay spoke sharply. 'I was led to believe that you were in the employ of Captain MacPherson and his wife.'

'Och, Mr Sutherland,' she said with mock reproval. 'It's my day off, surely everyone is entitled to that. I work my fingers to the bone at the laird's house and it's no easy matter trying to keep everything clean wi' all these bairnies getting under my feet.'

He coughed and dismissed the subject with a nod, Catrina threw Finlay one more laughing glance and her breasts brushed Ramsay's arm as she and Mattie went into the house.

Ramsay was left alone with his two sons. The three men looked at one another, Rob's jaw working as he gazed at the brother who was going to marry Morna and the father who was so wrapped up in himself that he couldn't even find it in him to utter a word of greeting to his elder son.

'I suppose you know about this fiasco between Morna Sommero and Finlay?' Ramsay began grimly. 'Or maybe it hasn't got round to you yet that the pair o' them are talking of getting wed.'

'I know.' Rob glowered at his brother as he spoke. 'These matters have a habit o' leaking out.'

'But they didn't leak out to me!' blustered Ramsay. 'If your mother hadn't told me over the breakfast table I would still be none the wiser.'

'We know what you're like, Father.' Finlay, who had said very little for the past half-hour, suddenly spoke up. 'We knew it would cause trouble and decided not to rile you any sooner than was necessary.'

'We! We! We!' Ramsay raged. 'Can't you ever open your mouth without including your mother in everything you say and do!'

A movement at the scullery window caught Rob's eye and he saw the face of Johnny Lonely peering out, absorbing everything that was going on. A thought struck Rob: could the hermit read lips? That way he had of staring at people, the intent expression on his face as he watched them, as if he knew what they were saying even when he was too far away possibly to hear anything, made him wonder.

Ramsay followed Rob's gaze. 'Ay, it's him, the godless one.' He spat scornfully. 'All nice and cosy in our house, supping our food, despite the fact that he was caught stealing it earlier. He should be punished, not fed, but you know your mother. Lame dogs. She would gather them all up if she could and allow them to eat us out o' house and home!'

With that he strode away and, seizing his chance, Rob grabbed a hold of Finlay's arm and hissed in his ear, 'I just want to say two things to you about Morna. Look after her, or you'll have me to deal with. If I hear one word—'

'That's three things.' Finlay, jubilant now that everything was out in the open, spoke cockily. 'And what's it to you, anyway? You don't own her even if you once thought you did. It's me she's marrying. I'm the one she'll be living with and lying with. I'll see her when she undresses and slips into bed each night, all smooth and soft as she presses herself against me . . .' He winced and let out a squeak of pain as Rob's grip on his arm tightened like a steel band. For a long suspenseful moment the two brothers glared into each other's eyes till Rob let go abruptly and strode into the house without another word.

But he wasn't to be allowed to cool down or forget his anxieties so easily. 'What's this we're hearing about Finlay and Morna Sommero getting married?' Mattie greeted him as soon as he was over the threshold.

'Ay, and why has it all been kept such a big secret?' Catrina added in aggrieved tones. 'Surely a wedding's something to be talked about. I know if it was me I would be shouting it from the rooftops! Good men are few and far between these days since the war went and took them from us.'

Rob looked at the women, sitting round the table, drinking tea and eating the remains of the toast left over from breakfast, and he found himself resenting them for being there, gossiping and prying, having nothing better to do with their time than poke their noses into other folks' affairs.

His mother appeared from the larder with a basket filled to the brim with home baking. 'Rob,' she cried, setting down the basket and rushing over to hug him. 'It seems such a long time since I've seen you – and if I didn't know better I'd say you've grown in the last few months!' She giggled and he had to laugh too, so pleased was he at the sight of her lively face with its pleasant regular features and dancing eyes. His annoyance evaporated. His mother of all people possessed the ability to make him feel that the world wasn't such a bad place to be in after all.

'Sit you down,' she said, taking his arm and leading him to the table. 'It's been a busy morning, the half of Calvost has seen fit to come visiting but there's sure to be another cup in the pot if I squeeze it hard enough.'

He did as he was bid, his temper restored. Mattie and Catrina smiled at him and pushed the toast rack towards him, his mother filled his cup, he began to relax and feel good and didn't even mind when the talk got round once more to marriage because by now it had become a generalised subject and Morna's name was only spoken in connection with a dress she had made for the laird's tiny daughter when she had been a flower girl on the occasion of an aunt's wedding.

In the scullery the farmhands were keeping their ears well cocked as they listened for snippets of family talk. They were well rewarded. Rita, excited and talkative, had been only too eager to tell her two women visitors about Morna and Finlay. The conversation that followed had been rich and interesting. Mattie had a loud voice, Catrina's was quieter but more piercing.

Ryan Du looked at Linky Jack and poked him in the ribs. As one they turned to Johnny Lonely. 'D'you hear that, Johnny?' Ryan Du said teasingly. 'Your favourite lass is getting hitched. Soon you'll no' be able to visit her as often as you would like.'

'Ay, she'll be too busy seeing to her man to let you in to sup at her table.' Linky Jack grinned, showing a row of tobacco-stained teeth in the process. 'You and she enjoyed a good blether too but maybe she'll no' be so interested in chat about wild creatures when she'll have a tame two-legged one to tend all her wee wants. From all I hear she's a ready sort o' girl – the bairn bears witness to that – and, of course, who knows what she gets up to in that lonely house down there wi' just the seabirds and the seals for company.'

The hermit, his face inscrutable, said nothing. The men made faces at one another and shrugged – and just about jumped out of their skins when Johnny suddenly leapt to his feet, thumped the table, and shouted. 'Dirty! That's all you're good for! Dirty talk! About other people! But I've seen you, Ryan Du, wi' Hic Gillespie's wife! Cavorting in the hay like a pair o' heathens while her man does his watch on the Kinvara Light! And you, Slinky Black Jack, pinching Mr Sutherland's chickens and selling them around the place. Does the butcher know where they come from? And all those others who think they're getting a bargain?

'Ay,' he went on relentlessly, 'there are things I could be saying about every one o' you so just you be mindful o' your tongue in future.'

'For God's sake, man, be quiet,' hissed Ryan Du. 'We didn't mean to upset you. I wasny to know that Morna meant so much to you or I would have kept my mouth shut.'

'Ay, it was only a joke,' supplemented Linky Jack, keeping his voice low while his broken nails rasped nervously against his chin. 'You'll no' be spreading talk about me, will you now, Johnny? I'll make it worth your while to hold your tongue, a nice juicy chicken wouldny go amiss in your larder, and maybe a few eggs to keep you going as well.'

For answer, Johnny planked his hands on the table and, leaning over it, he glared contemptuously at the pair for quite a few suspenseful seconds. Then, without a word, he straightened and stalked with great dignity out of the scullery, through the kitchen, and out of the back door, leaving behind him half a dozen puzzled and enquiring glances and several comments regarding his eccentricities and the lack of manners he had displayed in failing to thank Rita for the kindness and hospitality she had shown him that morning.

Chapter Nine

Mattie and Catrina hurried away down the track to the road, hugging themselves with excitement over the latest gossip to come out of Vale o' Dreip.

'Finlay's such a nice lad,' Catrina said thoughtfully, 'despite all the things folks say about him. I myself was glad he never went to war. I didn't like the thought o' him getting himself killed like all the others.' She gave vent to a heartfelt sigh. 'I mind them so well: Alex Dunn, wi' his nice smile and curly hair; Bert Smart, always money in his pocket and never stingy wi' it either; Billy Dunlop, such a fine big lad and never done chasing me ever since he got me behind the playshed at school. Oh, I had a fine time wi' Billy and just before he went away he asked me to wait for him . . . now he's gone, like a puff o' wind, and him just eighteen wi' everything to live for. Ay, indeed, there will be a scarcity o' eligible young men in Kinvara for many years to come.'

She sighed again, her eyes gazing unseeingly into the distance. 'Finlay would have made a good husband for someone like me, now here he is, marrying Morna Sommero, and her wi' a bairn out o' wedlock. It isn't fair and just goes to prove that being good and keeping your finger on your halfpenny doesn't mean a thing in the end.'

'You've aye been fascinated by the Sutherlands, haven't you?' Mattie said with conviction. 'I saw you giving even Ramsay the eye and you've never got over Rob. One o' these fine days you'll get yourself into hot water wi' your flirting and chasing after things you canny have.'

'They're very attractive men, all o' them.' An odd little smile hovered at the corners of Catrina's sultry, generous mouth. 'Ramsay too, for all his hot air. I've seen the way he looks at me, undressing me wi' his eyes, licking his lips, trying to pretend he's not interested even while his trousers are burning. Wanting's the word, it's all there, simmering under the surface, and all the religion in Christendom won't keep it from boiling over some day. And you're right about Rob, it was bad enough when he got himself hitched to Hannah from Ayr, now it's his brother's turn: three good men, all o' them tied to the wrong sort o' women.'

'Rita isn't a wrong sort o' woman!' Mattie hooted indignantly. 'She's a match for Ramsay and always has been! Oh, I know fine she's aye been too soft where Finlay's concerned but she's a mother and knows instinctively that he's the weak one o' her sons and has to be protected.'

Catrina let that pass but went on relentlessly, 'Ach, I'm no' talking about her being a mother, I'm talking about her being a wife. Ramsay's too much for her when it comes to the physical side o' their relationship. She lets drop wee hints to that effect when she's off her guard and I'm of the opinion she doesn't enjoy it one bit but only tholes it to keep him happy.'

'And I suppose you think you're an expert when it comes to matters o' that nature!' Mattie snorted disdainfully. 'Wait till you're wed yourself, my lass, you might no' be so ready to judge when you've a house to keep and a man like Dokie Joe to tend hand and foot, no' to mention a puckle o' bairns all screaming for your attention when you're just about done in and wanting only to put your feet up.'

Catrina looked at the older woman and her face softened. Mattie was, and always had been, a very able character, never afraid to say what she thought, always ready to defend herself and her family with a few well-chosen words. Her abrasive tongue had the power to shrivel the doughtiest of her fellow beings even while her witty observations about life in general ensured her popularity amongst them.

She and Dokie Joe already had five children and though she was now well into her sixth pregnancy she still went out cleaning four days a week for Lord and Lady MacKernon of Cragdu Castle, and also took in washing for other well-to-do families in the area.

Over and above all that she kept a cow, geese and poultry on a tiny piece of croftland attached to her house and still had enough strength left over to make sense of the organised chaos that frequently prevailed within the four walls of her home.

No one could ever accuse Mattie of being slothful, not least her very own easy-going husband who said that just to observe her 'fleering around' was enough to make his head birl.

With all that in mind, Catrina had the grace to look ashamed and linking her arm in Mattie's she grinned at her and said soothingly, 'Och, come on, don't go all sour on me. You know I don't mean half o' what I say.' Then she couldn't resist adding. 'I know what a busy soul you are with your man and your bairns but I don't intend to have a brood like yours nor a man like Dokie Joe. I want a bit of ease in my life and I'm not just going to take the first pair o' pants that comes along unless there's money in the pockets. I'm young, I can bide my time, meanwhile I'm going to enjoy myself as much as I can . . .'

She paused. Ahead of them was Father MacNeil on his bike, fair hair ruffling in the breeze, black coat flapping, long legs turning the pedals around with ease as he rode towards Calvost village. 'Now there's a fine man for you.' Catrina nodded, 'Young, strong, good natured – 'tis just too bad he happens to be a priest and isn't allowed to do the things that come naturally. It seems such a waste when Kinvara is full of girls like myself ready to tear each other's eyes out for a taste o' something different.'

Mattie shook her head. 'I can see that no' even the priest is safe with you around. But he's survived this far, and he's always got Minnie MacTaggart to make sure he doesn't get up to mischief. She's aye been a targe, that one. When she and me were bairns together I used to go and stay with her sometimes and her mother let Minnie boss us younger ones about. She made us polish our boots till you could see your face in them and at bedtime she lined us up to make sure we had washed behind our ears before making us get down on our knees to say our prayers. If anyone wet the bed she made them wash the sheets themselves so that everyone knew who had done it and called you "pee-the-bed".

'Now she's doing the same wi' the young curate.' Mattie chuckled at the startled look on Catrina's face. 'Ach no, I don't mean he has to wash his own sheets, but I hear tell she makes him take off his shoes at the door in case he gets dirt on her clean floors, and he's to wash his hands every five minutes for fear he gets marks on her brasses. Ay, he got more than he bargained for when he took her on as his housekeeper and is no' very likely to go astray while she's got him under her thumb.'

She looked at Catrina, Catrina looked at her, and they both burst out laughing. Behind them came the rumble of cartwheels and Effie Maxwell drew up beside them, shouting at them to hop on and she would give them a lift to wherever they were going.

In her late twenties, Effie was already a conspicuous figure in a black coat invariably speckled with cat and dog hairs, and a feather-bedecked black felt hat which, in winter, she wore pulled down over her ears, and in summer, tilted rakishly to one side of her head. Her mobile face, with its prominent nose, was full of character; her eyes so filled with an insatiable curiosity that Dokie Joe had once likened her to a 'ferret wi' colic', while Wilma Henderson of Croft Angus had sourly declared that Effie's mouth reminded her of a large-winged bird in perpetual vociferous motion.

Effie cared not what people said about her appearance: that was the least of her concerns. Despite the lack of a husband, her life was busy and full. Her position as district nurse kept her on her toes and also allowed her to indulge her interest in the affairs of others; her animals used up the remainder of her time and she had declared often enough that there were never enough hours in the day for her to do all the things that she would like.

Her mongrel dog, Runt, who travelled everywhere with her, was there beside her at the front of the cart, the only cratur' in Kinvara to have attended as many confinements as Effie herself. Very alert and straight, one ear erect, the other twisted to the back so that he might hear all that was going on around him, he had a haughty expression on his wiry face as he surveyed his surrounds from his lofty perch. When his mistress told him to 'jump in the back to make room for the ladies' he treated all three women to a baleful glare before rising unwillingly to do as he was bid.

'We're just going to the shop, Effie.' Mattie nodded as she settled herself on top of an old potato sack.

'Me too.' Effie tugged the reins and the cart moved forward. She looked quizzically at the two faces beside her. 'I saw you coming down the road from Vale o' Dreip and wondered how Rita is. It's a whily since I've seen her and was just going this very night to pay her a wee call. I've been missing all the talk and goings on of the place and now that Rob's home it will be busier there than ever.'

Catrina took a deep breath, Mattie did likewise, and both women plunged into an account of their recent visit to the farm. Effie's expression grew more and more animated as she ate up every juicy word that dripped from the lips of her companions.

The Calvost Village Store was looming closer. With a delicate little tug of the reins Effie made her pony go slower. It would never do to arrive at her destination until she had soaked up every little titbit of information before Bette MacGill got her teeth into it.

Big Bette MacGill, wife of Mungo, settled herself behind the counter of the Calvost Village Store and taking up a piece of wood she began to whittle away at it. Bette had never done any of the things that members of the fair sex were supposed to do, like knitting and sewing, darning and mending.

She was a complete individual and had always gone against the face of convention, even as a young girl when she was the despair of her parents who regarded her independent ways as lacking in the feminine graces. Bette had never listened to them; she had gone her own sweet way, growing bigger and bolder the older she got, free with her opinions, a good spokeswoman for those less fortunate than herself, an advocate of justice if she thought anyone was getting a raw deal.

In short, she was the battleaxe of the neighbourhood, worse even than the incorrigible Mattie MacPhee. If anything needed sorting out, Big Bette was in there with her ideas and sometimes her fists as well. Menfolk respected and feared her but tried not to let her see this since she had once dealt with one of their more troublesome brethren in a fashion that had branded him 'a mammy's boy' for the rest of his days. Coming upon the unfortunate creature drunk and disorderly, Bette had simply felled him and sat on him till Stottin' Geordie, the local policeman, had arrived to take over.

Her ways were inimitable; her appearance even more. Her arms were massive and dimpled; her billowing breasts like feather pillows; a white mutch cap framed her pleasant smooth face. Her girth was eye-catching to say the least yet she could move like lightning when she wanted to, a fact that commanded good behaviour in all but the cockiest youngster.

But she was good to children was Big Bette, bestowing on them the fruits of her labours in the shape of toys and little wooden flutes that had materialised under her carving knife.

She had taken over the running of the village store some years ago, after presenting her husband with two strong sons and one daughter, now eleven, ten, and six respectively, each of them showing every sign of becoming as indomitable as their mother.

Today they were in the shop with her, eating their breakfast apples before heading off to school, one perched on a sack of potatoes, two on the counter, sturdy legs swinging as they crunched and munched with great gusto while juice ran down their chins and on to the collars of their grey wool jerseys.

'Time to mop up!' Big Bette decided and without ceremony she grabbed the trio by the scruff of their necks and marched them into the back shop where she ran cold water over a rough towel, pasted it with carbolic soap, and proceeded to apply it to the row of tightly screwed-up faces in front of her.

'You're hurting, Ma!' yelled Tom, the youngest son.

'I've got soap in my eyes!' protested Joe, the elder, every fibre in him rebelling against treatment which he considered was only fitting for babies. 'I can wash my own face!'

'You washed us last night!' cried Babs, her chubby red face going an even brighter red while her big sensible shoes beat a tattoo on the wooden floor.

'Hold still!' came the sharp order. 'That Mr MacCaskill's got eyes on him like a hawk and I'll not have any bairn o' mine showing me up in front of the teacher.'

'His own face is no' so clean,' observed Tom, whimpering under his breath as his mother twisted his neck round in order to inspect it.

'Don't you dare say that about your teacher. Stuart MacCaskill's just got dark skin, that's all. Maybe his mother was a gypsy, or his father might have been a foreign mannie. Whatever way, there's no call to speak o' him wi' disrespect. When you come home tonight I'm giving you all a bath, just to teach you to mind your manners.'

'A bath!' Tom's eyes bulged. 'But we only ever have a bath on a Saturday, Ma.'

'I'll tell Da when he comes home,' blubbered Joe, the number one favourite son of Mungo MacGill. 'I don't want a bath, the soap makes my skin go all tight. You always do things like this to us when Da's away.'

'He'd better no' come any o' his snash wi' me or I'll wash him too,' Bette returned grimly, skelping her son's ear for his cheek. 'And don't you dare threaten me like that again, Joe MacGill. Tonight a bath – and maybe another one on Saturday as well. Cleanliness is next to godliness, my lad, so see you be in sharp from school this afternoon. It won't do any harm for you all to go to bed early for once so that you can be up at the crack o' dawn tomorrow, all bright and chirpy for school.'

'But it's the party in the hall tonight, Ma!' protested a horrified Babs. 'And we don't have any school tomorrow, the holidays are starting for Christmas, so we don't need to have a bath – because it will just be a waste o' good soap and water if Mr MacCaskill isn't there to smell us.' So saying she gave a defiant toss of her plaits and treated her mother to an almighty glower, actions which did not bode well for Babs's state of dignity.

With a snort, Bette hauled up her daughter's skirt, and was about to administer a good walloping to that young lady's generous bottom when the bell tinkled in the front shop and a voice called, 'Are you there, Bette?'

'Ay, I'm here!' Bette called back, adding under her breath, 'It's Father MacNeil, see you three mind your manners. I often think you're a mite too familiar wi' the priest just because he's young and new to the place.'

The boys' faces lit up. They, in common with many of the local youngsters, loved Father MacNeil. Full of boyish enthusiasm and zest he had soon organised a football team that included both Catholic and Protestant lads from the surrounding villages. People of all denominations were welcome to come and visit him in his home or in his church, with the result that his popularity had been quickly established, much to the disgruntlement of certain members of the Free Church who did not hold with this liberal behaviour.

This view was not shared by the Reverend Thomas Mac-Intosh of the Church of Scotland. He and Father MacNeil had soon become friends and often made social visits to one another's homes to indulge in a dram or two while they discussed local affairs.

The MacGill children had often expressed a wish to attend the tiny Catholic school in Vaul but had to content themselves with Stuart MacCaskill whose regime was strict and who didn't hesitate to use the belt on any miscreants who deserved it.

Father MacNeil's approach to the troublemakers in his school was softer, more subtle; he didn't rule with a rod of iron, rather he shamed his little rebels into obedience and made them pay for their sins with elbow grease and soap and water so that it wasn't unusual to see a boy or girl down on all fours, scrubbing the chancel floor or spring cleaning the house for an infirm parishioner.

In this, the curate was ably and adoringly abetted by Miss Aileen Dinkie, a gentle spinster lady who, feeling it was her duty to do so, had left her teaching job in Inverness to look after her ageing parents in Balivoe. Being still possessed of their more important faculties however, they had soon rebelled against her interference in their lives, and she, feeling like 'a spare fart in a commode' as Dolly Law put it, had soon established herself in the Catholic school in Vaul as a part-time teacher.

For all her genteel ways she nevertheless had a few tricks up her sleeve and was easily able to coincide her ways with those of Father MacNeil, which enabled them speedily to establish an excellent working relationship. Whatever Father MacNeil did, however he ruled, the youngsters of Kinvara thought the world of him and the MacGill children, glad to escape their mother's non-too-tender administrations, fairly scampered through to the front shop to greet him.

Chapter Ten

'You're on the road early today, Father,' Big Bette observed, eyeing the young priest who was bending down to study some jars of preserves reposing on a lower shelf in a corner of the shop.

He straightened and nodded, his ready smile beaming its rays upon the three MacGill youngsters who, thus encouraged, homed in on him to swing themselves by his hands and on any loose parts of his apparel that they could find.

'Ay, Bette,' he agreed. 'No rest for the wicked – if you know what I mean?' he amended hastily, annoyed at himself for never sounding as chaste as he should. 'I was over at Keeper's Row seeing the Morgans. It's time they thought about getting young Joss baptised.'

'Ay,' Bette nodded sagely. 'Janet's an easy-going lass but aye that nice and friendly. Big Morgan dotes on her and the pair o' them just love that bairn o' theirs. Pity about Hannah Sutherland. Janet has tried to make friends there but she might as well talk to a brick wall for all the good it does.'

'Well, things haven't been easy for her,' the curate hazarded carefully, his mind going to an encounter he'd had with Hannah and her positive rudeness when he had naïvely mentioned her son in connection with a crèche run by the young mothers of Calvost, and what a pity it was that she hadn't yet gone along to it.

Hannah had more or less told him to mind his own business

and ever since then he had been very wary of Rob's wife and tried not to cross her path if he could at all help it.

'Will you come to our party tonight, Father?' Joe's voice broke in on the priest's thoughts and he was glad of the change of subject since Big Bette was showing every sign of wanting to enlarge on it.

'Of course I'm coming, I wouldn't miss all that home baking for anything, and a little bird told me that Santa Claus just might be there. The minister has promised me a lift in his trap which means I'll be able to bring a few little tricks of my own to make the night go with a swing.'

'You mean you're bringing your magic stuff!'

'That's what I mean.'

'Could you make Mr MacCaskill disappear in a puff of smoke?'

'If he's there I might just do that.'

Three loud cheers followed this statement.

'Great! Great! Great!' yelled Babs excitedly.

'Out! Out! Out! School! School! School!' Big Bette retaliated, shaping her massive arms into a fleshy scoop in order to assist her offspring to the door.

'Can we go to Wee Fay's on the way home?' Babs got in one last shot, safe in the knowledge that her mother wouldn't dare to lift her skirt in front of the priest. 'I heard tell she's made lots o' different kinds o' sweeties for Christmas – and we wanted to get something special for you, Ma,' she ended in a triumphant burst of diplomacy.

'Ay, that's right,' Joe supported his sister. 'We wouldn't be long, we pass The Dunny on the way home, and Wee Fay's always good at helping us decide what to buy.'

'Ach, all right,' Bette relented, knowing that the children had been saving their pocket money for weeks. 'But don't be eating too much o' that tablet she makes, it will just put you off your tea and it's bad for your teeths as well.'

The MacGill youngsters released a united yell of triumph and flew to the door, only to collide with Mattie, Catrina and Effie making their way in. Confusion reigned for a few moments before the children made good their escape, leaving the new arrivals to unruffle their feathers and tut their annoyance at the swinging door.

'It's Christmas, the bairns are excited,' Big Bette explained in defence of her young.

Catrina treated the priest to a winning smile. 'We saw you on the road, Father, and Mattie and me were just saying what a pity it is that priests aren't allowed to take a wife to themselves. It seems a waste when young men are in such short supply at the moment.'

Father MacNeil, dumbfounded by her candour, opened his mouth and shut it again but Mattie had more than enough answers for the two of them and, dumping her bag on the counter, she rounded on Catrina to say grimly, 'I said no such thing, Catrina Simpson, you're the one who's looking for a man and will eye anything in breeks. Dokie Joe is more than enough for me to be going on with, so don't you be including me in your silly comments again.'

Catrina looked discomfited, the priest looked embarrassed, Effie shook her head and rushed into the breach with the expertise of one who was used to dealing with awkward situations. 'Och, never mind all that,' she said impatiently, 'I'm sure Father MacNeil understands that Catrina didn't mean to be insulting. Tell Bette the latest news from Vale o' Dreip, Mattie, you can explain these things better than anyone else I know.'

Mollified by the compliment, Mattie gave full reign to her explanatory powers. When she eventually finished speaking everyone was very thoroughly in the picture and Big Bette gave a satisfied nod. 'So, it's Finlay and the sea maiden, eh? Och well, the bairn will at last have a father and Morna a man o' sorts. I don't suppose Ramsay will be very pleased, getting a daughter-in-law who's an atheist and a ready-made granddaughter of unknown origin. Still, that's the way o' the world and Rita at least won't mind, she loves bairns and was really heartbroken when wee Andy was born without any o' his faculties.'

'Ay, but she loves him just the same,' Effie said sadly, 'even though she doesn't see very much of him. Hannah isn't for taking him anywhere and Ramsay doesn't encourage her to visit Vale o' Dreip, so all in all it's difficult for Rita and it will be just the same when Finlay marries himself to Morna.'

The bell above the door tinkled, making everyone jump, and Morna herself came into the shop, bringing with her the cold fresh air of morning, the tang of the sea in the ruffle of her hair, and the gleam of sunshine in the smile she bestowed on everyone as she said rather breathlessly, 'Did I hear my name? It sounded like mine as I came through the door just now.'

'It can't be denied,' Big Bette admitted shamelessly as she began putting groceries into Mattie's bag. 'We have just heard about yourself and Finlay and of course we were having a wee discussion about it.'

'Of course.' Morna couldn't hide a giggle. 'It was bound to leak out sometime and I'm glad it's out in the open. It's not as if it's anything to be ashamed of, and it will be good for Vaila to have a father figure in the house, she can be a handful at times and is getting to the age when she needs to have a bit of security in her life.'

Father MacNeil looked at Morna, a picture of young motherhood with her rosy-cheeked daughter in her arms, and a memory of a summer's day sprang to his mind, everything blue and green, lazy and hazy, the sands shimmering in the heat, himself walking, lost in thought, till he was awakened from his daydreaming by the plaintive sound of a seal pup crying by the water's edge. And there kneeling beside it was Morna, its head on her lap as she soothed it and sang to it in a small sweet voice that might have belonged to a child, while nearby, under a big yellow sunshade, her own little daughter slept in the drowsing heat of the afternoon.

Morna had looked very young that day, totally engrossed in what she was doing, her downbent head emphasising the innocent curve of her neck around which was braided a chain of daisies and buttercups; her glossy hair blowing in the breeze; her body encased in a shapeless smock that only added to the impression of a young girl still to bloom into womanhood.

So engrossed with the seal had she been she hadn't noticed the priest at first, and he had felt like an intruder when she had suddenly glanced up at him with a startled intake of breath and an expression of enquiry in the smoky grey-green of her eyes.

After that they had sat companionably side by side on a big rock, discussing the marvels of the day, the miracles of nature, the bounties of the ocean, while the seal pup played contentedly in a nearby pool and Vaila Marie continued to sleep peacefully in her nest of warm sand under the shade of the big yellow umbrella.

Father MacNeil had never forgotten that day nor the impression he'd carried away with him of a girl who had found her god in the wonders of the living world around her, a world which she obviously cherished and understood and was glad to welcome at the dawning of each new day.

Now he smiled at her and she responded with a look that conveyed to him that she too remembered their meeting on the shore and felt a kinship with him for having shared those moments of truth and beauty.

'Now, what can I do for you, Father?' The voice of Big Bette broke roughly in to his thoughts and in some confusion he tried to recall what Minnie MacTaggart had asked him to get from the shop.

'It was something to do with stuffing and jellies,' he said awkwardly. 'Things to put inside a turkey and others to go with it.'

'Stuffing!' Big Bette said promptly and banged a packet on the counter. 'I always make my own but it's no' everybody that has the knack, and while Minnie might be a dab hand wi' dusters and Brasso she's maybe no' all that good wi' flour and flavourings. By jellies you will likely be meaning sauces and preserves. I saw you looking at them when you came in so we'll just go over and help you to refresh your memory.'

For the next ten minutes a clamour of women's voices filled Father MacNeil's head as he received well-meaning advice from all quarters. In the end, and in desperation, he settled for a jar of cranberry jelly, some pickled onions, and a packet of gravy powder, all the while praying that he had made the right choices as Minnie MacTaggart wasn't backward at voicing her displeasure if anything wasn't to her liking.

'I just want some ingredients to make a clootie dumpling.' Morna, seeing the dazed look on his face, came to his rescue. Bette heaved her bulk to the other side of the shop to look for raisins, flour, and other such items, making the priest wait to pay for his groceries.

'Now where is that pair off to in such a hurry?' Mattie was peering from the window as she spoke. Outside, on the road, a cart containing Shug Law and Willie Whiskers, the blacksmith, was driving past at a spanking pace, saliva flying from the horse's mouth as she snorted and protested and worried at her bit.

'They'll be up to no good,' Effie stated with conviction. 'When that two get together it aye means mischief.'

'Ay, and it's even worse when my man's with them.' Mattie snorted. 'Rogues, the whole three o' them, as I've told them often enough to their faces.'

'Well, Dokie Joe's not there this time,' Catrina said sooth-ingly, glad of the chance to try and get on the right side of Mattie. 'He'll be doing his bit up at the laird's house and will be too busy to bother his head wi' Willie and Shug.'

'There isn't a lot to keep him going at Crathmor just now,' Mattie returned darkly. 'The MacPherson bairns haven't broken anything for a while, Mistress MacPherson has grown tired o' searching the spare rooms for furniture that needs fixing, and there isn't much work in the gardens at this time o' year.'

Bette had seen to the priest and was now ringing up the till for Morna who quickly paid for her purchases, scooped them into her bag, and hastily followed Father MacNeil outside.

'Phew,' she laughed. 'It's like a lion's den in there. Bette just swallows you up in one gulp and the others are no better.'

'I know.' He gave a rueful grin. 'I don't know which is the worst, Bette on her own or Bette with cronies. They all mean well, I know, but there are times when all I want is to go in there, get what I want and come out again without having first to go through an interrogation.'

'Och well, it's over now and we're still in one piece. I am now going to Balivoe to face Wee Fay in The Dunny. She only eats children so I'll have to keep an eye on Vaila to make sure she doesn't disappear.'

'The worst part for me is still to come,' he said with a grin. 'In a very short time I will meet my Donnybrook in the shape of Minnie MacTaggart. If I haven't got the right things for her turkey she will just wither me with a look and might make me polish the brasses for my sins.'

Uplifted by these nonsensical exchanges they parted in the best of spirits, he getting on his bike and riding away, she making her way over the Brig o' Shee and along the winding road to the hamlet of Balivoe, there to seek out the shop that everyone knew as The Dunny.

A stranger trying to find Wee Fay's shop would have had a hard time locating it, huddled as it was in between the Smiddy and the Chandlery, halfway down a cobbled lane that led to a fishery built on stilts at the water's edge.

The window of The Dunny was partially shaded by a black blind with a silver angel swinging on a glass star at the end of the pull cord. Displayed in the window on frilly lace doyleys was a tempting assortment of every kind of home-made sweet imaginable, together with glass jars crammed with colourful boilings of every shape and size.

Arranged in another section of the window was a captivating collection of hand-knits, embroidered linens, beautiful blouses and fascinating baby clothes, beside them a vast selection of fluffy toy animals and miniature figurines made out of shells and stones.

'Me get.' Vaila, utterly enchanted by the window, stretched out both her hands as if to grab all the contents.

'You get some, you wee whittrock.' Morna laughed and bore her daughter into the shop, out of the draughts that abounded in the narrow funnel that was Smiddy Lane.

The interior of The Dunny was indeed like a dungeon, softly

lit by red and green candles which served to make it all the more mysterious, and Morna found herself holding her breath as she entered the poky dark little shop. More fascinations awaited inside; carnival masks leered down from the beams, grimacing, grinning, garish; tapestries and pictures covered the many cracks and blemishes in the brickwork; baubles and beads, bows and buttons, trouser braces, ribbons, safety pins and elastic hung from nails on the walls and in bunches suspended from the ceiling.

On the counter sat trays of toffee apples; pink and white coconut squares; chocolate buttons; gingerbread soldiers; creamy tablet; buttery fudge; a mouthwatering array that was enough to melt the willpower of anyone, never mind the legions of children that had come and gone from the shop over the years.

Without exception they all loved and respected Wee Fay who wasn't much taller than the smallest child in Balivoe School but a regular little warrior for all that, agile and fit and perfectly capable of facing up to anybody, no matter how big or how daunting they might be.

At the tinkling of the bell she came bounding down a narrow flight of stairs from the living quarters that she shared with her husband, Little John, also a well-loved figure in the neighbourhood. The two of them had once roamed free with a band of Irish travelling people who came every summer to Kinvara, till the day dawned when Little John and his wife decided to settle down in the area and open up the shop that had quickly earned a reputation for the quality of its hand-made goods.

If anybody wanted anything special, be it a wedding cake, a baby's layette, or simply a woolly toy for a child's birthday, they ordered it from Wee Fay, the lady of Crathmor and Lady MacKernon of Cragdu being amongst her most regular customers.

Wee Fay was renowned for her adoration of babies and infants and as soon as she saw Vaila she snatched her from Morna's arms and began to dance round the room with her, singing to her in a deep melodious voice that totally beguiled

Vaila and stemmed any tears that might otherwise have arisen. A suger-olly twist worked the rest of the charm and Vaila did not mind in the least when she was deposited amidst a pile of fluffy soft toys, the tasty treat held very firmly in her plump little fists.

'You will be taking a seat to yourself, mavourneen.' Wee Fay turned her attention on Morna, drawing up a basket chair for her and pushing her into it. 'You look done in and puffing a mite too much for a lass o' your age. You're carrying the babe the wrong way. She should be happed in a shawl fixed over your shoulder and before you go out o' here I'm going to show you how to do it. It's the old way but it's the best, meanwhile just you sit there and rest a bit and I'll get you a nice brew of tea.'

'Och, no, I only came in to get some things for Vaila's Christmas stocking.' Morna's protest was only a gesture, it *had* been tiring carrying Vaila all the way from Oir na Cuan and she was very glad of the chance to sit there and catch her breath in the atmospheric quietness of The Dunny while Wee Fay went upstairs to make the tea.

When she came back, Little John was with her, dark-haired and cheery-faced, only half a head taller than his wife but like her possessed of such verve and vivacity he seemed to bounce along as he moved. Together they all sat and ate gingerbread soldiers and drank strong tea, and when Morna told them the news of her forthcoming marriage, Little John promptly got up to fetch a celebratory bottle of sherry so that they could all have a drink to the occasion.

'May all your troubles be little ones.' Wee Fay solemnly raised her glass though her eyes were sparkling with merriment as she looked at Morna over the rim.

'And may your man's slippers always be at your hearth and his boots never far from your door,' Little John supplemented gravely before getting up to do a little war dance of joy round Vaila in her bed of knitted dogs and soft woolly cats.

When Morna finally took her leave of The Dunny, Vaila was attached to her by means of a warm plaid shawl, fixed in such a way that it supported the child and left her mother's arms free to carry her shopping bags. Thus unfettered, Morna walked blithely along, revelling in the sunshine that was spilling over the land, delighting in the sight of the snow-capped hills soaring up into the blue sky, thinking of Robbie and how wonderful it would be if they could climb those hills together, free, happy, no one to see them, no one to know when they paused to kiss and speak of their love for one another . . .

Her heart missed a beat, it was wrong to think like that, wrong to want such things when she was marrying Finlay . . .

The door of Anvil Cottage opened and Mrs Whiskers, or rather Maisie MacPhee, sister-in-law of Dokie Joe and wife of Willie the blacksmith, came out to stand on her step. 'Have you seen my man?' she asked Morna in an ominous sort of voice. 'He went out a good half-hour back, just like that, without a word as to where he was going and him wi' half a dozen beasts waiting to be shod.'

Not wishing to get Willie Whiskers in trouble, Morna hesitated before saying cautiously, 'I saw him when I was in the Calvost store, going past in a cart.'

'Was he alone?' Maisie, whom Morna had privately christened Mrs Whiskers because she had quite a few sprouting from the moles on her face, glared at Morna in a way that dared her not to tell anything but the truth.

'Well, the cart was moving fast, I couldn't really see.'

'Was Shug Law with him?' Maisie asked heavily.

'He might have been, Bette has these blinds at her window and it's not all that easy to see out . . .'

'I knew it! I knew it!' Maisie sucked in her lips. 'Him and that Shug Law! And I wouldny be surprised if Dokie Joe MacPhee was meeting them somewhere. He might be my brother-in-law but a bigger rascal never walked this earth. Him and Willie egg each other on all the time and that wee runt, Shug Law, goes along with them for what he can get. Wait you till I get my hands on all three o' them, it will give me the greatest o' pleasure to bang all their silly heads together.'

'Oh, but I never said . . .'

She was talking to a closed door, Maisie had retreated inside, taking with her one of the big black cauldrons that were kept outside the Smiddy for the horses to drink from.

Bemused by the gesture, Morna went on her way, smiling to herself as she tried to imagine why the blacksmith's wife should want to take a witch's pot indoors, unless she was planning to brew a potion that would sedate her husband and keep him from his wanders – or perhaps one that might keep him permanently and meekly tied to her skirts for evermore, never again to touch a drop of whisky, or ogle a pretty young maid in the passing . . .

Chapter Eleven

A trio of men were gathering Christmas trees in the woods. At least, that was how they put it to one another because to say it any other way made it sound like stealing, when all the time it was for a good cause, that of bringing cheer and goodwill to the poorer children of the district, and if there was a few bob in it to reward the men for their labours then it would all be worth while.

Besides, it was only a few young spruce trees. The laird had been well recompensed for the timber that had been cut down on his land during the war and had been quite able to afford the planting of new afforestation since.

So the men eased any qualms of conscience they might otherwise have felt, except in the case of Dokie Joe who believed it was his entitlement to make a few extra shillings out of 'the mean old bugger' who was his employer and who hadn't given him a rise in wages for years, all the time pleading poverty and bemoaning the fact that he'd had to sell off some of his properties to make ends meet.

With that in mind, Dokie Joe swung his axe with vigour, assured that no one would hear the hacking in this deep thicket where sunlight filtered meagrely through the branches and the pine needles were like a thick russet carpet underneath.

An hour or so went by and the pile of fresh spruce grew bigger. The men were hot and sweating even though they had discarded their jackets some time ago.

'I'm buggered!' Shug Law declared at last, throwing down his axe and mopping his brow with the cuff of his shirt. Seated on the ground with his back to a tree he took his whisky flask from his pocket and treated himself to several gulps of its fiery contents, swilling them round in his mouth with the greatest of pleasure, his Adam's apple working rapidly in his thin neck, his tongue coming out frequently to mop up any stray drops that might have adhered to his straggly black moustache.

Shug was the head of a large poor family living in a tiny cottage in Balivoe, his eight children, ragged, barefooted, but seldom hungry, ranging in ages from two to ten with another one on the way. Known locally as the Outlaws, they lived mainly on their wits, knowing just how far they could go without actually breaking the law. If one of them did, they all closed ranks, as close-knit as any family could be. Wily, humorous, likeable, they accepted their lot without rancour, attending school when they weren't needed at home or could have a turn wearing the one pair of boots they shared between them. For the most part they did not mind if they missed their sums and their studying, all but Mary who was nine and wanted desperately to learn all she could so that she could get a good job when she grew up and buy herself a pair of winter shoes that hadn't been worn first by somebody else. Mary was the exception, however, the rest were too busy getting on with the business of survival to care very much about the scholarly aspects of life and were more than adequately occupied with matters pertaining to home and family.

Shug's wife, who went by the unlikely name of Dolly, seemed always to 'have one in the oven' so the older children were kept busy looking after the younger ones, fetching and carrying, lifting and laying, but still finding time for exploring the big wide world and keeping a lookout for anything that might be gainful to the family as a whole.

Shug himself was a sublimely contented man who had seldom worked very hard nor wanted for anything very much in the whole of his life. Possessed of a nature that was happy, carefree, and philosophical he rarely allowed anything to worry him, except perhaps when he'd had one too many and was inclined to take offence at the slightest triviality.

Today, however, he was in fine fettle. It was Christmas, the bairns would be expecting something a little bit special in the threadbare stockings that they hung up hopefully every Christmas Eve, stringing them out across the mantelpiece: big ones, little ones, bedecked by homemade baubles and bows that hid the worn bits and the holes in the heels. That was why Shug had allowed himself to be persuaded to come here today, to make some extra sillar to buy a pair of warm stockings for Dolly perhaps, or some tobacco for her pipe; a book maybe for Mary, a doll for wee Sheena – even a dram or two for himself.

It was hard work, though, damned hard work. At first Dokie Joe had said he just wanted the use of Shug's coal cart and would pay a small fee for its hire. But Shug had hummed and hawed at this and had said that he needed his cart to collect a cargo of coal he was expecting from *The Seahorse* when she called in at the harbour. The gentry, he said, relied on him to bring up their festive fuel supplies, the puffer was due in soon, and with it being so near Christmas he needed some extra money to keep his family happy at this special time.

'*Extra* money!' Willie Whiskers had exploded. 'You've never got *any* bloody money and should be glad o' the chance to lend out your cart to make even a penny or two. And it's for a good cause, remember, we're only going to take a few of the laird's trees, the sickly ones that he'll never miss. We're doing him a good turn really.'

'A good cause, my arse!' Shug had returned with asperity. 'Knowing you two you'll be selling the damt trees and I want my share o' the takings. Even if it is just to keep my mouth shut about what you're up to. I come wi' my cart, body and soul, and I'll expect to get paid for both it and me. After all, Willie's got a good enough cart o' his own but I know fine he doesn't want to be seen driving it through the village in case he gets caught wi' the laird's trees in it. Silence money, that's what I'm after, and I don't care who knows it.'

'Oh, ho! Blackmail, eh!' Dokie Joe had said half jokingly,

but in the end he and Willie gave in to Shug's persuasions, on the condition that he brought his own axe and did his share of the work and later helped them to sell the trees round the doors in the village.

Now here they were, up to their necks in wood shavings and pine needles, a helluva way to make an honest shilling! Shug felt quite aggrieved as he slugged at his whisky and examined a blister on his palm.

'Come on, man, you can't sit here all day sookin' the bottle!' Willie the Blacksmith, who owned the most magnificent set of ginger-coloured whiskers in Balivoe, stood glowering down at Shug. 'Get a move on, we're ready to start loading and we haven't got all day. My missus will be out looking for me on her witch's broom if I'm no' back by dinnertime.'

Reluctantly Shug heaved himself to his feet and began helping the others carry the trees down to a grassy lane where they loaded them on to Shug Law's cart while his dilapidated-looking mare, Sorry, waited patiently in her shafts, her face buried deep in an empty-looking nose-bag.

'Phew, it's hot when you're working this hard.' Dokie Joe took off his cap and wiped his perspiring brow. 'Still, we've just a few more to go then we can go home for our dinner before doing the rounds . . .' He froze in the action of replacing his cap as a crackling of twigs filtered through the woods.

'Someone's coming,' hissed Willie Whiskers, straining his eyes into the thick shadows that lurked everywhere.

'It's all right, lads, it's only me,' came a voice and suddenly Captain Rory MacPherson himself popped out from behind a pine trunk, his cat Sheba winding herself round his hairy legs, his dogs sniffing and snuffling among the debris of needles and pine cones that littered the forest floor. Shug nearly swallowed his whisky bottle, Willie Whiskers dropped his axe on his toes and let out a yell, Dokie Joe, his mind racing with the implications of being caught stealing his employer's trees red-handed, simply stared open-mouthed at the newcomer.

'Captain MacPherson, sir!' Dokie Joe found his voice and spoke with great deference while his companions looked on in amazement, expecting him to click his heels together at any moment.

'At ease, MacPhee,' the laird said drily. 'You're not in the army now, you know.'

'Please, Captain MacPherson,' Dokie Joe went on respectfully, 'we were just gathering up a few wee trees to give to the poor bairns at Christmas.'

'Ay, that's right,' Willie Whiskers nodded. 'A lot o' them have never seen a tree at Christmas, bar those growing in the forest.'

'It would be a beautiful sight for them, just,' Shug added his contribution, waxing lyrical as he went on. 'I can see their wee faces now, lighting up as they watch the candles flickering on the branches, all aglow by the light o' the fire, the holly boughs sparkling on the mantel, the—'

'Quite, quite.' The laird came forward and the men took deep breaths as they waited for him to pronounce the punishment that must surely follow their misdeeds. But Captain MacPherson seemed in no hurry to speak; instead he spent a few minutes thoughtfully rubbing his chin and stroking his moustache, stretching out the suspense, making the men sweat a bit before he said at last, 'You know, I'm really very grateful to you, lads, you have just given me an idea.'

'We have?' came the ragged, unbelieving chorus.

'Ay, indeed you have. As you know, it is my habit to give a little something to the more needy families at this time of year.'

The men nodded halfheartedly, 'little' being the operative word they would all have used in the laird's case because of his reputation for meanness.

'I'm glad you all agree on that.' Something that might have been a smile touched Captain MacPherson's mouth. 'Because I am of the opinion that the distribution of trees in the area is a brilliant conception. As you say, Shug, they would brighten up Christmas for the recipients and later on, they would have the added benefit of cutting them up for their fires.'

He went on to instruct the men to cut down as many trees

as they could, that day and on the next. 'Chop till you drop,' he said with a humorous chuckle. 'The more the merrier. No one can accuse me of being mean, and I'm doing this to prove it.'

Shug, for one, wasn't greatly impressed by these arrangements. The thought of all that hard work was too much for him to bear and his jubilation of the morning was wearing off fast.

'I know what you're thinking.' The laird was running his fingers through the spruce branches, sniffing in the balmy fragrance with the greatest enjoyment. 'And surely you didn't really think I wasn't going to reward you for your labours. When the job's finished I'll give you a round pound between you. I can't say fairer than that. As you said yourselves, it is for a good cause and a small price to pay for me catching you in my woods pinching my timber. But wait, the best part is yet to come.' He rubbed his hands together gleefully. 'I am personally going to supervise the distribution of my trees round the three villages: Calvost, Balivoe, and Vaul. The poorer families get them for nothing, the more solvent can have one for a few pence, I must cover myself, you understand.'

'*Three* villages!' The horrified chorus set the crows screaming overhead. 'But, sir,' stuttered Dokie Joe, 'that would take ages. We'd never get them all delivered this side of Christmas. Shug's old nag was just about knackered bringing us up here today and she'll collapse altogether if we work her any harder.'

'Never fear!' The laird was enjoying himself immensely. 'Not only will I come with you to do the job, I'll also drive you round in my very own AEC truck. She is capable of carrying loads in excess of four tons at a time and will be ideal for what we have in mind.'

The men were stunned. The truck that the laird spoke about was his pride and joy. Acquired from a surplus of ex-War Department vehicles sold in the civilian market, he treated it even better than his dignified old Lanchester, and didn't like to get it dirty, preferring to drive it on sedate journeys down to the harbour to collect genteel supplies from the puffers, or on runs round the countryside with his wife beside him at the front and his three children strapped into little wickerwork chairs on the tailboard. Once he had even driven it to church on a Sunday, much to the amazement of the Revd Thomas MacIntosh, and the amusement of the other parishioners. But the laird's wife, Emily, although something of a non-conformist herself, had none the less deemed it unfitting to take the truck to church and park it alongside the horses and the traps, the bicycles and the pony carts, and so her husband had reluctantly returned to the more respectable Lanchester, much to the disappointment of his children who had adored being the centre of attraction chugging up to kirk aboard the AEC.

Whatever its uses, no one had ever seen the vehicle doing what it was meant to do, which accounted for the men's astonishment as the master of the big house declared his intention of using it as a work horse. They made no comment however, by now so thoroughly disenamoured with the turn of events that nothing else could make them feel any worse than they did in those moments.

'Right.' Captain MacPherson cocked his head and looked at the three sinners. 'I'll go home now and get my dinner, you lot do the same but don't take all day about it. You can come back here and cut down a few more trees, I'll meet you at the foot of my driveway at one-thirty and we'll off-load Sorry's lot on to the AEC. That will give us about three hours of reasonable daylight for today's run. Tomorrow, if you start up here first thing, you should be able to fell enough trees for the entire Kinvara peninsula. I'll get you at my road end at eleven o'clock and we should be through by teatime – if we all work hard and willingly.'

With a wink and a laugh he was off, calling his dogs to his side, striding away down through the trees, swinging his crook, his kilt swirling round his sturdy knees as he went.

'Hard and willingly!' Willie Whiskers spat his disgust to the ground. 'He'll just sit in that truck o' his and watch us breaking our backs carting those buggering trees about.'

'Ay, and he'll get all the glory,' Dokie Joe said mournfully. 'Folks will see him and say "Aw, there's the laird, doing his good deeds, using his good truck too and him so proud o' it as a rule. It just goes to show what a fine generous man he is."'

'The mean old bugger's up to something,' Shug said with conviction. 'I don't know what it is, but he's got some mischief in mind, I could see it in his face.'

'Ay, he had that sly look about him,' Willie Whiskers agreed. 'I've seen it before, when he's up to one o' his dodges, making deals that can only profit him in the end.'

'Well, at least we got off lightly enough,' Dokie Joe said thankfully. 'He could have wiped the floor wi' us and if I lost my job at the big house, Mattie would have my guts for garters.'

'Lightly!' hooted Shug. 'More like a bloody year's work rolled into one. And here was me, wanting only to make a few bob for the bairns' Christmas, instead I'll be working my fingers to the bone for just a few measly pennies.'

Sorry, disenchanted with her empty nose-bag, gave a little whinny to draw a bit of attention to herself. In her searching in the bag for oats she had dislodged an ear from her old straw hat and Shug patted her head and adjusted the ear back into position. 'Poor old girl,' he said sympathetically, blowing gently into her nostrils. 'You at least have come off best. Come on, let's get you home. Dolly will be waiting for us. No sense in hanging around here any longer than we have to, we'll be back soon enough.' He unshafted her and led her away, the others following on his heels in disgruntled silence.

Chapter Twelve

Willie Whiskers was right. The laird did indeed cover himself in glory when later that day he drove through the lanes and the streets of the village in his smart cream–coloured AEC lorry, with its red-rimmed wheels and white cab roof, delivering his trees – or rather sitting in the comfortable cab of the vehicle while Dokie Joe, Shug and Willie carted them round the doors, giving some away free, selling the rest for just a little bit more than the price fixed by the laird, keeping the extra to console themselves for that which they had lost when their money-making schemes of the morning had backfired on them.

The sight of the AEC loaded up with Christmas trees, the laird at the wheel, attracted a good deal of attention as he wound his way along in a rather grand manner, lifting his hat and waving his hand to everyone he passed. Much to the dismay of his helpers he insisted on first driving to Keeper's Row because he wanted wee Andrew Sutherland to have a tree and also Morna Sommero for 'her fatherless bairn'.

'The sea maiden!' Shug cried in horror. 'But she lives miles down yonder in Mary's Bay!'

'That's right.' The laird smiled in full and calm agreement. 'A lonely spot for such a young lass. The sight of your bright and happy face will cheer her day, Shug, and the wee one will clap her hands with joy when she sees her very own Christmas tree coming through the door.'

'Let Willie or Dokie Joe do it,' Shug said hastily, the idea of tramping over wet sands with a tree on his back not appealing to him in the least.

'I've hurt my back.' Willie made a face as he rubbed at his supposed injury. 'Shoeing that big stallion brute of Dr MacAlistair's is never easy and I gave myself an awful twist when I was lifting up his hoof to look at it. Since then I canny seem to carry anything very far and the doctor himself said I was to rest it.'

'Ay, it's easy done.' Dokie Joe looked rueful. 'I myself hurt my own whilst going at it wi' a hoe in your very own vegetable garden, Captain MacPherson, so I'm like Willie, in a bit o' a delicate state at the moment and no' very able to indulge in too much heavy activity.'

The laird rubbed his chin. 'Ah, yes, the human back, abnormal posture, every one of us . . . never mind . . .' He turned the nose of the truck towards Keeper's Row. 'You are three stout men and all of you just bursting with festive goodwill. You will soon forget your wee aches and pains when you see the good you are doing. Willie, you get along there with Shug to give him a hand, and while you're at it take one of the smaller trees for Johnny Lonely. If you leave it with Morna she'll see he gets it, it wouldn't be very nice to leave him out, I often feel for the man down there on his own in that miserable hut of his.'

The men groaned and glanced tight-lipped at one another as the lorry came to a halt at Keeper's Row, its arrival creating quite a stir amongst the occupants of the houses. Moggy John's pre-school brood came running out, yelling with excitement, dancing round the AEC, making faces at the laird, jumping up and down and clapping their hands with glee when they saw the men bringing the trees down from the tailboard.

'Give them one too,' directed the laird. 'It will keep them busy and we've got plenty. They're a cheeky bunch but one has to make allowances when they're that young.'

Moggy John and Cathie, his wife, arrived on the scene, she to give tongue to her offspring for annoying the laird, he to help the men unload some of their cargo. Rob too appeared, followed by Big Morgan and Janet, all eager to find out what was happening.

Shug was making a great show about having to go to Mary's Bay with his burden, puffing and panting, coughing, staggering about as if the weight was too much for him to bear.

'I'll take it,' Rob offered, too quickly. 'It will save you a trek, Shug, and I can manage the smaller one as well if I tie them both together. I was going down there anyway to see Morna about the pup I'm getting for wee Andy's Christmas.'

The laird looked at Rob and saw a glimpse of something that wasn't meant to be seen, and in those moments Captain MacPherson knew that Rob's love for Morna was still very much alive. He couldn't blame the man; she was a lovely lass, natural and fresh. It was a pity they had ever separated. He had married Hannah on the rebound, of course, and Morna had come back with a babe born out of wedlock . . .

The laird leaned against the truck, thinking, thinking . . . Strange the twists of fate, that child, so dark and bonny . . . and now she was about to have a stepfather, Morna was going to marry Finlay . . . The laird glanced again at Rob. The child would be a Sutherland after all. He didn't quite know what had made him think that and something strange and sad clutched at his heart. He was acutely aware suddenly of the cruel turns life took. He himself was a sublimely happy man, he had Emily; children that he could be proud of; everything above board, open and honest. The thought that there were people around him who had to hide their true feelings from the world forcibly struck him. Forbidden love . . . A lump came to his throat and he straightened abruptly and called, 'Right, lads, that's taken care of! All aboard! We've got work to do and the sooner we get a move on, the better.'

The progression of the AEC through the village streets was no less sensational than had been its arrival at Keeper's Row. Windows opened, heads popped out, people paid willingly for the privilege of having one of the laird's trees gracing their home – and the coppers were going towards a fund that the laird had set up some time ago for the benefit of the local Fountainwell Orphanage.

'The good, kind soul that he is, he's just giving them away at that price,' was the general consensus and it wasn't long before word of his charitable gesture had spread throughout Calvost.

Later in the afternoon, when the children were released from school, they formed a triumphal procession behind the truck, one or two of the Laws in the lead, the MacGill three bringing up the rear, forgetting all about the horrors of bath night on this rarest of days: first the joys of poking and picking through Wee Fay's shop, now this, the truck, the laird, the trees . . . Christmas was coming, everything was joyous on that wind-fresh day with the clouds scudding along overhead and the scent of spruce needles in the air. Excitable members of the canine population, refusing to miss out on the fun, were joining in, and they all progressed along the street, skipping, barking, chanting, till no one was left in any doubt that Captain Rory MacPherson, the laird of Crathmor, had once more risen to the occasion and was, as an exhausted Willie Whiskers put it, 'So swollen-headed he just might burst altogether and serve him right if both him and his truck went up in a bloody great cloud o' steam!'

That evening, at the children's Christmas party in the Balivoe Village Hall, the laird covered himself with more glory. Mr MacCaskill wasn't there but it didn't matter, Father MacNeil had plenty of volunteers only too willing to take part in his magic tricks. The finale of his act was more than anyone could have hoped for when Captain MacPherson allowed himself to disappear in a puff of smoke, only to turn up later in the guise of Santa Claus, complete with a sack filled to the brim with exciting-looking parcels, personally wrapped by Emily, the laird's lady, who, like her husband, took a great interest in village affairs and a positive delight in entering into the spirit of local functions.

Pride of place in the hall that night was the Christmas tree that had been donated by the laird, hastily erected, hung with baubles and tinsel and dozens of striped suger-olly sticks generously supplied by Wee Fay and Little John.

The lights in the hall were extinquished, the candles on the spruce branches were carefully lit by Emily, a soft warm glow diffused the darkness, spreading itself gently over Father Christmas and his sack of toys.

A hushed ripple of awe ran round the gathering of youngsters. One by one they went up to meet Santa and receive their presents, some of the tinies bursting into tears with the joy and solemnity of the occasion.

'Ach, would you look at our very own lordship,' Mattie said with a mist in her eyes. 'He looks like an angel wi' the light o' the candles pouring over that nice face he has on him.'

'An angel!' snorted Dokie Joe. 'More like a bloody slave-driver if you ask me.'

'Nobody's asking you,' Mattie told her husband with asperity. 'And keep that big rough voice o' yours down. You're spoiling the atmosphere wi' your noise. I know fine you're mad at him because he asked you to help him this afternoon. It was the least you could do, it's what you get paid for, you aren't handyman at Crathmor for nothing, you know.'

Dokie Joe almost choked but could say nothing, neither could Shug nor Willie Whiskers who were standing nearby. They had all spun fine-sounding excuses to their wives for being out with the laird in his truck and the three of them were quaking in their boots lest the real reason behind the day's events ever came out.

'Ay, he's a fine man indeed,' Big Bette joined the other women in praise of the master of Crathmor, 'him and his wife both. 'Tis a pity The MacKernon wasn't as generous wi' his time and his money. There he is, gallivanting off to America wi' his family, too taken up wi' himself to be bothered wi' the likes o' us. We're very lucky to have someone like Captain MacPherson in our midst and I for one will be saying a wee prayer of thanks for him when I go to my bed this very night.'

The men knew when they were beaten and with one accord they retreated into the furthest recesses of the hall, there to take comfort in their own brand of Christmas cheer, in the shape of the hip-flasks that each one of them kept safely hidden in their pockets for 'emergencies'.

The last whispered secret in Santa's ear had been delivered, the last parcel handed out, so next on the agenda was food. Maisie MacPhee had not used her witch's cauldron to concoct an evil potion for her husband, in it she had made soup, the aroma of which now filled the hall and had everyone queuing up with bowls to be filled. This was followed by sandwiches and home-made cakes, jellies and trifles and thereafter by Christmas carols, led by Sunday School teachers, Tillie and Tottie Murchison, two energetic spinster sisters who ran the tiny draper's shop in Balivoe and were sometimes referred to as 'the Knicker Elastic Dears' because when a customer went in to ask for some they would shout to one another in loud penetrating voices, 'Knicker elastic, dear, do we have any?' before proceeding to rummage about in drawers and shelves looking for it.

The night was brought to a close by a vote of thanks from the Revd Thomas MacIntosh, a tall spare man with shrewd brown eyes and a habit of hooking his thumb into his lapel while staring thoughtfully into space, as if entirely unaware of his surroundings. He used this mannerism to great effect during Sunday worship when, in the middle of his sermon, he would pause abruptly, stick his thumb into the folds of his robes, and stare as if mesmerised up at the roof for minutes at a time, while down below in the pews the congregation would start fidgeting. Coughings; nose blowings; the surreptitious rustling of sweet papers; unexplained rumblings; feet shufflings; a small snore; eye-to-eye contact between young lovers; giggles; whispers; frequent glances at the man up there in the pulpit. Had he gone to sleep on his feet? Or was he perhaps seeing some sort of holy message written up there on the roof timbers? Silence, suspense, apprehension, then the shock of that still figure springing to sudden and vigorous life . . . the hand crashing down on the lectern; the accusing stare; the voicing of salient points and thought-provoking questions; the condemnation of all things that did not comply with the church and its teachings.

No matter how often this happened it never failed to surprise and shock the good folk of Kinvara into deep and anxious soul-searching as they wriggled in their seats and stared up at the robed figure in the pulpit as if he were some sort of demigod.

But for all his small foibles he had a good sense of humour and was a likeable and caring man who took time to listen to his parishioners' troubles and tried his best to solve them if he possibly could.

His Irish-born wife, Kerry O'Shaughnessy, blue-eyed, plump, fun-loving, had presented him with three lively children who had never stopped talking from the day they were born. They and their mother between them saw to it that the man of the cloth was first and foremost a man of the family and kept him on his toes with their eager hunger for life.

He had married late but had never regretted one minute of lost bachelorhood. From the first he had been besotted by Kerry O'Shaughnessy and still was, seeing himself as most fortunate to have wooed and won her. The more sober citizens of Kinvara regarded her as being 'quite unsuitable' for a minister's wife, but everyone else loved her, and the sturdy big Manse on top of The Knoll had never known so many visitors. The children brought their friends home from school; the minister and his wife regularly entertained theirs; and one large dog, two large cats, and a very large white rabbit completed the happy domestic scene. Altogether the staid orderly pattern of the minister's past life had disappeared under a deluge of family affairs.

So it was a good speech that he made, interspersed with little jokes that his own children had told him. No one was missed out: Father MacNeil whose magic box of tricks had kept everyone enthralled; Wee Fay and Little John who had supplied the mouthwatering sweets; Tillie and Tottie for leading the Christmas carols; Maisie MacPhee whose 'witch's cauldron' had produced such a savoury potion, the other ladies for donating the wonderful cakes and sandwiches, and last but certainly not least, Captain Rory MacPherson and his good lady Emily for their wonderful generosity and time so willingly spent.

The minister sat down, a loud burst of applause followed, and while it was still in full swing, the laird, fortified by 'a few wee sips' from his monogrammed hip flask, got to his feet to round off the evening with some appropriate words of his own, after which he drew his wife forward and with pride in his voice said, 'Here she is, my own dear Emily, without her I would be nothing, as fair a young English rose as you'd find anywhere, and blooming all the bonnier still for coming to live in the fresh pure air of this land that we love. Ladies and gentlemen, Bonny Scotland! May God bless her and all who live in her.'

Quite carried away he extracted his flask from his pocket, raised it, and took a good swig. 'Bonny Scotland!' The rallying cry echoed joyfully round the room before everyone went to get their coats in order to wrap up against the 'fresh pure air' that, as Shug said, 'could freeze the balls off a brass monkey' when it was blowing wild from the north.

The party over, the children lined up at the door, there each to receive an apple, a threepenny bit, and a suger-olly twist, handed out by the man himself, Captain Rory MacPherson. The laird of Crathmor was well pleased with his achievements of the day, the plaudits still ringing in his ears as he bundled his wife and his children into his Lanchester and drove away from the hall in a rosy glow of satisfaction.

But he had more surprises in store, just 'another little something' that he had been keeping up his sleeve, the recipients of which were the three wrongdoers whose punishment had almost broken their backs and their spirits for the last two days. The final tree had been delivered, the beneficiary Father MacNeil, who stood at his door saluting his gratitude, while Minnie MacTaggart made faces at his back and muttered darkly about the mess the spruce needles would make on her floor and how she wouldn't be the one who was going to clean them up, 'Christmas or no'.

'Well, lad, that's that.' The laird, looking well pleased with himself, started up the truck and grinned at the weary face of Dokie Joe whose turn it was to sit in the warmth of the cab. 'Full steam ahead to Christmas, and just to show you I bear no ill feelings for yesterday I want to share with you the spirit of the season, so sit back, relax, and – tally ho!'

Dokie Joe said nothing, too tired to even wonder what this latest ploy of his lordship was all about. But when the truck ground to a halt outside the Balivoe Village Inn he sat up and took notice. The two men in the back jumped down, and soon all four were comfortably ensconced in the Snug Bar, personally attended by Knobby Sinclair, the proprietor, whose lumpy face and irregular features had earned him his nickname.

Two hours later, Dokie Joe knew that it was time his employer went home when he turned to an ancient worthy and said in a mixture of Gaelic and English, 'Excuse me, but was it you or your brother who was killed in the war?'

The worthy, who had himself arrived at the stage of non-comprehension, looked more dazed than ever, and it was as well that Shug's wife, Dolly, entered at that moment, the only woman in the whole of the place who had ever dared show her face in the male-dominated shrine of the Snug Bar. But Dolly, a thin wiry little woman with a grimy face and straggly hair frisking out from the confines of a battered black hat with a felt daisy in the brim, was a match for any man with her coarse tongue and capacity for beer.

No sooner was she inside the Snug than she grabbed her husband's glass and downed the contents in two noisy swallows, wiping her mouth with the back of her hand, glaring witheringly at her spouse as she said in a voice that could have cut through coal, 'And what the hell do you think you're playing at, Shug Law? Your dinner ready, the fire lit, the bairns waiting to kiss their very own father goodnight.'

Shug did not flinch. His dinner was seldom ready at the proper time, the smouldering wood fire was only worth sitting at when there was coal in the bunker to give off a good heat, his children only kissed him goodnight when they knew he had money in his pocket and wanted some before he and Dolly spent it on beer and tobacco. So Shug was not impressed by his wife's showy comments, instead he fondly patted her pregnant belly and said cheerily, 'You came at the right time, lass, Captain MacPherson will have to be taken home and we will need all the hands we can get to hoist him on to the cart.'

The laird staggered to his feet, hiccuping loudly, doffing his hat and muttering unintelligible farewells as he was led away outside to where Sorry was waiting resignedly in her shafts, knowing only too well the procedure and what was expected of her whenever her master emerged from one of his frequent visits to the inn.

Dolly had been using the cart that day for collecting laundry from the gentry houses and delivering it to the various 'washerwomen' of the area. Some of the sacks were still on the cart and on top of them the laird was deposited, there to lie quite comfortably, singing a sea shanty, a bottle of whisky cuddled to his bosom with all the tender care he might have applied to a baby.

With Dolly at the reins the cart moved off, Shug in front beside his wife, the laird in the back with Dokie Joe and Willie Whiskers who had decided that they had better come along as their help would be needed when they arrived at Crathmor.

The cart rumbled along the quiet dark road, with Sorry needing only an occasional flick of the reins to keep her moving. Above them the moon was floating in and out of the clouds, the stars were beginning to twinkle, moon diamonds sparkled on the sea, and on the horizon the Kinvara Light was flashing, reminding everyone of the men out there on that bleak forbidding rock.

'It's a terrible way to make a living,' Dokie Joe said, shaking his head, 'cut off from the world like that. I myself couldn't do it. The sea is no place for man nor beast on cold nights like these.'

'They'll be warm enough,' Willie Whiskers said. 'I went out there once to see it and it was quite cosy. I wouldny like to be shut up wi' Mungo, though, he'll be trying to fill the others up wi' religion. Him and Donnie Hic will maybe have a fight and Jimmy Song will drive them all daft wi' his singing.'

At that, Dolly began to sing in a grating, off-key voice and the others joined in. The merry band proceeded steadily along, over the Brig o' Shee with its tumbling white waters, past the Mill o' Cladach, and on towards Crathmor.

No one was prepared for the sudden appearance of Stottin' Geordie, the local policeman, but suddenly he was there, getting off his bike, calling on them to halt, and when they did, peering at them suspiciously and saying in an accusing voice, 'Ay, ay, what's all this, then? Drunk by the look o' it and riding without lights.'

'Away you go now.' Shug pretended great surprise. 'It must have got blown out in the wind.'

'There is no wind,' retaliated Geordie, extricating his note-book from some inner recess of his black cape. 'What's more, there is no bloody lantern! It must have been a helluva wind indeed, to have blown away the light and the lantern!'

At that moment he spied the laird lying sprawled amongst the washing in the back of the cart and his tone immediately changed. Geordie never crossed swords with Crathmor if he could help it; he liked the laird and felt he owed him a favour since that same man had once rescued him and driven him home in the Lanchester when he'd had one over the top and could hardly walk straight, never mind find his way homewards.

'Right, I'll say nothing more this time.' Geordie put his notebook away. 'But see you get a lantern fitted to your cart, Shug Law, or I might no' be so lenient the next time.'

'There will be no next time, Geordie,' Shug said meekly. 'Thanking you and bidding you goodnight.'

'And a merry Christmas when it comes,' roared the laird and lay back, chortling and singing for the rest of the journey up to the big house. Once at his own front door, supported by Willie Whiskers and Dokie Joe, he fumbled in his pocket and withdrew some notes. 'There you are, lads, just to show there are no hard feelings, a round pound for each of you to give your families a good Christmas, and may God bless you all.'

The men took the money, Captain MacPherson was delivered safe and sound into the arms of his good wife, Emily, who fortunately saw the funny side of the situation and let him off with just a mild scolding when he called her his bonny English rose and said he was sorry for all the bother he was causing.

'Ach, he is a good man, just,' Willie Whiskers commented in a complete about-face as he and the others departed into the night. 'Though, mind,' he added relentlessly, 'I still say there's more to all this than meets the eye.'

Dolly sucked thoughtfully at her pipe, Sorry gave a little snicker, Dokie Joe wondered what explanation he could give Mattie for coming home so late, Willie Whiskers wondered how he was going to face Maisie and hoped she might be safely tucked up in bed when he got in, and Shug fingered the pound in his pocket and decided it was going to be a good Christmas after all.

Chapter Thirteen

Christmas morning dawned calm and peaceful, dark still except for a streak of silvery light lying across the vast reaches of the eastern sea. Rob woke early and lay still for a moment, something warm and sensuous stealing into his heart, filling the quiet corners of his mind. This was the day he was going to collect Andy's puppy from Oir na Cuan. In a short while he would see Morna, talk to her, touch her. It seemed ages since he had last been in her company but, in fact, it was only three nights ago, the Morgans having invited her to their little son's birthday party. Quite a few of the neighbours had attended, all except Hannah, who had said she was too busy to be bothered.

No one had missed her, she was far too much of a recluse for that and her presence would probably only have blighted the proceedings anyway. As it was, everyone had enjoyed themselves, especially the children, and no one had made any difference about Andy, young Joss readily accepting him as a playmate after an initial stage of summing up.

Andy had squealed, drooled, made faces, threshed about a bit, but he had quickly been accepted into the fold and had thoroughly revelled in all the attention he had received.

Afterwards, the adults had entertained one another with songs and stories, and Rob remembered how Morna had looked when her turn came to sing. She had not got up, but stayed sitting there by the fire, the lamplight shining on her hair, shy and hesitant at first but her voice soon soaring out, like larksong, sweet, pure, unaffected.

'The sea maiden can sing,' Moggy John had said appreciatively and Rob's love for her had made him feel as if his heart was bursting inside of him. He had longed to have her on his own after that but opportunities to go and visit her were rare these days: there had to be reasons, excuses. Finlay never seemed to be away from the house, gloating about it whenever he and Rob met, inciting jealousy and anger in his older brother, making it hard for him to hold his tongue or keep his fists to himself.

But no one would be about at this hour, it would be just Rob and Morna and Vaila, together on the morning of Christmas; his family, the one that he had to keep secret from the eyes of the world even though there were times when he wanted to shout it from the rooftops, let everyone know that they were his and he didn't care who knew it.

But he had to care, everything had changed, only his love for Morna remained the same . . . no, not the same, deeper, more precious than it had ever been.

He was very conscious of this feeling as he slipped from bed and got dressed. It was freezing cold, the window was open a peep and he went over to shut it, remaining there for a moment to gaze out over the machair to Mary's Bay and Morna's house sitting down there at the edge of the ocean, so small and white against the dark waters of the bay, beyond it the black finger of Kinvara Point . . . and . . . wasn't that an orange glow up there, high on the headland? Beside the ruins of the old Chapel Light?

Johnny Lonely was at it again, lighting his bonfires, perhaps to usher in Christmas Day or just to console himself in his own peculiar way. Strange, sad, lonely man, finding some sort of comfort in these little rituals of his. He wasn't a religious type, no one had ever seen him in kirk, yet he seemed to derive an odd kind of pleasure in trawling through the ancient seventeenth-century remains of the old chapel and probably knew more about them than anyone else.

Occasionally he even lived there, keeping warm by lighting

fires in the old stone hearth, unafraid seemingly of the strange lights that some folks claimed to have seen and of the ghostly monks that were reputed to haunt the place. It was said they had been seen flitting in and out of the crumbling apertures, extending their activities as far afield as Calvost Harbour where they had once collected tolls from the ships coming in.

When Johnny was 'in residence' the smoke from his fires could be seen issuing from the chimney, the only part of the structure that remained reasonably intact; it was an odd sensation that, to see the chimney in use and to watch the smoke pouring out of it as it must have done so long ago.

Rob shivered. Drawing his gaze away from the Point, he fixed it on a farther horizon, to that other light, the great flashing octagon of the Kinvara beacon, in itself over fifteen feet high, its powerful beam winking out over the sea, and he thought of the weeks he spent out there when he was on duty, cut off, a part of him longing only to leave it and return to the life he knew best, the other part finding solace in that loneliness because when he was here there was so much conflict in his heart, so many people who sapped his emotions and his energies.

Behind him the bed springs creaked, Hannah muttered something in her sleep and changed her position. He froze, not wanting her to waken, to start asking questions as to what he was doing up at this hour, where he was going. He stayed perfectly still for a few more minutes till her even breathing told him it was safe for him to move.

He crept out of the room and carefully eased the door shut, wincing as the hinges squeaked, making him pause for a moment to listen. Harriet was in the next room and the last thing he wanted was for her to waken. She had come two days ago, arriving when he was out, her voice meeting him the minute he opened the door on his return.

With her she had brought enough supplies to last for a month, seasonal fare that had certainly filled the larder to capacity and had ensured that they would all be well fed over Christmas. But Rob had resented this, not seeing it as an act of generosity but more as an indication that he was unable to provide adequately for his family, even though he knew in himself that this attitude of his had been brought about by her previous disapproval of his abilities as a wage-earner and her view that her daughter should never have married a man so unsuited to her station.

He had been careful to make himself as scarce as possible, not wishing to be in her company any more than was necessary, her presence in his home being just a bit too stimulating for his peace of mind. Yet, he had to admit, in her own forceful way she had certainly livened things up. She had taken charge of Andy, bundling him into outdoor clothes and taking him for walks in his pram, at the same time urging her daughter to get out of the house.

'You mustn't mope, Hannah,' she had said firmly. 'You're far too pale and ought to get out of the house more. The fresh air will do you good.' Hannah had shown her rebellion in her usual ineffectual way, sulking, making excuses, protesting that it was too cold outside. But to no avail, her mother simply didn't listen, and for the last two days she was more outside her own front door than she had been for weeks.

Rob smiled a little to himself at the remembrance of Hannah, muffled to the eyeballs in collars, scarves, and hats, her feet encased in stout boots, her hands enclosed in two pairs of gloves, trailing along at her mother's back, returning home windblown and fresh, with colour in her cheeks and a healthy appetite for some of Harriet's plain but wonderfully wholesome home cooking, the way it had been when she was a girl living at Dunruddy Farm in Ayrshire.

One good thing about Harriet: when she went to bed she slept like a log, and all was quiet as Rob made his way downstairs and into the kitchen where Andy breathed gently in his sleep and made no move when his father stooped to kiss him on one pale soft cheek. At the foot of his cot Rob had hung a little stocking; in a corner of the room the tree stood green and fragrant, giving off the scent of the forest, silver baubles hanging from threads on its branches, rotating gently round and round, a sight that had entranced Andy and held his attention from the minute he saw them.

'Wee man,' Rob whispered softly, 'so small and helpless, so easily pleased, you'll never want while I'm around, be assured o' that. Rest easy, little lad, I'll make sure you'll never feel lonely, soon you'll have a friend, one who'll look after you and see that you'll come to no harm.'

He let himself out of the house to find all was quiet and peaceful. There was no wind, the sun was low yet over a sea which was like a sheet of glistening metal shot through with dazzling shafts of golden light. One or two puffers and some fishing boats were bobbing tranquilly in the harbour; the relief boat, which had recently taken mail and seasonal supplies out to the Kinvara Light, including one of the laird's trees complete with all the trimmings, was tied up alongside the pier. Filling his lungs with the bracing air Rob made his way to the beach, skirting the endrigs of the croftlands that he shared with the other light keepers. Behind him, the bens rose sheer against the blue-black of the sky, the purpled shades of night still lingered in the cradles of the hills and hovered dark and quiet in the sleeping vales beneath the snow-filled corries.

Further down in the foothills, the dawn light was glinting on the russet red of the bracken; sparkling on the burns frothing amongst the rocks; brushing gold over the pale winter grasses in the fields.

It felt good to be alive on such a morning. As he went along, Rob was acutely aware of the life forces throbbing within him, everything that was around and about him seemed sharper and clearer: smells, sights, sounds, the piping of the oyster catchers, the curlew's plaintive call, the salt fresh tang of the sea in his nostrils . . . the fragrance of peat smoke rising up from yon chimney, Morna's chimney, telling him of the life that bloomed inside the walls, letting him know that she was up and about . . .

*　　*　　*

She answered the door in her dressing gown, a soft green garment that enhanced her eyes and clung to the enticing swell of her voluptuous young breasts. Her hair was the colour of a raven's wing that morning, clinging around her lovely little cameo of a face, tumbling down about her shoulders in glossy curls that hadn't yet been brushed but were all the more attractive in their disarray.

'You look good in the morning, young Morna Sommero,' he said teasingly, trying to sound nonchalant but unable to ignore the feelings that the sight of her was doing to him; the stirring in the pit of his belly, that raw deep ache within his heart, the dreadful sensation of sadness because she would never be truly his, his Morna, his love, pale somehow in the morning light, the roses gone from her cheeks, the sparkle from her eyes.

'Merry Christmas, my darling,' he breathed, unable to stop the words of endearment tumbling from his lips.

The tears sprang to her eyes. 'And to you, my dearest, dearest man. I hoped you would come, I prayed you would come. I rose early to light the fire, peats for Christmas morning, I love the smell of the smoke coming out of my chimney.'

She drew him inside and shutting the door she pulled his head down towards her and kissed him tenderly on the lips. Her body was warm, so warm, he wanted only to crush her to him, to tell her of how he pined for her, how much he loved her, but the time for that was not this moment. He sensed the gentleness in her, the need just to be there with him, like this, on Christmas morning, with the sparks from the peats crackling up the chimney, the little tree shining in the corner, the small pile of parcels beneath its boughs, the pups and the dogs spilling from their baskets, coming forward to greet him with sleepy yawns and wagging tails.

She smiled and pulled away from him. 'I'll make tea, then we'll talk, Vaila isn't awake yet, when she is there will be no time for any . . . o' this, so we must make the most of it.'

They sat at the fire, drinking tea and eating buttery oatcakes, laughing at the antics of the pups. He had already chosen an inquisitive big character with spots dappling its nose and paws and a white tip at the end of its feathery tail. 'I'll call it Breck,' he decided, 'the spotted one, Andy will go daft altogether when he sees it. Hannah and Harriet will go daft too but in a different kind o' way. It doesn't matter what they think, Andy's the one who counts. He and the pup will grow up together, the lad will have at least one friend he can count on.'

'Only a little bitch left after Breck,' Morna nodded. 'The Henderson sisters took the last dog pup but yours. I went over to Croft Angus with it yesterday.' She paused, remembering her visit to the home of Wilma and Rona Henderson. Pebble, the 'big collie brute' who had fathered Mink's pups, had come bounding to meet her and sniff curiously at his offspring which cowered in the protective shell of Morna's jacket.

'Lovely,' Rona had beamed in her gruff but well-modulated voice. 'He'll make a wonderful sheepdog, the eagerness of the collie, the patience of the labrador, such a clever mix. We've decided to call him Rebel. Pebble and Rebel, a nice ring to it, don't you think?'

Without knowing why, Morna had always experienced an odd sense of disquiet whenever she encountered 'the Henderson Hens', a name bestowed on them by the locals because of their enthusiasm for keeping poultry of all kinds. No one knew very much about the two. They had only been in the area for about eight years, newcomers by Kinvara standards. They were vague about their origins, 'the south' Wilma was wont to say absently, blinking nervously through the large glasses that made her eyes look enormous.

They were great clumpy women with large hands and feet, both dressed to the neck in black which they covered over with striped butcher's aprons when they were stomping around the croft in their big stout boots, bawling out orders to their dogs, their cows, their fowls, and to each other. They were, however, kind and harmless and quite secular in their views, rarely attending church but enjoying an occasional local event such as the annual Highland Games; the fêtes given each year by both the laird and the Clan Chief of The MacKernons. Once they had even turned up at a ceilidh in the summer camp of the travelling people and had surprised everyone by a song and dance routine that no one had ever forgotten for its wit and originality.

The Henderson Hens, two jolly sisters who were inclined to keep themselves to themselves yet who could be so entertaining when they set their minds to it. Morna had always felt that there was more to them than met the eye, that somehow the image they portrayed to the world was only put on to hide the depths of their true characters. Lonely, Morna decided, a feeling that she herself had experienced often enough and with which she could sympathise.

'A penny for them.' Rob's voice broke into her thoughts and she laughed.

'I was just thinking about the Henderson sisters, they're calling their new pup Rebel to rhyme with Pebble. Strange ladies, loud, obvious, yet somehow sad and lost.'

'Morna,' he reached out and took her hand. 'Never mind about them, what about you? We're all going to Vale o' Dreip for Christmas dinner, why don't you come too? My mother would be glad to see you.'

She shook her head. 'Your father wouldn't, Finlay has already asked me but I know when I'm not wanted. Don't worry so, I'll be fine.'

'What will you do?' he asked, quietly, helplessly, an anger in him against the man whose dogma affected so many people. 'I cannot bear the thought o' you being here on your own today of all days.'

'I won't be on my own, I'm having dinner with Johnny Lonely. I've invited him to share my table.'

'Johnny Lonely?'

'Ay, Johnny Lonely. He hasn't got anywhere else to go and everyone needs someone on Christmas day.' She shook her head. 'Poor Johnny, in many ways he's like me, a bit o' a conundrum, misunderstood by society.'

'He won't be much company.'

'That's where you're wrong, we get along fine, Johnny and

me, and have a lot in common. You'd be surprised at how he opens up and talks. He knows so much about everything and he's a great reader too. Did you know that, Rob? Everyone thinks he's illiterate just because he's different, but he isn't. Robert Burns, Chaucer, Sir Walter Scott, you name it, he's read it.'

'Folks will talk about you, consorting with a hermit, having him here in your house when there's no one else around.'

'Och, Robbie,' she chided with a smile, 'they talk anyway – and I know fine it's not them you're worrying about, it's yourself, jealous of any man I keep company with.'

'What else does he get up to – besides reading these highbrow books you mentioned?'

'Oh, lots o' things. He loves music too and has an old gramophone in his bothy which he plays very quietly when he thinks no one is around. I've heard it, floating out softly into the bay, and something inside of me cries for him and the loneliness o' his existence. Don't ask me where he got the books and the records, who knows what his life was before he became so disillusioned with it he wanted only to be on his own. He never talks about it and I never ask, I only know he has intellect and a sensitivity that few here will ever see or understand.'

'You seem to know a great deal about him.' Rob frowned, envious suddenly of a man who hitherto had raised in him only emotions of frustration and resentment.

'I told you, we talk,' she said simply and closed the subject at that.

Chapter Fourteen

Rob, very conscious of time passing and of how precious these moments alone with Morna were, wasted no more breath discussing Johnny Lonely. Instead he took something from his pocket which he held on to briefly before opening his palm to reveal a beautiful mermaid brooch carved out of polished wood.

'I made this for you,' he told her a trifle self-consciously. 'It isn't much, but it's from the heart. Something personal for my own little sea maiden.'

Tears glinted on her lashes as she pinned the ornament to her dressing gown. 'This means more than the world to me. With your own hands you made it and whenever I wear it, I'll think of you.'

Shyly she handed him a tiny corn dolly. 'It's meant to be you and me,' she explained softly. 'Keep it close to your heart, my darling Robbie, for that's where I'll be, through all the days o' my life, no matter what else happens. You're my man. From the first minute I saw you I loved you – and so it will be till I am no more of this earth.'

There was something about the way she spoke that made him draw in his breath, he saw pleading in her eyes, the catch of her teeth on her lips . . . lips like blaeberries, soft and sweet. To taste them was to hunger for more – and he had never been able to resist them, not even now, when he knew that she had promised herself to somebody else, that somebody being his own brother who would very soon share her life – and her bed. None of that seemed to matter just now, today it was just Morna and Rob, here in this room on Christmas morning with the peat fire glowing in the hearth and the rug at their feet, so warm and inviting.

His hunger for her gnawed at his belly. Reaching out, he touched a lock of her hair, his eyes very tender as he gazed into hers, his pulse beginning to race when she caught and held his hand, her long slender fingers gripping it with an almost desperate strength.

When their mouths touched it was like the merging of two fires, burning and consuming them in its heat, leaving no space for rhyme nor reason as it swept through them mercilessly.

His lips blew into her ear and tingles of pleasure ran down her spine. She gave one small protesting cry when his hands moved inside her dressing gown, but it was no use, he was cupping her breasts, his fingers feathering the swelling peaks of her nipples.

Tears ran down her face as helplessly they sank to the floor where the fire bathed them in its warmth and it seemed that they could never get close enough to one another, no matter how hard they tried. Flesh pressed against naked flesh, limbs entwining as their bodies throbbed with an unashamed yearning to be fulfilled and released. No other world existed but theirs, time was forgotten, reality slipped away from them as locked in each other's arms they spun together into a sphere where only Rob and Morna lived and breathed and loved.

So Morna Jean Sommero gave herself willingly to Robert James Sutherland, her lips and breasts offering him their nectar, her soft flesh opening to him like the petals of a flower as he searched and plunged and cried out his love for her when, as one, they reached the pinnacles together, locked as they always wanted to be in mind, soul and body.

Reality, when it came, was as tender as the aftermath of their lovemaking. Slowly, lazily, they gazed at one another, smiled and kissed, delighting in their closeness, savouring the warmth of each other's bodies.

'We're so lucky,' she whispered, 'to have found this wonder, we might never have met, might never have known what it was like to be so loved by another human being. As it is, we will always have these precious times to remember − when we're apart and can't be alone as we are now.'

Her voice faltered, and placing a finger over her lips he murmured, 'Hush, my sweet darling, don't think about tomorrow. I'll never be far away from you and will be here for you whenever you need me.' He stroked her hair and held her close, the echo of his own words empty and meaningless inside his head while she lay passively against him, her thoughts deep and distant as she saw her future stretching before her like a long grey road leading to nowhere.

Her throat tightened. There was so much she wanted to say to him, so many things she wished she could tell him that might make him understand why she had pledged herself to a man she didn't love. Her breath caught . . . wildly she wondered if she could go through with her marriage to Finlay, she would have to lie with him, let him touch her, allow him to do the kind of things that any man would expect of his wife. Panic seized her, she could never do it − never! Then she thought of Vaila, and knew why she had to carry on. Tears fell silently down her face, but Rob didn't see, and he never knew of the ceaseless turmoil that churned inside the heart of his beloved Morna Jean as she lay quiet and still in the warm enfolding circle of his arms.

Together they went upstairs to wake Vaila, flushed and innocent in her sleep, long lashes fanning her rosy cheeks, the curls that framed her face making a dark halo against the whiteness of her pillow.

For a moment they both stood, arms entwined, gazing down at their child, the daughter they had conceived in the wild wondrous days of their careless lovemaking, never knowing what fate would hold for them but letting tomorrow bring what it might, just as long as they went on with each other, loving, caring, sharing.

'She's beautiful,' he said simply. 'I'm proud to be her father.'

'Robbie.' Morna bit her lip. 'Perhaps one day she will call you that. Life has a way of twisting things and who knows what lies in store for any o' us? Oh, God, I wish, how I wish . . .'

'Hush, my baby.' He kissed away the tears from her eyes. 'I hate to see you tormenting yourself like this. I can't bear it either, but if we're to go on we have to be strong for one another, and for Vaila.'

As if aware that her name had been spoken, the child stirred in her cot. 'Wobbie!' she cried as soon as she opened her eyes, stretching out her arms for him to lift her up and bear her away downstairs to the tree and the presents that awaited her.

She explored everything, the parcels, the wrappings, the colourful gift tags, and only when she had finished with these did Rob show her what he had brought her, a silver pendant in the shape of a tiny lighthouse and when he fastened it round her neck she fingered it for a long moment before saying solemnly, 'Lighthouse. Wobbie's lighthouse.'

'That's right, sweetheart,' he said huskily. 'Robbie's lighthouse, whenever you look towards it you can picture me, lighting the lamps, gazing from the windows, thinking of my little Vaila Marie and wondering what you are doing.'

Young as she was, she seemed to understand everything that he had said because she nodded her full agreement and said again, 'Wobbie's lighthouse', and it was a joy to watch the expressions that flitted across her intelligent small face as she looked first at him and then pointed to the window with a quaintly knowing nod that made Morna and Rob laugh aloud with delight.

After that they all got dressed in outdoor clothes and took the dogs for a walk along the shore. The sun had risen higher, spilling its welcoming rays over a sea that was so calm it was like a looking-glass, mirroring the white clouds, the little islands, the fingers of land jutting out along the shoreline, even reflecting the misty isles of the Hebrides far away in the distance.

Vaila was entranced by everything she saw and heard and went toddling away with the dogs, splashing into pools, falling over, picking herself up to go on her determined way again, clapping her hands at the frolics of the pups, her laughter gurgling happily in her throat.

Her parents stood watching her, Morna's fingers clinging to Rob's inside the pocket of his jacket. 'She's tough, that wee one,' Rob observed admiringly. 'Just look at her, never a moan out o' her when she skins her knees and hurts herself.'

'She's a Sutherland,' Morna reminded him. 'She's got your blood in her, Robbie, she's inherited a lot o' your traits, stubbornness, wilfulness, a liking for getting her own way . . . she is also caring, thoughtful, loving – a marvellous combination of everything that makes her into an exciting and wonderful little human being – just like her father.'

'I'm glad you added the nice bits,' he said ruefully, kissing the tip of her nose. 'To me she's perfect, wilful or no, and I just hope Finlay will know how to get the best out o' her, he's never been renowned for his patience or his tact, he's far too immature himself for that.'

A seal suddenly popped its head up in the bay and Morna was very glad of the chance to swing the talk away from Finlay. 'Oh, look, it's Kelvin, the seal pup who used to come into the bay last summer. Father MacNeil found me here talking to it and so I called it Kelvin after him. I'm sure it's the same one, he had these enormous wet eyes, as if he had cried a lot and couldn't stop the tears falling. I hope he's found his mother since then, he was so unhappy on his own.'

'The priest or the pup?' Rob spoke sarcastically and she looked at him quickly.

'Why, the seal of course.'

'Are you sure? And how come you know the man's Christian name? It's the first time I've heard it.'

'Because he told me,' she faltered. 'There was no harm in it, we talked for ages, right here on the beach. I found him very interesting, he's a fine man, compassionate and considerate.'

'Johnny Lonely, Father MacNeil, my brother Finlay, is there no end to the men you feel compelled to speak to and take pity on?'

'Stop that, Robbie, just stop it! I can speak to whom I like, men or women. I enjoy getting to know people, there's no harm in it, you're jealous of everyone who comes into my life, that was the reason I ran away from you, and look where it led, to this, me without a husband, Vaila without a father she can openly claim as her own. Don't hurt me like this, Robbie, it's taking all my will-power to go on with what I have to do and you're only making it worse for all of us.' Her face was ashen as she spoke, her breath coming quickly and unevenly.

'Oh, God, I'm sorry!' he cried harshly. 'I don't know what I'm saying, it's being here like this with you and Vaila, all the while knowing that soon I must go away and leave you . . . forgive me, you're the last person on earth I want to hurt.'

Taking her in his arms he crushed her to his chest, murmuring her name over and over, kissing away her tears, unashamedly displaying how he felt about her, unthinking of who might see them out here in the open with no shelter of any kind to hide them from prying eyes.

'Me go home now.' Vaila's voice, small and uncertain, filtered through to them, a forlorn expression on her face as she stood gazing up at the two people in the world she had never expected to see crying.

They were immediately filled with remorse at having turned her outing into an unhappy one. 'Come on, it's time we all went back,' Rob said, and hoisting her up on to his shoulders they returned to Oir na Cuan where Vaila, tired out after her walk, fell asleep on the couch amidst a heap of canine and feline bodies.

The moment of parting had come. Rob was reluctant to leave, but Morna took his arm and went with him to the door where they stood facing one another.

'Robbie,' she said slowly, 'before you go I have something

to ask of you and I don't really know how to put it. I've lain awake at nights, the words going round and round in my mind – now the moment has come I feel even worse than I imagined I would.'

'What is it?' He gripped her arm and stared down into her face. 'Surely you know you can say anything to me.'

She took a deep breath. 'I want you to give me away, Robbie, at my wedding. Your father most certainly won't do it, there's no one else I feel close enough to turn to. It's a lot to ask I know – oh, God, it's all so difficult!'

He was staring at her incredulously. 'Give you away? How can you ask that o' me? Give away the woman I love, hand my daughter over to another man? It's too much, Morna, it's bad enough knowing that you're getting married without this as well. Why don't you just change your mind about Finlay? You don't love him. God knows he can be a bastard at times, but he is my brother and it doesn't seem fair to be using him like this.'

'When you say fair, Robbie, you aren't really thinking of him but of yourself. He's happy to be marrying me, it's what he wants and I'll do everything I can to make him a good wife. Please, oh, please, try to understand. We have to think of Vaila now and what's best for her.

'We've had our time, Robbie, all that was meant for us. I will never stop loving you, never cease to remember how it was between us, you're part o' me and always will be. You're my great love, Robbie. I will live and die with you in my heart, but I can't go on with things as they are – the waiting, the hoping, the long hours when I don't see you.' A sob caught in her throat. 'This is the only way out for me. I can't face the future alone. The step I am about to take is inevitable but I need you there by my side, Robbie, and I'm begging you to do this for me – and for Vaila.'

His raging emotions engulfed him, anger, hurt, sorrow, all seethed within him till he felt he would go mad with the pain. Then he saw her face, pale and tragic, her huge dark eyes reflecting the same sort of feelings that were tearing him in two.

But he couldn't bring himself to comfort her, it was enough for him to stand there in front of her and hear himself say, 'All right, if it makes you feel any better, I'll do it, but don't expect me to kiss you and shake Finlay's hand afterwards. It will take me all my time just to be there with you and my daughter and watch you both walking away with another man.'

Turning on his heel he slammed out of the house, banging the door behind him. Moments later it was wrenched open again and Morna came running out to catch up with him. 'You forgot to take Breck!' she panted, handing him the floppy little bundle. The pup's tail was wagging furiously, anxious to please. It whined and licked his face, its moist eyes gazing into his before it buried its nose in his neck and gave vent to a huge soulful sigh.

In spite of everything, Rob had to smile. 'He'll be well taken care of,' he said briefly, adding, 'thanks for letting me have him,' before striding away down the path to the gate.

Morna stood watching him go, feeling the morning on her face, the blackness of night in her heart. He didn't look back and she returned to the house feeling shaky and unreal. Her pulse was fluttering rapidly, she felt breathless and strange, there was a dull heavy pain in her chest, like a band of steel growing ever tighter. From a cupboard on the wall she took a bottle of pills and swallowed one of them. Doctor MacAlistair had prescribed them for her when he had discovered her weak heart during a bad bout of flu. His face had been serious when he had bundled up his stethoscope and put it back into his pocket. 'How long has this been going on, lass?' he had questioned her kindly.

'I took rheumatic fever as a child. Afterwards the doctor said it had weakened my heart and told my parents to mollycoddle me a bit. Of course they tried, but I was always on the go and after a while everybody treated me as normal. But I had a bad time having Vaila and felt breathless a lot and now it's worse since taking this flu.'

'Ay, ay, that would explain everything, you have a very

distinct heart murmur which means a damaged valve. If you take life easy it should be all right, no heavy lifting and laying, and it might be best not to have any more children, another pregnancy wouldn't be wise in your condition.'

The bluntness of his words took her breath away.

He was an amiable, white-haired bewhiskered man of middle age, portly and pink-faced, his purple-veined nose showing his liking for a good dram, the pipe that protruded from his tobacco-stained moustache looking like some benign growth because it was nearly always there, lit or otherwise. In his tweed cloak and deerstalker hat he was a very distinctive figure, 'an auld rascal' according to his wife who nevertheless tended him hand and foot and patched the holes 'in the arse of his combinations' with a devotion that had earned her the nickname of 'Long John Jeannie'.

Doctor Alistair MacAlistair had tended the population of Kinvara for twenty years and was as much at home supping broth with one of his patients as he was downing a dram at his own fireside. Everybody liked, respected, and trusted him, even though he was renowned for being outspoken, and had 'scared the shat' out of many an ailing soul by telling them exactly what was wrong with them in plain-spoken English mixed with some Gaelic when he'd had one too many.

Now it was Morna's turn to be on the receiving end of his frankness, and all she could do was to stare at him for a few startled moments before saying, 'Och, come on now, Doctor, surely it can't be as bad as all that.'

'Take it or leave it, lass,' he had replied, patting her arm with a big hairy hand. 'It's your choice. I can only give you my advice, the rest is up to you – but don't say I didn't warn you.'

The echo of his voice seemed to ring in her head as she sat there in Oir na Cuan on Christmas morning, staring at the pill bottle in her hand.

'Please God,' she whispered, 'give me the strength to carry on for my daughter's sake, I ask nothing more of you than that, except for one thing, never let Robbie's love for me die, no matter how difficult it might be for both o' us in the days and years that lie ahead.'

Then she lay down on the couch beside her little daughter and fell asleep with the rays of the sun warming her through the panes of the window.

Chapter Fifteen

Rob let the pup precede him into the house, reasoning that the diversion it would cause might take some of the attention away from him and help to ward off too many searching questions regarding his activities of the morning.

He hadn't said anything to his mother-in-law about the pup, not wishing to precipitate an argument any sooner than was necessary. Hannah hadn't said anything either, almost as if she had forgotten the whole thing or was hoping that if she didn't mention it he might forget also.

So it was with mixed feelings that Rob watched as the little dog marched boldly into the lobby and straight through to the kitchen, whiskers bristling, eyes aglow, tail a-wag, everything about him alert and confident because already he knew that this was how to face the world, head on, softening opposition before it had a chance to take root, giving that first vital good impression before youth and inexperience let him down.

Hannah was at the table, setting it for breakfast. Harriet was at the stove, cooking bacon and eggs. Breck lifted his speckled nose and sniffed the delicious aroma, just as the womenfolk spotted him sitting there on the threshold, a tiny cheeky black-and-white bundle surveying his new domain with great aplomb, giving every impression of having lived on the earth considerably longer than his mere nine weeks.

Hannah's reaction was typical, dropping a heap of forks on the table, she rushed to fill a bucket at the sink and to fetch a mop from the broom cupboard. Holding on to it like a lance, she stared fixedly at Breck as if expecting him to soil her floor at any given moment.

Harriet, on the other hand, behaved in a most uncharacteristic fashion. Her strong-featured face showed astonishment as she shook her head and said, 'I can hardly believe it! He's exactly like the dog I had when I was a girl growing up at Dunruddy Farm. We did everything together, he came everywhere with me, his name was Ben Pepper and I've never forgotten him.'

Stooping down, she snapped her fingers at Breck, but he took not the slightest notice. Instead he gave a squeaky tongue-curling yawn, then made straight for the child lying on the fireside rug. There he began to sniff him and lick him and roll all over him in a flurry of tail and tongue and paws while Andy shrieked with laughter and in turn rolled all over the pup.

'Get him out o' here!' Hannah shouted, trying vainly to sweep the pup away with her mop while he, thinking it was some kind of game, jumped up and grabbed it in his jaws, worrying it as if it were a rat, shaking it from side to side, the growls and whines rising in his throat with mock ferocity.

'Get him out o' here!' Hannah repeated to her husband. 'I won't have a vicious creature like that in the house, he can sleep in a kennel outside.'

The 'vicious creature' had now abandoned the mop and was cuddling sleepily up to Andy whose arms came round to hold this new and wonderful playmate close to his heart.

'Sorry, Hannah,' Rob said calmly, 'this is one Christmas present that's here for keeps. The bairn loves him already and that's all that matters.'

'Oh, is it!' Hannah turned furiously on her husband. 'And what about me? Left to clean up the mess after each o' them! The pup piddling and skittering all over the place, the baby doing the same! He'll never learn to be clean like other bairns, he'll go on filling his nappy till the day he dies and I'm the one who'll have to bear the burden till the day *I* die!' With that she threw herself down on a chair and burst into a flood of self-pitying tears, rocking herself back and forth, muttering over and over, 'I won't do it, I was never meant to be a skivvy, I'll be left here while you go gallivanting . . .' Her head came up, she glared at him accusingly, 'Just where *have* you been half the morning? You weren't here when I got up, I was left to see to *him* and attend to everything else into the bargain. It's my Christmas too, you know, but for all anyone cares it might as well be any other day o' the week.'

'Och, come on, Hannah.' Harriet jumped into the fray, not to rescue her son-in-law from his wife's wrath but to indignantly defend herself against her daughter's unfair complaints. 'All you did was see to the infant, I did everything else in case you haven't noticed. It's high time you took stock o' yourself and started behaving like a grown woman. All you ever did was bury your nose in a book and pretend the rest o' the world didn't exist. Well, you've made your bed, my girl, and you'll just have to lie in it.

'Given time, the boy will improve, he's as human as the rest o' us and we all shat our nappies when we were his age. He's certainly unusual, I'll grant you that, and I find it hard to accept that he's got Houston blood in him, but where there's life there's hope and though he might look as though he isn't all there, his eyes say differently. As for the dog, he's a cross collie, and if he's anything like my Ben Pepper he'll end up training *us* before he's very much older.'

Silence met this outburst. Rob was so taken aback he was speechless, Hannah was equally dumbfounded, and there wasn't so much as a whimper from either the baby or the puppy as they lay side by side on the rug.

'Well, I've said my piece.' Harriet adjusted her apron and turned back to the stove, 'Finish setting the table, Hannah, before the bacon gets burnt to a frazzle. If we're to get ready in time for kirk, we'll have to get a move on. Bette MacGill said she would give us a lift in her trap and we can't keep her waiting.'

'I'm not going.' Hannah stated sullenly, the idea of sharing a trap with Big Bette and her brood of three was almost too much for her to bear. 'I've got too much to do here and besides, I cannot abide all that whispering that goes on in kirk. I don't like the people here and they don't like me, so you go yourself and welcome to it.'

'Nonsense, girl,' Harriet rattled the hot plates on to the table and began serving breakfast, 'you can't miss the Christmas Day service, the Reverend MacIntosh is a good minister and a fine speaker, and you won't have too much to do here, you never have, and today you'll have even less since we've been invited to Vale o' Dreip for dinner, so there's no excuse for you not to go to kirk.'

Hannah looked miserable, she wasn't looking forward to dining at Vale o' Dreip: Ramsay Sutherland trying to be polite when all the time he resented having her in the family; the rest of them putting a jolly face on things even though she knew they spoke about her behind her back because she'd presented them with Andy and were ashamed that he was kin. She also hated the idea of going to kirk; Tillie and Tottie Murchison wearing their Sunday School faces; that Bette MacGill with her big fat nosy face, thinking she was something because she ran the village store; Mattie MacPhee, rough and uncouth, eyes goggling with interest at everyone who came into her line of vision; Maisie MacPhee folding her lips; the Simpson sisters eyeing her with jealousy and dislike; Wee Fay and Little John, staring at her as if *she* was abnormal . . . and that man, the minister, gaping at the ceiling in crazed contemplation, thumping his bible like one demented; that Irish wife of his gazing at him as if he were God; their children looking like a row of cherubs, when all the time they were dropping sweet papers on the floor and whispering mischief to one another . . .

Hannah drew her knife through her fried egg and glared at the yolk running over her plate. She wouldn't go. She had to make a stand at some point in her life and this was one time that Harriet Houston wasn't going to get her own way, and that was final!

*   *   *

In the end, after much argument, Hannah gave in to her mother's persuasions, and while she was upstairs getting dressed, Rob turned to his mother-in-law and said softly, 'You are indeed a woman o' surprises, one who once had a dog called Ben Pepper, a truly unique name for what was obviously an outstanding animal.'

'His spots inspired it, of course, he was literally peppered with them, and he wasn't all that outstanding, just another cross collie who slunk about rounding up the hens when he had nothing better to do with himself. But he was clever, so wise he could run rings round all o' us, and to me he was the best dog that ever lived . . . of course, I was only a girl,' she added hastily, 'young and foolish and liberal with my feelings. People grow up, they change.'

Despite those careless last words she had allowed her guard to drop, and Rob had glimpsed another side to Harriet Houston that he hadn't known existed, seeing a warmth about her that had softened the determined lines of her face and made her more likeable somehow.

When Hannah came downstairs her mother was herself again, brisk and bossy, telling her daughter that her hat was squinty and her hair untidy, that her overall appearance left a lot to be desired, and to cheer up, it wasn't a funeral she was attending but a service in praise of Christ's coming.

She was still talking when she hustled Hannah out of the door and Rob felt a pang of sympathy for his wife even though he now saw his mother-in-law in a clearer light. Hannah needed somebody like Harriet in her life and he wondered if it had always been like that, or if it was something that had developed over the years as Hannah withdrew more and more into herself.

He watched them from the window, walking along to No. 1 of the row where Big Bette was emerging from her house, resplendent in black wool from head to toe, haranguing her three children to 'stay clean, stay quiet, and speak nice to the minister if he speaks to you'.

Rob could hear her voice plainly and he could imagine

Hannah visibly shrinking from the onslaught that awaited her when she climbed into the trap beside the MacGill family. It was obvious that Harriet had been getting to know the neighbours in the short while she'd been here, and knowing Bette, she would be making the most of any opportunity to find out more about the Houstons, since, in common with everyone else, there was little she'd been able to extract from Hannah in the few years that she'd lived in Calvost.

Almost everyone from Keeper's Row was making for the kirk that morning. The farmhands were coming from the bothies, among them Ryan Du and Linky Jack Black, polished and shiny-looking, meeting up with Moggy John and Cathie MacPhee as they came piling from their house with their family of six.

Mollie Gillespie appeared on the scene. The allegations of Johnny Lonely regarding Hic Gillespie's wife were very fresh in the mind of Linky Jack and he tried not to look too interested in her as she came over to join the others.

She was a fresh-skinned, brown-haired young woman in her mid-twenties, quiet, attractive and well-spoken, giving every impression of someone who was always cool and calm and self-contained. As yet she had no children and was often lonely when Donnie Hic was away, and sometimes even lonelier when he was at home as he drank too much and was inclined to spend a lot of his time at the village inn with his cronies. Despite his faults, however, he doted on his wife and was jealous of any man who looked at her with more than a friendly eye.

But Ryan Du had wakened fires in her she hadn't known existed, and whenever she and he met they were carried away with a helpless need for one another. Yet they had been careful never to be seen together. Ryan Du never came to her house, she never went to visit him over yonder in the farm bothies beneath Blanket Hill. In the eyes of the world they were no more than good acquaintances, but they hadn't been careful enough it seemed – Johnny Lonely knew about their liaisons and he had given the game away to Linky Jack Black who was now eyeing her in rather a sly fashion and nudging Ryan Du knowingly.

Rob watched the scene for a few minutes longer, smiling a little when two of the MacPhee children ran to catch up with Big Bette in her trap in order to hitch a lift on the tailboard. Hannah would be having a fit altogether! All those children, talking at once, Big Bette shouting to make herself heard, Harriet having her say at the top of her voice.

Rob drew away from the window. It was very quiet in the house, Andy and Breck were snoring companionably on the rug, the yule logs were hissing in the grate, the clock was tick-tocking lazily on the mantelpiece. Wonderful blessed peace, a breathing space in which to be alone with his thoughts for a while. Sitting down at the fire he took out the little corn dolly given to him by Morna, and with tears in his eyes he gently kissed it, wondering as he did so what the New Year would bring for all of them.

For Captain Rory MacPherson it brought Lord MacKernon from the ancient seat of Cragdu Castle, storming down to the stronghold of Crathmor where the master of the house was sitting with his feet by the chimney enjoying a celebratory dram by the comforts of his own fireside.

The New Year was one day old. The previous evening, on the stroke of midnight, every house in Kinvara with a bell had rung it, and Shug Law had driven his cart through the village streets swinging a big hand bell and shouting 'Happy New Year' at the top of his voice.

The noise had brought Stottin' Geordie on the scene but he had let Shug off with a warning because he was in a festive mood himself after consuming a fair number of drams in the privacy of his tiny office in the police station.

Afterwards, there had been a great deal of traditional first footing and Crathmor had seen its share of visitors, song and dance had been the order of the day, the whisky had flowed, the bagpipes had skirled, well into the small hours of morning.

Even so, Captain MacPherson had been out walking his dogs after snatching only an hour or two of sleep and only now, many hours later, were the effects of the festivities taking their toll. He confided to Emily that he could still hear the pipes reverberating inside his head, to which she laughed and told him he was simply suffering from a good old-fashioned hangover.

'Oh well, a hair of the dog,' he decided, but had no sooner settled himself by the fire with a stiff dram than Catrina came in to say that Lord MacKernon of Cragdu Castle was outside in the hall.

'Well, show him in, show him in, lass,' he said affably. 'This is no time to be standing on ceremony. Oh, and bring more logs for the fire while you're at it, it's freezing outside and we must keep our visitors warm.'

Emily's voice filtered through the door, trying to be heard above those of the children who had come downstairs *en masse* and were being very vocal in their curiosity regarding the caller.

There was a scuffle, and the next moment the door was thrown back on its hinges. The MacKernon as he was known, was not standing on ceremony as he came striding into the room, complete with his two deerhounds who pulled up short at the sight of the laird's spaniels stationed beside him, chins resting on his knee, eyes lovingly following every move he made. Sheba, who had just settled herself on the Captain's lap, was greatly perturbed by the intrusion of the deerhounds and wasn't slow to show her annoyance in a display of gleaming fangs and unsheathed claws.

'Rough! Irish! Here, lads! Down!' The MacKernon snapped his fingers and his dogs folded their lithe haunches to the floor as their master threw himself into a nearby chair.

'MacKernon, this is indeed a pleasure.' The laird extended his hand and half rose from his seat. 'I had thought you still to be over the pond or, at least, setting sail for home. I'm delighted to see you and glad to have this opportunity to wish you all the best of the season.'

His visitor, however, was having none of the pleasantries, New Year or no. 'I got back yesterday and I'll come straight to the point, MacPherson,' he said heavily. 'It's about trees, my trees, somebody's been pinching them and I'm here to ask if you know anything about it.'

'I'll get Alice to make tea.' Emily poured the newcomer a whisky and hastily withdrew from the room, shushing the children away from the door as she went.

'And I'll get the logs.' Catrina, eyes flashing with interest, took her time leaving the room and it was only when the laird cleared his throat and looked pointedly in her direction that she unwillingly departed.

'You were saying . . .'

He turned back to the visitor who nodded and said drily, 'You heard, MacPherson, about my trees, I went down there this morning and couldn't believe it when I saw this bloody great clearing in *my* woods. You must have heard the timber coming down, surely you're not going to sit there and tell me you know nothing about it.'

'Ah, yes, your woods, dear me.' Sadly, the laird shook his head. 'I don't really like to say this but that's a debatable point, MacKernon. As you know, the piece of land you mention has never been clearly defined as yours, so the question of ownership rears its ugly head once again. However, there's no need to get het up about something that's been going on so long, so let's just sit back and discuss the matter reasonably.'

'Reasonably! Reasonably! And just what do you call reasonable, MacPherson? People plundering my land, taking what isn't theirs, not even having the decency to clear up properly after them.' The Clan Chief's face had turned red. He was a tall, handsome man in early middle years, dark hair slicked back from a thin aristocratic face, the lower half of which was covered with a large black moustache and an abundance of beard.

Unlike his neighbour, The MacKernon hadn't actively fought in the war, but had done his bit behind a desk. The laird didn't allow him to forget this fact, sounding so innocuous when he dropped his little hints and innuendoes that even The

MacKernon couldn't help smiling, though there were occasions when he itched to get his own back, but felt he could never be a match for a man of such wiles.

'Calm down, old chap,' the laird spoke soothingly, 'I know all this must seem intolerable to you but in actual fact it isn't as bad as it seems. Some lads from the village took your trees to sell round the doors for Christmas, you know what they're like, always anxious to make a bob or two. Good prospered in the end however, I persuaded them to *give* the profits to a worthy cause, they agreed, and in that way saved face and honoured you, MacKernon.'

At that moment Alice came in with the tea, Catrina with a basket of logs, a gift from Shug and the others for the generosity that Captain MacPherson had recently shown them. Catrina heaved the basket on to the hearth, the laird cleared his throat and shifted his feet to allow her to top up the fire, his face taking on a slightly sheepish look as she did so.

The MacKernon eyed the logs. 'Keeping the home fires burning, eh?'

'The time of year, MacKernon, there's plenty more where they came from. And to show there are no hard feelings, why don't you allow me to send up a cartload to your goodself? I'm sure the hearths of Cragdu would greatly benefit from some hardwood and there's nothing to beat the smell of woodsmoke coming from your chimneys.'

Catrina and Alice departed, The MacKernon looked at the laird and knew when he was beaten, though he didn't give in without a fight. But gradually the drams mellowed him, he even began to appreciate the funny side of the situation, though not for one minute was he taken in by the other man's plausibility. He would pay MacPherson back – by jove and he would! At that moment in time he didn't know how he was going to do it, but he would think of something . . . Meanwhile . . . he held up his glass, it winked golden in the firelight, the laird held his up also and both glasses chinked together.

'Happy New Year, MacKernon.'

'And to you, MacPherson.'

Sometime after midnight the Clan Chief took his leave and Emily came in to question her husband about the visit.

'It's a long story, Emily, a very long story.' He shook his head thoughtfully, a lock of hair fell over his brow, giving him a rakish look. Emily laughed and kissed him, and poured herself a drink before settling beside him to hear what the long story was all about.

It wasn't long before Mattie got to know about The MacKernon's visit to Crathmor House and being Mattie she soon put two and two together concerning the part her husband had played in the affair. 'You silly bodach!' she scolded Dokie Joe furiously. 'I could have lost my job at the castle if his Lordship had found out you were involved, and still could if the laird lets it leak out.'

'Ach, come on now, Mattie,' Dokie Joe said soothingly, 'he will never tell, after all, he is a saint in the eyes o' Kinvara, Santa Claus himself, handing out The MacKernon's trees and taking all the credit for it. And don't forget, it was for a good cause, everyone benefited, even the bairns in the orphanage, and the fires o' Kinvara have never burned so bright as they did when the trees were cut up for logs.' Dokie Joe paused and looked thoughtful. 'He's a helluva man, the Captain, but he is a kind soul too, that ten shillings he gave me allowed us a few wee luxuries that we would never have had otherwise.'

'Ay, that was generous right enough,' Mattie agreed. 'Though a pound would have been better.' She stuck out her hand, 'Come on, Dokie Joe, I wasn't born yesterday, Dolly told me what you, Shug and Willie got, and I want my share of it, the new bairn is coming soon and will need some warm goonies and things for when it arrives.'

'But Mattie, I spent it! That mean old bugger, MacPherson, worked us till we nearly dropped and if he'd had any common decency he would have given us double the sillar after all we did for him.'

'Is that so? A minute ago he was a good kind soul wearing

a halo.' Mattie's lips twitched, the look of tragedy on her husband's face was truly comical.

He glanced at her and saw the softening of her expression. 'Mattie, lass, you're a witch,' he grinned and they fell against each other in a fit of laughing that erased all traces of the animosity that had sprung up between them.

'The subject of The MacKernon's trees is closed forever,' Mattie said decisively.

'Ay,' Dokie Joe agreed fervently. 'And long may the houses of MacKernon and MacPherson reign in harmony – at least until the Clan Chief thinks up a way to pay the Captain back. No man in his right mind would let a thing like that slip by without a fight, and it will be interesting to see the outcome.'

'Ay, interesting right enough,' Mattie said drily and went to put an enormous pan of potatoes on the fire in order to feed her hungry horde.

SHETLAND

March 1923

Chapter Sixteen

Rob would always remember the journey to Shetland, even though parts of it seemed to pass without making any impression on him at the time. Sitting in the rickety little post bus that picked up passengers twice weekly from Kinvara, he stared from the windows, never seeing the scenery meandering past, a numbness taking hold of his mind as one thought gripped it. He was going to Shetland to give Morna away to another man, the man who sat beside him now, his brother Finlay, who had not had much to say for himself since boarding the bus, except for a few complaints about the hardness of the seat and a few more regarding the peculiarities of an ancient fellow passenger who was avidly eating something from a greasy paper bag and belching loudly in the process.

'Dirty old pig,' Finlay muttered in disgust.

Big Jock Morgan, who had agreed readily to be the best man at the wedding, grinned from the seat behind, and leaning forward he hissed in Finlay's ear, 'Wait till it starts coming from the other end, then you really will have something to girn about, laddie.'

Finlay snorted. 'If Ma was here she'd soon sort him out, she never could abide anybody with filthy manners.'

'Our mother isn't here,' Rob growled. 'You've grown into a big boy, Finlay, and now that you're about to be married, you'd better start behaving like one.' Rob paused, thinking about his mother. She had gone on ahead with Morna and Vaila a few days ago to help out with the wedding preparations. Ramsay had refused to accompany her. 'I told you, Rita,' he had stated bluntly, 'I will not have any part in my son's marriage to a lass who is little more than a heathen.'

'Morna is no more a heathen than I am,' Rita had argued wearily. 'She was a regular church-goer when she lived in Shetland, but felt she needed something else when she came here. She's a good lass, one who has found her god in the world around her. She doesn't need four walls to make her believe in the Lord.'

'For all that she has a bastard child and she didn't get *that* inside the Lord's house! You seem to know a lot about her, Rita, I hope you haven't been consorting with her behind my back. I told you, I want no part o' her, even if she is about to become a Sutherland – God help us all!'

'Of course I've been consorting with her, as you call it. In a short while she'll be my daughter-in-law, and besides, I've grown very fond of her and her bairn and if you weren't so blind with religious prejudice you would see the good in her for yourself. It isn't really Morna that worries you, it's the fact that she's being married in a church that isn't of your denomination, and I know you hate the idea of Jock Morgan being the best man just because he's a Catholic. It would be better if you learned to take the Free kirk less seriously, Ramsay, it warps your way o' thinking. You've set yourself too many standards and one day you won't be able to live up to them. We all have our weaknesses and like it or no', you're as human as the rest o' us.'

Rita's ability to speak her mind had always annoyed Ramsay, and now it infuriated him. 'Don't you dare talk like that to me, woman,' he had raged. 'You have no respect, either for me or the church, and it's thanks to this liberal outlook o' yours that our sons go their own sweet way with no regard for anybody, far less their father. It's also thanks to you that Finlay's the namby-pamby he is today, he thinks he can get away with anything and in marrying this girl he is making a fool o' himself. All she wants is someone to look after her and her bastard and I will have no part in it. I will not go to the wedding and that's final, Rita, and if you had any feelings for me at all you would back me up on this.'

'And if you had any for me you would forget your pride and start behaving like a husband and a father. Part o' me will never forgive you for this, Ramsay, and to hell with your sulks and moods! One o' these days, Finlay will turn on you and tell you what he thinks of you and I'll be right there beside him putting the words in his mouth. Tonight you can get your own tea! I'm going out and won't be back till I'm good and ready.' With that she had tossed off her apron, jammed on her hat, and had flounced away down to Purlieburn Cottage to visit Effie, leaving a fuming Ramsay to drum his fingers on the table and glare at the window as if the devil himself was outside looking in.

Hannah, too, had declined to go to Shetland, despite the fact that her mother had offered to come to Kinvara to look after Andy for a few days. 'No, Rob,' she had said vehemently. 'Why should I travel all that way just to see Morna Sommero being married to your brother? Oh, I like her well enough as a neighbour, but other than that she means nothing to me and he means even less. He only speaks to me when he has to and makes it quite plain he cannot thole having me in the family.'

'It's all in your mind, Hannah,' Rob had told her angrily, 'Finlay and the rest o' the family have tried to include you, but you're too wrapped up in yourself to notice anything that's going on around you.'

'Your father and me are tarred with the same brush then,' she had returned darkly. 'He loves only himself and his own selfish pursuits and to hell with what anyone else is feeling. He doesn't even think enough o' his own son to attend his wedding and he refused to give Morna away, even though she has no one else she can ask. It's just a pity that she had to get herself entangled with the Sutherlands, she will be as welcome as a piece o' dung, your father will surely see to that.'

Rob had no answer to that and so he let the matter rest, comforting himself with the fact that Janet, who was staying behind because Joss was laid up with a head cold, had promised to look in on Hannah and Andy to make sure they were all right. 'Though she won't thank me for it,' Janet had added with a toss of her fair head, 'I know she sees me as just the nuisance from next door but I'm not as soft as I look, and it's high time she saw that for herself.'

'You *are* soft,' Rob had said with a laugh, putting his arm round her and kissing her on the cheek. 'But everyone loves you for it, myself included, and even if Hannah doesn't yet, she will, given time. You might look as though butter wouldn't melt in your mouth, but for all that there's a persistent streak in you and I know you will never give up trying with Hannah.'

The people of Kinvara shook their heads when word of all this leaked out. 'Ramsay Sutherland will get his comeuppance one o' these days,' Big Bette said grimly, an expression on her face that suggested she would love to be there when it happened. 'Fancy refusing to go to his own son's wedding. He should be tarred and feathered and strung up on yon headland for all the world to see.'

'Ay,' agreed Mattie, whose latest addition to the MacPhee household was happed tightly in a shawl strung round her shoulders. 'Morna and Finlay should have wed themselves here in Balivoe kirk and never mind Ramsay and his opinions.'

Dolly Law sniggered at this. 'Better still, they should have turned Catholic and got Father MacNeil to bind them together. That would have made Ramsay sit up and take notice.'

'Sure to goodness,' nodded Wee Fay, 'Father MacNeil would have enjoyed that. He's taken a fair liking to the sea maiden and I know for a fact he gave her a white bible to carry into church on her wedding day.' She sighed. 'I myself would have made her a cake if she'd married here, blue and green icing like the sea, decorated with seals and all the other creatures that she loves.'

'You can still make it,' Effie put in eagerly.

'Ay, and we could have a ceilidh at my house when she comes back,' added Mattie. 'The laird himself would maybe turn up to watch her cutting the cake. He's fond o' Morna and asked her up to the big house to have tea with himself and her ladyship a few days ago. Dokie Joe just happened to be there when they presented her with a wedding gift, a whole set o' bed linen edged with Irish lace and finished with silk embroidery. It was beautiful just, I went along to her house to see it for myself and she had tears in her eyes at the very idea of everybody's kindness towards her.'

'I wish I could have seen her wedding outfit,' Connie Simpson said dreamily, 'I hear tell she made it herself, along with one for her sister. Maybe when I get married Morna will make me a wonderful dress with all the trimmings, white, of course, I've aye fancied a white wedding.'

'Ay, well, you'd better hurry up and find yourself a man,' Big Bette said cuttingly. 'White wouldn't look well on you when you're fat and forty and maybe by that time kirk weddings will have gone out o' fashion anyway.'

Connie reddened and was about to make a defensive remark when Mattie nodded towards the shore and said sadly, 'Would you look at that now, there goes Johnny Lonely, poor soul, he'll be lonelier than ever now that the sea maiden has gone and got herself another man.'

'Ay, Johnny canny very well go in about wi' Finlay in the house,' agreed Effie, pummelling her nose with a large hanky and giving out one of her loud honks in the process. 'It was strange, the way he took to her, a man like that, never a word to say to anybody else, but plenty to say to Morna.'

'Maybe he's in love wi' her,' Cora Simpson put in hesitantly, glancing at Big Bette as she spoke, as if anticipating one of that lady's sarcastic remarks.

But Big Bette said nothing, neither did anybody else, as silently they watched Johnny Lonely scrambling along above the tide line, looking for the driftwood he burned to keep himself warm. But that wasn't its only use – from it he made simple bits and pieces to furnish his ramshackle hut, and, more recently a rocking chair for Morna to 'rest herself in' when she got tired.

'Don't be telling anybody about it,' he had warned, 'they would just laugh and make their foolish remarks. It's our secret, yours and mine, and though it's nothing very grand it's special, because I made it with my own hands for you.'

But to Morna it was something 'very grand', beautifully fashioned and comfortable, the old wood telling of the wind and the waves and the long ages it had taken to make it as smooth and as white as it was. Was it from some distant land, she wondered. Or from somewhere nearer at hand? She didn't know, she didn't care, in it she drifted and dreamed and thought about things that she wished she had, even while she knew they would never be hers.

When she kissed Johnny's cheek in gratitude he hurried away and she was sad for a man so clever and so lonely as he, because she knew he deserved better things but was too shy and too wary of life ever to seek them.

The old man had finished eating and was now noisily sucking at his pipe, thick smoke invaded the air, and something else that made Finlay's lip curl and an oath to issue from his mouth. Big Morgan let out a shout of laughter. It was the release Rob needed. He too began laughing, and for the next few miles he and Big Morgan kept up such a relentless flow of banter even Finlay had to smile and join in the light-hearted nonsense as the bus wound its bumpy way over the hilly road to the tiny railway station at Achnasheen.

The landscape of Shetland was patterned with cloud shadows and sunlight, overhung with vast dramatic skies that swept the ocean and brushed the earth with banners of wispy vapour. So bright was the light it was difficult to tell where the sea met the sky, and the visitors from Kinvara shielded their eyes from the glare as they stepped from the boat at Lerwick Harbour. The journey from the west coast mainland had been long and tiring. They had stayed their first night at the station hotel in Inverness, and from there they had travelled to Aberdeen on the Great North of Scotland Railway to spend the following night in the granite city before boarding the steamer to Lerwick.

None of them had slept very well on the boat, Finlay was in a bad mood because of it, Rob was quiet as he wondered what the days ahead would bring for him, only Big Morgan was his usual cheerful self as he dumped his luggage on the cobbles and gazed around him expectantly.

A young woman detatched herself from a little group on the pier and came towards them. 'Hallo, I'm Mirren, I won't ask if you've had a good journey since I know from experience what it's like to travel such a distance from the mainland. If you'll just come this way.'

This was when Rob met Morna's sister for the first time. As fair as Morna was dark, her eyes were clear, direct and honest, and there was a quietness and a stillness about her that suggested inner strength and depth of character. She gave the impression of a young woman possessed of a self-controlled nature, but there was a hint of fire in her blue eyes and pride in the way she held herself, and Rob knew right away that she was the sort who would stand no nonsense from anyone.

She wasted no time on any of the usual pleasantries, instead she led them straight to where a sturdy pony waited in the shafts of a big wooden cart in which sacks of straw had been placed for seating.

'We don't run to anything fancier here,' Mirren briefly explained. 'Even the summer visitors have to make do with this.' There was a strange sort of defiance in her words, almost as if she was defending herself against criticism, and her eyes when they met those of Rob were cool and rather distant.

'Don't worry, lass.' Big Morgan was heaving the luggage into the cart as he spoke. 'My bum thinks it's been sitting on rocks for the last two days, so a bale o' hay will make a nice change.'

Mirren smiled at him, warming to him instantly, then she

took up the reins and they were off, rumbling away from the harbour, the gulls dipping and diving in the glimmer and the gleam above the windswept vista that was Shetland stretching away before them as the pony carried them steadily over the bare bony road to their destination.

Chapter Seventeen

Burravoe House was a fine big place, standing stark and dour on a spit of land beyond Bridge of Walls on the west side of the island.

'There it is,' Mirren said with a soft pride in her voice. 'The house of Burravoe. It's been in our family for a long time, my father worked very hard to keep it going and now I try to do the same. He and my mother were killed out there in the bay, the tide took them. He had been handling boats all of his life, but in the end the sea got him.' She spoke in a matter-of-fact voice, yet her words carried such drama they made the men look at one another and then out to the sea that tossed restlessly beyond.

Finlay shifted uncomfortably in his seat. The journey from Lerwick Harbour had seemed to worsen with every passing mile, and they were all glad when they at last stopped outside Burravoe House and could get out to stretch their legs.

The door opened and Rita came forward to welcome her sons. 'It's good to see you again, Ma,' Finlay held on to her arm as if he hadn't seen her in weeks, and Rob couldn't help but think that his brother often behaved like a schoolboy, the way he clung to his mother and hated to let her out of his sight for any length of time.

The tiny figure of Vaila stood framed in the doorway for a moment before she came toddling to meet the new arrivals. Finlay held out his arms to her, but she went straight past him to Rob who picked her up and swung her round and round while she giggled and screamed 'Wobbie' in an ecstasy of delight.

Finlay watched them, a frown touching his face, then he turned on his heel and went to help Big Morgan carry in the luggage.

At the sound of voices in the hall, Morna came out of the kitchen, wiping her hands on her apron as she hugged Big Morgan, gave Finlay a kiss on the cheek. Then Rob appeared with Vaila in his arms, there was silence for a moment, Rob hardly dared look at Morna, nor she at him. When their eyes finally met they were laden with emotion and she was the first to turn away.

'You must be tired and hungry,' she said in a muffled voice. 'Later I'll show you where you'll be sleeping, but first you must eat.'

'*After* you have all washed your hands,' Rita chimed in. 'Tired or no, there are some things that mustn't be neglected.'

Finlay began to tell her about the old man they had travelled with on the bus to Achnasheen. 'You would never have stood for it, Ma,' he said with conviction. 'He was filthy and smelly and his manners were atrocious.'

'Ooh, that would be old Sandy MacManus from along Ullapool way, he often travels down to Achnasheen in the bus to visit his sister who lives there. Oh, ay, I used to know Sandy well, he was a fisherman in his younger days and was as handsome a rogue as anyone could meet. He courted me when I was just a bitty lass living in Poolewe, then he went to fight in the Boer war. Oh, he must have been a bonny fighter because he was aye a fearless soul when I knew him. Then he got shot in the head and when he came home he just got dafter and dafter as the years passed. But I still remember him as he was, and if it hadn't been for the war, he and I might have wed and my life would be very different from how it is now.' She sighed. 'Poor Sandy, he was aye that clean and fussy about himself in the old days, if he could have seen what was ahead o' him he might have stayed a fisherman and where would we all be if that had happened?'

The look of complete astonishment that these revelations brought to Finlay's face was comical to say the least, a touch of light relief was added to the atmosphere as everyone laughed and went to sit round the table in a cheery mood.

Later that day, Rob, with Vaila held firmly on his shoulders, walked with Morna to the bay beyond Burravoe House. Finlay had opted not to come, saying that he was exhausted after all the travelling, and it was with a feeling almost of reprieve that they stood side by side, gazing out to sea, acutely aware of one another, silently thinking their individual thoughts as the wind whipped them and the seabirds wheeled in the sky above.

'Look out there, Robbie,' Morna eventually spoke, pointing towards a small island beyond the bay. 'That's Vaila. I used to go out there with my father in the boat and always loved it. When our daughter was born it inspired her name, whenever I look at it I think of you and how I longed to see you when we were apart.'

'Why did you ever leave here in the first place?' Rob spoke abruptly to hide his feelings. 'Burravoe House is a fine place with plenty of good arable land, you should surely have stayed to help your sister run things.'

'Life here was never easy,' she replied slowly. 'My father was a good farmer but he also had to go out with the fishing to make a living. When he and my mother died it seemed impossible to go on, I was eleven years old, a dreamer and a drifter, Mirren was fifteen, determined, strong, and practical. She wouldn't give in to anything and took over the running of the place, eventually letting part of the house so that she could make enough money to renovate the shepherd's cottage that you see from Burravoe House. Now she lets that out to summer visitors and has the house to herself again. She has achieved so much in just a short space o' time, everyone here admires her and have always helped in any way they could. The farming side is well run and so is the house, and my parents would be proud if they could come back and see how well Mirren has coped with everything.'

'You still haven't answered my question, why did you leave here to go and live a life of near solitude in Kinvara when you had a sister as capable as Mirren?'

Morna looked at Vaila playing happily among the rock pools on the shore. 'That was just it,' she answered slowly, 'she was too capable, in her determination to prove to the world that she could bring me up properly she smothered me. She was always worrying about me and protecting me and it got too much for me to bear. I had to get away, to be an independent person in my own right, and as soon as I was old enough I left. Then I met you and my whole life changed, all I wanted was to be near you . . .' Her voice faltered at this point, and he couldn't resist taking her hand in his and squeezing it reassuringly. 'Mirren thought I was too young to know my own mind,' Morna went on, 'and when I went back to Shetland, thinking it was over between you and me, it seemed to prove her point. Then Vaila was born and after a few months I couldn't wait to return to Kinvara and to you – now – it's all changed, I'm marrying Finlay and Mirren knows what a muddle it all is and thinks more than ever that I should never have left home.' Her fingers curled round his. 'Perhaps she's right after all, I *have* made a mess o' my life, she knows that Vaila is your daughter but will never say anything to anyone. Mirren's like that, staunch and true to her own and I'll never cease to be grateful for everything she has done for me.'

'She doesn't like me,' Rob said decidedly, 'I felt it this morning when we met for the first time, it was in her eyes, the mistrust, the resentment. Perhaps it's no more than I deserve, she's your sister and doesn't like to see you getting hurt.'

Morna fingered the mermaid brooch pinned at the neck of her shawl. 'If I had to go back to when we first met I wouldn't change any o' it – except the bitterness that drove us apart and altered our lives for ever.'

They gazed at one another for a long time, gently he smoothed a lock of dark hair from her brow, then his fingers uncurled from hers, and calling on Vaila they made their way back to Burravoe House.

That night the menfolk slept in the shepherd's cottage. The silence of the sleeping house enclosed Rob like a dark blanket.

Tired though he was he tossed and turned in the strange bed, restless of mind, body and spirit, hearing the clock ticking on the mantelshelf, the sound of Big Morgan snoring from the room next door.

Eventually he fell into a fitful sleep, only to wake as the first grey fingers of dawn came creeping over the night sky. A sense of terrible unrest seized him. Throwing back the bedcovers, he got up and went to the cold window – and there in the garden of Burravoe House was Morna – a still shadowy figure, leaning pensively against the wall, her hands clasped to her mouth as she gazed into the distance.

Morna. His heart spoke her name, he wanted only to go to her, to hold her close and tell her how much he loved her, but he did none of these things. Instead he turned away from the window and went back to his lonely bed, there to lie till he heard the others moving about, bringing a sense of normality to the beginning of the day – yet – how could anything be normal on this day of all days? Morna was about to marry Finlay – and nothing would ever be quite the same again.

The wedding was held in a quiet little church, attended by a few neighbours and friends, conducted by the white-haired minister of the parish whose soft voice had a calming effect on everyone.

Rob was a striking figure in his Sutherland tartan Highland dress, his eyes as black as his hair as he looked at Morna who was wearing the simple blue suit that she'd made herself with a little veil that hid her eyes but couldn't conceal the solemn expression on her young face.

Rob thought he'd never seen her looking more lovely and he had to swallow hard as he crooked his arm to her and began to lead her into church. Mirren walked along behind them, holding on to Vaila's hand, a tiny flower girl dressed in white, clutching a bunch of daffodils, wondering what all the fuss was about as she followed along behind Rob and her mother.

Rob felt unreal as he led Morna down the aisle. It was

happening, really happening. He was giving Morna and his daughter away to another man, and even though that man was his own brother it didn't help matters in the least, rather it made everything worse somehow, and it was only by a great strength of will that he forced himself to carry on – for Morna's sake. This was what she wanted, her way out of a situation that had become unbearable to her – to give Vaila the Sutherland name . . . Pray God that it would work . . . that Finlay would love Morna enough to put her happiness before his own . . .

Morna was trembling a little, he was as aware of the tension in her body as he was of his own, and he held her arm a little tighter as they went on, past the people in the pews, Rita sitting in the front, a bit strained and tired-looking after all the preparations of the last few days.

Whispers in the local community about Morna and her fatherless child had taken a long time to die down, and even yet there were those who maintained that she had a cheek to get married in church and that the minister should never have consented to his part in the affair. Even so, a fair number of those who disapproved of Morna and her 'unholy ways' were present that day, even if out of mere curiosity, while the more broad-minded of the population had turned up because they genuinely liked her and had always respected her family.

Rob didn't know any of them and he was glad to see the familiar figure of Jock Morgan waiting at the altar, magnificent indeed in his Black Watch kilt and lovat tweed jacket, his beard flowing over his sark, his hair pulled back and tied with a little black band.

And there was Finlay, dressed like his brother in the Sutherland tartan, his sandy red hair slicked back from his forehead, pale blue eyes flickering rather anxiously as Rob appeared with Morna, a small smile touching his mouth when she turned her head to look at him. He was fidgety and nervous, despite the fact that he had consumed a fair number of drams before leaving Burravoe House. The reek of whisky was on his breath, beads of perspiration were popping out on his brow, but then the minister began to speak in his soothing voice, everybody calmed down, murmurings and scrapings died away and the wedding ceremony began.

It was over. Everyone was moving outside. Clouds were skudding across the tumble of the March skies, occasionally torn apart by the wind to allow brilliant shafts of sunlight to beam down on the wintery landscape.

Mirren was taking photographs, a group picture was called for, Finlay tried to pick Vaila up but she squirmed away from him and went to cling to her mother's skirts, her thumb in her mouth, her eyes brimming as she looked at her new stepfather from lowered brows.

'Give her time, Finlay,' Morna said quietly. 'This has all been a bit much for her, she isn't two yet and doesn't really know what's happening.'

Finlay nodded, 'Don't worry, she'll soon get to know me better, she's probably too used to getting her own way and will have to learn to adjust, a father's hand is what she needs.'

There was something in his voice that made Morna look at him quickly, she couldn't make up her mind if it was hardness or firmness and a chill went through her at the realisation that she was his wife of only a few minutes and already he was trying to lay down the law.

She was very tired, the excitement of the last week or so was beginning to tell on her and she prayed for the strength to carry on as the wife of Finlay Sutherland . . . she glanced at Rob, standing there on the fringe, lonely somehow . . . apart from her as he had never been before. A sob rose up in her throat, she bit her lip and forced herself to behave normally. Mirren was growing impatient, trying to herd members of the family into the group, calling on Rob to come over and stand next to the best man.

Rob hesitated, the last thing he desired was to be there in that photograph, trying to pretend that he was a willing member of the wedding party, when all he wanted was to turn on his heel and walk away. But to do so would be churlish and suspicious and so he went to stand beside Big Morgan who threw an arm around his shoulder and murmured in his ear, 'Don't worry, man, it will soon be over, this part o' it anyway, so do your best to look happy, if only for the sake o' the lass and her bairnie.' There was something in his voice that made Rob wonder what he meant. The big man was no fool, he gave the impression of always being jovial and carefree, but he was also a deep thinker and had often surprised Rob with his astute observations about the people around him.

But no, how could he know more than anybody else? Rob took a deep breath. He was letting his imagination run away with him . . . the shutter clicked . . . damn Mirren and her buggering pictures!

'Rob, don't go away, I want one of me with my two sons.' His mother's hand was on his arm, Finlay was coming over to pose on one side of her, Rob took up his stance on the other . . . like a couple of kilted bookends he thought wryly, just as the shutter clicked again and he was free to wander away from everyone and light his pipe in peace.

'Rob!'

Bugger it! It was Mirren's turn, coming up behind him and extending her hand to him as he spun round. 'You're my brother-in-law now and I think we should try to be friends.' The expression of sympathy in her eyes caught him off guard, 'I know how hard this has been for you,' she went on, 'and all we can hope for now is for Morna and Vaila to be happy, in the end that's all that really matters.'

His throat was dry, his voice unsteady as he replied, 'Ay, that's all that matters, they both deserve to have that in their lives and at least Vaila will at last have a father.'

Mirren looked back to where Finlay was standing talking to his mother, and a frown creased her brow. 'I suppose so,' she said doubtfully, her eyes clouding.

Morna was waving at them, Vaila followed suit. Mirren turned her attention once more to Rob and gazed at him steadily. 'They're all the family I have left, keep an eye on them for me,' she said softly before walking over to where everyone was getting ready to climb into the various forms of transport that would take them back to the reception at Burravoe House.

KINVARA

Spring and Summer
1923

Chapter Eighteen

Hannah awoke with a feeling of dread. This was the day that Rob was going back on lighthouse duty and the thought of the empty months that lay ahead of her was almost too much for her to bear. There were times when she felt that she couldn't go on with her life the way it was, and once or twice she had even thought about ending it – or running away – anywhere away from this house, this place where she'd never been accepted and was often so lonely she simply sat down and wept with despair.

Rob was still asleep by her side, breathing gently and evenly. She stared at his back. Such strong shoulders he had on him, and that bonny dark head of his making the pillow look so white in comparison. She caught her breath, her hand came up to touch the nape of his neck, hovered for a moment, then fell away again. She couldn't allow herself to get involved in any of *that* again! It would be easier for both of them if they didn't share the same bed. After Andy's birth she had suggested that Rob should sleep in one of the spare rooms, but he had refused, saying that he was damned if he was getting out of his own bed just to please her and why didn't she go instead. But she had shrunk away from that proposal, the other rooms in the house were small and sparse, here at least there was space and air and light . . . and Rob's company when he wasn't away on duty.

She could feel the heat of him burning against her skin and she remembered how it had been with them in the beginning

. . . his physical attraction couldn't be denied and it was small wonder that the womenfolk of Kinvara batted their eyes at him and vied with one another to get his attention. They seemed to be able to say things that made him laugh – that deep laugh of his, ringing out – she wished she could make him as happy as that, but part of a man's happiness involved things that she wasn't ready to give – if she ever would be.

Lately he had been quieter than usual, ever since he'd returned from Shetland and Morna Sommero's wedding – except she no longer went by that name, she was Mrs Sutherland now – the same as Hannah herself.

Hannah lay on her back and thought about Morna, she was a pretty one and no mistake, that cloud of raven hair, those green eyes, and a nature so sweet it made everyone want to be near her, as if some of her goodness might rub off on them. Even that strange dour creature, Johnny Lonely, had taken to Morna as he had to no other and it was said that he had become more withdrawn than ever because he could no longer visit her as freely as he used to when she was living on her own at Oir na Cuan.

Hannah frowned. Morna hadn't been nearly so blithe of spirit since her marriage to Finlay, and who could blame her for that? He was a mother's boy and always would be, the opposite of Rob with his independent nature and strength of will.

Then there was Vaila, a truly beautiful child, the same hair as her mother, so curly and dark . . . and those eyes, something so familiar about the expression in them . . . Hannah didn't allow her thoughts to wander further. Throwing back the blankets she slipped silently from the bed. Grabbing her dressing gown from a chair she shivered herself into it and pulled it tightly round her body. It was a bitterly cold morning, outside the window it was still dark, but she could see the waves heaving and foaming as they hurled themselves against the rocks. That was another thing about this place, the endless freezing winters, the feeling that the sun would never again touch the land with its warmth.

Down in the kitchen Breck looked up from his basket but he didn't come to greet her, he reserved all that sort of palaver for Rob and Andy, and only tholed her on sufferance. Brute! If she'd had her way he would be outside in a kennel where he ought to be . . . perhaps when Rob wasn't here to pamper him she could put him out in one of the huts at the back. As for taking him walking, she had more than enough to do here without the added burden of exercising him as well.

Andy stirred in his cot in the corner. Rob had wanted to move the boy upstairs to a room of his own, but she had insisted that it was easier to see to all his wants down here in the kitchen. 'He's getting too heavy for me to carry him anywhere, let alone up and down stairs,' she had said sourly. 'He'll never walk like other bairns and I'm not going to start anything I can't finish.'

Walk! Her lip twisted. He couldn't even crawl yet, just lay where he was put, twitching and slavering, meaningless sounds issuing grotesquely from his throat.

A changeling! That's what he was! Some evil force had taken her own child away and left this useless lump in its place. She could never have produced anything so ugly and she knew she would never get to like him – never mind love him – it was too much to ask of any human being . . .

She looked again at the sea swelling in the distance and the loneliness of the coming months seemed to smother her and force the breath from her lungs. Panic rose up inside her. She couldn't stay here alone, she couldn't! Perhaps if she went to spend some time with her parents in Ayr – but no – she shrugged away the idea. It would mean lugging *him* with her and who would look after the brute?

It all involved too much effort – she would just shut herself away with her books and think what it might have been like if it hadn't been for *him*.

Morning was breaking. From her bed Morna watched as the eastern sky became streaked with gold and silver, infusing the dark reaches of the sea with a quiet ethereal light. Night had at last departed yet she wished it would go on for ever because when it came again Robbie would be gone from her, far away over that lonely sea where only their thoughts and their longings could join them together.

Lying here, in the silent hours, she had gone over in her mind everything that they had done when they were together, the things they had said, the glow she had felt when they had kissed and laughed and imagined that was how it would always be with them. Now she lay here in this bed with this other man, Robbie's brother, so different from him in every respect.

In his own way he was a good man, kind and eager to please, and she knew it was wrong to compare him to Robbie, but she couldn't help it. She had only been married to Finlay a matter of weeks, yet already she wished only to be alone to think her thoughts and enjoy just pottering around the house with Vaila and the animals. Finlay was like a child, always wanting her attention, sulking and taking himself off to visit his mother if he didn't get enough of it.

It had all started on their honeymoon, spent in the shepherd's cottage near Burravoe House. He had wanted to be with her constantly and had resented it when Mirren brought Vaila to see them or invited them to Burravoe for a meal.

'Why can't she leave us alone?' Finlay had said peevishly. 'I'm your husband now, Morna, and I have a right to have you to myself for a while. It *is* our honeymoon after all and I'm damned if I'm going to share you with Mirren or anyone else while we're here.'

Morna had been glad to return to Kinvara where she could at least have some freedom when Finlay took himself off to work at Vale o' Dreip. It also meant she was near Robbie again, even if only to talk to him occasionally or wave to him from a distance. Now he was going back on lighthouse duty and she wouldn't see him again for months – yet – in many ways it would be a relief, for to be so close was a constant torment to her and she knew she was being unfair to Finlay, wanting his brother, making any excuse at all in order to see him.

Turning her head on the pillow she could see another light glowing in the skyline, the remnants of Johnny Lonely's fire up there on Kinvara Point. More than ever of late he had taken to living in the old chapel ruins and to kindling his fires on the cliff-top. Big Bette said it gave her the creeps to see lamplight in the crumbling window apertures, and Janet Morgan didn't like to go out after dark because Johnny's behaviour was scary when he went into one of his brooding moods, isolating himself from everyone yet doing things that ensured they were aware of what he was up to anyway.

But Morna knew what was wrong with Johnny. He had no one to talk to now that she was married to Finlay, who had made it very plain that the hermit wasn't welcome anywhere near the house. In some strange way Morna missed the talks that she had shared with Johnny, some of his thoughts and opinions had been very profound and soul-searching and she had found herself listening to him avidly, and believing in a lot of the ideas he put forth on so many interesting subjects.

Poor Johnny, she thought, I miss you too, it was good to talk to you, so good. Beside her Finlay stirred, and turning over he threw one heavy arm around her and moved closer. She froze, not wanting him to wake, knowing if he did, he would start touching her and then grow angry when she didn't respond. It wasn't so bad in the morning, she was usually up and about before him, it was the night hours that she dreaded most – lying here in bed beside him, hearing his heavy breathing if he'd been drinking too much, the arguments they had because he told her she was like a piece of wood when they were making love, his cajoling, pleading and arguing and finally his rage when she failed to satisfy his demands.

But nothing he did could arouse her, his lovemaking was as ineffectual as were his day-to day decisions. It was over in minutes and he would roll off her and be snoring soon afterwards, leaving her wakeful and wide-eyed and empty inside . . .

The weight of his arm was imprisoning her and her heart fluttered in her breast when he grunted in her ear and began to move against her. 'Morna,' he murmured, 'let me do it. You're so soft in the morning, that's when I want you the most, but you're never usually here, always it's Vaila or the animals needing you, but you're married to me now and I have my rights before anybody.'

His hands crept down to her thighs and roughly he pushed up her nightdress, his sinewy legs were hard against hers, painfully he began to knead her breasts . . .

Moisture bathed her brow. 'No, Finlay,' she gasped. 'Please let go of me, I must get up!'

'So must I,' he laughed crudely, his hands digging into her shoulders, pinning her down.

At that moment the door opened and Vaila stood there, a tiny wisp of a child in her white gown, dark hair rumpled about her face, eyes big and dark as she stuck her thumb in her mouth and stared wordlessly at the man and woman in the bed.

'Vaila.' Morna struggled up, never so glad to see anybody as she was to see her little girl in those moments.

'Damn her!' Finlay cursed, falling back on his pillows to glare belligerently at his stepdaughter. From the start she had rejected him, moving away whenever he approached, struggling from him when he tried to pick her up, tears flooding her eyes when his bewilderment made him snarl at her and push her away, then blame Morna for spoiling her.

Finlay was fast realising that marriage to Morna wasn't going to be as easy as he had at first imagined. For a start she always seemed to be too busy to pay him much attention, though he couldn't fault her when it came to filling his belly and attending to his bodily needs – all except for one – when they went to bed she seemed only to want to sleep, while all he wanted was to possess her and have her completely for his own.

But he was learning that wanting Morna and having her were two very different affairs. She was stiff and cold and unresponsive in his arms, at night she took her time about coming to bed, almost as if she were hoping that he would be asleep when finally she crept into the room. He sensed in her an unhappiness that nothing he said or did could reach, and he was already doubting if he had done the right thing in marrying her.

'Give her a chance, Finlay,' his mother had told him when

he had voiced his feelings to her. 'Marriage is a big step for anybody to take, treat her gently and don't go rushing at her like a bull at a farmyard gate. Morna is very young yet, and a lot has happened to her in just a few short years.'

'I know, I've wondered a bit about the bairn, who her father is, for instance. It didn't worry me before, but now I'm beginning to think Morna might still be hankering after him because she doesn't seem able to settle herself with me.'

'Ay, the bairn,' Rita had nodded, her face softening for she had come to look forward to seeing the little girl who was now her step-granddaughter. 'Such a wise wee thing but she's still just a baby, you'll have to be patient with her, son, she's known only her mother since she was born and must be finding it strange having someone else living in the house. As for her father, you'll have to try and forget about him, Finlay, it's all in the past now and Morna knew what she was doing when she turned to you for comfort and companionship.'

'I thought it might have been for love,' he had said in hurt tones, but had nevertheless taken his mother's advice and had tried to hold himself back more where Morna was concerned. And it had been good, sitting beside her at night while she darned or knitted, the room cosy and warm around them, Vaila at their feet playing with her toys, the animals sleepy and contented on the rug after a run by the sea.

He hadn't made any demands on Morna when they went to bed at night and she had begun to relax more with him and even to laugh at some of the things he said and look at him with a new respect in her eyes. It hadn't lasted very long though, she was so bonny and winsome and all he could think about was the way she smiled and moved and how warm and smooth she was under the quiet sober clothes that she wore . . .

'Bwuddy man!' Vaila suddenly spoke the words, loudly and clearly, gazing quite innocently at Finlay as she spoke.

'Where the hell did she learn that?' Finlay demanded incredulously.

Morna tried to be serious. 'I don't know, she picks things up, when we go to the village everybody wants to talk to her.'

'It's that Bette MacGill!' Finlay raged. 'That bloody mouth o' hers is so big she could open it up and swallow a battleship. The sooner that man o' hers is home the better. I don't like him much myself, he's so full of his own importance he might choke on it someday, but at least he keeps a watchful eye on her and makes sure those three snotty horrors o' his do as they're damned well told!'

He hopped from the bed and began pulling on his trousers. 'I just hope Ma doesn't hear such language coming from her new granddaughter, she would start wondering what sort o' upbringing the girl is getting and might blame *me* for teaching her to blaspheme!'

The door banged behind him. Morna knelt down to her daughter, and taking her in her arms, she gazed into the face of the child she so loved and who had the power to make her forget her weary heart even while reminding her so much of the man she loved.

'Vaila,' she tried to sound strict, 'you mustn't use bad words like that, Finlay doesn't like them and neither do I.'

Vaila looked as if she understood exactly what was being said. 'Finlay no like,' she nodded confidingly. Then in the next breath she uttered loudly and clearly, 'Bwuddy man!'

Morna let out a shout of laughter and buried her face in the child's neck, giving herself time to regain her composure before going down to get Finlay's breakfast.

Chapter Nineteen

All along Keeper's Row doors were opening and shutting as the wives of the lighthouse men were going either to meet those who were returning or to say goodbye to the ones who were leaving.

The moment had come for Rob to depart and he stood with Andy in his arms and cooried the wobbly little head against his shoulder. 'You'll be a wee man when next I see you,' he said softly. 'Don't give up trying to do the things I've been teaching you so that you can show me how you've got along when I come back.'

Breck nuzzled his hand, and stooping down he ruffled the dog's head affectionately. 'Ay, Breck, you know what I'm saying, you look after him for me and see he comes to no harm.'

He looked at his wife. 'Don't give up on our son, Hannah, talk to him, try to show him what to do and help him to learn about the world around him. He knows what we say to him, never make any mistake about that.'

'And what about me, Rob?' she said tremulously. 'Who's going to be here to help me bear the burdens I have in my life? It's bad enough when you're here and a million times worse when you're away.'

'I didn't know you cared that much. When I came home at Christmas you made me feel as if I didn't belong here in my own home.'

'I just can't show my feelings like other folk, you ought to know that by now.'

'Ay, you've made that plain enough, but everyone needs love in their lives, Hannah, and I hope you realise that before life passes you by altogether and you'll wake up one morning and wonder where the years have gone.'

Leaning forward he kissed her on the cheek, she turned away from him quickly and pretended to busy herself at the stove. 'Go away, Rob,' she said in a muffled voice, 'I can't stand it when you talk like that, just go away.'

'Very well, if that's how you feel.' He laid his hand on her arm, then picking up his bag he went to the door, opened it, gazed briefly back into the room, then with a soft little snap the door closed behind him and he was gone.

Hannah sank into a chair and sat there staring into space as if she was mesmerised. Glancing up at her, Breck whimpered, before slinking away to flop down beside Andy on the rug. The child threw one convulsed arm round the dog's neck and emitted a low moaning sound, as if he were trying to say a name but couldn't get the word to form properly.

'Come on, Rob!' Big Morgan greeted his neighbour as he came out of the house. 'Janet and Joss are seeing me off and it looks as if everybody else is doing the same. Spring must be in the air right enough for there wasn't a soul to be seen when we came home at Christmas in brass monkey weather.'

Cathie MacPhee was coming out of No. 3 with Moggy John and her children, Annie MacDuff, a stringy-looking young woman who invariably wore her hair in curlers and her stockings rolled to her ankles, was emerging from No. 2. Today she had spruced herself up because Jimmy Song was coming home, even though she claimed he drove her daft altogether with his habit of singing all round the house and blowing away on his mouth-organ.

Of Donnie Hic's wife there was no sign and Rob wondered about that. Surely she wanted to be down at the harbour to welcome her husband back after three long months of absence. But then, maybe not, the rumours had grown stronger about her and Ryan Du, and it was more than likely that he and she were having a last rendezvous while they still had the chance.

Big Bette was puffing up the brae, herding her three children in front of her because they had said they were hungry after school and wanted 'a piece' before setting off to meet their father.

Only Hannah remained indoors, shrinking away from the idea of joining the others. 'It's silly anyway,' she had told Rob, 'better to say what has to be said in private without people goggling at every move you make.'

'Walk with us, Rob.' Janet took hold of his arm, 'I hate these goodbyes as well, but Joss wanted to wave his father off.' Her voice faltered. She looked very young with her fair hair falling around her shoulders, so small beside Big Morgan, trying to be brave now that he was leaving, but unable to hide the fact that she'd been crying.

'Ay, let's go.' Part of Rob was glad to be leaving his house in Keeper's Row for a while, and he didn't look back as he walked with the Morgans down to the harbour to await the arrival of the relief boat.

Of necessity, the old harbour of Calvost had known its origins well before the lighthouse had come into existence. The pink granite that had been used to build both structures had been quarried in Kinvara where the stonemasons had cut and shaped it, ready for it to be towed in barges thirty miles out to sea where a squad of men had set up temporary accommodation on the rock upon which the lighthouse was to be erected.

In those days there had been sluice gates so that the barges could be floated in and safely loaded. Now it was no longer a tidal harbour, the gates having been removed when work on the lighthouse was completed, but it was a picturesque place nonetheless, where thrift grew thickly amongst the pink stones and the children of the families who now lived in the old quarrymen's cottages sat in rows on the walls and caught fish when the tides were right.

Now that the days were lengthening it was busier than ever, dawn had seen the return of the fishing boats, a cargo vessel was unloading its supplies, and a cheery little puffer with a red funnel aptly named *Blithe Spirit* was discharging a load of coal on to the pier.

People from all over had come with a variety of vehicles, some with squeaky old prams, others with bogies, Captain MacPherson was there with his AEC lorry and Shug and Dolly Law had arrived with their cart to take on a load that was to be delivered to the gentry of the area. Heavy work of this sort was not to Shug's liking and he made a great fuss about having to do it, despite the fact that Dolly was up there on the cart, heaving on the sacks with her skinny arms as her husband filled them, all the while puffing away on her clay pipe and removing it every so often to spit on the cobbles.

'Better than any man any day,' laughed Big Morgan as he helped the little woman with a particularly heavy bag. 'Maybe you'll drop some off to Janet while you're about it.'

Dolly stuck out a filthy palm. 'Anything to oblige, and with the price o' tobaccy as it is now I don't mind doing anything to help a friend.'

Big Morgan dropped some coins into her hand just as the laird came up to wish him well on his 'voyage', while he nodded good day to Dolly and made the observation to Big Morgan that she was as strong as a horse for such a small woman, and it was a wonder that Shug didn't get her to pull the cart as well.

Laughing at his own joke he indicated Dokie Joe who was filling the AEC up with coal. 'I had to pay him extra for that, too bad Emily hasn't got Dolly's strength, but lady wives and all that, mustn't get their hands too dirty.'

His keen eyes raked the gathering. 'Hmm, I see the Henderson sisters are down to collect, strange pair that, can never make up my mind about them, theatrical if you know what I mean, never could quite fathom what it is . . .'

Rona and Wilma had finished piling up their tiny donkey-cart and were preparing to leave. 'Good day, ladies,' the Captain lifted his hat, a lock of hair fell becomingly over one eye, his kilt lifted up in the breeze, the sisters stared at him nervously, then, all lisle stockings and striped aprons, they climbed aboard their cart and trotted quickly away.

'That's what I mean about them,' the laird was obviously intrigued by 'the Henderson Hens'. 'They never mix too well, do they? Nobody knows much about them, which is a pity because they look as if they might be interesting. I must get Emily to invite them up to Crathmor for a bite of dinner some time, see what they're made of and all that.'

'They won't come,' Janet put in. 'Everyone else has tried to be friendly, but they seem to just like their own company – of course, it might be different if you asked,' she added hastily as the laird's face fell. 'Emily is so nice and natural I'm sure she could bring anyone out o' their shell.'

Rob had moved away from the hub and sat on a bollard to light his pipe, trying not to think about Morna down there in Mary's Bay, but hoping all the time to catch a glimpse of her before he went away. He felt very alone and cut off from everyone who meant anything to him. Last night he had said goodbye to his parents at Vale o' Dreip and Finlay had stopped by to wish him well and to promise that he would send some reading material on the first monthly mail to the lighthouse.

Both brothers had forgotten their differences as they chatted over the supper table and Ramsay too had been in an amiable mood. Spring was in the air, the first lambs would be arriving soon, and the master of Vale o' Dreip liked it when the longer days meant that he could be out there in the fields manning his affairs after being cooped up over the winter.

A cry went up, the relief boat had been sighted, soon it was tying up, women and children surging forward to claim their menfolk.

Mungo MacGill, head keeper of the light, was the first to set foot on the cobbles. He was a big burly man whose impressive whiskers and arrogant expression singled him out as a person of some importance in the community.

'Full of himself,' was the general opinion. 'Thinks he's Neptune himself ruling the waves.'

'Ay, and bossing the rest o' us about the minute he's got his feets on dry land,' Tottie Murchison, the younger of 'the Knicker Elastic Dears', was always quick to add, never having forgiven Mungo for interfering with her script for the Sunday School nativity play, even though more than three years had passed since the event.

Big Bette was not exactly enamoured to have her husband back. In certain respects she enjoyed herself better without him. He was far too sanctimonious for her liking, and took his role as church elder very seriously indeed, often irritating the minister with his insistence that certain duties should be carried out his way and interfering even with the arrangement of the church flowers, much to the annoyance of Tillie Murchison, who took great pride in organising this particular duty.

'And what have you been doing while I've been away?' were Mungo's first words to his children.

'Behaving ourselves!' came the united chorus.

'And what will you be doing while I'm here?'

'Behaving ourselves!' Before the words were out of his mouth the chorus came again, Tom and Joe looking as if butter wouldn't melt in their mouths, but Babs making a face at her father when he turned away to say something to his wife, whose billowing breasts were larger than ever that day because she had omitted to squeeze their generous proportions into the restraining confines of a corset.

'You're looking well, Bette,' Mungo glanced at her bosoms and moistened his lips. 'No need to ask if you've been managing without me, since I know very well that you always do.'

An oddly coy look flitted over Bette's round, expressive face. She always knew how to get the best out of her husband. 'A wife aye misses her man, Mungo, it's been sore doing without you all these months.'

'Ay,' he nodded, his voice gravel-hard with meaning. Their

eyes met, if there was one thing that Mungo and Bette had in common it was a lustful appetite for the more basic needs of life, and without further ado they bade their children to 'play outside for a while' and made with all haste to the pleasures that awaited them in the bedroom of No. 1 of The Row, where they had installed an extra-large feather bed to accommodate them in comfort.

Annie and Jimmy Song were also departing from the scene, several others were drifting away, of the returning keepers only Donnie Hic remained, disappointed that Mollie wasn't there to meet him. Then suddenly she appeared, hurrying down past the signal tower, ruffled and breathless as she reached her husband and stood looking uncertainly up at him. The eyes of Donnie Hic lit up. 'It's good to see you, lass,' he said in a relieved voice. 'I felt foolish waiting here, but better now that you've come.'

Taking her arm he led her away. Rob and the others boarded the boat. Willie Whiskers was accompanying them on this trip, having been kept busy over the last few weeks making double straps of wrought iron for repairs to the lighthouse stairs. His wife Maisie didn't like it at all when Willie had to go away like this, and she had come down to the harbour to give him a last piece of her mind before his departure. Willie didn't trust the sea, but on this occasion he was glad to leave the shore behind, if only to be rid of Maisie's nagging tongue for a while.

The water was calm and smooth with only a slight swell beyond the breakwater. Rob looked back as they skirted Mary's Bay and sailed out past the point – and there on the headland was Morna, the scarf in her hand fluttering in the wind as she waved it back and forth, back and forth. His throat tightened, poignancy raw and terrible tearing at his heart. She was running, down the slopes and along the shore of Camus nan Gao, waving, waving. And then all he could see was a tiny dot in the distance, and after a while even that disappeared and there was nothing. His eyes smarted, he turned his face away and gazed seawards, the long weeks of lighthouse duty stretching before him like eternity.

When at last they reached the bare rock on which the

lighthouse was built, a numbness had crept into his being and he wondered, as he had so often wondered before, what had possessed him to have sought a life of near seclusion in this wild tormented place which was often awash at high tide and only allowed for a limited amount of exercise when the reef was exposed.

The boat was tying up at the landing-stage on the leeward side of the light, the men were getting out, making their way up to the entrance where the mural stair, built into the thickness of the walls, led up to the various levels inside the tower.

'Why do we do it, lad?' Big Morgan asked, dumping his bag on the floor and throwing an arm round Rob's shoulders.

'To get away from wives like Maisie,' Willie supplied readily, happier now that he was on relatively dry land.

Big Morgan shook his head. 'My Janet isn't like that, she's a soft wee lass and only goes sour on me when I'm getting ready to come back on duty.'

'She's young yet,' was Willie's succinct reply, and the other men laughed as they went to reacquaint themselves with the lamp rooms where carefully prepared timetables informed the keepers of the exact times of lighting and extinguishing the lanterns.

The business of tending the light had begun and Rob was already feeling that a million miles separated him from Kinvara and all that it held dear to him.

Chapter Twenty

It was a fine night in April when Donnie Hic went storming down to the Balivoe Village Inn to confront Ryan Du with the business-end of a double-barrelled twelve-bore shotgun. Several of the village menfolk were sitting quietly in the Snug Bar as was their wont of an evening, supping ale and talking of everyday affairs. Dolly was in there with the men, downing beer and smoking her pipe in a seriously contented manner, her battered black hat sitting rather lopsidedly on her head since she'd just used it to swat a dusty fly which had been enjoying a dribble of liqueur on the stained tabletop.

Now the fly was no more, and feeling very satisfied about its demise, Dolly had jammed her hat back on to her head without regard to her appearance. The atmosphere was smoky and ami-able: Jimmy Song was playing his mouth-organ, accompanied by one or two of the gathering, singing in hearty off-key voices; snatches of conversation detached themselves from the various small groups and drifted around The Snug in a desultory fashion; Knobby Sinclair, the proprietor, had seized a quiet spell to sit down beside Ryan Du with an enormous glass of beer to fortify him after his evening's labours.

Outside the inn, Sorry stood in her shafts, face buried deep in a nose-bag filled with oats that had been mixed with beer – something she'd had a taste for ever since Dolly had left a glass half-filled with the stuff on a shelf in the tumbledown hut in which the horse was wintered.

The arrival of Donnie Hic on the pavement outside the inn made little difference to the mare's enjoyment of her meal, since she couldn't see much of what was going on anyway, but when Donnie made his entrance into The Snug with the barrels of his shotgun clearing the way, the effect was electrifying. Music, talk and banter tailed off till complete silence filled the room. Eyes bulged, faces whitened, because the look on Donnie's face spelled out Murder with a capital 'M', and nobody fancied getting in the way of the menacing twin barrels of his gun.

There was, however, no need for any of them to worry. It was Ryan Du who was the quarry, and it was to him that Donnie insidiously made tracks. Hoisting the gun to his shoulder, he pointed it straight at Ryan Du's chest, his nostrils flaring with rage as he ground out, 'Leave my wife alone, you bastard! And don't try to deny that you've been seeing her, I *know* for a fact you've been tom-catting around behind my back, and if you don't leave her alone in future I'll run you out o' Kinvara wi' the barrels o' my gun up your arse! No woman would ever look at you again wi' your balls in smithereens and a voice on you that would better suit a castrated ram!'

Ryan Du could have flattened Donnie Hic with just one blow from his mighty fist, but on this occasion he had no intention of moving one muscle. He stayed as still as a mouse in his corner as he heard the other man out and noticed how unsteady his trigger-finger was in those fraught moments of blind and unreasoning fury.

'Well, bugger me!' After his initial astonishment Knobby Sinclair had found his voice, his irregular features turning an unhealthy shade of purple as he went on with some authority, 'I will not have this kind o' violence going on in my own establishment, and I would ask you, Donnie Gillespie, to take your gun and yourself out o' here this very minute before I am obliged to call in the law.'

But before anybody else could speak, Ryan Du got in there first, telling Knobby to go easy and going on to try to appeal to the better side of Donnie Hic's nature, ending with, 'Come on now, Donnie, I know you're a reasonable man. Put that gun away and let me buy you a dram and maybe we can shake hands on it and call it a truce like two grown-up sensible men.'

'Don't you dare try and soft talk me, you swine!' Donnie's arm was beginning to tremble, his finger on the trigger noticeably quivered, beads of sweat were popping out on his brow and altogether he had the crazed look of a man who was about to explode at any minute.

The tension in the room grew till it oozed from every pore of every man there, then Dolly, who had been holding her breath for the last minute or so, choked on a mouthful of smoke and beer and made a terrible noise as she retched and wheezed and gasped for breath.

'God save us all! God save us all!' Shug cried as he thumped his wife on the back with more enthusiasm than feeling, till she turned round and thumped him right back between the eyes so that he recoiled from her like a spring and promptly passed out on the seat beside her, remaining where he was for a split second before slithering under the table with all the grace of a landed trout.

'Now see what you've done!' Dolly screeched at Donnie as she got down on her knees beside her husband and fanned him with the hem of her grubby apron. 'You've knocked my man for six, and him only here to enjoy a wee rest after working hard all day long. It isn't right to harass hard-working folks like us and I'll never forgive you, Donnie Gillespie, if Shug isn't able to do another honest day's work for the rest o' his life.'

The blatant exaggeration of this accusation put Donnie off guard, the gun swung slightly off target, giving Ryan Du the chance to draw in a lungful of smoky air and gather up his senses. Seizing his opportunity he began to rise slowly to his feet, everyone else shuffled to theirs, Donnie Hic, however, was immediately alert again and ordered that the room be seated or he would blow them all to kingdom come, and even though Jimmy Song was as scared as anyone else by this threat, he extracted just a tiny note from his mouth-organ, making Donnie glower at him and warn him that the next blow would be his last.

Ryan Du shook his head. 'The folks here have got nothing to do with this, Donnie, just you let them go peaceably and say what you have to say to me.'

But Donnie Hic wasn't listening. 'I've got nothing more to say to anybody here, from now on Mollie belongs to me and me alone.' His voice was even and deadly calm. 'And I'm going home this very night to bairn her. Ay, by God! I'll give her something to keep her occupied while I'm away, and after one there will be another, and maybe another. A puckle o' bairns at her skirts will soon sort her out and might keep any other man from wanting to get up them.'

With that he lowered his gun and took himself off as abruptly as he had come, leaving everyone to look at one another meaningfully. 'He is a poor demented cratur right enough,' hazarded Dokie Joe. 'I think he really means what he said just now, and I would like to be a fly on the wall when he arrives home to deliver his message to Mollie.' So saying he went to the door and with one accord everyone else followed, Shug having recovered sufficiently by now to make a reasonably straight exit outside where Dolly gave him a leg-up into the cart before proceeding to remove Sorry's nose-bag.

'All aboard!' She uttered the rallying cry as she got into the driver's seat and took up the reins. No one needed any second bidding, as many as possible piled on, others ran alongside, one or two on bikes caught on to the end of the tailboard so that they went sailing along without effort as Sorry got under way with a small snicker of annoyance as she strained to take the extra weight behind her.

The inn was suddenly empty, only Ryan Du remained where he was, contemplating the bottom of his glass, Knobby having gone to the door to shake his head as he watched the ragged procession fading slowly off into the distance.

The people who had congregated outside Keeper's Row watched avidly as Donnie Hic disappeared into No. 4.

'Ay, by God! He'll be telling her a thing or two this very minute,' Jimmy Song said gleefully.

'Ay, ay, there goes a dish or two,' Dokie Joe put in, his eyes popping as there came the sound of breaking glass from the house in question.

'Ach, my.' In her excitement Dolly was puffing furiously at her pipe and sending clouds of smoke into the air. 'I hope he's no' doing the lass an injury for he's as much to blame as anyone for her carrying on as she has. He's never paid her much attention and wi' her being such a bonny lass it was only a matter o' time before she went off the rails wi' another man.'

'It will just be some wee bit things getting knocked over by accident,' Shug said knowledgeably. 'Donnie would never raise a hand to Mollie, he thinks the world o' her and though he's as tough as leather when it comes to a fisticuffs, it isn't in his nature to knock any woman about.' He glanced belligerently at Dolly. 'No' like some women I could mention who think nothing o' hitting their very own man between the eyes.'

'Ach, I'm sorry about that,' Dolly had the grace to look ashamed, 'but you punched my back so hard I thought my teeth were going to fall out my head at any moment.'

'Donnie Hic won't hit Mollie,' Dokie Joe affirmed. 'He might be a wild bugger wi' the drink, but never in the whole o' his life has he lifted his hand to a woman and would blacken the eyes o' any man who did.'

'That's as may be,' agreed Conrad O'Conner, the miller of Bruach, 'but it would be sore on any man to find out that his wife had been deceiving him. Donnie wasn't in a normal kind o' temper when we saw him. Blind rage would be a good description o' the way he was when he spoke to Ryan Du – his eyes were bloodshot and insane, he was foaming at the mouth, and he looked as if he might do anything to anybody in a mood like that.'

Quite a crowd had gathered at the scene by now, all anxious to see what the fuss was about, and caught up as they were in the exhilaration of the moment no one thought it unusual when Hannah Sutherland came outside, curiosity getting the better of pride as she took up a stance some discreet distance away from the rest.

Even so she felt uneasy and out of place among the folk who were her neighbours – they were all so attuned to one another, so able to exchange banter and talk and laugh amongst themselves with the ease of people who had known one another all their lives. She could never be like that, never! And then Morna came up from the shore with Vaila in her arms, smiling at Hannah in that nice way she had, a breathless greeting tumbling from her lips as she came to stand beside the older woman and ask her what was happening.

Something strange stirred in Hannah's heart then, a sense of relief that she was no longer alone, a feeling that here was someone who was new in Kinvara like herself and who understood what it was like to be watched and talked about because she was different.

Then Janet came to join them as well, friendly and talkative as she explained to them what had happened in the Balivoe Inn with Ryan Du and Donnie Hic.

'Surely not!' Hannah spoke in shocked tones, the idea of anyone threatening anyone else with a gun confirming her belief that most of the people in the surrounding communities were mad as well as bad.

'Donnie Hic was always jealous o' Mollie,' Janet returned, 'I suppose in a way Ryan Du got off lightly, because we all thought that Donnie would kill anybody who ever looked twice at his wife.'

The sound of raised voices came drifting out of No. 4. 'She's getting a piece o' his mind right enough,' Dokie Joe nodded, wishing to himself that he could give Mattie a piece of his when she was in one of her difficult moods.

'Serves her right,' sniffed Cora Simpson. 'One man ought to be enough for anybody. As for Ryan Du, he should never have looked at a married woman when there are so many spare single ones about. Mollie was just being greedy when she got her hooks into him.'

'Ay, she had it coming,' was Annie Song's opinion, despite

the fact that she'd sympathised with Mollie often enough over Donnie Hic's shortcomings. 'Mind you,' she glowered at her own husband whose red face gave away the fact that he was a man who enjoyed a dram, 'I know only too well what it's like sitting at home knowing that the housekeeping is being pee'd up against a wall. They're all the same when it comes to drink and Mollie was only taking on more trouble when she had her bit fling wi' Ryan Du.'

Stottin' Geordie appeared on the scene, having been informed of the incident in the pub by Knobby Sinclair, who had taken fright when he saw how matters were heading. Geordie was only too ready to ask Donnie a few questions, since that same man had often made life difficult for him on his drunken wanderings. On one occasion removing the lamps from his bike, on another letting his tyres down, once even resisting arrest and punching Geordie on the nose in the process. So, all things considered, the policeman felt an odd sort of pleasure at the idea of being able to get his own back on Donnie Hic, and it was with the greatest of zest that he pedalled up on his bike, propped it against a fencepost, and made his way to the front of the gathering to ask in an authoritative voice just exactly what was going on.

Nobody answered, nobody uttered a word, not even when he removed his notebook from his pocket, licked the end of his pencil, and waited with it poised at the ready. But, save for the lights that glowed softly from the windows of Keeper's Row, it was too dark now to see anything, and by the time he asked someone to fetch a lantern and hold it over the paper, the drama of his actions had paled into insignificance compared to that which was taking place in Donnie Hic's house.

At that moment a cheer went up from the throng, the lights had gone out in the bedroom of No. 4 of The Row and not another sound was to be heard coming from the house – much to the disappointment of the onlookers who had been enjoying the whole episode thoroughly and were in a frame of mind for the entertainment to continue.

'Heathens,' Hannah muttered in disbelief. 'How they can

all stand there prying into other folk's private affairs is beyond my understanding.'

'We're doing it,' Janet reminded her gently.

Hannah's face flared. 'If I had known what it was all about I would have stayed indoors and minded my own business,' she told her young neighbour smartly.

Janet sighed, she had put her foot in it again, after promising Rob that she would try and make friends with his wife, and she had been doing so well a moment ago, Hannah had really seemed to be taking an interest in the world outside her door. Now it had all turned sour, and Janet sighed as she laid her hand on Hannah's arm to bid her goodnight before walking away to seek more agreeable company.

Everyone began to disperse, Geordie too, though he wasn't finished yet, having promised himself that he would interview Ryan Du at the first opportunity to find out what he had to say about being threatened by a shotgun during a peaceful night out with the lads.

'I'd better go too.' Morna took hold of Vaila's hand and prepared to depart. 'I came rushing out o' the house when I noticed all the folk gathering up here. Finlay was asleep in a chair when I left and he will be wondering where I am by now.' She glanced at Hannah, and choosing her words carefully she went on, 'Why don't you come and visit me at Oir na Cuan? Finlay is out during the day and you and me could have a cup o' tea together and keep one another company.'

A quick refusal sprang to Hannah's lips, but she never spoke the words. Instead, impelled by some feeling of kinship towards the girl who was now her sister-in-law, she said gruffly, 'Ay, that would be fine, the house does get quiet when Rob's away, with only the bairn and the brute for company.'

Morna ignored that last remark. 'Vaila will enjoy playing with Andy, and bring Breck as well, it will be interesting to see Mink's reaction to her pup after all these months.'

Ever since her son had been born, Hannah had tried to keep him hidden away, fearing that all anybody wanted to do was 'gape at him as if he were some sort of freak in a sideshow'.

When she was forced to take him to the village shops in his pram, she kept him so well wrapped up that anybody looking in at him could only get a glimpse of his face. Yet somehow, with Morna, she felt no such anxieties, and the two women parted on a friendly note as they wished one another goodnight and headed off to their separate homes.

No one saw Johnny Lonely down there among the dunes, watching Morna as she made her way along the shore, and no one heard him when he muttered to himself, 'I miss you, lass, they were good times we had, now *he's* got you, and you and me can't talk any more.'

Nor did anybody see Ryan Du wending his silent way along to the farmworkers' bothies beneath Blanket Hill. Ryan Du had a score to settle, and he knew exactly where he was going and what he was going to do when he got there.

Linky Black Jack turned up late for work at Vale o' Dreip next morning, sporting a black eye and looking very subdued. Ryan Du didn't turn up at all, and it was reported from a reliable source that he was still in bed in his bothy, nursing his grievances as well as a hangover as big as his head. As for Ramsay, he was furious with both men and threatened to sack them for bad timekeeping, but they were two of his best workers and so he contented himself by giving Linky Jack a dressing down and delivering a lecture to Ryan Du regarding his involvement with a married woman, which, in Ramsay's book, was one of the great cardinal sins.

'Don't worry, I've learned my lesson, Mr Sutherland,' the big man said decidedly, 'I don't think I'll be seeing Mollie again after this.'

'Ay, well, see and keep your word, there was no need for you to spend your time with a woman like Mollie Gillespie when there are plenty o' presentable single young women in Kinvara only too anxious to be seen walking out with a man like yourself.'

Ryan Du had looked decidedly uneasy at this point. 'That's

just it, Mr Sutherland, they're too anxious, if you see what I mean. I have no intention of getting myself hitched to anyone just now, and the lassies that you talk of only have that one thing in mind.'

'So you thought you would be safer with a married woman! Already hitched and only out for a cheap thrill behind her husband's back! Well, let me tell you this, my lad, to my way o' thinking, Donnie let you off very lightly indeed by just threatening you with his gun, many another man would have used it, even if only to knock some sense into that great silly head of yours. Don't let it happen again, Ryan O'Donnel, or I'll run you off my land with my own gun between the cheeks o' your backside!'

Ryan Du never pressed charges against Donnie Hic, telling Geordie that the matter had sorted itself out and that was the end of it, much to the chagrin of the village policeman, who regretfully put his notebook away whilst consoling himself that next time he would 'get his man'.

Chapter Twenty-One

When spring came that year to Kinvara it had started off well enough, only to disintegrate into weather that was wild and stormy, with cold winds blowing in from the north bringing flurries of snow that settled on the peaks and corries of the hills to give the landscape a Christmas-card appearance.

The farmers, in the middle of the lambing season, cursed the snow and the wind, while everyone else cursed it as well and moaned to one another that they were mad to stay in a place like this even though most of them had been born and bred there and had no intention of leaving.

But to some it wasn't all bad news. Wee Fay's shop became busier than ever as the locals sought to comfort themselves with her home-made sweets, while the Knicker Elastic Dears did a roaring trade in hanks of wool, warm vests and combinations, and more knicker elastic than ever since there were those who, for some reason that the sisters had never been able to comprehend, went through more of this commodity in winter than at any other season of the year.

There was, however, one thing that kept the people of Kinvara in a reasonably hopeful frame of mind – cold as it was, the days were growing longer, the skies widening and brightening. Night no longer spread such a thick dark blanket over the land, and that reason alone was enough to make everyone a little more buoyant.

By early summer the days had grown warm and golden.

Bluebells and primroses carpeted the woodlands, the breezes brought the scents of wild thyme from the hills, pink sea-thrift sprouted among the rocks on the seashore, every crack and cranny in the old harbour became filled with it, and the fields were deluged with acre upon acre of golden buttercups and dazzling white daisies, so that wherever you looked there was colour and perfume and wide blue skies all combining with the blue of the sea to make the Kinvara Peninsula a perfect and desirable place to be.

For Hannah Sutherland, the weeks after Rob's departure had been some of the best she had ever spent since coming to live on this rugged north-west coast of Scotland. She and Morna had become good friends, and some of Hannah's happiest hours were spent down there in the homely kitchen of Oir na Cuan. The two women drank tea together, and did so much talking that Hannah surprised even herself for being able to discuss topics that she hadn't given much thought to before Morna brought them into the open, speaking in the easy natural way that the older woman was coming to know and admire.

When they weren't doing that, they were out with the dogs and the children, walking along the shore, Morna pointing out the seals and the birds and the charms of the island-strewn sea, opening Hannah's eyes to the beauties that surrounded her and which she had never seemed to notice before.

Janet also made a breakthrough with Hannah during a visit to Mary's Bay to see Morna, and when Harriet came to stay with her daughter she too fell under the sea maiden's spell, and it became commonplace for them all to meet up at her house to talk and drink tea and sit outside to watch as the afterglow of the sunset spread dazzling colours over the ocean.

It was during this time that Rita, who was a regular visitor to Oir na Cuan, really began to get to know the elder of her two daughters-in-law, even though Hannah displayed a certain reserve towards her, since she was directly connected to Ramsay – the one man Hannah tried to avoid if at all possible.

And all the while Vaila played with Andy, and in her innocent child's way she taught him things that he would never otherwise have learned. With Joss and Vaila and the dogs as his companions, he blossomed that summer of his second year, responding to them with expressions of delight in his eyes so that before long he was attempting to crawl and speak and do other things that his mother had thought would be impossible for her 'changeling of a son'.

Finlay did not approve of all these women 'clecking away like demented hens' in his house, the feeling growing in him that he had never had Morna to himself and never would as long as she found it necessary to surround herself with so many others. He didn't mind his mother, in fact he positively welcomed any appearance she made, and was glad that she had taken the stand she had against his father's wishes.

Hannah and her mother were different kettles of fish, one clamming up whenever he showed his face, the other telling everybody else what to do, himself included – on one memorable occasion informing him that it was high time he snapped out of the sulks when he had so much to be thankful for, including a wife who was like a ray of sunshine about the place, and a little stepdaughter he should be proud of.

Finlay took great umbrage to this last remark. He was not proud of Vaila and was sure he never would be, she was the daughter of some other man who had been in Morna's life before him. He had never taken to her and she showed very plainly that she felt the same way about him – shying away whenever he approached, displaying affection to anyone else but him, gazing at him out of those great eyes of hers for long periods of time as if trying to convey some sort of message that she was as yet unable to put into words. Small she might be, but there was something about her that made him feel uncomfortable, a strength of feeling that she might not understand herself, yet was there just the same, waiting to grow bigger and stronger as she herself grew in size and strength.

Morna had told him that he was imagining things, that the child needed time to adjust to the changes that had taken place in her life, that if he behaved naturally towards her and didn't try to rush her, she would eventually come to him and be happy to have a male figure to whom she could turn when she needed help and comfort.

Rita had already told him much the same thing, and if there was anyone that Finlay listened to it was his mother. So he had tried hard to be patient and kind to Vaila, and for a while it seemed to be working. Then one night he and Morna had argued about something that had started off as a triviality and had ended up with the two of them facing one another in heated verbal battle.

Neither of them had heard Vaila coming downstairs, but all of a sudden she was there, standing in the doorway in her nightdress, clutching a teddy bear to her chest as she stared at them for a long, long, endless moment. And he would never forget the look on her face as she came over and started to beat his legs with her tiny fists, fear and rage contorting her features because she thought he was hurting the one person in the world who spelt love and security in her life.

After that Vaila trusted him less than ever. Then something happened to change everything – he discovered that Morna was pregnant with his baby, and so euphoric was he that he went about in a haze for days, convinced that everything would change in all of their lives now that he was going to have a child he could call his own.

When Rob came home at the end of June he found a very different situation from the one that he had left behind. Hannah was more contented than she had been for ages, Andy had made notable progress, making huge efforts to express himself in many ways, getting about with the help of Breck – who didn't seem to mind his tail being used as a lever. Then, one memorable day, Andy very slowly and painfully formed the word 'Dadda.'

Rob was delighted. Picking up his son, he held him aloft while Hannah looked on, surprise making her mouth fall open even while she pretended to take the whole thing calmly, telling her husband never to expect too much or he would end up being sadly disappointed in a child who would never 'look or behave right' no matter how devotedly anyone tried with him.

Rob knew her cynicism was a reflection of her continuing disappointment in Andy, and he realised then that the fight was not to try and get Andy to do the kind of things that a normal infant of his age would do but to get Hannah to behave like a normal mother towards her own flesh and blood.

There were undercurrents towards Rob as well, old resentments simmering away, her emotional rejection of him, her conviction that she was the wronged party in their marriage because she had borne such a flawed child, her lack of physical demonstrativeness that told him plainer than words to keep his hands to himself: she wanted no part in 'palaver like that'. There was, however, one bright ray on his horizon. Hannah's acceptance of Morna as a friend meant that he and she could meet up without raising any suspicions. Just to be near one another, to talk and walk and laugh and occasionally touch, in some small measure helped them both to bear the love they had for each other in their hearts.

Every moment they spent together became a cherished interlude in the dimension of time, and because there was space now to pause and reflect, their vision of one another became clearer so that they drew closer than ever in mind, body and spirit, 'like a quiet sea undisturbed by tempests and storm', she once told him with that childlike smile he knew so well. He had wept within himself for what he and she might have known together, but for foolish jealousy and pride.

Some of those painful feelings touched him again when he found out that she was carrying his brother's child, until the acceptance came that she was as married as he was now and that the twists of fate were playing their tricks again and somehow they were all being swept along on a road marked out for them in the beginning.

Gradually he even learned to feel an extra special tenderness towards her because of the helplessness of the situation she had created for herself over concern for their daughter's future. 'Hush, my love,' he told her when she voiced her fears to him, 'you did what you felt had to be done, there's no turning back now, and just remember, I love you no matter what, and I'll try always to be here for you whenever you need me.'

KINVARA

Winter 1923–24

Chapter Twenty-Two

Rob couldn't be there for Morna on the November night her son, Aidan John Sutherland, was born. He was many miles away on lighthouse duty on a boiling sea that lashed the shores with fury while the wind howled over the waves to shriek and roar round Oir na Cuan, where Morna lay upstairs in childbirth, wishing in the midst of her pain that Rob was here to comfort her with his strength and love.

'But he is here, he is!' she cried aloud in her confusion, holding on to Effie's arm and staring at her wildly, as if willing the nurse to verify her words. 'He's always with me in spirit, no matter how far away he might be.'

'Ay, lass, of course he's here,' Effie said soothingly as she stroked the girl's hair from her brow, thinking that Morna was calling out for some spiritual sustenance in her distress. 'He's here with us all, whenever we're in need o' Him, so just you lie back and rest all you can. The doctor wasn't in when I stopped by at his house, but I left a message with Jeannie so he shouldn't be long. If you're in a mood to pray, you might say one for him and hope he gets here safely. That big stallion brute o' his is as highly strung as a Shetland fiddle and would think nothing o' throwing the doctor off his back just to get rid o' him.'

Effie's dog, Runt, was sitting on the rug staring thoughtfully into the fire, as unconcerned about Morna and the noises she was making as he was about the weather. Runt had attended many a confinement in his four years of worldly living, and this one was nothing new to him. Even so, his wiry face was wearing a long-suffering expression since he'd had no dinner that night and was feeling mightily annoyed about it. He had tried to convey this to his mistress for the last half hour, but for all the attention she had paid him he might as well be invisible. He was therefore very glad when she at last turned from the bed and bade him follow her downstairs to 'get something nice to eat'.

Finlay was in the kitchen, needlessly poking the embers of a fire that was already giving off a good heat. His face was flushed and anxious-looking, the muscles in his jaw taut with tension. The whisky bottle on the table by his side was almost half empty, but he could hold his drink could Finlay, and it always took more than a few drams before the effects began to show.

At Effie's entrance he jumped to his feet and demanded, 'Well is it here? Is it born yet? Can I go up and see Morna?'

'Ach! Sit yourself down, you daft gowk!' Effie admonished with a flash of her somewhat horsy teeth as she pushed him back into his chair. 'Babies don't just pop out like corks from a bottle! It's well seeing you're a man with no idea o' the workings of a woman's body. Give the lass and her bairn some breathing space! Her waters haven't long broken and you should know all about that, working as you do with the beasts o' the field.'

'Her waters, ay, her waters.' Finlay put a hand to his eyes. 'I'm sorry, my mind isn't functioning properly, and the noise o' that wind is getting me down. I've never spent a winter here by the water's edge. I thought it was bad enough up at the farm, but at least it had the shelter o' the trees round about it.'

'It is fierce tonight,' Effie admitted, pulling her hat further down over her eyes as if unconsciously warding off the wiles of the weather. She patted Runt, who was eyeing Tink and Mink in a way that suggested he was so hungry he could easily eat them. 'I was wondering,' Effie went on, 'if you have got anything nice to eat in your larder?'

Finlay looked at her dazedly, but without question he got up once more and went to rummage in the food cupboard at the back of the house, returning with the remains of a meat pie which he set down on the table. 'I'll get you a knife and fork,' he said politely, mindful of his manners towards the nurse who most folks respected for the cheerfulness and efficiency she displayed when dealing with her patients.

'Och, don't bother yourself about that, laddie,' Effie said with a laugh, 'Runt is surely a mite more clever than most dogs, but he hasn't yet learned good table manners.' So saying, she made a dive at the meat pie and set it down on the floor under her dog's nose, standing guard over him as he ate, in case the two drooling labradors decided they wanted some too.

Finlay stared. 'For the dog! I thought it was for you! That was for tomorrow's dinner! If I'd known I'd have given him some bits o' scrag-end from our own dogs' supply.'

'Don't foul your breeks,' Effie said without a trace of contrition. 'I'll make sure you get your dinner tomorrow, and sit down before you fall down! You've had a bit too much to drink, and I'm going to make you a cup o' good strong tea to sober you up. We'll maybe need your help before the night is over and much good you would be lying down here drunk and insensible and Morna upstairs struggling to bring your bairn into the world!'

At her words, Finlay immediately came to his senses, and when the tea was made he took a cup up to his wife and stayed with her for quite some time, talking to her gently, bathing her brow, holding the cup to her lips so that she could take a sip of her tea.

When he got back downstairs he was white-faced and shaken. 'Shouldn't you be up there with her?' he demanded of Effie. 'She doesn't look too good and – and she's having pains. I hate to see her like that, she doesn't look like Morna somehow.'

'Finlay,' Effie laid a hand on his arm, 'your wife is having a baby in case you didn't know, she's bound to have some pains, it is the natural way o' things when the wee buggers are fighting to get out into the world. And don't you worry your head about either of them, I've never been a body to neglect any o' my patients, and the sea maiden will be no exception.

But she's got a long way to go yet and it will serve no good purpose to have us up there, perpetually fussing around her. So far everything is going fine, the doctor should be here soon and between the two o' us you can be sure that Morna will get the best o' attention.'

Finlay cleared his throat. 'If truth be told, I'm shit-scared sitting down here on my own and I'll go mad altogether if I have to wait here for much longer.'

'Don't wait here then,' Effie said as she calmly sat down at the fire to remove a shoe that had got wet in a puddle. 'Take my cart and get along up to Vale o' Dreip to fetch your mother. Rita is aye good at keeping cool when the need arises – be it a wedding, a funeral, or a confinement – and she'll surely want to be here to see to Vaila in case she should waken in the night and ask what's happening to her mother.'

Finlay brightened at once. 'Ay, Effie, you're right. It would be good having Ma here. I'll get going right away.'

Bolting outside, he ousted Effie's pony from the shelter of the woodshed to harness her up to the cart. In a very short time he was bumping along the winding track that led to Vale o' Dreip and his mother, the woman who had always understood him best, and who knew exactly what to do in any situation.

Chapter Twenty-Three

Doctor MacAlistair's face was grim when he arrived at Oir na Cuan, and he went straight upstairs to see Morna. He hadn't wanted her to have another baby, and had told her this quite plainly when she had come to him in the advanced stages of pregnancy.

'I warned you against this, lass,' he had told her bluntly, 'and now here you are, as big as a house and too late for me to do anything about it. It's going to put a great strain on your heart and I want you to rest as much as possible, put your feet up whenever you can, go to bed early and get up late, make Finlay do all the lifting and laying, the fetching and the carrying.'

'Please, Doctor,' she had laid a hand on his arm then and had looked at him pleadingly, 'Finlay doesn't know about my heart condition, nobody knows except my sister Mirren.'

'Well, they'll have to know now, it isn't the sort o' thing you can keep to yourself forever. You need help to get through this and if you don't rest more then I can't answer for the consequences.'

'No, Doctor,' she had told him with a stubborn lift of her chin, 'I don't want anybody to find out, they would only start fussing and treating me like an invalid. It is my choice to go on as I've always done and I want you to give me your word that you won't say anything to anybody, least of all Finlay.'

Doctor MacAlistair's bewhiskered countenance bristled a bit at this. 'You don't need my word, I am bound by my profession to honour the trust o' my patients, that much I've known since I took the Oath attributed to Hippocrates when I was a raw young doctor. It hasn't always been easy to hold my tongue, but somehow I've managed it and I don't think I'm likely to change my ways now. Your secret is safe with me, Morna, and I will do everything I can to assist you and look after you in the days that lie ahead.'

He had been as good as his word. In his straightforward but kindly way he had done everything he could to ease her difficulties so that she soon came to regard him as a father figure as well as a friend – someone she knew she could turn to whenever her physical and mental burdens became too hard for her to bear alone.

She had also grown to love Long John Jeannie, the doctor's wife who, despite having had no children of her own, knew how to deal with every childish temperament that chanced her way. Whenever Morna had reason to visit Butterbank House, Jeannie would whisk Vaila away to the kitchen to ply her with milk and biscuits and amuse her by bringing out the prized collection of china figurines she had gathered in her travels round the world.

Jeannie was of good farming stock and her husband often joked that she was better than a plough horse any day, with her strength and her patience in dealing with all the ills that came to her doorstep, even if it was just to listen to the woes and worries of the doctor's patients while they were waiting to see him.

But she was more than just 'the doctor's wife'. As a young girl she had determined to broaden her horizons beyond the farmyard gate and had saved every penny towards this end. That, combined with a legacy left to her by a favourite aunt, had enabled her to pack her bags and set off on her travels, soaking up knowledge and experience as she went, so that by the time she returned, she was quite a lady of the world and was a popular figure at social events for her wit and stories of adventure.

She was a great help to the doctor in his day-to-day work,

and he was the first to admit that the walls of Butterbank House would have fallen round his ears long ago if it hadn't been for her. As well as all else, she was a great reader and when she wasn't darning, or mending the 'arse of his combinations', she was to be found with her nose buried deep in a book. She enjoyed cooking, but disliked housework and was glad of the fact that Connie Simpson came thrice weekly to help with the dusting and the sweeping, the ironing and the polishing. A dreamer and a romantic, Connie hated housework too, but somehow she muddled through, talking of the day when she would find herself a rich husband to 'keep me in comfort for the rest of my days'.

Morna was often invited into the kitchen to partake of tea and jammy scones with Jeannie and Connie and sometimes Cora and Catrina too, while Vaila played with the cat – who nearly always had kittens – and clapped her hands with glee when Tubby, a large mournful-looking basset hound, came in to gaze reproachfully at the scones on the table till Jeannie relented and flipped one in the air which he expertly caught in his drooling jaws.

During these little gatherings in the cosy kitchen of Butterbank House much gossip and talk was exchanged and Jeannie always had some entertaining story to relate. Morna too had her tales to tell, of her childhood in Shetland, and of the wild animals of sea and shore that she had rescued since coming to Kinvara. Jeannie and the Simpson sisters listened avidly as she spoke, and came to have a very high regard indeed for the sea maiden. Never mind that she was an incomer and quite a recent one at that, she fitted in very well with the ways of the place and it didn't matter that she had no fixed religious beliefs to speak of. She believed in her Maker and that was the main thing, and the Simpson sisters weren't the only ones who found her a fascinating and likeable young woman who always had a good word for everyone, even Johnny Lonely despite his sly and unsociable ways.

*　　*　　*

Now she was having her baby, three weeks earlier than expected, and all night long Effie and the doctor were with her as she struggled to bring her child into the world while the waves crashed against the rocks in Mary's Bay and the wind continued to howl round the house, 'like a banshee wi' the colic' as Effie so neatly put it.

Down below in the kitchen Finlay had fallen asleep in a chair while his mother presided over pans of hot water on the fire and the never-ending cups of tea required by the wakeful members of the household.

Tink, Mink and Runt, having buried their differences over an earlier contest for supper scraps, had collapsed together in a companionable heap on the rug and were now snoring away in deep contentment, to be joined by Vaila in the early hours of the morning, after she had awakened in the night in some alarm at the sound of her mother moaning softly in the next room.

Rita had tried to soothe the little girl's fears, but she wouldn't be calmed till she was taken in to see Morna for herself, and only when it was explained to her that the baby she had heard so much about in recent months was at last coming, did she allow herself to be led downstairs where she cooried into the animals and was soon as fast asleep as any of them.

Just before dawn, too weak to deliver her child herself, Morna lapsed into a state of semiconsciousness, leaving the doctor and Effie between them to apply their collective skills in assisting Aidan John Sutherland into the world – a little boy who looked like a cherub from the start, making no murmur after his first instinctive cries, boxing his tiny fists in the air as Effie cleaned him with olive oil, put him in a 'goonie' and wrapped him up snugly in a shawl before placing him in the cradle at the foot of the bed.

'Thank God it's over – for her sake.' Alistair MacAlistair indicated the girl in the bed, pale as the sheets upon which she lay, damp tendrils of hair clinging to the moistness of her brow, vulnerable-looking in her youth and helplessness.

'Ay, she had a hard time o' it, poor lass,' Effie nodded, gazing at Morna sympathetically. 'Some just drop them like rabbits out o' a hat, Big Bette had Babs in between making two wooden flutes and a pea-shooter, and was up at the crack o' dawn next day to get breakfast for the family. No two women are alike and you never know what to expect from one confinement to the next. I had always thought the sea maiden to be strong with that nice rosy face she has on her, but seeing her lying there makes me realise she's a bittie more delicate than I would ever have imagined.'

The doctor had nothing to say to this and Effie nodded her head meaningfully, 'Och, c'mon now, Alistair, do you think I'm daft as well as stupid? Don't forget, I'm as much at home in your house as I am in my own, I've sat in Jeannie's kitchen drinking tea with Morna and knew fine her visits weren't purely for sociable reasons. I'm mad at you for trying to keep me in the dark about her, me who's worked beside you for a goodly number o' years now and who has every right to know what's going on.'

'You're right and I'm sorry, Effie,' the doctor shook his head, 'I should have taken you into my confidence about Morna, but she made me swear not to tell anybody of her heart condition. Now that you've guessed for yourself I want *you* to hold your tongue on the subject, even to her husband, it's what she wants and I'm bound to honour my word to her.'

Effie looked hurt, 'As if I would ever break a confidence. I might enjoy a bit o' chitchat like anybody else, but as the nurse I have my own codes to stick by and you of all people should know the truth of that.' She grinned at him suddenly and went on to say in a cheerier vein, 'You know, it's a pity they aren't all like my Queen Victoria.'

The doctor looked startled at this statement. 'Queen Victoria?' he questioned in some confusion.

'Ay, my bonny sow, she had thirteen sucklings last summer, all popping out one after the other like wee pink sausages from a machine and their mother none the worse for the experience.'

'Tea – and maybe a dram to go with it!' Doctor MacAlistair decided quickly, giving Effie no chance to enlarge further on the maternal abilities of her beloved pig.

It wasn't long before everyone knew that Morna had given birth to a son, and those that couldn't get to see her personally for one reason or another were anxious for news of the event, especially when it became known that she'd had such a difficult time giving birth.

Effie had naturally been the target of much questioning as also was Jeannie, whom many believed knew all there was to know about the medical history of Kinvara as a whole, 'with her being so close to the doctor'. Tottie Murchison was no exception, and when Jeannie appeared in the tiny draper's shop in Balivoe to buy some long johns and a pair of winter combinations for her husband, his old ones being past repairing, Tottie was in there at the double, peering at Jeannie through her pince-nez as she probed the doctor's wife for information.

'Well, when I went to see Morna she was sitting up in bed looking as bonny as ever,' Jeannie said in a deliberately low voice, all the while enjoying the sight of Tottie's fingers hovering over the small ear trumpet lying on the counter, which actually belonged to Tillie but which Tottie sometimes used if she felt the occasion demanded it, simply because she was rather hard of hearing herself but didn't like to admit to it.

'Ay, ay, that's as may be,' Tottie leaned across the counter and stared at Jeannie's lips as if trying to read them, 'but a body can look well and still be at death's door and Catrina Simpson was saying that Morna had been over at the doctor's house quite a lot when she was carrying her bairn.'

'Ay, she was that,' Jeannie replied carefully, 'a lot of pregnant lassies go to see their doctors, it's only right that they should get advice and attention, both for themselves and their unborn infants.'

'And the doctor, what has he to say about a lass who can't

get up out o' her bed more than three days after the birth? Surely there must be something wrong there?'

'The doctor doesn't discuss his patients with me,' Jeannie said firmly and rather coldly. 'You know as much as me, Tottie, Morna didn't have an easy time giving birth to her son, a lot of women have the same problem, it's quite a natural state o' affairs and doesn't mean to say there is anything wrong with them. I myself have unfortunately never had children, but I can well imagine how the experience must be a drain on any young woman.'

'And the baby?' Tottie probed relentlessly, 'is everything all right there? You know, a Sutherland and all that. Well, look at what happened to Hannah from Ayr, that poor wee mite that she bore to Rob. I was just wondering if maybe there is something that runs in the family that isn't quite right, on the male side perhaps. Finlay himself isn't very robust when it comes to the bit, look at that queer illness he took when the war was on. I mind fine he couldn't get out o' bed for months and we all know he isn't quite the full shilling the way he hangs on to his mother's apron strings and can't make up his mind about anything, though mind, I blame her for that, she should have made him stand on his own two feet long ago instead of pampering him the way she has.'

Jeannie treated Tottie to a withering glower at that junction and she might have brained her altogether if the doorbell hadn't jangled to admit Big Bette looking for vests and knickers for Babs and some sensible undergarments for the boys. Since she was in a hurry to get back to her shop, Jeannie allowed her to go first and wandered away to browse through a display of shop-soiled goods going for half-price.

'An unrepeatable bargain,' Tottie beamed at Jeannie as soon as Big Bette had departed, 'Tillie wanted only ten per cent off, but I thought they might go quicker with the fifty per cent tag on them.'

'I doubt it,' Jeannie returned sourly, still smarting at the Sunday School teacher's vindictive remarks regarding Rita Sutherland. 'They look as if they've been in the shop since it opened and that wasn't yesterday if my memory serves me right. I came in for some things for Alistair and would like to see a good selection of your men's underwear.'

Tottie rummaged in various drawers and laid out the contents on the counter till soon it was littered with vests and long johns of all shapes and sizes.

Tottie picked up a set of combinations and fondled them lovingly. 'These are good quality wool and will keep the doctor nice and warm – the soul,' she added solicitously, anxious now to get on Jeannie's right side, 'with him being out in all weathers he needs the best protection he can get from the cold.'

Jeannie made her choices and Tottie was wrapping them up when Tillie, the elder half of the Knicker Elastic Dears, appeared from the back of the shop and was quite unable to stop herself saying curiously, 'If you don't mind me asking, Jeannie, the doctor does seem to go through a lot o' long johns and combinations and I was wondering what he does to wear them out so quickly.'

'It's the horse,' Jeannie said promptly and with a perfectly serious expression.

'The horse?' The sisters spoke in unison as they gazed at Jeannie in confused anticipation.

'Ay, that big stallion brute o' his has a hard hide on him and would wear the breeks off anybody. As well as that, the doctor has some peculiar wee ways about him and does a lot o' thinking with his backside.'

'His backside!' Tillie and Tottie were agog by this time and Tottie, unable to resist the temptation any longer, picked up the ear trumpet to hold it against one quivering lug, much to the annoyance of her sister who had been on the verge of doing the exact same thing.

'Just that,' nodded Jeannie. 'When we were first married I myself noticed this terrible habit he had of standing with his back to the fire tearing away at his breeks. Being young and shy at the time I couldn't bring myself to say anything, but later on, when I asked him about it, he just said in a rough sort o' manner, "some folks scratch their heads when they have things on their mind, in my case I think with my arse and a warm arse is better than a cold one to get the grey cells going. Besides that, wool itches, Jeannie, especially in the nether regions, and if a man can't have a decent scratch in the privacy o' his own home then God help us all and that's my last word on the matter".'

The sisters stared dumbfounded at Jeannie and it was all she could do to keep a straight face as she paid for her purchases and ran outside to lean against a wall and roar with laughter at the memory of the expressions on the faces of the Knicker Elastic Dears.

When she went home and told her husband about the incident he too threw back his head and said he would have to remember all this and play on it next time he came across the sisters. 'Instead of raising my hat to them I'll scratch the seat o' my pants and wait to see what their reaction is to that. You've taken away some of their innocence, Jeannie, my lass, and Sunday School will never be the same for them again.'

'Not so innocent,' Jeannie said grimly and went on to recount Tottie's comments regarding the Sutherlands.

'Ay, Sunday School teachers or no, they have big mouths on them that pair,' the doctor agreed. 'But they're just repeating what they've heard and you know what gossip is in a place like Kinvara.' He smiled at his wife and dropped a kiss on her cheek. 'And now I must put on a pair of my best woolly combinations and go and see how Morna is faring. There's a wind blowing out there that would cut you like a knife and whatever else we might say about the Knicker Elastics, they do stock good warm underwear.'

'Ay, Morna,' Jeannie said thoughtfully, 'you know I try never to pry into your medical affairs, and God forbid I should ever become a Tillie or a Tottie, but all this talk about Morna has got me wondering. She isn't a strong lass, is she, Alistair?'

'No, she isn't a strong lass, Jeannie,' he returned softly, 'but she's got youth on her side and tremendous courage and fortitude. I've grown very close to her in the last few months and a more spirited young woman I have yet to meet.'

Jeannie didn't pursue the matter further. Her husband had

extracted his pipe from its hairy nest of moustache and beard, and was tapping it out on the bars of the grate, a sign that he was preparing to go forth and face the wintery wiles of the November day. Jeannie went to fetch his cape and hat from the stand in the hall and helped him to shrug himself into them.

For a few moments he stood looking at her, his eyes twinkling, 'Ants in my pants, eh? I'll say this for you, Jeannie, you're never short of answers, and real corkers at that. I would love to have been there when you said all that to the sisters and even more, the things *they* had to say to one another after you left.'

Jeannie gave a snort of laughter. 'I'll make a bargain with you, Alistair, when you come back from your rounds we'll have a nice cosy evening together – you scratch my backside and I'll scratch yours, after all, as I've said before, who knows what goes on in the privacy of a couple's own home?'

'It's a deal,' he nodded and went off chortling to the stable where his 'big stallion brute' Dandy, was only too pleased to be saddled and let out to stretch his legs in the great wide grey yonder that was Kinvara in winter.

Chapter Twenty-Four

Morna was exhausted and ill for weeks after the birth of her son, and was told bluntly by Doctor MacAlistair that it would be a long while before she regained her strength. 'You'll need someone to look after you and the babe,' he went on to say. 'I know that Hannah has been a good help to you as has Rita, but they can't be here twenty-four hours a day to see to all the demands of the household. Effie will look in as often as she can, but it won't be enough and I might have to arrange for someone to come here and live in for a while.'

'We could never afford that, Doctor,' she had told him with a sigh. 'It takes us all our time to make ends meet as it is and it will be even harder with a new baby in the house.'

'Leave that worry to me,' he had said kindly. 'You have enough o' your own to be going on with. I have one or two good contacts, women who have retired from nursing for one reason or another but who are only too willing to earn a bob or two for the sort o' job I have in mind.'

But the problem was taken out of their hands. As if on cue Mirren arrived from Shetland to look after her sister, breezing in and taking over the running of the place, making it plain from the start that she would be doing it *her* way and wanted no interference from anybody.

Morna wasn't too sure if this was a good idea. For a start, Mirren wasn't at all pleased about her sister having had another baby and said that Finlay should have known not to get her pregnant again.

'It's my fault,' Morna protested, already feeling herself irritated by Mirren's presence. 'He doesn't know about the illness I had as a child and I don't want him to know – or anyone else for that matter.'

'Oh, Morna,' Mirren sighed, 'you always were too stubborn for your own good. But yes, I promise not to tell anybody, though I do think you're being rather silly about the whole thing.'

'I just want to lead as normal a life as possible,' Morna said, feeling as though lead was flowing through her veins, so tired was she with all the useless talk about how she should conduct her own life. 'I'm me, Mirren, and I'm all grown up now and at liberty to make my own decisions.'

'Of course you are, my dear little sister, I just want what's best for you, it's all I've ever wanted since our parents died and you know that better than anybody.'

She sounded pacifying and slightly martyred and Morna gave up arguing simply because she knew that Mirren would always have the last word, and that the only way to bear the situation was to keep out of the way as much as possible and let her sister run the house in the same efficient manner that she handled everything else.

She was wonderful with Vaila and Aidan, but had scant patience with Finlay who was so full of himself these days that he seemed to be floating on air and had been drinking far too much since the advent of his son. He was bursting with camaraderie towards his fellow men and spent a lot of his spare time and his money in the mellow atmosphere of the Balivoe Village Inn, 'wetting the baby's head' so regularly that even beings like Shug Law felt moved to comment that in all his days he had never known anything like it, and that it was little wonder Morna was so ill after 'having a bairn with more heads on it than a crop o' boils ready for the bursting'.

Rita gave her son a lecture on his drinking habits, but all he said in retaliation was that it wasn't every day a man became a father and she gave in to this because he looked so happy as he held his newborn infant in his big strong arms. 'He's mine, Ma,' he said, his face glowing with pride. 'For the first time in my life I feel I've achieved something worthwhile and I just can't help wanting to shout it to the rooftops. Let me have my moment o' triumph. I'll go back to being sober and serious when I'm good and ready, but for now I'm enjoying myself.'

'As long as you remember to stop, son, you have a growing family to keep now and you know what your father is like when you drink too much, especially if it interferes with your work.'

'I could drink all night and still be fit for work the next day,' Finlay boasted. 'Don't worry, Ma, I'll give him no reason to find fault with me. I'm as good as him any day when it comes to doing my job and damned fine he knows it.'

'Ay, we'll see,' was all Rita said, and left it at that.

During her enforced confinement to the house Morna was never allowed to weary, visitors came to Oir na Cuan in a regular stream, particularly her neighbours from Keeper's Row, including Mollie Gillespie, almost ready to have her own baby now, much to the delight of Donnie Hic, who said it might be the first but wouldn't be the last, and bragged that he was going to be there personally when it arrived since it was bound to be a boy with all the kicking it had done in the last few months.

'And how would you know about that?' Mattie had said sarcastically. 'If any man had to carry and birth a bairn the way a woman does the human race would become extinct.'

Donnie was undeterred, 'I put my hands on Mollie's belly and *felt* it,' was his cheery comment, 'and don't forget, Mattie, Mollie might be carrying it, but I had a big part in putting it where it is, surely you're not overlooking that side o' the matter.'

'As if anybody could,' Mattie said with a snort. 'And don't *you* forget how much you enjoyed doing what you did, with half o' Kinvara watching and listening to you behaving like a heathen.'

'I didn't ask you to come, you were all there because you liked the wee drama of it all, and Dokie Joe told me afterwards it gave him such a thrill it was well worth the dram he bought me.'

'He bought you a dram for that!' Mattie screeched. 'The dirty bodach, just wait till I get my hands on him and we'll see what kind o' thrill he gets with one o' his very own socks tied tightly round his silly neck.'

'Now, now, Mattie, calm down, there is no need for threats o' that sort,' Donnie returned placatingly, and hastily vacated the scene in case Mattie might take it into her head to wrap one of *his* socks round *his* neck.

It wasn't only the neighbours who came to see Morna, Father Kelvin MacNeil called one morning, putting his head round the door and shouting, 'Anybody at home? It's only me, Father MacNeil.'

'In here, Father,' Morna shouted back, and in he strode without any second bidding, peeping at the baby in his cradle as he passed, ruffling Vaila's curly head affectionately.

'I haven't come to try and save your soul,' he greeted Morna with a boyish grin as he settled his rangy frame into the chair opposite, laughing when his lap was promptly commandeered by a large white cat that Morna had recently found starving in her shed. 'I heard that you weren't feeling so good and wanted to see how you were for myself – and – I can't tell a lie – I had to escape Minnie's tender administrations for a while. Something gets into her at this time o' year, she goes mad altogether with the dusters and the polish and she keeps asking me to get her seasonal supplies from the village shops. I always seem to lose the list and can never remember if she asked for suet or lard, and when I go into Bette's it's always full of women giving me well-meant advice which only ends up confusing me.'

Morna's dimples showed. 'Like last year? When I was in the shop with you?'

'Exactly. I've never forgotten how you rescued me from the lion's den so to speak, and wish I could take you shopping with me every time. It's a daunting experience coping with so many women at once, all trying to make themselves heard above one another.'

They both burst out laughing and she was glad that Mirren was out shopping and that she was able to make tea for her guest without her sister grabbing the pot from her and insisting that she would do it.

The dogs got a biscuit each, the cats got milk, Vaila was given a buttered oatcake, and after that Morna sat down and poured tea for her visitor and herself, feeling better than she had done for ages as a sense of renewed independence returned to her.

She thoroughly enjoyed talking to the young curate, he was a man after her own heart, so easy and natural to get on with, never standing on ceremony, seeing the funny side of many things that others might have taken too seriously, able to discuss a wide range of issues in a wise and worldly way that appealed to Morna's own sense of curiosity about life's purpose and meaning.

After the first light-hearted exchanges, the conversation swung round to other matters. 'I met Johnny Lonely the other day.' He helped himself to a large sugary doughnut as he spoke. 'He asked me to tell you he sends his regards and hopes you will soon be well.'

'Oh, poor Johnny,' Morna sighed. 'I've felt so guilty about him, I looked for him all of last summer, but he never seemed to be around and I knew he was hiding himself up there in the ruins of the old Chapel Light and me too pregnant to climb up to talk to him.'

'I was wondering,' the young priest hesitated, 'I worry about Johnny and often wish I could help him more than I seem able to, he is wary whenever I approach him and as far as I can see you are the only person in these parts who he trusts. Would it be possible for him to come and see you here? I know how much he valued his friendship with you and how sorely he misses his visits to your house. He's taken a step backwards, Morna, and has retreated into a lonelier shell than ever.'

'Of course he can come,' Morna said at once. 'But we'll have to conspire a bit on this. Johnny won't put a foot near the place if Finlay is here, but as he's away at the farm most of the day it should be all right. If Johnny makes it an afternoon, I'll have the place to myself and will be able to put him at his ease.'

'What about your sister, Mirren, does she know about Johnny? You know what he's like, he doesn't take kindly to strangers and will shy away altogether if he sees your sister, though, of course, if she's anything like you he'll have nothing to worry about.'

'No, she isn't like me,' Morna said honestly. 'Mirren is practical and unsentimental, I'm the opposite, soft as putty and easily moved to tears over the most trivial matters. She has a good heart however and would never willingly do anyone a wrong turn.' She looked at him and her green eyes glinted mischievously. 'She also goes out most afternoons, so it's more than likely that Johnny and me will have the house to ourselves – except of course for the children and the animals, and not forgetting one large white cat who has covered your knees with bits of her fluff.'

He smiled ruefully and stood up to brush crumbs and cat hairs from his dark trousers. 'It's been worth it, I've enjoyed my visit.' He extended his hand to her. 'I'll go home now ready to face the mops and the dusters and I'll make a point of speaking to Johnny as soon as I can.'

And so Johnny Lonely made his pilgrimage to Oir na Cuan, trimmed, brushed, and washed – looking really quite handsome without the wild hairiness that everyone had come to associate with his appearance – bearing in his large brown hands a little pot filled with shells and pebbles he had gathered from the seashore, presenting them to Morna with a gruffness that hid his terrible shyness.

'Oh, Johnny, they're lovely!' Morna cried in genuine appreciation. 'Just look at the colours of these little stones! And the shells.' She held one to her ear and there was silence for a moment. 'I can hear the sea,' she said at last, 'sweeping gently to the shore, washing the rocks in the bay. I miss it all so much, but you have brought it in here for me in this bonny wee pot.'

Reaching up she kissed him on his cheek and he closed his eyes and tried to hold back his tears. She had become so pale since he'd last seen her, yet more beautiful than ever, with her black hair falling to her shoulders, her green eyes brilliant with the life-force that flowed so eagerly within her, one that had seemed to inject itself into him and infuse him with new hope when she and he had shared so many small interludes of confidence and caring. His throat tightened. Precious days, ones that he could never forget. No one else had touched him as the sea maiden had done, and she would never know how much he'd worried about her or how often he'd thought about her in the long months since her marriage to Finlay.

'Johnny,' she said softly, 'how have you been? It seems so long since we talked together. I've thought about you a lot, what you were doing, how you were faring. Are you well, Johnny? Are you happy?'

He didn't reply, but stood by her chair looking embarrassed, awkward, and strained, and she took him by the arm and led him over to the fire. 'Sit down, Johnny,' she said gently, 'and please don't be shy of me, remember how we once talked and trusted one another. Nothing of that has changed, we can still be friends. I'm going to get stronger. Having the baby wasn't easy, but it's over now and I'll soon be back to my old self.'

'I miss the talks we used to have!' he burst out suddenly as his pent-up emotions came flooding to the surface. 'I miss coming here to see you and the wee one. They were good those days and then you got married and they stopped and after that I had nobody.'

'Johnny, there are things, many things that have happened in my life about which I can tell no one. I wanted it all to be different, but nothing turned out as it should and I have had to go along other roads that weren't of my choosing. Sometimes we have to make decisions in order to protect people we love, even though others we love might then be hurt. So it was with me, Johnny, and nothing I can do will alter how it is now.'

'I know,' he spoke quietly, secretively, 'I know why you had to do what you did. I've always known about you, Morna, ever since you came here as a young lass of sixteen and didn't know anybody in the place. I watched over you and saw that you came to no harm, and I'll always go on doing that for as long as I have to.'

'I know you will, Johnny, and I'll go on caring about you too, so relax and just enjoy being here, nobody else is in the house, just me and the babies.'

She made him tea and they sat talking companionably together as they drank it. He had taken a liking to Father MacNeil, and spoke warmly about the encounters he'd had with him, saying he wished all clergymen were like that, natural and approachable and unbiased in their outlook.

Vaila had always been somewhat bewitched by Johnny, and now she climbed on his knee and played with his beard and the buttons on his jacket while he spoke to her in that nice easy way he always had with her.

It was cosy in the house with all its little homely touches, and he was at ease to begin with, but after a while he became nervous and kept looking anxiously towards the door, as if he were afraid that someone might appear at any moment.

'I'll have to go.' He got up abruptly. 'It isn't the same here now, and I doubt if I'll be back to see you again.'

'I'll come to see you instead,' she promised softly, 'when I'm stronger and able to get outside as I used to. Go back to living on the shore, Johnny, it's quite a scramble up there to the point, and if you move back down I'm more likely to come across you when I'm out walking in the bay.'

He gazed at her for a long moment, twisting his cap in his

hands, seeming always to be on the verge of saying something. But in the end he left without a word, his steps firm enough, but the hunch of his shoulders giving away the heaviness in his heart.

'Goodbye, Johnny,' she whispered, standing at the door with her hand raised in a farewell that he never saw because he didn't turn round once.

Mirren passed him as she came along the track through the dunes, and as she drew close to her sister she said with a frown, 'Who on earth was that? I saw him leaving the house, and now that I come to think of it, I've seen him wandering about on the shore, gathering driftwood and other bits o' rubbish.'

'His name's Johnny, people around here call him Johnny Lonely because he lives by himself on the shore. He's a nice and kindly man, and I've always got on well with him.'

'He looks like a tramp to me.'

'Not a tramp,' Morna tried to keep her voice even, 'just a man who likes to keep himself to himself and does no harm to anyone.'

'Really, Morna, you seem to make a point of gathering lame dogs around you, both animal and human. Why can't you be like everybody else and just leave the Johnny Lonelys of this world to their own devices?'

'Because I'm not like everybody else,' Morna replied with a defiant tightening of her mouth. 'I like lame dogs. I like Johnny Lonely. He knows more about the things that count than anybody gives him credit for – and I'll go on caring about him in spite of what people have to say, yourself included – so put that in your pipe and smoke it!'

Mirren had to smile at this. 'All right, I give up, into the house this minute before you catch cold. I stopped off at The Dunny while I was out and bought a walnut cake from Wee Fay for our supper. I've never met anybody like her, she talks at the speed of light and not even her husband can get a word in. She says to tell you she'll be along whenever she has a moment, it seems she's been knitting for the baby and wants to deliver the results personally.'

Harmony was restored. The sisters laughed together over the snippets of village talk that Mirren had brought home with her and Johnny's name wasn't mentioned again that day, a fact for which Morna was heartily thankful as she knew she could never have convinced Mirren of his worth as a man of knowledge and learning.

Chapter Twenty-Five

No one was more surprised than Morna when Ramsay appeared on her doorstep one cold sunny morning a week before Christmas, striding into the house without preliminaries to stand in the middle of the kitchen, tapping one foot impatiently as he waited for her to shut the door. But it wasn't her he had come to see and he wasted no time in telling her so.

'I want to see my new grandson,' he imparted curtly, gazing over her head as if she weren't there. 'I've been too busy to come before, but I'm here now and I can't spare too many minutes o' my time.'

Morna was immediately on the defensive at his tone. 'Well, like it or no, you'll just have to wait. My sister has taken him out in his pram – he needed to get some fresh air into his lungs and I don't know when Mirren will bring him back.'

His icy blue gaze fell on her and it was as if he were seeing her for the first time. 'Hmm, so you're Morna, my wife has spoken of you quite a lot, so today I thought I would take the bull by the horns and see what you're made of for myself.'

Her face flushed crimson at this and sparks danced in the green of her eyes. He had made her sound like some creature under a microscope and she was quick to react. 'I've been married to your son since last March, you could have met me properly then, but you didn't think I was good enough to even come to our wedding, so why bother now!'

Ramsay Sutherland looked at the younger of his daughters-in-law and he liked what he saw. She was bonny all right: that black hair, skin that was peachy and pure, a figure that was curved in all the right places – and those eyes, flashing fire and defiance at him, every bristling line of her telling him that here was someone who would fight tooth and nail for the things she believed in.

He was about to take a stand down when he remembered – she was a person of no fixed religion. Some said she was an atheist though Rita claimed that she was more a child of God than some people who went to kirk every Sunday and called themselves Christians, yet didn't seem to carry the Lord's teachings into their day-to-day lives. He hadn't liked that one bit, it was as if his wife were implying that *he* was at fault by diligently attending kirk and believing implicitly in his faith. In his book there was something lacking in people like Morna. He didn't hold with the liberal attitudes that were beginning to float around these days – they hadn't done this young woman much good, her morals were loose, she had borne a child out of wedlock and God knew how it would turn out . . .

'I had my reasons for not attending my son's wedding,' he said with a jutting of his beard. 'Some matters are best ignored, and that was one o' them. Time, however, has a habit of healing and so it is with me. I bear you no ill will for wanting to marry into a respectable family. Your daughter has a name now and you have provided me with a grandson, that alone is good enough reason for me to forgive and forget.'

Morna was flabbergasted. 'Forgive and forget!' she all but yelled, and she would have said a whole lot more had not the door opened at that moment to admit Mirren with Aidan in his pram, and Vaila – who had adored her little brother from the start – hanging proudly on to the handle. Her cheeks were frost stung, her eyes big and bright and questioning as she looked at the visitor. But he had no interest in her, the pram was no sooner over the threshold than he strode over to scoop his grandson into his arms and carry him over to the window to examine him as if he were some sort of specimen. A grunt of satisfaction escaped

Ramsay. The boy was perfect in every way that he could see, well formed, good big fists on him, a hint of red in his hair, undoubtedly a Sutherland through and through . . .

Mirren was looking enquiringly at her sister, a hint of annoyance in her eyes at this sudden intrusion.

'He's a fine boy.' Ramsay returned the infant to his pram and swung round on Morna. 'But I don't like the name you gave him, it's Catholic and not a fitting name for a Sutherland.'

'I wouldn't care if it's the name of the man in the moon!' Morna returned with spirit. 'I'm not bigoted, I like the way it sounds and chose it for that reason.'

A slow flush was creeping over Ramsay's face. 'As you like,' he said coldly. 'What's done is done and it seems I have no say in that particular matter. There are some things I may be able to correct however. A child like him will need space to grow up . . .' His critical gaze took in the room in one sweep. 'It's far too cramped here for him. I'm willing to let you and Finlay have one o' the bigger houses on the farm, it will be handier for my son and easier for my wife and myself to have access to our grandson.'

'No!' The refusal sprang from Morna's lips before he had finished speaking. 'This is my home. It's been good enough for my daughter and it will be good enough for my son. You can keep your house for I want no part of it nor of you, and it would give me the greatest o' pleasures if you were to disappear up your own backside this very minute! Forgive and forget indeed! It's I who should be saying that to you but I won't, because I don't, and if you want to see your grandson you'll do so when I'm good and ready and not before!'

Ramsay drew himself up to his full height and glaring down at her he spat out, 'You're showing yourself in your true colours now, my girl, but I tell you this, it is my right to see the boy and I mean to do just that, so see you let Finlay bring him to me whenever I take the notion to have him at Vale o' Dreip – and that is not a request, it is an order!'

With that he slammed out of the house, leaving a stunned silence behind.

Vaila was round-eyed, Mirren open-mouthed, Morna was white and shaken, and without a word her sister made her sit down and take a sip of some brandy which she quickly found and poured.

'So, that was your father-in-law,' Mirren said at last.

'Ay, that was him,' Morna confirmed. 'A fine performance from a not so big man. But he's got the trump card, Mirren, it *is* his right to see Aidan – but I won't be the one to set foot inside Vale o' Dreip. I like Rita and I'm sorry that it's turned out this way, but these things happen and there's no turning back the clock.'

'Ay, these things happen,' Mirren said uneasily and went to put the kettle on. A moment later she turned from the stove to look at her sister. 'I shouldn't say this, but I loved that bit about you wanting him to disappear up his own rear end! His face was a picture.'

Morna giggled. 'I'll never forget it. I suppose I didn't really know what I was saying and it all just came pouring out. He'll resent me worse than ever now, but at least we both know where we stand, and – strangely enough – I feel better for having got it all off my chest at last. He's the sort o' man who needs firm handling and I know now why Rita feels that she always has to stay on top, if not she would just be trampled underfoot by all his demands. I also see why Finlay is so close to his mother, it must have been hard for both him and Robbie to have been brought up by such a tyrant.'

Mirren opened her mouth as if to speak, but quickly shut it again, knowing that if she got going on the subject of Finlay she might never stop, and Morna had been through enough that day without adding further to her burdens.

When Hannah heard of Ramsay's visit to Oir na Cuan and how he had fussed over Aidan, she was furious. In almost three years of marriage and motherhood he had never been able to bring himself to visit her.

'He didn't come to see me, Hannah,' Morna pointed out, 'it was only Aidan that he was interested in.'

'Ay, it would be,' Hannah returned bitterly. 'He has never so much as looked at his other grandson – perfection is the thing that matters in Ramsay's eyes. It would never even enter his head that Andy's faults might lie on the Sutherland side, and I'm sure he sees me as some kind o' freak who has done nothing better than produce another freak.'

'Hannah, don't speak like that!' Morna cried in dismay. 'Andy isn't a freak, just a little boy unlucky enough to have been born with a few handicaps . . .'

'A *few* handicaps!' Hannah rounded on her. 'He's a vegetable who will never be good for anything! Oh, I know Rob thinks he can work miracles on the boy, but no one can do that and . . . and it would have been better for everybody if he'd never been born at all!'

'That's enough, Hannah!' Morna had never seen this side of Hannah and she was horrified by it. 'Give Andy a chance, give yourself and your husband a chance. Of course your son will never be perfect, none of us will ever be perfect, but give him the credit o' the doubt. Tell yourself that he's got intelligence and understanding, convince yourself that one day he will be able to speak and walk, and if he does, at least you will have the satisfaction of knowing you helped him get where he is. Most of all, Hannah,' she added softly, 'give him love. That's the one thing in life we all need, for without it we are nothing and we have nothing to give in return.'

Hannah sat down suddenly and putting her face in her hands she burst into a fit of weeping. Morna let her have her moments of emotional release, and then she put her arms round the older woman and said, 'You'll feel better for that. I do it often myself when everything gets too much for me, and afterwards I feel as if a great weight has slipped from my shoulders leaving me free to get on with living.'

Hannah caught and held Morna's hand. 'You're my real friend, Morna – oh yes you are. Since getting to know you

I feel as if I'm beginning to belong here – when before I hated everybody and everything in the place.'

Morna bit her lip. Guilt tore her in two. She prayed that Hannah would never find out about the love that burned in her heart for Robbie – a man who didn't rightly belong to her but who would go on living within her as long as there was breath in her body.

Gradually things started to settle down at Oir na Cuan. Finlay sobered up, Morna slowly got well, and Mirren began to relax a bit more. She and Morna talked and reminisced about childhood days in Shetland and how good it had been when their parents had been alive. In the evenings they all sat round the fire, Finlay and Mirren tolerating each other better now, sharing the chores, looking after the children.

At bedtime Mirren would go to her sister's room and brush her hair as she had done in years gone by, and in the daytime they went for walks along the shore with the dogs and the children, Morna revelling in the freedom of the wide open spaces after being cooped up indoors for so long.

When Christmas came it brought with it a heavy fall of snow that draped the countryside with tracts of virgin white and made the peaks of the hills sparkle against the cold blue of the sky.

On Christmas day Hannah came to Oir na Cuan with Andy, giving Rita the opportunity to see both her daughters-in-law together. 'Killing two birds with one stone.' A smile sweetened Hannah's face as she spoke.

'There's only one dead bird in this house and it's almost ready for the eating,' Mirren said, withdrawing the crackling turkey from the oven and putting it on the table to rest before carving.

Nobody mentioned Ramsay's name, not even Finlay who had been rather peeved at Morna for refusing the offer of a bigger house, but was understanding enough to see her point of view on the matter. He had, however, honoured his father's

desire to see his grandson, and had taken the baby to Vale o'
Dreip whenever it was feasible to do so.

Now it was Christmas, a time for giving and receiving,
forgiving and forgetting, small differences were overlooked,
bigger ones temporarily pushed aside. Ramsay was acting as
lay preacher at the Free Kirk in the minister's absence, so
Rita didn't feel guilty about enjoying herself without him.
She threw all restriction to the winds as she partook of port
wine and after-dinner brandy, thoroughly revelling in the fact
that her husband wasn't there to frown at her lack of personal
restraint in things he considered to be 'unseemly' in the female
of the species.

It was a family Christmas, convivial and enjoyable. Even
so, Morna couldn't help but remember the last one, when
Robbie had come to visit her on Christmas morning and they
had exchanged their small gifts. Her breath caught, her hand
went up to the little seal brooch at her throat, and she thought
of how they had made love, the sweetness and delight of it
mingling with the terrible sadness they had felt knowing that
it might be the last time for them.

A whole year had passed since then. A year! She could
hardly believe the months had gone so quickly, yet it seemed
an eternity since she had lain in his arms, felt his kisses on her
lips. So long ago, so far away and out of reach now. She had
sent him a Christmas letter, and her thoughts were with him
out there on the barren lighthouse rock. She tried to picture
him as he went about his duties, perhaps thinking of her as he
gazed out over the wintery seas to the lights of Kinvara winking
in the distance . . .

Soon after Christmas, Mirren went home to Shetland and
the house was quiet for a while, a fact much appreciated
by Finlay who stretched his feet to the fire and told Morna
it was good to have her to himself at last. 'It seems as if
we haven't been alone for years,' he murmured, eyeing her
longingly as she sat quiet and still on her favourite little

tapestry stool by the hearth, shivering slightly despite the heat.

She was tired still, wanting no part of that which seemed constantly to occupy Finlay's thoughts, and she was glad when the turn of the year brought more visitors to Oir na Cuan, popping in and out, ceilidhing into the small hours.

But the person Morna most longed to see didn't come home till the end of January. His leaves, and those of Big Morgan and Moggy John, had been staggered to allow the other men to spend Christmas and New Year with their families. His arrival home was further delayed by violent storms that lashed the coast and made it impossible for the relief boat to get out to the rock.

Then came a day of blessed calm, mild too for the time of year, and Morna was out there on the shores of Mary's Bay, waiting for a sign of the relief boat, not daring to light her fires any more but waving her scarf when she at last sighted the boat rounding Kinvara Point on its way into the harbour.

Her throat tightened. She wanted to run to him, to stand before him and just look and look at him, to kiss him and tell him how much she had missed him – but she could do none of these things. The eyes of the world were always watching and in them he belonged to another woman, one who wouldn't be there to meet him, but who would be waiting for him just the same as he trod the well-worn path to No. 6, Keeper's Row.

Rob came to her the following day, the earliest he could get away. When she opened the door he saw her as she had been when he had left her, rosy and bright and smiling, and he never really knew how ill she had been. He had heard that she had been unwell, and she told him a little of it herself, but she didn't want to spoil their moment with tales of sorrow and sickness.

Her eyes were glowing with delight as she bade him inside and shut the door behind him. And inside were the children and the animals, Vaila shouting her pleasure at seeing him again, saying 'Robbie' without hesitation. Gone was her babyish pronunciation, it came out loud and clear and he laughed his deep laugh as he swung her up into his arms and kissed her soft cheek.

They exchanged small, belated Christmas gifts and then he went to look at Aidan lying asleep in his cradle. 'You've given my brother a lovely son,' he told Morna quietly.

'And I gave you a lovely daughter,' she said quickly, not wanting anything to spoil the precious minutes they had together.

'A lot o' good that has done, who will ever know she's mine, least of all Vaila? Finlay can shout his feelings aloud, no one will ever hear o' mine.'

'We know, my dearest Robbie, and who can tell what the future will hold? Now is what matters, this lovely moment of being together.'

'I can't stay long, Hannah doesn't know I'm here and I want to be off before Finlay appears. I'm not yet ready to hear him crowing about his fatherly achievements and wanting to celebrate with yet another wetting of the baby's head. Hannah told me all about that and now that he's been sober for a while it's best to keep him that way.'

'Did you miss me?' She was hungry for his words of reassurance and love.

His hand came up to stroke the dark hair at her temples. 'Every minute of every day.' His voice was husky, the pain of their forbidden love touched him anew. 'I couldn't wait to get home, and yet, now that I'm here, I feel so helpless, wanting to touch you and hold you and knowing all the while how hopeless it is.'

Dusk was creeping over the landscape and it was soon time for him to go. Briefly their fingers entwined, then he opened the door and was gone, into the night and the darkness, a tall figure moving in the shadows, and then it was just the stillness and the emptiness with only the wind whispering in from the sea to break the silence.

Alone and desolate she stood by the door. Echoes of his voice seemed to come to her. Tears pricked her lids, she kissed her hand where his fingers had touched it, and then she went back inside and softly closed the door.

KINVARA

Summer and Autumn
1925

Chapter Twenty-Six

Willie Whiskers, the blacksmith, was shoeing a horse in the forecourt at the front of the smiddy, shaded by two large chestnut trees that had somehow managed to survive the winter gales and salt-laden sea spray.

Outside Anvil Cottage, Maisie Whiskers was taking her ease on a bench, fanning herself with her hanky and muttering every so often that it was 'hot, hot' as she languidly watched her husband working.

Summer had come to Kinvara; the sun was beating down in the glens, the purple-hazed hills drowsed against the azure sky, and the sea looked like a millpond with the little islets of Stac Gorm, Eilean Crocan, and Eilean Orsa showing almost perfect reflections in the glassy mirror of the water. Dogs ran on the shimmering white sands, sea-birds called from the cliffs, and the children on their summer holidays from school roamed barefoot through the leafy woodlands or sat fishing in rows on the harbour walls.

Further inland, the harvesters were whirring as the plough-horses plodded up and down the rigs, releasing the heady perfume of newly-cut hay into air which was already heavy and sweet with warm summer scents.

Everybody was taking advantage of the good weather to catch up on all the outside jobs that had been piling up during the winter. Up on the moors the peats were being cut and stacked; farmhands and crofters were down on the shore with their carts gathering the seaweed that had been flung up at the last high tide; Effie was in the yard of Purlieburn Cottage cleaning out Queen Victoria's pen; Rona and Wilma Henderson were doing likewise in the chicken runs that littered the field outside Croft Angus; within the walled garden of Butterbank House, Doctor MacAlistair and Jeannie were spreading dung on the roses that were their pride and joy, stopping every so often to rest from their toils and gaze appreciatively towards the serene blue reaches of the Atlantic Ocean.

Willie's hammer rose and fell, rhythmically, steadily, seeming to find its echo in the shed behind No. 6, Keeper's Row where Rob was making a little cart for Andy so that he might enjoy some freedom in his restricted life.

The back door of the house, seldom opened in winter except for access to coal and wood, now gaped to allow currents of air inside. The muslin curtains fluttered at the window in the lobby, a bee droned against the panes, a newspaper rustled on the bench, a stray cat that had wandered into the house lay on the floor in a ray of sunshine and lazily snapped at a fly that was buzzing around its nose.

But nobody was in the house to chase the cat or squash the bee. If Hannah had been there she would most certainly have done both, but like everyone else she was outside in the sun, having been persuaded by her mother to help with one of the cows that was calving in the nearby field.

Harriet was really beginning to enjoy her visits to Kinvara. She and her son-in-law were getting on better these days. She had proved her worth to him by mucking in with whatever needed doing, both in and out of the house. The families of Keeper's Row all helped one another with their small patches of land at harvest time, and Harriet liked nothing better than to join them, wielding her scythe with energy, and afterwards making the corn into stooks, the rows running north to south to even up their chances of drying.

She also had a way with animals, and the geese, the hens,

the ducks, came waddling or running whenever she hove into view, some even following her as she went about her work. At Easter she had been out every day helping with the lambing. Now Thrift, one of three cows that Rob owned, was calving for the first time, and Harriet had been up at the crack of dawn to be with her should she need assistance.

Hannah wasn't in the least keen to be present at this event, but her mother had flatly told her to 'grow up and buckle down' since part of her income depended on the well-being of her husband's livestock. And so it was that she now sat on a grassy hillock, swatting away the flies, trying not to look too hard at Thrift who was showing the whites of her eyes as Harriet pulled the calf from her body.

The little creature slithered to the ground and Harriet rubbed it briskly with bunches of dried grass. Hannah felt sick as she looked at the messy bits attached to both calf and mother, though even she couldn't suppress a small twinge of empathy as the new mother strove to clean and fuss over her offspring.

'There, that's done.' Harriet stood with her hands on her hips and grinned indulgently at the animals. 'She managed most of it by herself but just needed a little help at the end. We can leave them to it now. I don't know about you, but I'm that thirsty I could drink a whole pot o' tea to myself and come back for a second one.'

They were half-way down the field when Breck, now a big strong dog, came running to meet them, noticeably making more of a fuss of Harriet than he did of Hannah.

'You should get to like animals more, Hannah.' Harriet rubbed Breck's ears and looked askance at her daughter. 'Sometimes they make better friends than humans and they're good company if you happen to be alone a lot.'

Hannah had nothing to say to this and in silence they walked over the fields to the small enclosed garden behind the house. Andy was asleep under the dappled shade of a gnarled apple tree in his own little rocking chair that his father had made, simply because none of the other chairs in the house were suitable.

Harriet looked at her grandson and shook her head. 'He's so small for three, but he's a bonny boy despite everything. I used to be so ashamed of him being in the family, but now it doesn't seem to matter so much. People get used to anything after a while, and I just wish your father could see it that way. He's never got over having a grandson like Andy, which is a pity because the boy has intelligence, if only he could express it more.'

'Ay, if only he could,' Hannah's lips tightened. 'But he can't, he gives nothing in return for all the work he causes, and I don't blame Father for not wanting to see him. He isn't the only one, his other grandfather . . .' she inclined her head in the direction of Blanket Hill, 'has never looked the road he's on and I *do* blame him, because he's nearer and he makes such a fuss o' his other grandchild – because he's perfect as befits a Sutherland.'

'Och, don't be so bitter, Hannah,' her mother scolded. 'Ramsay Sutherland isn't worth bothering about and isn't blood kin – not *our* blood anyway. Your father is, and should be ashamed o' himself for his attitude as should you, but then, you and he always did harbour grudges and resentments, and I'm off this minute to make the tea before I say too much on the subject.'

She reappeared a short while later bearing a tray set with a large pot of tea and a plate of her own home-baked shortbread which she put down on a table under the apple tree.

'Come and get it!' She raised her voice in a lusty shout and Rob came from the shed, wiping his brow with a duster. He was grimy and sweating but looked well pleased as he flung himself down on the grass and accepted the mug that Harriet handed him.

'Nearly finished.' His dark eyes glowed with satisfaction. 'Tomorrow should see it done and then we'll have our little launching ceremony to get Andy and Breck on the road.'

Hannah looked at him sharply. 'You're surely not going to make too much of this. I don't want every Tom, Dick and Harry coming here to look at us as if we were some sort o' performers in a peep-show. It is our business, after all, and it's bad enough you taking it upon yourself to put Andy into a cart and letting a dog pull him along like some monkey in a circus!'

'For heaven's sake, Hannah!' Harriet intervened before Rob could speak. 'Andy has very nearly been a prisoner in his own home since he was a baby. Other children o' his age are running about like hares and leading a normal life . . .'

'That's just it,' Hannah broke in furiously, 'he *isn't* normal, he'll never be able to run about like other children, he isn't fit to be outside and I for one hate the idea o' him going on show so that everybody can gape at him and whisper to each other about how ugly and deformed he is. It's just not fair to do this to me when it's taken me all this time to make some headway in the place. Now I'll be a laughing-stock again and won't be able to go into the village without people pointing their fingers at me.'

'So that's it,' Rob said with a shake of his head. 'The same old theme, not what's good for Andy but what's good for you. You aren't thinking about him, all you're worried about is the effect it will have on you and what folks might have to say about you behind your back. Well, I tell you this, Hannah, the people o' Kinvara have got bigger hearts and minds than you have and will welcome Andy into the community, so whatever you say and think doesn't carry a bit o' weight, and I'm going this very minute to finish making that cart and to hell with what you want.'

Angrily he got up and went back to the shed, and Harriet sighed and looked at her daughter. 'Really, Hannah, why do you always spoil everything? Rob's a good father to Andy, I've watched him these last few years and have seen for myself how much he cares and worries about his son. He's accepted matters as they are and made the best of a raw deal. Why can't you do the same? Join forces with him, help for a change instead of always hindering. You're such a fatalist, forever seeing the black side, never encouraging your man in anything he tries to do that's good and right.'

Hannah had the grace to look ashamed. 'I know,' she whispered, staring down at her hands, 'I hate myself for it sometimes and want to bite my tongue out, but I can't seem to stop myself saying the things I do. Rob *is* a good father to Andy, he's patient and kind and understanding, but I know I'll never be able to match up to him. You've no idea what it's been like, the fear, the anger, the loneliness. I want to reach out to Rob and tell him how I feel, yet whenever I think the time has come to confide my thoughts, I shrink away from facing him. I can't really explain it too well, I just feel safer the way I am, I don't want ever again to open myself up to more hurt and pain. I'm a good wife, I do everything I'm supposed to do . . .'

'Except for one thing,' Harriet nodded meaningfully, 'perhaps the most important thing of all between a man and a woman. Oh, don't try to pretend to me that I'm wrong, I know the signs. You and Rob never touch, there's no warmth or affection in the way you behave towards one another, and I don't think I'm mistaken when I say the fault lies with you, Hannah. I've seen him sometimes, looking at you as if he would like to be closer to you but you always turn away from him.'

Hannah's face flared. 'That's nobody's business but mine and I'll thank you not to interfere, Mother. How can you possibly set yourself up as a judge on other people's marriages when you and my father were so busy making money you never seemed to have time to spare for one another – and hardly any at all for me?'

'So that's it,' Harriet's strong face hardened even more, 'blame somebody else, never yourself. You were always like that, even as a very young child, never giving anything o' yourself, growing tighter and less responsive as the years went on, shutting yourself away more and more till all you seemed to want was to be by yourself with your books and your dreams.'

'That was because you and Father shut me out,' Hannah faltered, her heart beating fast because she had never spoken to her mother in this way before. 'You were always so strong, both so close, there was no room for me in anything you did. Then you bought the hotel and things got even worse, and now I think you and he have become strangers to one another as well as to me. I can't get close to him, I can't do anything right in your eyes, all you ever do is nag at me and tell me I'm wrong. I'm heartily sick of it and have wanted to tell you so for a long time!'

Harriet was somewhat taken aback at this outburst. Hannah was close to tears. She was twisting her hands nervously in her lap and looking as if she would like the ground to open and swallow her up.

'All this is news to me, Hannah.' Harriet managed to squeeze the words out as she tried to maintain her equilibrium. 'I had no idea you felt this way about your father and me. Perhaps you've been reading too many books, immersing yourself too much in other people's lives.'

'No, Mother.' Hannah's voice came out in a croak but became stronger as she went on to say, 'When Rob came along I thought I saw a way out o' my miserable life, I was desperate to escape, and I suppose I used him to help me to do it. I had never known a man like him, so strong, kind and gentle too, something wonderful about his nature that made me want to be with him all the time. Then he brought me here and I hated it, I became lonelier than ever and when Andy was born I knew I was doomed never to escape misery and heartache.'

Harriet took a deep breath and composed herself for a moment before reaching out to clasp her daughter's hand. 'I never knew you were so unhappy, perhaps your father and I *were* too wrapped up in ourselves to be bothered about you. I suppose sinking everything into the business wasn't such a good idea after all, and you're right about us, we have drifted apart these last few years.' She sighed. 'It's too late for us to change, but it isn't for you and Rob. You're young, you have time on your side, but don't wait too long, a man like Rob needs a woman, and sooner or later he'll get one – if he hasn't done so already,' she added darkly.

At this, a strange expression flitted across Hannah's face, she said nothing however and was really quite glad that Andy chose that moment to wake up, giving her the excuse to get up and go to him and hold a drink of milk to his mouth, not minding for once when he slobbered into the cup and held trustingly on to her wrist with one of his bony yet surprisingly strong little hands.

The moment had come for Andy's first trial run in the cart. Rob had brought it round to the front of the house and it sat there in all its splendour, fashioned out of plain wood but, bedecked as it was with painted garlands of flowers and colourful pennants, fitted out with bicycle bells and one large motor horn, it was a carriage fit for a little king.

The safety side of it had not been neglected. Willie Whiskers had fixed straps to the seat and a simple braking system to the wheels which could be worked with one finger and he was there that day to make sure that everything went smoothly.

Maisie Whiskers and some of her cronies were there as well and were soon joined by several others of their ilk. The children from Keeper's Row and those from Quarry Cottages were curiously examining the cart and loudly wishing that they could ride in it until Big Morgan came out of his house and scattered them with a few well-chosen words.

'This cart belongs to wee Andy, he can't get about like the rest o' you. To begin with he'll just be using it here, but later, when he's older, he'll be going further afield and when that happens I want you all to promise to look out for him and help him if you ever see him in difficulty. Will you do that for him?'

'Ay, Mr Morgan!' came the enthusiastic yell.

'And we'll no' let anybody else touch him or hurt him or we'll punch their noses for them,' Babs MacGill added her contribution, an expression of mutiny on her face that was a facsimile of her mother's in fighting mood.

'Right now, clear the way for Andy,' Big Morgan ordered and with one accord the youngsters moved respectfully back a pace, their attention now riveted on No. 6 of the Row from whence Rob and Harriet were emerging. Between them they supported Andy, a tiny figure with contorted limbs, able only to walk by scraping one foot in front of the other, his legs half bent but getting there just the same, Breck anxiously hovering nearby as every painful step of the way was slowly negotiated.

Ever since puppyhood the dog had been instinctively aware of the dangers that existed on the road, he was intelligent and wise and had been quite intrigued when Rob had recently tied him to a wooden sledge and induced him to pull it along so that soon he was quite used to wearing a harness and obeying short commands.

Today he seemed to know just what was expected of him and stood patiently as he was harnessed between the cart's shafts. By this time Morna had arrived with her children, Vaila immediately breaking away to join Joss Morgan while Aidan, now a sturdy toddler with bright golden hair flecked with red, went to seek out Mollie Gillespie's beautiful little black-haired daughter, Runa.

Despite Donnie Hic's efforts to increase the Gillespie line, Mollie had not produced another child, a fact which had caused Donnie a good deal of anxiety. He had begun to suspect that Runa had sprung from his wife's former liaison with the black-bearded giant who worked at Vale o' Dreip.

Whatever he thought, whatever he had to say, didn't matter to Ryan Du who was now leading a respectable life as the husband of Cora Simpson, who hardly let him out of her sight since she had 'hooked' him and was as unprepared as he was to allow him to take the blame for anything that had happened in his wild and carefree past.

Mollie didn't listen to Donnie either, she had no desire to have reams of children at her feet and was quite content with just Runa, who had been a great comfort to her from the start and showed every sign of remaining that way.

Rob was lifting his son into the padded seat of the cart, but the little boy stiffened, rolled his eyes, and let out a screech of protest.

'I'll show him! I'll show him what to do!' One of the MacPhee boys made to climb in, but was abruptly stopped in the act as a hand shot out to clamp itself round his arm.

'Leave him be! He isn't daft and can do it himself.' Hannah had come out of the house and was suddenly there in the front line, glowering at Billy who was about to make a face at her when his mother promptly grabbed him by the scruff of his collar and bulldozed him away.

'Can we do it? Can we do it?' shrilled Tom MacGill, jumping up and down with excitement.

'No, you can't.' Big Bette cuffed her youngest son on the ear but the action lacked its usual enthusiasm, so taken up was she by Hannah's appearance on to the scene and the untypical manner in which she had just spoken up for Andy.

Everybody else was looking at Hannah too, not least Rob and Harriet, and she further surprised them by placing a calming hand on her son's dark head and saying soothingly, 'It's all right, you can do it, Breck will look after you, he'll keep you safe.'

Andy relaxed and allowed his father to lift him into the seat and strap him in. Rob showed him how to work the brake, the reins were placed in his hands.

'Go.' He uttered the word in a distorted croak, but the dog was well attuned to everything that the little boy said and understood perfectly. Slowly and easily the cart moved off, another screech escaped Andy, this time of excitement, his eyes were glowing, his body twitching. The wheels glided beneath him, the little flags fluttered merrily in the breeze.

A cheer went up from the onlookers. There were tears in Harriet's eyes, Rob swallowed a lump in his throat, Hannah showed no emotion except for a slight tightening of her hands as she held them rigidly at her sides.

'You'll no' keep him indoors now,' Moggy John observed, nodding in Andy's direction. 'Once he's had a taste o' the big wide world there'll be no holding him back.'

The laird was coming along the track with his dogs and his cat, the sight of which caused a stir of unease amongst the canines in the gathering. They knew her temperament well, most of them having been acquainted with her sharp claws at some point in their lives, and as the laird and his hairy entourage came nearer, the dogs drew back, contenting themselves by baring their fangs at Sheba from the safety of the convenient forest of ankles and feet nearby.

Sheba, however, was in one of her haughty moods, and sitting herself down in a patch of sunlight she curled her tail round her dainty feet and looked loftily down her nose at the defensive antics of the dogs, as if to convey her superiority as a top cat who knew how to conduct herself when the occasion demanded it.

She did not remain stationary for long. Breck was coming back, and if there was one creature Sheba respected, it was him, ever since he had sent her smartly about her business when she had tried to intimidate him years before in his callow youth. Never by one bristle of his whiskers had he shown any fear of her, and ever afterwards she had given him a wide berth in order to retain the dignity that befitted a feline of her status. Now she arose and beat a stately retreat to her master's side to take shelter under the folds of his kilt as he stood there watching the return of the cart.

'Well, well, just look at that! Just look at that!' The laird was thrilled as he examined the combined efforts of Rob and Willie. He tooted the horn, rang the bicycle bells, made Andy laugh, and finished up by patting Breck on the head and telling him what a clever dog he was. And all the while Sheba skulked and sulked in the background.

The resident canines of Quarry Cottages and Keeper's Row dared to come out of the shadows and everyone began speaking at once. Willie Whiskers supped the glass of beer that Moggy John brought out to him while Hannah and Harriet looked at one another and smiled.

Over the laird's head, Rob's eyes sought those of Morna. Without a word passing between them they conveyed their love to one another. Nobody saw, nobody gave them a second glance.

Sheba had grown tired of taking a back seat. Claws unsheathed she made a dive for the nearest black nose, a howl rent the air, the laird shouted, the dogs barked, and order was only restored when the laird picked up his cat, stuffed her unceremoniously inside his jacket and went on his way, his crook scrunching on the gravel as he made haste to reach the road at the foot of Keeper's Row.

Chapter Twenty-Seven

Rita let herself into the house, a strange sensation seizing her as she sat down at the table and removed her hat. It was very warm outside, there was barely the breath of a breeze to stir the trees. The smoke from a fire in the grounds of Crathmor House hung in the still air; a dog barked somewhere in the distance; Linky Black Jack was chopping wood by the shed and singing in an off-key voice; the hens were clucking in the yard; the sound of horses' hooves rang on the road below.

Rita knew that she ought to start preparing the midday meal. The men would be in shortly, and Catrina Simpson had said she would drop in about now to collect a knitting pattern for the minister's wife, who would only tackle the hilly farm road when she was able to get the use of her husband's pony and trap.

'You could always come on your bike and leave it at the bottom of the track,' Rita had suggested, but Kerry had just laughed in her easy-going way and said she only ever used it around the village and even that was sometimes an effort with all the extra pounds she had put on since having to cook for herself when Cora left to get married.

Ramsay didn't wholly approve of Kerry O'Shaughnessy, he said she was too flamboyant to be the wife of a clergyman, and he didn't hold with the teachings of the Church of Scotland, of which establishment she was very much a member. Yet he had to smile at some of the things she came away with and was always pleasant to her whenever she came to visit at Vale o' Dreip.

Rita thought about her life with Ramsay. When she had first met him he had been the most charming and good-looking man she had ever encountered. Plenty of other women had thought so too and she had been overwhelmed when it became obvious that his liking for her was more than just a passing fancy. He had been a bit of a lad in those days, wild with the drink, able to hold his own with any man who ever said anything that annoyed him. Strike first and think later, that had been Ramsay's philosophy. Men respected and feared him and made a point of keeping out of the way of his ready fists. Women were drawn to his charismatic personality and it was only later that Rita found out he had bedded a string of them and probably had fathered quite a few bairns on the wrong side of the blanket.

He had laughed a lot in those days, and all had seemed perfect when they had married and settled down to their life at Vale o' Dreip. Then everything had changed. As if to compensate for his misspent youth he had taken to religion in a big way and, believing that the Church of Scotland was too liberal in its attitudes, he had broken away from it to join the wee Free Kirk whose teachings seemed to satisfy the strict moral rules he had laid down for himself.

Perfection of mental and physical form were two very important factors in his book. When Finlay failed to come up to the standards that he had set, he saw it as a direct reflection on his own unruly behaviour as a young man and that he was receiving his punishment through his son's shortcomings. The same rule had applied when his first grandchild had come into the world, flawed and imperfect. He couldn't bring himself to associate with such an obvious reminder of 'the sins of the father', and so he shunned little Andy and his mother and held Finlay at arm's length because of the guilt he felt at having produced such a weak link in the Sutherland line.

But it was his arrogance that Rita found so hard to bear. Despite his so-called self-condemnation, he treated everybody else as if they were the ones at fault. She was of the opinion that contempt for his fellow men had become a way of life with him and there was no way he could climb out of the pit until he saw that fact for himself.

A tear ran down Rita's face, for things passed, the happiness she had once known as a young girl. Even now she could feel some of that joy touching her, he had been such a wonderful man, full of vigour and life, kind and gentle, thoughtful too, Rob was very much what his father had been like in those far off days . . .

Catrina swung her basket as she made her way up the track to Vale o' Dreip. The blackbirds were singing in amongst the blossom on the hawthorn trees. She couldn't see them, but she could hear their sweet outpouring of song. The scent of the flowers was like nectar. Catrina put her nose to a blush-pink spray and sniffed deeply, then on impulse she snapped it off and fixed it into her shining red hair before going on her way, her steps light, feeling so good to be alive on this bonny morning with the sea shimmering in the distance and the hills looking like giant warriors slumbering against the misted blue sky.

'I want to reach up and touch you,' Catrina cried, buoyant in her youth and delight of life. 'I would marry you all and let you fight over me and then I would lie down on each one of you and feel your strength and hardness beneath me.' Her voice rang in the stillness. She put her hand up to her mouth and giggled. It was daft, daft, to act like this, but it was such a lovely day and she just felt good and happy to be alive.

Linky Jack was outside one of the big sheds chopping wood. He stopped what he was doing when he saw Catrina coming towards him with flowers in her hair and her blithe steps carrying her along. 'Fine day, Catrina,' he greeted her with a flash of his stained teeth. 'You get better lookin' every time I see you.'

'Flatterer,' she smiled, 'I suppose you say that to all the girls.'

'Only the good-looking ones.'

He grabbed her and kissed her before she could stop him.

'Don't do that,' she cried. 'I hate men who think they can paw me whenever they feel like it.'

'Aw, come on, Catrina,' he gave her a sly smile. 'You know you like it, wi' a figure and a face like yours men just canny help themselves. You would be lying if you stood there and told me you don't enjoy the thrill you get wi' a man, and from what I hear you've never run short in that respect.'

Catrina knew she should have shown annoyance at this, but she was easily swayed and could never resist a bit of flirting. 'Ay, you could be right there, Jack, there was a time, just after the war, when lads were thin on the ground, but a few have moved in or grown up since then and I just enjoy myself with them as nature intended I should.' Her dimples showed. 'But I'm not a free woman any more. I've been walking out with Colin Blair who works at the fishery in Balivoe, and woe betide any man who tries to get off with me when he's around.'

Linky Jack grinned. 'Sounds a bit fishy to me. I always understood you to be aiming higher than that. Wedding yourself to Colin Blair will never buy you any o' the things you ever fancied.'

'Whoever said anything about marriage?' Catrina gave Linky Jack one of her coquettish looks. 'I have no intention o' tying myself down to Colin or anybody else just yet. I mean to enjoy myself first. I'm only twenty-two, I've got plenty o' time to look around, and if you've got a fortune stowed away under your mattress you might easily be the one I'm looking for.'

She let out a peal of laughter and fluttered her lashes at him as she left him to make her way to the kitchen door. 'Rita! It's me, Catrina!' she called, opening the door as she did so. There was no answer and she went further inside to see Rita sprawled on the floor, the folds of the tablecloth lying over her like a shroud, dishes strewn everywhere.

Catrina rushed forward, and getting down on her knees she grabbed Rita's wrist and felt for her pulse. Then without ado she ran outside and yelled, 'Jack, go and fetch Doctor MacAlistair, something's wrong with Rita, I'll stay with her till you get back.'

Linky Jack immediately dropped his axe. Jumping on the nearest bicycle he went clanking away down the track while Catrina returned to the kitchen to place a cushion under Rita's head. A shadow fell over her and she looked up to see Ramsay standing there, gaping down at his wife.

'She's fainted – or something,' Catrina explained quickly. 'We'd better not move her till the doctor has seen her.'

'Fainted?' Ramsay continued to stare at his wife. Rita ill! But she was never ill! And it was nearly lunchtime! She always had his meal ready and waiting for him when he came in . . . He transferred his attention to Catrina who was behaving in a most cool and rational manner as she made Rita as comfortable as she could.

'You seem to know what to do, Catrina,' he said dazedly.

'When I was a young girl during the war I took a course in first aid . . . just in case,' she added laughingly, 'any stray airmen might drop from the sky to receive my tender ministrations.'

'This is no laughing matter, Catrina.'

'I was only making conversation – och – don't just stand there, help me put her on her side then go and fetch a blanket.'

With a meekness that was surprising in a man like Ramsay he did as he was bid, coming back to kneel down beside Catrina and tuck the blanket round his wife's inert form. His hand brushed against Catrina's and something impelled him to look at her. Her face was inches from his, her breasts were straining against the flimsy material of her blouse, he could smell the flowers in her hair. Hawthorn! Memories came to him. Boyhood. Young girls. Warm summer fields. Discoveries. Smooth flesh. The musky sweet scent of hawthorn blossom driving him wild . . .

He came back to reality with a start. How could he be thinking of such things at such a time? Rita ill. The doctor coming. Getting up from the floor he retired to the table to drum his fingers impatiently while Catrina stayed by Rita's side and in silence they waited for the doctor.

$$\star \qquad \star \qquad \star$$

'Stroke.' Doctor MacAlistair made his diagnosis in his usual blunt fashion as he folded his stethoscope and put it carefully away. Rita was coming round, disorientated and unable to speak, one side of her body paralysed. The doctor smoothed the hair from her brow and said soothingly, 'There, there, Rita, lass, don't worry about anything. You've had a mild stroke. You're in your own bed in your own house and we're all here to look after you, so just you relax and let us do the caring and the sharing.'

He drew Ramsay aside and said in a low voice, 'I really mean that, Ramsay, she won't be able to do anything for herself for quite a while, so see you make sure she isn't disturbed, and don't allow her to get upset on any account.'

'Will she recover?' Ramsay's voice was taut with anxiety. 'Fully, I mean? The way she was before?'

'Ay, she should be all right, but I warn you, she'll need good care and attention and all the rest she can get. No visitors to begin with, except family. Effie will call in every day of course, and I myself will check up on her regularly. She could be left with a weakness in her left side and her speech might be affected, but Rita's got spirit and I'm sure she'll make an excellent recovery.'

Despite these reassurances Ramsay looked stunned and the doctor gripped his arm. 'Patience, man, you'll have to have patience. Knowing the sort o' man you are that will be difficult, but in a case like this there's nothing else for it. Go about your work as usual, there's no point in hanging over Rita and willing her to get well, she'll do that at her own pace.' So saying he picked up his bag and went downstairs to find Catrina hovering in the hall, waiting for news.

Quickly he explained the situation to her, ending, 'You did a good job this morning, lass, I didn't think you had it in you, which just goes to show none of us really knows one another till an emergency like this crops up. If you can look in on Rita from time to time, all to the good. Ramsay too will need bucking up. This has come as a shock to him – I don't think he's had to face serious illness before.'

Catrina nodded. 'I'd better get word to the family, unless of course Linky Black Jack has already told the whole place, and knowing him, that wouldn't surprise me a bit.'

When Doctor MacAlistair got home, the first thing he did was pour himself a stiff dram. 'Rita of all people,' he confided in Jeannie. 'Small she might be but she's always been wiry and fit and gave the impression that she was as strong as a horse. It just proves that you can never tell with people.'

'No wonder, being married to a man like Ramsay would sap any woman's strength,' was Jeannie's opinion. 'He's a very demanding sort o' person and thinks he only needs to snap a finger to bring everybody running to his bidding, let alone Rita.'

The doctor shook his head sadly. 'I don't doubt he will have difficulty coping with this, on the other hand, he could surprise us all. He's made o' stern stuff is Ramsay and if he practises what he preaches he'll not fail his wife in her hour o' need.'

When Finlay heard that his mother was ill he went to pieces and drank enough to 'kill a horse' as Dokie Joe was quick to observe. But after Effie and Doctor MacAlistair had each given him a piece of their minds, telling him that he would be no use to anybody in the state he was in, he soon rallied and was never far from Rita's side. It was quite touching to see him with her, brushing her hair, holding her hand and talking to her, willingly taking his turn to massage her limbs to keep them from cramping.

Rob was given leave from lighthouse duty to be with his mother, and as soon as the relief boat got in he went straight to Vale o' Dreip so that she had both of her sons at her bedside and was greatly comforted by their presence.

Hannah and Morna went to see Rita too, but always when they knew Ramsay would be out of the house as neither of them had any desire for a confrontation with the man who had all but ignored them since they had married into the family.

Rita was a well-liked figure in the community and many visitors came to see her as soon as the doctor said she was strong enough to receive them – the Simpson sisters; Mattie; Jeannie; Dolly Law smoking her clay pipe – much to Ramsay's disapproval as he regarded 'the Outlaws' to be little better than tinkers with none of life's graces to their credit. Dolly ignored him. Filled to the brim with cheek and cheery chatter, she made Rita smile and the doctor said that she was probably one of the best tonics his patient could have at this crucial period in her life, though he also told her very discreetly that pipe smoke did little to enhance the air that Rita breathed in the bedroom.

Dolly was not offended by this, instead she promptly produced a little tin filled with 'baccy' which she proceeded to roll into skinny cigarettes with her grimy fingers. The doctor gave up, the fascination on Rita's face telling him that she was enjoying a procedure that brought some light relief into the boredom of her long days.

Most surprising of all perhaps was the appearance of the Henderson Hens into the scene, wearing their striped butcher's aprons and big baggy cardigans, sporting shoes in place of their usual boots since they had agreed with one another that visiting a sick-room was much the same as going to church and commanded the same sort of respect.

Awkward and shy, grinning at Rita with their big teeth and peering at her from behind their spectacles, they entertained her with anecdotes about their ducks, their chickens, their turkeys and their geese, in the end producing a clutch of pale green duck eggs which they said would get Rita on her feet in no time since they were chock-full of nourishment and goodness.

Rita hated duck eggs. She wasn't all that keen on eggs of any sort, but the kind intentions of the sisters were not wasted on her and when they seized her hand to heartily shake it there was a tear in her eye as they said their goodbyes and clumped downstairs well pleased with themselves.

*   *   *

Ramsay gazed morosely at the pile of dirty dishes in the sink. It was too much! The house filled with visitors from morning to night, marching in, leaving trails of muck on the stairs, all that meaningless chatter, the most unlikely beings cropping up, people who had never before crossed his door, making the excuse of visiting Rita when all the time they were just being nosy, like vultures at a killing.

It wasn't as if any of them did any good, not one would have thought of offering some practical help, all they did was disrupt any remnants of routine left in the place. And the offerings they brought by way of a passport! Duck eggs of all things! The buggering farm had enough eggs to sink a battleship! About as original as giving a leg of lamb to a sheep farmer.

And that Effie. Sitting in the kitchen drinking tea till it came out her lugs, talking about that silly pig of hers as if it were some sort of creature to be revered and pampered. What did she want with a pig anyway? Surely she was kept busy enough nursing the people of Kinvara without the added work of keeping a sow.

As for those two daughters-in-law of his. Fat lot of good they were. Creeping in when he wasn't there, not doing a hand's turn to justify their position in the family, probably talking about him behind his back and telling everyone what an ogre he was . . .

The door opened and Catrina put her head round. 'Mr Sutherland. I was hoping to find you in.' Her voice was light, her eyes warm. She came further into the room, all smiles and rosy cheeks, her yellow summer dress seeming to bring sunshine into the house. She looked around, her glance taking in the dusty furniture, the mess in the sink, and she shook her head indulgently. 'Och, I knew it, you're needing some help, a busy man like yourself shouldn't have to worry about all this. How would you like me to come and do my housekeeper for a wee while? I could look after Rita too and cook for you and the rest o' the menfolk. It would leave you free to get on with your work and I promise you I wouldn't get in the way.'

'I thought you worked for MacPherson.'

'I do, but the whole family is away for a spell, so I'm not

needed there at the moment. I thought the laird would have mentioned to you that he was leaving.'

'Ay, ay, he did – but with all that's been happening here I completely forgot about it.'

'And who can blame you for that, Mr Sutherland? It's been terrible for you these last few days and that is why I came today to offer my services.'

Ramsay took a deep breath. 'All right, I would be glad of your help,' he conceded gruffly before he could change his mind. He swallowed. 'I'll pay you, of course.'

'Of course,' she agreed with a pert smile and went at once to enclose herself in one of Rita's aprons before tackling the mountain of greasy plates in the sink.

Chapter Twenty-Eight

The Vale o' Dreip farmhands were delighted that Catrina had come to look after them and enjoyed flirting with her and teasing her as she served them up with imaginative meals in the scullery.

'You'll make a grand wee wife for somebody some day,' Linky Black Jack told her, grabbing her round the waist and squeezing her in a most familiar manner.

'Ay, the Simpson girls are all right,' agreed Ryan Du. 'A bit giddy sometimes and aye wishing for the moon, but they certainly know the way to a man's heart – and are experts at getting into their trousers forbye.'

'Hold your tongue, Ryan Du,' Catrina scolded. 'Just because you're married to my sister doesn't give you the right to judge us all the same.' She laughed. 'I myself have never hankered after the moon, there are better riches to be found here on earth, and neither myself nor my sisters will ever find them in a man's trousers. A girl can get into trouble that way and end up with nothing.'

'Och, come on now, Catrina,' Linky Jack's hand lingered on her bottom. 'You canny stand there and tell us you're as pure as the driven snow, it's all there in the way you wiggle your fanny and tease a man wi' your smiles and dimples.'

'That's none o' your business,' Catrina returned ably. 'And I'll thank you not to be so rude to me in future. And another thing, while I'm working here for Mr Sutherland, it would be better if you were to keep your hands to yourself, he wouldn't like it if he found you pawing me the way you do.' She put her nose in the air. 'Colin wouldn't like it either, I'm his girl and the sooner you get that into your head the better. If I were to tell him about the things you say and do to me he would be that angry he might just come up here and sort you out.'

But she never mentioned any of this to Colin when she rendezvoused with him in Smiddy Lane where they would steal a few kisses before going on to a dance or a ceilidh in the village hall and thereafter to the barn attached to Willie Whisker's stables.

Colin Blair was a young man whose small stature and smooth boyish face totally belied his hearty sexual appetites. Once roused it was well nigh impossible to stop him getting his own way. But Catrina did just that, allowing herself to be kissed and mauled to a point of almost no return then with a great strength of will, she called a halt and tore herself free, leaving Colin gasping and panting and begging for more.

'No, Colin, I don't know you well enough. If you love me the way you say you do you'll wait and enjoy it all the more for that.'

'Aw, hell, Catrina,' he would explode, 'I've asked you to marry me umpteen times and you always keep putting me off. I'm only flesh and blood and I can't wait forever, so you'd better make up your mind soon or I'll – I'll find somebody else.'

'No you won't, Colin, you want me and only me and you'll get me when I'm good and ready and not before.'

And this was how she had treated all the young men she had ever gone out with, playing one off against the other, keeping them on a string, using them as a sort of collateral for the future should her unwearying search for a man of means fail to pay off.

Her would-be suitors, past and present, never liked to admit to each other that they had never made it with Catrina, and it didn't matter if some of them got tired of waiting and married somebody else. There were always others only too willing to take their place, and Catrina would go home to her soft-hearted

Granny Margaret and feel glad that she had kept herself intact 'until the right man comes along'.

The farmhands weren't the only ones to enjoy having Catrina about the place. Rita's day was brightened by the girl's cheerful presence, while Ramsay was feeling really pleased with himself for having taken her on to look after the running of the house which she dusted and polished and kept shining like a new pin. She saw to all the tiresome little chores that he had no patience with, and produced tempting meals for everyone, singing as she went about her business, as blithe a spirit as anyone could wish to have in their home.

This fact he conveyed to her one day as she breezed into the kitchen and laid his meal before him, smiling at him as she did so and asking what sort of morning he had had.

'All the better for coming in here and seeing you, Catrina. I'm grateful to you for all you're doing here and . . .' he placed his hand over hers, 'I'll make certain your diligence is rewarded, you know. I'm a man who always keeps my word.'

'I know that, Mr Sutherland.' His thumb was caressing her palm, his cool blue gaze was on her, and an odd little stab of response went through her before she drew away from him. 'But you're already paying me enough for what I'm doing, I don't need anything else, and besides, I'm enjoying it here. Those MacPherson bairns drive me daft altogether sometimes and while I love them every one, it makes a nice change to be getting away from them for a wee while.'

'Of course.' Ramsay was himself again, brusque, self-contained, bending his head to his soup plate, dismissing her with a slight flick of his hand.

'I'll take Rita's up to her,' she turned at the door with the daintily set tray, 'it's that nice to see her eating again. She was getting so thin we were all worried about her, but now she seems to have perked up and Effie says there is some life coming back to her weak side.'

'Ay,' was all he said as he broke bread and supped soup,

seeming to be a million miles away, so aloof and distant was his manner.

Catrina purported not to care. She took the tray up to Rita, helped her to spoon food into her mouth, wiped her face afterwards with a cool cloth and then brushed her dark hair till the soothing rhythm of it made Rita close her eyes and drift away. Only then did Catrina sit back and think of her little interlude with Ramsay. She was annoyed to feel a shiver go through her – especially as she wasn't certain if it was unease – or anticipation.

It was raining, a harsh heavy rain that quickly soaked the parched countryside and turned the dried-up ditches into overflowing streams. The heavens crashed, thunder and lightning rent the darkness, the animals in the fields cowered against the onslaught and sought shelter wherever they could find it.

Catrina looked in dismay from the farmhouse window and wondered how she was going to get home. She was still wearing the light cotton dress she had arrived in that morning and her shoes were not of the sort made for wading through puddles. The farmhands had retired to their bothies some time ago but she had waited on, hoping for an improvement in the weather, but it had only worsened. Ramsay had gone out a half-hour before to see if the roads were flooded, if not he had promised her a ride home in his trap.

Suddenly the door was wrenched open and he stood there, soaked to the skin, his hair plastered around his face, drips running down his chin and into the collar of his waterproofs.

'The ditches at the foot o' the track have burst their banks,' he reported heavily. 'There's no chance o' taking anything down there tonight, never mind a horse, so you'll just have to bide here till we can clear it.'

'When will that be?' she asked, her mind running ahead to small insignificant things like a change of underwear for the morning, the promised return of the half-crown that Cathie MacPhee had loaned her a week ago. She wasn't all that worried about Granny Margaret or Connie. They were used to her being out late and when she didn't come home they would assume that she was staying with a friend till the storm abated.

'Who knows,' he said shortly, divesting himself of his wet things as he spoke. 'We'll have to wait till this goes off. We certainly can't do much in the dark anyway, so you can borrow some o' Rita's night things and take your pick o' the upstairs rooms. There are plenty to spare since my sons left home.'

Catrina pulled the folds of her crocheted black shawl across her chest.

'Perhaps I should walk home, Mr Sutherland. It isn't all that far and if I borrowed some waterproofs I should be all right.'

'Don't be silly, lass.' He sounded kind, concerned somehow. 'You would get swept away in yon torrent. Far better to remain here and go home nice and dry in the morning. I'll show you where you can sleep, you'll be cosy enough in Finlay's old room, the window rattles a bit but otherwise it's draught- and rainproof.'

Grabbing a paraffin lamp he led the way out of the kitchen and up the stairs. The staircase took on a new aspect, his shadow leapt on the walls, everyday objects looked distorted and threatening, the stairs creaked, she caught a glimpse of herself in the landing mirror and gave a little half-scream.

'In here,' Ramsay pushed open a door, the hinges squeaked, a jagged streak of lightning lit up the window. 'I'll leave the lamp with you.' Ramsay put it down on the bedside table and lit the candle that sat there. 'Don't worry, Catrina, you're safe here, go in and get a nightdress from Rita's room, you know where they're kept.'

'No, I'll be fine, Mr Sutherland.' She found her teeth chattering slightly, though it wasn't cold. 'I don't want to wake her if she's asleep.'

'As you like. I'll leave you to it, then. Sleep well, Catrina, it's a quiet house at night and you won't be disturbed.'

He departed, the flickering light from the candle making his shadow look bigger and more frightening than before. She stood for a moment listening. A door clicked softly but she wasn't sure which one it was, then she closed her own and stood with her back to it for several minutes before she went slowly over to the bed. But she didn't get undressed. Removing only her shawl she lay down and covered herself with the quilt, feeling strangely on edge as she listened to the wind raging outside.

Rita was restless. The thunder was reverberating against the hill peaks. It was something that she had been familiar with all her life, but tonight it was somehow menacing and she was unable to get to sleep. Compared to the turmoil outside, the house seemed very silent and still. She tried to move the arm that had been affected by the stroke. Little by little some life was returning to it, but not nearly enough to allow for any useful mobility. Frustration seized her. She had never thought that anything like this could ever happen to her. It was so terrible lying here all day, unable to move or speak or do anything for herself. Yesterday, Doctor MacAlistair had said she could get up and sit in a chair for a while, and that had been a small step forward – a very small step. She had become very tired in just a short time and had reluctantly allowed Catrina to put her back to bed. She had become very fond of Catrina in the last week or so. It had been lovely having her here, like a breath of fresh air, showing a side to her nature that no one had suspected was there until now. She had always given the impression of being empty-headed and flippant, with nothing more on her mind than boyfriends and parties.

Voices floated up from below. Ramsay's and Catrina's. Minutes went by. She lifted her head to look at the door and saw a wisp of light passing beneath. Catrina must have decided to stay, just as well, on a dreadful night such as this . . .

Voices again, the light coming back, she waited, hoping that Ramsay would come in to see if she needed anything. A cup of tea would have been lovely. The light went past, a door clicked shut, he had retired to the room in which he had slept since she had been taken unwell.

She moistened her dry lips. Effie had told her to get a

handbell and ring it as loud as she could for attention. She could well imagine Ramsay's reaction to that. He was the one who was used to snapping his fingers to bring everyone running. He had been distant towards her since the onset of her illness, almost as if he blamed her for having allowed it to happen. He had never liked anything to do with sickness, he said it made him feel uncomfortable and avoided contact with it if at all possible. Now he couldn't avoid it, and she felt that more of a gap existed between them than ever, one that she knew wouldn't be bridged till she was able to get up and about as she used to.

Reaching out with her good arm she picked up the photo of herself and her two sons that Mirren had taken at Morna's wedding in Shetland. She smiled to herself as she remembered how Rob had said afterwards that he and Finlay were like a couple of kilted book-ends with her sandwiched in between. Memories, that was about all she had now to keep her going, and lying back on her pillows she cuddled the picture to her chest and let her mind wander.

Catrina was unable to settle. The bedroom that Ramsay had shown her was at the back of Vale o' Dreip and looked on to the huddled black shoulders of Blanket Hill, so different from the daytime, dour and forbidding, lit every so often by flashes of lightning that gave only momentary respite from the rain-drenched night. The burns were frothing down, glinting on the wet rocks, the wind had risen to gale-force and the trees were tossing hither and thither, those near the house creaking and groaning as their tortured branches were blown about.

She lay in the strange bed, her nerves tightening with every passing minute, thinking of Granny Margaret and Connie in cosy little Struan Cottage on the outskirts of Balivoe, wishing that she could be there with them instead of here, an odd creepiness about the place with Rita lying helpless in her room, Ramsay lying somewhere else – anything but helpless. She remembered his hand touching hers in the kitchen and she was glad that she had made it plain she wanted nothing to do with him. It was all right leading him on a bit when there were plenty of other people around, she did that with a lot of men, only fun on her part but the trouble was, they all took it so seriously. She sighed and thought of Colin. He was a good man, he treated her with kindness and consideration and she wished he was here now to keep her company with his cheery talk.

She could stand it no longer, she needed something to help her sleep. Granny Margaret always made cocoa at bedtime, perhaps if she went down and made some . . . throwing back the quilt she seized the paraffin lamp and quietly opened the door . . .

Ramsay was brooding by the remains of the fire in the kitchen, his head jerking up at Catrina's entry into the room. With a startled intake of breath she drew back. 'Mr Sutherland,' she gasped, her heart galloping into her throat, 'I thought you were in bed. I came down to make cocoa, I couldn't sleep.'

'Me neither. Come, Catrina, shut the door, don't be afraid of me, let us comfort one another, it's been lonely here since Rita took ill.'

She stood hesitating, and, getting up, he took her hand and led her gently into the room. 'Make your cocoa, lass, I'd like a cup too, it might help us both to get to sleep.' His voice was hushed and reassuring.

Telling herself that she had nothing to fear, she filled a pan with milk and set it to heat on the cinders.

'Catrina,' his hand shot out to grab her arm, 'you're such a bonny girl, I've always admired you and I know you like me too, I've seen it in your eyes when you look at me.'

'Please, Mr Sutherland, I do that with all the lads, it doesn't mean anything . . .'

He was standing over her, big and looming, the glow from the fire emphasising every hollow in his face. Without a word he pulled her roughly against him and undid her hair, his hand running through the thick rich tresses. 'Red, I always liked red hair in a lass,' was all he said before his mouth clamped down on hers, hard and smothering.

A strange kind of thrill ran through her, a mingling of pleasure and suffocating apprehension. This was different from anything she'd ever experienced with the young men she had known. With them she had always exerted a certain measure of control – now she was the one who was being overpowered – and she knew, even as she struggled to free herself, that there would be no stopping Ramsay Sutherland.

His hands were on her, tearing at her clothes, her breasts sprang out, white and full in the dimness. 'This is what you've been asking for,' he grated, flinging her across the table, pinning her down with one big heavy hand, stemming her protests with the other. She lay spreadeagled, powerless to move, her outflung hands gripping the tablecloth as he undid his trouser buttons and drove himself into her. Pain shot through her, she closed her eyes, hating him for what he was doing, taking away the one thing that she had tried all her life to save 'till the right man comes along'.

He was sweating, grunting and groaning, the weight of his body holding her down as he strove for the release of his ungodly urges. It was over in minutes. Breathing heavily he threw himself into a chair and put a hand over his eyes.

She lay where she was, sobbing quietly, bruised and sore.

'Get dressed,' he ordered, 'and stop crying. No harm's been done. You got what you came down for. Make your cocoa and go to bed.'

'No.' She struggled to her feet 'I won't stay in this house a minute longer. You can get someone else to come in and look after you. I'm sorry about Rita, she doesn't deserve any o' this, but I – I can't go on as before – not even for her sake.'

He made no attempt to stop her as she wrenched open the door and ran off into the howling night. A feeling of self-loathing had seized him. He had let himself down, all those years of self-control – and now this – and to a lass who meant nothing to him . . .

Getting up, he went into the parlour and unlocked the drink's cupboard to withdraw a bottle of whisky. Returning to the fire he remained there for the rest of the night, drinking, dozing, hardly a thought to spare for Catrina and how she was faring. All he could think about was himself – and how he had betrayed all the values that he had held sacred for as long as he could remember.

The silent tears ran down Rita's face. All the things that had ever been said about Catrina were true after all – those sounds from the kitchen after she had gone downstairs with only one thing on her mind – to seduce a man who had for years teetered between self-righteousness and self-gratification. The lusts of Ramsay Sutherland had simmered away for years, hidden under the surface. Rita had always known that a time might come when they would erupt, but to do this, in his own home, with his wife lying ill upstairs, was beyond anything that Rita could comprehend, and the tears that she shed were not of sorrow but of the anger that she felt for a man who had robbed her of so many of life's pleasures.

He couldn't, however, take away her fighting spirit, as long as she had that she would win through – and as if to prove to herself that she could do it she made a mighty effort and moved the fingers of her left hand. She would show him that she wasn't finished yet, by God and she would!

Catrina never knew how she got home. For hours it seemed she struggled through blackness, bent double against the bullying wind and the driving rain, never seeing another living soul, not wanting to see anybody in the state she was in. Shame! Such shame! Tearing her apart. Her clothes dishevelled and half hanging off her. She prayed that Granny Margaret and Connie would be in bed. She couldn't face them. Not yet, not until she could face up to herself and the thing that had happened to her.

Somehow she reached Struan Cottage. Opening the door she let herself in, never so glad to get back to the homely things that she had known all her life. Stoking up the fire she set pans of water to heat, fetched the zinc tub from the scullery, towels from the cupboard beside the fireplace, all the while trying to be as quiet as possible.

But she hadn't been quiet enough. The door opened and Connie appeared, filled at once with sisterly concern when she saw the state Catrina was in.

'You're soaked through, what on earth made you come home on a night like this? We thought you would surely have stayed with someone till morning. Oh, let me help, you're all thumbs and you're shaking like a jelly.' She helped Catrina to peel off her wet layers of clothing. Shivering, Catrina got into the bath, letting the warm water cleanse her, trying to shut out the memory of Ramsay's face as he pounded into her like a wild beast.

'Catrina, you're bleeding,' Connie said in dismay.

'I know, it's the usual,' answered Catrina, who had had no idea that she was until now, 'that's why I'm having a bath.'

'You know Granny Margaret doesn't like us to bathe when we're like that.'

'Oh, she's just old-fashioned.' Catrina tried to keep her voice steady. 'Please, Connie, don't fuss, I'm cold and wet, I'm having a bath, and that's all there is to it.'

'All right.' Connie's sweet face took on a crestfallen look. 'I'll go and make us some cocoa, it will help to heat you up a bit.'

Catrina put out a wet hand and took that of her sister. 'I'm sorry I snapped at you Connie, it's just – I don't feel very good at the moment and it's lovely just to lie here and soak for a while.'

Connie's face cleared. She went to get milk from the pantry and Catrina lay back in her bath and gave a sigh of thankfulness to be warm and safe in her own home surrounded by people she loved.

Chapter Twenty-Nine

The MacKernon had waited a long time for his revenge on the laird but his chance came during that gentleman's extended absence from Crathmor.

Notices were distributed in the villages of Calvost, Balivoe and Vaul, to the effect that a fishing competition was to take place within the estate of Cragdu, everyone could keep the salmon that they caught, and there would be a prize of five pounds for the biggest fish to come out of the river.

This announcement created a great deal of interest in the community. Everyone, it seemed, wanted to take part in the event − it was a good opportunity to stock up on supplies of food, and the added lure of the prize money was the final sway for most folk.

'Well, he's no' such a bad soul, after all,' Big Bette decided as she sat behind the counter of the village store whittling away at a piece of wood.

'Ay, he has his good points,' Mattie agreed. 'It is very generous o' him to let everyone have a go in his river and over and above all that to hand out five pounds to the winner.'

'Of course, it is rather strange too.' A frown touched the face of Annie 'Song' MacDuff. 'At this time o' year he normally has his own high-falutin' friends staying at Cragdu for the fishing. I wonder what's made him change his mind now.'

'Och well, that isn't our worry.' With a flourish, Big Bette pared off the last flake of wood from the toy horse she was making. 'I for one will go along there to try my hand for that prize money. A fiver isn't to be sneezed at – the bairns are always needing something and seem to grow out o' their clothes as soon as they get them.'

'Can we go, Ma?' Joe asked excitedly. 'I'm the best at fishing in the whole o' the village.'

'The best at poaching, more like,' his mother said meaningfully. 'And no, you can't go, it isn't for children.'

'It isn't for women, either,' Cathie MacPhee put in quickly. 'You'd best leave that side o' it to Mungo, it's a man's place to take part in rough sports like fishing.'

Bette withered her with a look. 'Fishing isn't a rough sport, and I'm much better at it than Mungo could ever be. It would be too undignified for the likes o' him and he never liked water o' any sort, never mind a freezing river wi' the midgies biting his ears off.'

'Well, you had better watch out for my Dokie Joe.' Mattie lifted her shopping bag off the counter. 'He's a dab hand wi' the rods and where sillar is involved he would drown himself to get it and that's a fact.'

But when she went home and regaled her husband with the gossip in the shop and how she had sung his praises he was less enthusiastic than she had expected. 'I'm no' that good, Mattie,' he said uncomfortably. 'A lot o' the other lads are much better than I am. And besides, there's something wrong about this whole business. The MacKernon is up to mischief, it's no' like him to be so generous, and I don't want to take part in anything that isn't above board.'

Mattie let out a hoot of laughter. 'Listen to the man! A cherub without wings! Only thing is, your halo's slipped a bit over the years and it would take more than some fancy talk to convince me that you're an angel. Don't be silly, Dokie, I'm your wife, I know what you're made of. I want that fiver, and you're the very mannie who just might help me get it.'

*   *   *

The day of the competition dawned, mellow and golden, the trees in the Cragdu Estate were wearing their autumn hues and it was altogether a most desirable setting for the event. It was good fishing weather, the rains of September had swollen the river, the flies were in abundance, the fish were leaping.

The MacKernon's rich American-born wife, Dolores, affectionately known as Roley to her husband, was there that day, helping to get everything organised. She was of wealthy New England banking stock and had injected a good part of her fortune in the Cragdu Estate. But she loved being Lady MacKernon, she enjoyed living in a Scottish castle with a real lord who behaved in a manner that befitted his title and had introduced her to a way of life that was, to her, utterly satisfying. She had one son from a previous marriage, currently at boarding school, and another to her present husband, a little boy of six who was quite enchanted that day to meet and mingle with the lads from the surrounding villages.

Roley had often said to her husband that she would like to mix more with her neighbours and today was a perfect opportunity to do so. She went among them, a glamorous figure with her blonde hair and immaculate clothing – for all that very down-to-earth and able to put everyone at ease with her voluble chatter and ready laugh – 'quite human', as Shug Law observed, his conception of anyone from beyond the boundaries of the British Isles being rather vague.

Wives and sweethearts of the participating menfolk had brought baskets of food with them and the atmosphere was festive as they draped themselves on the banks at dinnertime, eating, drinking, laughing, comparing catches and wondering who would be the lucky prize-winner at the end of the day.

Not all, however, were in lighthearted mood. 'I am seriously worried, Mattie,' Dokie Joe confided to his wife. 'In all the time I have worked for the laird I took this stretch o' the river to be his, now here is The MacKernon behaving as if it were on his land, hooking out salmon as if his life depended on it and inciting everyone else to do the same. It's no' right, Mattie, it is just no' right.'

Mattie looked consideringly at her husband. Over and above his other duties to Crathmor he was also the water bailiff, and if anybody should know what was correct on that score it had to be Dokie Joe. Mattie was a fair sort of person herself and didn't like to see anybody being cheated out of what was rightfully theirs – there were exceptions to that rule however, and this was one of them. 'Five pounds, Dokie,' she said softly, 'just think what we could get the bairns for that. No one would blame you for getting mixed up about the boundaries between Cragdu and Crathmor, they themselves fight about it all the time. So just you stop worrying yourself and do your best for me and your family, who surely should come first before everyone and to hell wi' your halo!'

Dokie Joe gave in, and for the remainder of that afternoon he cast his rod with the rest of them, the tension mounting along with the numbers of landed fish as the minutes ticked by.

The weigh-in was even more nerve-racking, followed by a terrible silence as The MacKernon opened his mouth to pronounce the winner. When Shug Law heard his name being shouted he nearly fainted, and it was only the reviving contents of Dolly's hip-flask that saved him from doing so.

'Quite an achievement for such a wee man,' Mattie commented, swallowing hard at the sight of Shug and Dolly gleefully counting the money. 'It takes Dokie Joe all his time to make that amount o' sillar in a month and here's Shug Law doing it in just one afternoon – without having to work for it.'

'As long as he spends it on his bairnies and doesn't pee it up against a wall,' Big Bette said with a martyred sniff. Her cronies nodded their somewhat subdued agreement and everyone went home, laden down with sacks of fresh salmon, no small consolation to many of the poorer families who often found it hard-going to fill the bellies of their children.

Revenge was indeed sweet for Lord MacKernon. That night he dined on best salmon – caught from his own river and all entirely above board – ostensibly of course. MacPherson would be furious when he returned to find his fish stocks depleted, but he had asked for it with that Christmas tree business a couple of years ago, and had to learn that he couldn't get the upper hand every time.

Lord MacKernon put his hand over Roley's and was glad that she had never quite grasped the intricacies of land rights and ownership.

The fish that couldn't be immediately consumed by the local people found their way to the Balivoe fishery to be smoked – the men who worked there being only too happy to do this in return for some of the spoils. Colin gave Catrina a share of his but she wasn't all that keen to take it, saying that the thought of it made her sick. 'Give it to your folks then,' he urged. 'I'm sure your sister and your granny would be only too glad o' the chance of some smoked salmon.'

Colin was worried about Catrina these days, she had lost her sparkle, was quiet and on edge for most of the time. When he asked her what was wrong she just snapped at him and told him to mind his own business, and then she had run away crying, leaving him scratching his head in bewilderment.

'Pregnant!' Ramsay spat the word. 'Why come and tell me? I'm not a doctor, there's nothing I can do to help you.'

'It's your baby, Mr Sutherland.' Catrina twisted her hands together nervously. She was pale and exhausted-looking with dark circles under her eyes, so different from the rosy laughing girl that everyone knew. 'And you'd better do something about it because I'm that sick with worry I don't know what I'm doing.'

'*My* child!' Ramsay was thunderstruck. 'Don't be silly, Catrina, it could be anybody's, you have a reputation for letting anything in trousers get up your skirts and I'm not going to take the blame for what has happened to you because o' your loose ways.'

'I'll have to tell on you then,' Catrina burst out. 'You can't deny what you did to me and you'll have to pay for it.'

'Go ahead and tell, your word against mine, no one will believe a servant girl against a man of principle like me.'

'I'm a respectable girl, Mr Sutherland,' she cried desperately. 'You can't treat me as if I were a piece o' dirt to be trampled under your feet.'

'Respectable! You're the village bicycle, everyone knows that, and I won't stand here and listen to any more o' this foolish talk when I have important work waiting to be done.'

'You'll have to help me.' Her voice was soft with despair. 'I don't know what I'm going to do, who to turn to. You raped me, Mr Sutherland, and you can't just turn your back on me as if I don't exist.'

'Here.' He rummaged in his pocket and threw some money on the table. 'That should sort things out for you. There surely must be some old witch woman in the place who'll do anything for a few bob.'

'Keep your money! And I hope you choke on it!' Catrina threw at him, and bursting into tears she wrenched open the door and fled.

'That was all very interesting.' Ramsay jumped. Rita had come into the room and was standing there looking at him, an expression on her face that didn't bode well for him. Doctor MacAlistair had been right about her. She had made an amazing recovery, her powers of speech were rapidly returning and she was getting about reasonably well with the aid of two sticks.

'It was just Catrina, raving on about some triviality,' Ramsay blustered, unable to look his wife in the eye.

'Rape is hardly a triviality, Ramsay.' Rita's voice was deadly calm. 'It's a dirty word and an even dirtier deed. I couldn't sleep that night o' the storm. I might not have been able to speak but by God! I heard everything that was going on under my own roof! I thought at first it was all Catrina's fault, now I know it was you. She ran from you in panic, I found her shawl in Finlay's room where she'd left it, too afraid to come back upstairs and get it – afraid o' you, Ramsay, and what you did to her.'

'You don't know what you're saying, Rita,' he parried, a muscle in his jaw working.

'Oh, I know, all right, only too well. I've been expecting something like this for years, now it's happened and I hope you get your just punishment for what you did to that girl. You'll pay, Ramsay, in the end you'll pay. Catrina will not be cast out into the wilderness, if necessary she can come here and have your child and I will stand by her every step o' the way.'

Ramsay had turned white, he had no chance to say anything, however, because Johnny Lonely chose that moment to put his head round the door.

'Excuse me, Mr Sutherland,' he said respectfully. 'I just came to give these flowers to Mrs Sutherland. She's been good to me and I was very sorry when I heard she'd been ill.'

He laid a bunch of bronze chrysanthemums on the table. 'Been robbing graves again, I see,' Ramsay said sarcastically.

'No, Mr Sutherland.' Johnny was using the placating tones that never failed to annoy the master of Vale o' Dreip. 'Mattie MacPhee gave them to me when she heard me mentioning that I would like to come and visit Mrs Sutherland.'

Rita picked up the flowers and held them to her nose. 'They're lovely, Johnny.' She put her hand on his arm and smiled at him. 'I haven't been able to get out much since I took ill, and these are just what I need to cheer me up.'

Johnny touched his hat. The door closed behind him. A terrible sense of unease crept into Ramsay as he wondered just how much the hermit had heard of the conversation between himself and his wife.

Catrina had been in a state of turmoil since her confrontation with Ramsay the previous day. Both Granny Margaret and Connie had been alarmed when they saw how upset she was and the latter had begged her to tell them what was wrong.

But for Catrina the idea of that was too terrible to contemplate. How could she bring such disgrace on the dear grandmother who had raised her and her sisters from an early age? How could she tell Connie who was always so considerate towards her and tried her best to give good advice in her role of elder sister? They had become closer than ever since Cora had married Ryan Du, and Catrina couldn't bear the thought of letting her down.

There had been no rest for Catrina since she had discovered she was expecting a baby, and now she wandered along the shore and down towards the great grey rocks that rose up out of the sea beneath Kinvara Point, slippery and wet with the seaweed thrown up from the autumnal equinox. Here the water was black and deep, swirling ceaselessly around the reefs, booming into the many caverns that pitted the cliffs on this rugged side of Mary's Bay. Catrina scrambled on to a huge overhang of rock and stared mesmerised into the deep glassy pool beneath. Her mind became blank. A wave of dizziness washed over her and she swayed on her feet . . .

'No! Don't even think the thing!' Morna's voice rent the air and she came running up. Grabbing hold of the other girl's arm she hurried her away from the spot and made her sit down. 'This isn't the answer, Catrina,' she said breathlessly. 'Have your baby, love and care for it and never heed what folks will say. It will be a comfort to you in days to come, and you will never be alone as long as you have a child to keep you company. I know,' she went on softly. 'When I discovered I couldn't have the man I loved, my daughter became all to me, a treasure greater than anything else in the world.'

Catrina stared at her. 'Oh, Morna, I'm so unhappy. I don't know what I'm doing, what I'm thinking.' Her eyes grew bigger. 'But how did you know about me? I never even told my sisters about this.'

'Johnny Lonely passed you yesterday coming from Vale o' Dreip in a terrible state. Later he heard some of what Rita said to my father-in-law. He was so shocked he couldn't keep it to himself. You know Johnny, he hears everything, but don't worry, I won't say anything to anybody else and neither will he. Only thing is,' she smiled sympathetically, 'you can't keep it to yourself for much longer anyway, you'll have to tell someone.'

'Oh, Morna,' Catrina sobbed. 'It's so good to talk to you. You of all people understand what I'm going through.' The two young women embraced and cried together, then Morna got up and held out her hand. 'Come on, I'm taking you back to Oir na Cuan for a cup of tea and maybe something stronger. You'll feel better once we've had a good blether.'

They went back along the beach, taking one each of Vaila's and Aidan's hands, the dogs running in front, barking and frolicking as they went. The Henderson Hens were down in the dunes, hacking away at the marram grass in order to repair the thatch on their crofthouse roof. At sight of the girls they stopped what they were doing to smile and wave and shout a greeting.

'I know what bothers me about those two,' Morna said as she waved back. 'They do everything alike, they talk alike, they each wear similar clothes, when one changes into boots or shoes the other follows suit, they even think alike and come out with what's on their mind at the same time.'

Catrina nodded. A smile touched her face. 'Like me and my sisters. When we were little, people used to call us the Simpson triplets, Granny Margaret dressed us the same and we went everywhere together, never one without the others, as close as any sisters could be.' She sighed. 'Too bad we have to grow up and grow apart a little, there are some things that can't be shared with those that are nearest and dearest to you.'

'I know,' Morna agreed softly. 'I know only too well.'

The girls linked arms and went on their way, Catrina's heart much lighter now that she had found someone she could confide in and who could give her comfort at a time when she needed it the most.

Ramsay was in the hayshed when a bolt from the blue knocked him for six. Only it wasn't a bolt from the blue, it was Colin Blair, pouncing from the shadows, dancing nimbly around like a boxer in a ring, a small mean bundle of fury, fists held aggressively in front of his face, nostrils dilated, eyes staring. 'That's for Catrina and what you did to her, you filthy hypocritical swine! She told me all about it, Sutherland, how you took advantage of her when she was here helping you to run your life. I know Catrina, you see, all that flirting was just bluff with her, deep down she was as innocent as a bairn – till you took it away from her.'

Ramsay was shaking his head, trying to clear it, his hand going up to his nose to stem the flow of blood.

'Don't just lie there feeling sorry for yourself,' Colin taunted. 'Get up and fight like a man – show us what you're made of, Sutherland, I'm waiting.'

Ramsay struggled to his feet, panting and dishevelled. 'Get off my land, you little runt,' he blazed, 'before I throw you off.'

'Try it, just try it.' Colin was still dancing around, only too anxious to take another swing at the older man's jaw. But Ramsay was having none of it. Leaning against the door for support, he straightened his clothes and made to depart, only to be grabbed by the collar and swung round.

'Listen, and listen good,' Colin said through gritted teeth. 'I'm going to marry Catrina, but I want you to pay for what you've done. Upkeep, in return for keeping my mouth shut. And I don't want a pittance. You've got plenty o' sillar and can surely spare a few bob. It's either that or your reputation, Sutherland, pay up and no' another word will be said – and you have my promise on it.' With that he took himself off, leaving Ramsay to stagger across the yard and into the house.

'So,' Rita greeted him as soon as he was inside. 'I see you've had a visitor, Ramsay, an angry one from the look o' you. Well, you had it coming, that's all I can say, and you'd better clean yourself up before lunchtime. The laird sent a message, he came home yesterday and wants to discuss some business matters with you. That means an extra place at table, so make sure the cutlery is arranged properly and remember to put the milk in the china jug. I would do it, but, as you know, I'm just not quite ready to take over the running of the house – especially since Catrina left and you didn't get anybody else to take her place.'

Rita was enjoying herself, Ramsay wasn't, and it was with very bad grace indeed that he went to try to repair the damage to his appearance before Captain MacPherson arrived for lunch.

Soon after that, Colin and Catrina travelled to Inverness to be married in the registrar's office. It was nothing like Catrina had visualised her wedding day to be – there was no white dress, no uplifting organ music, no flower girls, only her sisters and her Granny Margaret to watch as she made her vows and promised to be a good wife to Colin.

As Mrs Blair, she kissed him and wept a little for that which was lost to her, but that was life, as Granny Margaret said, and there was no turning back now. Colin was a loving and kindly man, he had a steady job at the Balivoe Fishery – she could have done better for herself and she could have done a lot worse. One thing was sure, he loved her and she knew he would take good care of her and her child, and in that respect he was perhaps Mr Right after all.

KINVARA

Summer 1926

Chapter Thirty

June. Golden and warm. The countryside burgeoning with new and glorious life, each day longer than the one before, sunset merging into sunrise with hardly a break in between. But today was even more special for Morna. Robbie had come back from lighthouse duty yesterday and she knew he would be here to see her very soon. She had walked with the children and the dogs to wait for him in their special place in Mary's Bay, a hidden hollow amongst the rocks, the sand was warm under her bare feet and she could hear the rhythmic rattling of the tiny pebbles in the shallows as the waves washed them to and fro, to and fro.

Out beyond the bay the sun was silvering the sea, further inshore the seals were calling from the rocks, plaintive, sad, lost somehow. She fingered the little seal brooch at her neck and drew a shuddering breath as a life stirred within her. Robbie's child. But she wasn't going to tell him about it because it would make matters too complicated for everyone.

For the last year Finlay had been impotent. She knew it was the drink that was to blame, but he said it was her fault for not loving him enough. There might have been some truth in that – Robbie had been right all along, she should never have married his brother when she didn't love him. It hadn't worked, he was unhappy and so was she. He had never taken to Vaila nor she to him and she hated to see the hurt in her little girl's eyes when he made such a fuss of Aidan and none at all of her.

That was why she had decided to go back to Shetland to live once more. She wouldn't be staying at Burravoe House with Mirren, though, she wanted to bring her children up in her own way and had saved some money towards this end. She was a good seamstress and had lately acquired a little treadle sewing-machine. There was always work to be had from some of the bigger houses in Shetland, and she had written to a lady who was offering a small cottage for a reasonable rent that would be free for occupancy in the autumn, giving her enough time to enjoy the summer with Robbie, yet allowing her to leave Kinvara before her pregnancy really began to show.

It would break her heart to leave him, she couldn't begin to imagine what it would be like, but she couldn't go on with her life as it stood, loving him, never truly having him, stealing moments that weren't rightfully theirs to steal, all the while feeling guilty about the deceptions, the lies.

It had come full circle. In Shetland she would have Robbie's second child, only this time she wouldn't be coming back to Kinvara. Finlay of course would have to see his son, Ramsay and Rita their grandchild. The details weren't clear in her mind yet, she had told no one of her plans, she just knew she had to get away from a love that was tearing her apart every time Robbie went away, each time he came home.

The children came up to her to show her the tiny shells they had gathered at the water's edge, their faces shining as they emptied their treasures on to her lap and waited for her response, laughing with her as they listened to the sea-like sounds in the bigger shells and examined the delicate colours in the smaller ones.

She drew them in close to her, Aidan with his serious little face and affectionate nature, Vaila so bonny and bright and smiling, nearly five now – how the years had passed, it seemed only yesterday that they were both babies. They were devoted to one another and were always together, hand in hand, arguing, laughing, playing.

Morna kissed the two small faces and stroked the dark curls from Vaila's brow. 'I wish I could have heard you calling Robbie your father. He's a wonderful man and someday I will tell you about him and what he really was to you.'

'Robbie.' Vaila nodded and pointed upwards to the tall chimneys of Keeper's Row prodding into the blue sky. 'Father Robbie.'

'That's right,' Morna said huskily. 'But for now you must call him just Robbie. He will be here soon and will want to see all the nice things you found on the shore.'

They wandered off once more, leaving their mother sitting in her little hollow of dry sand, her back to a sun-warmed rock. She stared across the water and listened to the seals. Life was all around and within her. Special and precious. She thought of Robbie and how it had been with them in the beginning. A fire had burned within her in those magical days. Pictures flashed through her mind, images of the past, the two of them running like children, splashing in the sea, stealing kisses in dappled woodlands, her Robbie, the only man she had ever loved . . .

She gasped suddenly. Pain seized her, a band of steel seemed to be tightening around her heart and she fumbled for the little bottle of pills prescribed to her by Doctor MacAlistair. But her fingers wouldn't work, she couldn't get the top off the bottle and it fell and disappeared under a crevice in the rocks where she couldn't reach it.

'Vaila. Aidan.' Desperately she called their names. They came running. She put her arms around them and held them till all the strength that was in her ebbed away. The sand was warm beneath her. Warm and soft. Her last thoughts were of Robbie and how she had lain with him here, loving him, never wanting to part with him. 'Robbie.' His name was a mere breath on her lips. And then her body relaxed, the thoughts and dreams and longings that had tormented her in life slipped away from her, and peace, dark and silent, took their place.

It was Johnny Lonely who found Morna, lying where she had died, the wavelets lapping at her feet, a breeze lifting the corners of her wispy black shawl, her hands spread out as if to gather earth and heaven to her before she had slipped away, leaving one behind, journeying on to the other.

Vaila and Aidan were sitting huddled together nearby, bewildered and afraid, but Johnny only had eyes for Morna.

'Lassie, oh, lassie, what have they done to you?' he whispered as he got down on his knees gently to touch her pale cheek. For a long moment he remained like that, motionless, just staring down at her, then he did a strange thing, gathering the dead girl in his arms he bade the children follow him and went stumbling away along the shore, towards his humble bothy beneath the cliffs of sullen Ben Du.

Here he laid Morna down on his bed of straw and sacking and folded her arms across her breasts. After that he smoothed her hair and straightened her clothes and tenderly kissed her cold lips.

The children weren't afraid of Johnny, rather they were fascinated by him and were always glad to see him when they met him on his wanders. Today was different, today he was acting in a way that made them feel uneasy, and they cuddled close to one another and began quietly to cry.

Johnny was too incensed with grief to notice. Getting down beside the bed he clasped his hands and began rocking back and forth, the tears running silently down his face, calling Morna's name over and over, never knowing or caring about anything that existed outside the agony of his own personal sorrow.

A shadow darkened the door. 'Robbie!' Vaila cried, running to him to take his hand and gaze beseechingly up into his face. Robbie took one look inside the hut.

'What the hell do you think you're playing at, man!' he cried, even as dread filled his being.

'She was as much mine as yours,' Johnny cried. 'As any o' you! You all thought you owned her but you didn't, all you ever did was sap the strength out o' her till she could take no more.' Putting his face in his hands he shook his head from side to side. 'I found her! Down there among the rocks where she died. I brought her back here – to say goodbye to her. She was my Morna, my lass, she aye listened to me when no one else did and in here . . .' he placed his hand over his heart '. . . I loved her and would have died for her.'

Rob couldn't speak, his mind had gone numb. He saw the evidence of his own eyes, Morna lying dead on Johnny Lonely's bed, the children white-faced and big-eyed, the tears streaming down the hermit's face, but the true impact of what had happened didn't fully penetrate his shocked consciousness.

Wordlessly he picked the children up, put his arm round Johnny's racked shoulders, and then he began to cry too, helplessly, hopelessly. Morna was dead and his world had gone black, even though the sun was beating down outside and the sea shone like silver.

Father MacNeil found them like that and it was he who took charge, lifting the children into his arms, leading Rob outside, telling Johnny to wait where he was till he got help to take Morna home, home to Oir na Cuan where she had known some of the happiest and saddest years of her life.

'We'll take the boy,' Ramsay decided as soon as the news came to him. 'He is after all your son, Finlay, and my grandson – and besides – he'll be more use about the place when he's older. Not the girl, though, there's no place for her here, she'd be better off going to live in Shetland with her aunt – and if that fails there's always the orphanage.'

'Over my dead body!' Rob blazed.

'Oh, and what's your interest, then?' Ramsay shot back. Every day he was becoming more like the Ramsay of old. His confidence had taken a knock over the affair with Catrina and for a while he had kept in the background, but now his arrogance was returning, though Rita didn't intend for one moment to ever allow him to get the upper hand again.

'Vaila's a dear little girl, Ramsay,' she said firmly, 'and has as much right to be here as Aidan. I for one would never stand back and allow her to go to any orphanage. I'm fitter than I ever was and we can always get help if necessary. Meanwhile, it's far too early yet to make arrangements for their future, and the children will stay here until we are all more able to face up to the dreadful loss we have suffered. I thought the world of Morna and so did everyone else, and if you had any decency in you, Ramsay, you would be mourning for her too instead o' trying to cast out her daughter as if she were some stranger.'

At her words Ramsay remembered the flash of Morna's eyes, the spirited fire of her tongue, and a pang of remorse went through him. 'Ay, you're right, Rita,' he nodded. 'Let matters stand as they are for the moment. I shouldn't have said what I did – and I'm sorry for letting my tongue run away with me.'

A little smile touched Rita's mouth. She would make him eat humble pie all right – till it was coming out of his ears – and of course, Catrina's tiny new baby, Euan, was always there to remind him – should he ever get out of hand.

Later that day, when everyone else was out of the house, Rita said softly to Rob, 'Vaila is your daughter, isn't she? She's so like you, Rob, the way she has of smiling, her eyes when she's hurt or angry.'

'Ay, she's mine,' Rob admitted. 'She was born to Morna after we argued and she went back to live with her sister in Shetland. By the time she returned I was married to Hannah, there was no way out – for either o' us.'

'Why don't you tell Ramsay that she is his grandchild?'

'I can't, the time isn't right. Morna can't be hurt any more but there's Hannah and Andy to consider. He needs his mother, and if this came out she might up and leave with all that pride she has in her.'

'As you wish, son.' His mother put her hand on his arm. 'But it is Vaila's right to call you father – and before I'm very much older I want nothing more than to hear her say it.'

When Mirren arrived from Shetland to sort through her sister's things she handed Rob a letter.

'Morna sent this to me a long time ago, asking me to give it to you should anything happen to her. Well, it has, she's gone now, and all that's left are memories and heartaches. Oh, God, I feel so alone without my little sister.' Her voice broke, she turned away to hide her grief, leaving Rob to seek a quiet corner where he could read his letter in peace.

My dearest Robbie,

It is night as I write this, Vaila and Aidan are asleep, the house is quiet and still around me, and I look from my window and see the flashing of the Kinvara Light, reminding me of you out there. You are the one I think about in my darkest hours, what we had together was something rare and my life would have been nothing if you hadn't come into it.

You will know what I kept from you when you get this letter. I never told you I was ill because it would have served no useful purpose and would only have caused you a great deal of worry in a situation that was difficult enough without adding to the burdens.

My strong handsome Robbie, you are my love, the only man in the world I ever cherished. I thank you for sharing your life with me and I know you won't forget what we meant to each other. But you have a lot of life to live yet and I want you to go through it fulfilled and happy.

It is our little daughter that I fear for most, I know Aidan will be looked after but she will be adrift when I'm no longer here to take care of her. I can only hope she will not land up in some strange place. She belongs in Kinvara and it is my dearest wish that she will remain here.

Goodbye, my precious love, in my mind I feel the touch of your hand, in my heart I sense the power of your love, in my soul I am aware of the Divine Greatness that brought us together and will never allow us to part – even unto death.

Forever yours,
Morna

* * *

Rob crushed the letter to his chest. Putting his dark head in his hands he cried for his beloved Morna Jean, never to see her again, no more to know the touch of her lips on his . . . like blaeberries . . . so soft and sweet . . .

'She never told me,' he cried to Mirren, 'I thought she looked tired sometimes but I had no idea that she was so ill.'

'It started when she took rheumatic fever as a child. If she had lived her life quietly she might be here now but that wasn't Morna's way, she did things she shouldn't, she took life with both hands – and in the end it killed her.'

'You hate me, don't you? You think I was to blame for what happened.'

'No.' Mirren gazed steadily back at him. 'She found love with you, Rob Sutherland, and I can never hate you for that, also you gave her Vaila, a child who brought her comfort and joy in her lonely hours. Now Vaila will do the same for me, I've lost my sister, Vaila is all that matters now and I'll be taking her back to Shetland with me as soon as everything here is settled.'

'No!' The protest was torn from Rob. He was remembering what Morna had told him about Mirren's smothering, what she had said in her letter regarding wanting Vaila to remain in Kinvara. 'You can't do that, Mirren, Vaila is my daughter and I won't let you take her away from me. You have no right to do this.'

'I have every right, I am her aunt, after all.'

'And I am her father,' he flashed back.

'You have no option, Rob,' she returned softly. 'Oh, I know you're her father, but nothing's changed regarding your position here, you have your other life with your wife and your son and they must take priority over everything. Don't worry, Vaila will have a good upbringing at Burravoe and you can always come and see her whenever you get the chance.'

In stunned silence he walked away from her, out of Oir na Cuan, along the sandy path that led up through the dunes and past the fields of Keeper's Row. He couldn't part with Vaila. Not now, she was all that he had left of Morna. She was his little girl and he had every reason in the world to keep her and bring her up as his own. But Mirren had played the trump card, he couldn't make any claims on his own child, it was all as it had been when Morna had been alive, hidden, tormented, unresolved.

The answer to his prayers came to him from the most unexpected quarter of all. When he told Hannah of Mirren's plans to take Vaila to Shetland she shook her head and said calmly, 'I don't think so, she can come here. She's a fine bright wee lass and I've grown fond o' her over the years. She's always been good with Andy and she'll be company for me when you're away on light duty.'

He just stood there, unable to speak, staring at her as if she had gone mad.

'I'm not as daft as you think, Rob,' she said with a shake of her head. 'I know she's your daughter, perhaps I've always known but didn't want to admit it to myself. At first it wasn't easy to accept, then I began to see it as a way out – Morna was taking the burden off me, giving you what I should have given you, love, companionship, comfort. Despite myself I grew to love Morna, like everyone else I loved her, and when I told her I considered her to be my best friend I really meant it.'

She looked at him and a tremulous smile touched her mouth. 'I'm sorry for all the hurt I've caused you, Rob. Morna's death has made me stop and take stock o' myself, she was so young, so eager for life, so unselfish in the way she lived. She's made me realise I'm just frittering my own life away in useless bitterness, but I think I'm now ready to look to the future – that's if you feel you can face it with me,' she added hastily.

There was no need for further words. He drew her to him and held her close, and it seemed to her that she had at last found a safe harbour in which to rest after all the storms of the past years.

'Do you know what?' she said with a little catch of her breath. 'I would love to see your father's face when he finds out that Vaila is a blood Sutherland after all.'

'So would I.' Rob smiled when he thought about it. 'And I'll make damned sure I'm there when he hears it, Finlay too for that matter. The pair o' them turned up their noses at Vaila, now she will have the last laugh after all.'

Chapter Thirty-One

The minister paid tribute to Morna in his Sunday sermon, saying that she had touched the lives of all who knew her with her goodness and love, and that she would be remembered in Kinvara for many years to come.

Afterwards, the Simpson sisters cried in each other's arms and recalled the happy hours they had shared with Morna, Catrina in particular thinking about the day in Mary's Bay when she had so badly needed someone to turn to and Morna had been there with her advice and friendship.

Everyone else wept for the girl they had called the sea maiden and told one another that the place would never be the same without her.

'She always had time to spare for everyone,' Mattie said as she wiped away the tears from her eyes.

'Even Johnny Lonely,' Catrina said quietly.

'Ay, no matter how she herself was feeling,' agreed Effie.

'She loved people,' Wee Fay said simply and that summed it up for everyone as sadly they said goodbye to the minister and made their way homewards.

Later that day, Catrina walked to Johnny Lonely's hut in Mary's Bay and handed him a bunch of flowers. 'For you, Johnny,' she told him kindly, 'from Morna's garden. I know how much she respected and liked you and she would have wanted you to have these – in memory of her.'

Johnny took the flowers, his big hands closing gently over

the stems, his fingers caressing the rose petals. He couldn't speak, he could only shake his head wordlessly as a mist of tears came into his eyes. Then he put his hand on Catrina's shoulder by way of thanks before turning back inside, closing the door on the world, a world that meant very little to him now that Morna was no longer in it.

Morna was buried in Shetland beside her parents, in a small graveyard overlooking the windswept places that she had once roamed as a child.

Finlay was there to say his farewells to the young wife whose heart he had never really owned, Rita was there too, with Ramsay beside her, a man who had refused to accept Morna in life and who was only too well aware of that fact as he scattered his handful of earth on her coffin and silently asked for her forgiveness.

Rob didn't attend. He couldn't bear to think of his beloved Morna Jean lying in the cold ground, far better to remember her as she had been, warm, vibrant, loving, a spirit who would roam free in death as in life and would always remain young and beautiful.

Hannah's father had died and she travelled to Ayr for the funeral. Rob didn't go with her. He and her father had hardly met, had never got to know one another. She didn't cry at the graveside, neither did her mother, though her strong face showed the emotion she was feeling – she still loved her husband despite them having grown apart in their later years.

'I don't know what I'll do now, Hannah,' she said when it was over. 'I'll sell up here, of course, I couldn't manage to run the place without your father. Afterwards I might go back to Dunruddy Farm to live with your grandparents – or I had thought of moving to Kinvara to be beside you, Hannah. I've grown very fond o' the place and seem to have made quite a niche for myself.'

'Whatever you think best, Mother,' Hannah took a deep breath, 'just as long as you live your own life and let Rob and me get on with ours.'

Much to her surprise her mother beamed at her. 'That's a girl, a fighting spirit at long last! I'm glad that you and Rob have grown close again, it's what I've wanted for ages, and far be it for me to ever come between a husband and wife! Have no fear, my lassie, if I do decide to come to Kinvara I'll buy a croft and join forces with the rest o' them. Meanwhile I have a lot o' sorting out here to do and won't be ready to make my mind up about anything till the business is tied up.'

With her mother so busy, Hannah wandered alone through the streets and promenades she had once known so well. Nobody knew her, no friendly hand was raised in greeting. She was a stranger, one who didn't belong, who didn't fit in. Her home was after all in Kinvara – with Rob – Andy too. She still found it hard to accept him, but she was learning. It would take time, but with Rob beside her it would be all right. Then there was Vaila – little as she was she seemed to understand about Andy, already she was settling in at No. 6, Keeper's Row, a bright spark if ever there was one, keeping everyone on their toes, intelligent, loving . . .

Hannah couldn't wait to get back on the train, back to Kinvara and all it held dear to her.

Rob stood on the headland, remembering Morna. In his hand he held the little corn dolly she had given him on the Christmas of 1922. He would never forget how she had looked that day, radiant, bonny, sad too knowing that she would soon be starting a new phase in her life, that of her marriage to Finlay. Now it was over, everything that she had been, joy, vibrancy, laughter, was gone, only the memories remained, memories that were breaking him, giving him no rest, filling his heart with such terrible poignancy he wondered how he could go on with his life as it was. Perhaps in time the pain would lessen, but not yet, it was all too near, too unreal for him to fully take in the fact that he would never see her again.

The sun was breaking through the clouds of evening, beneath him the sea was filled with sparkling light, and in the sigh of the wind he seemed to hear the echoes of Morna's voice . . . that beloved voice he remembered so well.

'Morna,' he whispered, 'I miss you so.'

Down below in Mary's Bay the waves were curving gently to the shore, lapping the white sands . . . and over yonder was Oir na Cuan, empty now. The lamp that had burned there had been extinguished, but he would never forget his Morna, his love, a love that he would keep in his heart for all time to be . . .

'Robbie!'

A voice was calling him. For a moment he thought it was Morna, only she had ever called him that – but no – there was one other. He turned to see Vaila running towards him, and as she drew nearer he caught her and lifted her up and kissed her rosy cheek. 'You can call me father now,' he said huskily. 'It's all right for you to do that.'

She nodded. 'Father – Father Robbie,' she said solemnly and a smile of mischief lit her face.

Over her head he saw Hannah standing a short distance away, beside her was Andy in his little cart with Breck in harness, wagging his tail, all of them watching as Rob took Vaila's hand and went walking towards them.

'Your tea's ready, Rob,' Hannah said briefly. 'You'd better come down before it gets cold.'

'Ay,' he nodded. His hand slid into hers and together they made their way along the point and down towards the lights that were beckoning from No. 6 of Keeper's Row.

Far out to sea the lighthouse was flashing, a beacon in the dark turmoil of sea that surrounded the wild and beautiful peninsula of Kinvara.